Sex at the Sports Club
A Wicked Words erotic short-story collection

Look out for other themed Wicked Words Collections

Already Published: *Sex in the Office, Sex on Holiday*
Published in November 05: *Sex in Uniform*

Sex at the Sports Club

A Wicked Words short-story collection

Edited by Kerri Sharp

BLACK LACE

Wicked Words stories contain sexual fantasies.
In real life, always practise safe sex.

This edition published in 2005 by
Black Lace
Thames Wharf Studios
Rainville Road
London W6 9HA

Typeset by SetSystems Limited, Saffron Walden, Essex
Printed and bound by Mackays of Chatham PLC

ISBN 0 352 33991 8

Contents

Introduction

What is often described as beautiful, graceful, athletic, sensuous and just plain good for you? Sport of course. And what is considered daring, obsessive, thrilling, exciting and entertaining? Sport again. But can you think of another pursuit that is also an intense combination of the physical, mental and emotional states, described in exactly the same terms?

And despite the cost and sacrifice required to make it as an athlete – the gruelling training, superhuman dedication, the injuries, the no-sex before a game rule, the sweat, blood and dirty laundry of the sporting world – few activities attract the glamour, média coverage and money as sports. And, whenever something is blessed with such acclaim and attention, before long, sex is sure to be a member of the club.

Dating experts recommend sports clubs as an ideal place to meet future partners, professional athletes are often celebrated philanderers, and the ideal and most attractive physique is generally agreed to be one that is fit and toned. Sport creates heroes and champions, it is the realm of the muscular, the strong and the assertive, saint, sinner, gifted amateur and valiant underdog. It creates a worship and adoration in its followers befitting the church and temple in past times. And for as long as physical prowess is considered the pinnacle of human achievement, and one of the fastest methods of achieving fame, money and the love of the people, it will inspire erotic fantasy.

So it comes as no surprise that, when the opportunity

presented itself for talented writers to produce imaginative fiction about sport and sex, we were deluged with stories full of diversity, colour, perspiration and action, in the same way that good games are made.

And it's an interesting squad assembled here. For lovers of equestrian pursuits combined with heavy wagers, look no further than Maya Hess's exotic Polo story, *The Game of Kings*. For tough girls competing against and levelling the field with men, Alexandra Cole's *Taming The Tigress* hits the spot by taking you all the way to Japan and unleashing you into a world of martial arts and cedar hot tubs. Fans of the strong, silent rugger boy will be delighted by the unusual, highly imaginative and intensely erotic *Tighthead*, by Nuala Deuel. We also have sport's writers taking interviews to their furthest extremes: the showers in the changing room; sports widows crossing the touchline with toyboy, pin-up heroes of the astro turf; tennis bunnies going at it like rabbits; golfers out practising their 'swinging'; and even the dedicated grounds man gets to be number one in this anthology.

So next time rain stops play – and lets face it, there will be plenty of opportunity – slip a copy of *Sex at the Sports Club* into an inside pocket, picnic hamper or sports holdall. It's a winner.

Kerri Sharp, Editor, Spring 2005

Want to write for Wicked Words?

We are publishing more themed collections in 2006 – made in response to our readers' most popular fantasies. The deadline for the next anthology – *Sex in the Kitchen* has, I'm afraid, already passed. Keep checking our website for information on future editions.

Sex on the Move (transport) – deadline end of October 05
Sex and Music – deadline end of December 05
Sex and Shopping – deadline end of February 06

- Your short story should be 4,000–6,000 words long and not published anywhere in the world – websites excepted.
- Thematically, it should be written with the Black Lace guidelines in mind.
- Ideally there should be a 'sting in the tale' and an element of dramatic tension, with oodles of erotic build-up.
- The story should be about more than 'some people having sex' – we want great characterisation too.
- Keep the explicit anatomical stuff to an absolute minimum

We are obliged to select stories that are technically faultless and vibrant and original – as well as fitting in with the tone of the series: upbeat, dynamic, accent on pleasure etc. Our anthologies are a flagship for the series. We pride ourselves on selecting only the best-written erotica from the UK and USA. The key words are: diversity, surprises and faultless writing.

Competition rules will apply to short stories: you will hear back from us about your story <u>only</u> if it has been

successful. **We cannot give individual feedback on short stories as we receive far too many for this to be possible.**

For future collections check the Black Lace website.

If you want to find out more about Black Lace, check our website, where you will find our author guidelines and more information about short stories. It's at www.blacklace-books.co.uk

Alternatively, send a large SAE with a first-class British stamp to:

Black Lace Guidelines
Virgin Books Ltd
Thames Wharf Studios
Rainville Road
London W6 9HA

The Taming of the Tigress
Alexandra Cole

Black pine, cedar and rich loam soil infused the autumn air with the cleansing essence of nature. There was scarcely a wisp of cloud to obscure the pristine blue sky that framed Mt Fuji and the forested hills at its base.

'We're going to be here an entire week, are we?' Michelle nudged her friend Emiko as they walked a leaf-strewn path towards a sprawling wood-frame inn built into a hillside. 'I don't think I ever want to go back to Tokyo. This is the real Japan.'

Emiko laughed. 'There is no "real Japan", any more than the changing of the guard is the real England, or a cottage on a loch is the real Scotland. Anyway, as for not wanting to leave, we'll see what you think about that after you've had four straight hours of training. This is my second martial-arts retreat. It will take you a month in Tokyo to recover, trust me.'

Michelle snapped her fist into Emiko's stomach, stopping just at the point of contact. 'I reckon I can tolerate a week away from those leering, pudgy salarymen in my classes. Come to study English, they say. Not bloody likely, they come to stare at these, is what they come for.' Michelle pushed her fingers into the tips of her breasts.

Emiko flashed her hand to one of Michelle's cushiony mounds and squeezed. 'Well, you've got something to stare at, haven't you? Look at me.' She cupped her hand under her modest cone. 'Any time you want to trade, just tell me.'

'You Japanese are shameless.' Michelle kissed Emiko's neck just below her ear. 'That's why I love your country.'

The forest path became a walkway lined with pebbles, as they approached the inn.

'We're here,' said Emiko.

They entered a stone-floored foyer. *'Gomen kudasai!'* Emiko called out.

A tall Japanese man, raw boned with angular features and an aquiline nose, came to answer her call. His black eyes had the focus of a raptor, no nonsense, no flirtation.

As if by instinct, Michelle squared her shoulders and thrust out her chest. Somewhere in the back of her mind she wondered, What's wrong?

The man obviously didn't hear Michelle's private thoughts. He glanced once more at her face before he entered the names of Michelle and Emiko into his register and led them to their room.

'Training begins in twenty minutes.' Before he left, he looked at Michelle as though she were a somewhat unappealing insect. 'It will be hard,' he said in English and closed the door.

'It will be hard,' Michelle repeated in a nasal falsetto and sneered. 'Fucking twit. I speak Japanese well enough. He can talk to me in his own language.' Again in falsetto, she said, 'Training's hard.' Groin high, she raised her knee and whipped a kick into the air so fast that her trousers slapped loudly against her leg. 'How's that for hard, you shirt-lifting bugger.'

Emiko smiled and whispered into Michelle's ear. 'Are you sure you're not angry because he didn't look.' She caressed her friend's glorious pillow and gently pinched its tip.

'I don't like to be taken lightly,' said Michelle.

'He doesn't take you lightly. He knows all about you, European champion in *karate*. Of course he knows you. The idea of this retreat is cross training, isn't it? You've signed up for *aikido*. You want grappling to complement your striking skills. That man's name is Yoshi Sakamura. He is the resident grand champion of *aikido*. He will be your *sensei* for the next week.'

'Gawd, almighty!'

'Put on your *do-gi*, Michelle-san. We don't have much time.'

The padded *aikido* jacket was uncomfortably heavy compared with the thin *karate* top that Michelle was used to. The white belt that she tied around her waist was new and stiff. Her own black *karate* belt was pliant and pitifully frayed from years of use. Its white core showed through the black, but nevertheless it was black to the fourth degree. She missed that old friend but would do without it for the next week. She hurried to the *dojo* and took her place at the front of the room.

At the blow of a stick wielded by an advanced student, a great drum resounded to announce the start of class.

'*Yoo-ii! Kamae!*' Sakamura shouted and gestured to his assistants, who rushed among the students pairing them for practice.

Sakamura himself walked towards Michelle and a tall muscular Caucasian man who stood next to her. He gestured towards each of them to indicate that they would pair off.

'Thus!' He pointed to Michelle's hand and to the tip of his own noble nose.

Michelle needed no other encouragement. She brought her hands head high, slid her front foot forwards and flicked a fist square at Sakamura's upper lip. She had expected to see the master grimace in pain; instead, he snared her wrist with astonishing speed. He turned his body in a circle that sent Michelle diving face first into the mat. He followed her to the ground and wrapped one leg around her arm. Next he secured the hold with his other leg. He could break her arm at will, if he chose. He did not. Rather, Michelle's arm was forced into the master's crotch.

From her own experience and from folklore, she had believed that all Japanese were small down there. However, the thick cord that she felt with her forearm belied that notion. The man was cushy and limp, but quite, quite large.

Keeping Michelle's arm in a pin, Sakamura looked at the Caucasian man. 'Do you understand?'

'*Hai!*' The man danced on his toes as Michelle got to her feet. He snapped a fist to her face.

Michelle batted the blow away and countered with a smashing punch to the man's stomach. He grimaced and lurched forwards.

'No!' Sakamura shouted and demanded that Michelle attack him. Again, he took her to the mat. He wrapped himself around her, but quickly released his grip.

Michelle took her time extracting herself. She ran her arm between his legs and pressed her hand along his cord into his balls. Again, she was impressed with the size of both.

She sprang to her feet and pointed to the fist of the man next to her and to her own nose. 'Attack me!' She said in a silent voice. The man lunged forwards. Michelle grabbed his wrist and turned her body, leading him down sprawling on to the mat. She wrapped her legs around his arm. It was long and reached to her breast. He pressed his palm into her cushion.

Michelle stared down at him. 'What do you feel?'

The man stammered. Still he tightened his grip on Michelle's exquisite mound.

'Is that it? Squishy, squishy; titty, titty. You're American, right?'

The man nodded.

'You're cute but, if you want me, you have to take me.' Michelle let him go and sprang to her feet. He attacked to no effect. She took him down again. His elbow popped at the pressure of her legs. His hand pressed into her labia. 'Enough?' Michelle asked.

The American patted the side of his leg to indicate submission. Even as he waited to be released, however, his thumb pushed to the core of her sex. Michelle started to let him go but, instead, decided to make him fight for his freedom. He was no flaccid salaryman. From his neck to his thighs, he was as hard as a man gets.

A sharp gust of air exploded from Michelle's lungs. 'Enough?' she asked. 'I can easily break this arm, you know.'

The American ran his thumb to the pearl of Michelle's sex and pressed. He shook his head.

As he struggled to free himself, she saw his mouth move and heard his unspoken words: 'I . . . want . . . you.' Even as she held the American helpless, she looked away into the eyes of the grand master. They were cold as steel.

The attacks and techniques changed and changed again until Michelle's legs and back quivered in exhaustion. There was no clock, but she could see the sun slide down towards the horizon. How many hours? She looked around her. Most of the students had given up. They lay prone or panted on their hands and knees. Was this the first day's test, then, to outlast the others?

Sakamura stood in front of her and extended his arm slowly, palm up. The invitation was to grab his wrist. To accept that was to accept defeat. Sakamura was stronger than she. He was a master in joint manipulation.

Michelle relied on her own expertise. She slapped the back of her wrist into Sakamura's hand and in a single motion stepped towards him. In lightning speed, she snapped a back fist to his face. On instinct alone, the master caught her wrist. It was too late. At the same moment that Michelle had attacked with her hand, she had thrust a kick to the master's groin. It nearly struck home.

Sakamura pressed his thighs together but only partially avoided the flashing ball of Michelle's foot. The master was clearly in pain as he called an end to the class.

Emiko was waiting in the room when Michelle returned. 'You look like you've been run over by a train, except for the smile. What happened?'

'I stayed with it until most everyone else was whimpering like an exhausted baby. At the end I kicked grand master Sakamura in the bollocks.'

'You what? Michelle, you can't –'

'Maybe not, but I did anyway. He had it coming.'

Emiko just shook her head. 'You're always competing, Michelle. Let's go take a bath. There's a *yukata* for you.'

Michelle changed out of her rough *do-gi* into the light cotton robe provided by the inn. 'I'm ready.'

Emiko tossed Michelle a length of terry cloth the size of a face towel and led the way down the hall to the front entrance. 'Here, use these outdoors.' She set out a pair of rubber sandals.

'Where are we going? Is the bath in another building?'

'Not exactly.' Emiko looked over her shoulder and smiled.

Michelle breathed deeply and flexed her sore shoulders as they walked along a narrow path. Her eyes followed a hawk drifting on the breeze. It banked to the left and swooped down across the disc of the sun turning red-orange. 'I guess I know what kind of bath we're going to.'

Emiko chuckled. 'Yeah, what we call *rotenburo*, a bath under the heavens. Have you been to one before?'

'No, but shouldn't we have a bathing suit or something?'

'Since when did you become so prissy? Anyway, what was that talk about the real Japan?'

'OK, Emiko-san, you're the boss.'

They came to a sharp decline and had to hold on to a rope strung along the path until they reached level ground and the hot springs pool. It was long and narrow and twisted back under the trees.

'These waters have minerals that will help your skin and achy muscles,' said Emiko.

'I could use that. I have mat burns on my elbows and shoulders and probably other places that I haven't discovered yet. Where do we put our robes?'

No sooner had she asked the question than she heard a ripple of water. 'There's a good rock. Hi there, ladies.' It was the American she had paired with for *aikido* practice.

'Hi.' Emiko grinned and waved.

Michelle was aghast. 'I can't do this,' she whispered into Emiko's ear.

'Do what?'

'Bathe with a man, that man. In practice, he touched me here and here.' She pointed to her breast and pubic mound.

'Aren't you the lucky one? He's adorable.'

'But . . .'

'Michelle, you are the best friend a girl could have, but I really do not want to spend a week with you in the same room, if you are not going to bathe.'

'Can't we –'

Emiko rolled her eyes and untied the *obi* of her *yukata*. 'This rock you say?'

The American nodded.

Emiko laid the *obi* on the rock and let the robe fall loose. She looked the man straight in the eye as she reached for the edges of her only garment. 'How's the water?'

'Perfect. What's your name?'

'Emiko.' She pulled the *yukata* open and watched the man's eyes slide down to her furred vee. 'What's yours?'

'Joe, what else? All Americans are Joe, right?'

Emiko laughed and pulled the robe wide. Her breasts were indeed modest, but they were exquisitely contoured, high and capped by pinkish-beige tips that were marshmallow soft. Despite the unabashed display of her body, Emiko's smile was coy as she let the robe slide off her shoulders. 'What do you train in, Joe?'

'*Shorenji kempo.*'

'Do you?' Emiko folded the *yukata* and laid it on the rock. 'That's a bit of a cheat, isn't it? *Shorenji* uses techniques similar to *aikido*, right?' She dipped her foot into the water to test its heat.

Joe's nostrils flared as he watched. 'It isn't exactly the same, but you're right. There are some similarities in the grappling. I wanted *bojutsu*, but there were no openings.'

'Oh, sorry.' Emiko stepped into the water knee deep. 'I'm afraid I got your spot in stick-fighting class. It's always popular.' Emiko raised her arms high overhead and swung them in a circle as though she held a staff. She looked back at Michelle. 'Are you coming?'

Her friend was having uncommon difficulty removing her *obi*.

'Do you need help with that?' asked Joe.

Emiko pinched her nose and made a face. 'A week is a long time, Michelle.' She pointed towards the water.

'I'm coming.' Michelle's face flushed pink as she unknotted the *obi*. What else could she do? She could hardly walk away. She would look like a fool or even worse a timid girl. She kept her back turned to Joe as she slipped off the *yukata*. She folded it carefully and laid it on a rock. There she stood naked as the day she was born at the edge of a forest in front of a stranger who only an hour ago had been fondling her during their workout. She could hardly complain about that. She had been doing the same to Sakamura, hadn't she? The sun was low and cast sharp angles of light and shadow. She wondered how her backside looked to Joe. She knew he was staring. What to do now? Cover herself with her hands? No, that would be as bad as walking away. Slowly Michelle turned with her arms at her sides and her chin straight. The sunlight burnished her flesh in bronze.

'Whoa,' Joe whispered. 'Where're you from?'

'Bristol.' Michelle stepped into the water.

'England.'

'Last time I checked, yes.'

Emiko shot her a glance. 'Stop competing. It's time to relax.'

Michelle lowered her body into the hot water and grimaced as it intensified the pain of her mat burns.

'I know how that feels,' Joe said. 'Look at this.' He turned the side of his hip towards Michelle and stood high enough for her to see a large red scrape. When he stood, the muscles of his back and legs snaked under his skin like steel cables. He wasn't brawny, just lean and hard all over.

Well, maybe not hard *everywhere*, Michelle smiled at the thought. She noticed that Emiko saw Joe from a different angle and her gaze had dropped to his lower belly.

'Don't be babies,' Emiko said. 'Look at this.' She was still standing and walked towards Joe with her palms out. They were raw and blistered at the base of each middle finger.

'Ouch.' Joe took her hand in his for a closer look. As he did, he stood to full height. 'Maybe I'm lucky I didn't get a slot in the *bojutsu* class after all.'

'Yeah.' Emiko made a facetious snarl. 'I might have whacked you.' She swung an imaginary staff at Joe's head.

He turned away by instinct and faced Michelle whose gaze took in the front of his body. A thin cover of hair crossed his chest and tapered to a narrow vee between the ridges of his abs. The water covered only the tip of his cock. When Joe caught her watching, she looked quickly into the sky as though she had just seen another fascinating hawk. She could not believe he and Emiko were so casually chatting as though they were not stark naked.

'Show me how you hold it,' Joe said.

'Hold what?' Emiko glanced at his groin.

Joe grinned and held out his hand. 'Pretend my arm is the staff.'

Emiko held his arm in the four basic grips and then offered her own arm for Joe to practise. 'It's getting cold.' She sank into the water.

'Sorry.' Joe looked into Emiko's face as he lowered himself until the water was just below his chin. 'It must be tough handling a stick for hours straight.'

'After a while, the staff felt like it was made of lead. I ache here.' Emiko touched her shoulders. 'And here.' She ran one hand along her forearm.

'Maybe I can help. Turn around.' Joe slipped his hands under Emiko's arms and pulled her towards him. When he did, he must have touched more than her underarms.

She leant her head back and looked up at his face. 'I'm not so sore there.'

'Excuse me.'

'It's OK.'

'I'm not so sore there.' Michelle repeated in her mind. Joe was a lecher. During class, he touched her tits, arse and quim every chance he got. However, after a few minutes of Emiko sashaying her trim body in front of him, things took quite a turn. He was now completely focused on her friend.

'Mmm, that feels good.' Emiko hummed a moan of pleasure as Joe sank his thumbs into her shoulders and down her spine.

'Face me,' he said and wrapped his legs around her hips when she turned towards him. He took one hand and kissed her palm. 'Your hands can't take another day like that. The skin is about to tear here.' He kissed her hand again.

'I'll tape it.' Emiko emitted a series of shallow gasps as Joe began massaging her forearms.

'Did that hurt?' He frowned and lightened his touch.

'Yes, but in a good way. Don't stop.'

Joe continued on Emiko's arms and the front of her shoulders until her head hung limp in relaxation.

'I guess we'd better go,' she said. 'It's almost dark.'

'I'll walk with you,' said Joe.

Michelle didn't move.

'Aren't you coming?' Emiko asked.

'A few more minutes. I'll be along.' She floated back in the mineral-rich water and watched Emiko and Joe dry themselves and each other's back with the small towels. They had to wring them out several times before they were done.

'Bye-bye.' Emiko and Joe waved as they started back to the inn.

Michelle was glad she didn't have to display her body in front of Joe again. She gave them just enough time to get well ahead of her then she stood to leave. When she did, she saw in the dying rays of the sun a silhouette of a man's face. He sat in a secluded niche of the hot springs pool. His face was serene, his eyes closed and his nose aquiline. She stood facing the man, but looked towards the horizon and slowly stretched her arms over her head and behind her back, jutting her wonderfully sculpted breasts forwards. She turned and splashed nosily through the water towards the bank and stepped out.

The orange remnants of refracted sunlight had faded to night, but a full moon washed Michelle's skin in a glow of blue light. With her back to the man, she bent at the hips and ran the towel down one leg and then the other. The man's silhouette was lost in shadow, but she faced where he had been and slowly, deliberately, she finished drying. She put on her *yukata* and started along the path. 'This time, did you look at me, Sakamura *sensei*?'

When Michelle got back to the room, Joe was on his stomach covered only across his hips by a towel. Emiko still wore her *yukata*. She sat astride him and was working her hands into his back.

'Hi,' she said smiling. 'I had to return the favour. He knows *shiatsu* very well. You should let him work on you.'

Michelle smiled and shook her head. 'Should I –?' She gestured towards the door.

'No! This is your room. I'm the one who should ask. Is it OK?'

'Of course, don't mind me. It's still early, but we were up at dawn and after today's workout I'm exhausted.'

The room was traditional Japanese with reed *tatami* mats for flooring. While Emiko continued massaging Joe, Michelle pulled a thin foam-rubber mattress from a closet and laid it on the floor. She covered that with a thickly padded futon and took out two lighter futon to use as quilts. The pillow was an oblong bar that felt like a beanbag on one side and a foam cushion on the other. Michelle turned it cushion-side up and lay down on her back.

'Turn over,' Emiko said to the man under her.

Michelle opened her eye only a slit and peeked at her friend. Joe was on his back now and Emiko straddled his hips as she leant the heels of her hands into his shoulders and upper chest.

Lucky Joe, Michelle thought as she turned her back to them. An image of Joe's rock-hard stomach, the lush curls at its base and the flesh below formed in tantalising detail in her mind. Lucky Emiko.

'Do me again,' she heard her friend say.

'All right, but you have to take that off. We have only one dry towel and it's small.'

'It's OK.'

Michelle listened to the rustle of cloth and quiet moans. More than once she wanted to say, 'Do me too,' but that would admit weakness. She had the pride of a champion, a competitor. At the bath, Emiko had said, 'Stop competing.' Her friend didn't understand. The moment she stopped competing, even for an instant, was the instant she stopped being a champion.

Emiko's moan turned to a giggle. 'That's not a *shiatsu* pressure point.'

'Maybe you've just been reading the wrong books.'

Michelle heard a sharp intake of breath, followed by another moan deep in Emiko's throat. Next came a series of sharp breaths and a low keening sound. Suddenly, she felt her friend's breath in her ear.

'Do you mind if he stays tonight?' Emiko whispered. 'He has three roommates. There is nowhere else to go. We'll be quiet.'

Michelle didn't answer. She just reached up and patted Emiko's cheek.

'Thank you,' said Emiko.

They were not exactly silent, but they were subdued vocally. Nevertheless, Michelle followed every moment. She didn't know what Joe was doing but, whatever it was, the man had staying power. It was nearly midnight before she heard their rhythmic breathing and let herself succumb to sleep. Just before she did, she saw the silhouette of a man with an aquiline nose.

'You have a hard kick, Michelle.'

'You aren't the first to tell me that.'

'I expect not.' Sakamura had paired Joe with another student and told Michelle that today he would work with her personally. 'Your victories in tournaments speak for your courage and strength, but do you know what "*aikido*" means?'

She nodded.

'I'm sure you know what the *words* mean. "A meeting of the spirit." But, do you understand them, here?' He pointed to the centre of Michelle's chest. 'Morihei Uyeshiba, the founder of *aikido*, said that never competing means never losing.'

'That doesn't sound like *bushido* to me.'

'There was once a great swordsman who was also a tea master. It was said that he could conduct an entire tea ceremony and never leave himself open to attack. He was serving a group of *samurai*, among which was a young man who sought to test him. At one point the tea master was vulnerable. Just before the young man attacked, however, the tea master looked at him, complimented his bearing and praised the *samurai*'s lord. After that, the *samurai* could not possibly attack. There are many aspects to the Way of the Warrior, Michelle.'

'I think I took the wrong class.' Michelle squared her shoulders, but her voice lacked its characteristic bravado.

'You're free to go but, before you decide, you should know that you took exactly the right class.'

Michelle evaded the issue. She wanted time to think. 'How do you know English so well?'

'My grandfather was German. He made sure I was educated in Bonn and London. Now, if you don't mind, I have a class to conduct. Are you, or are you not, my student?'

She didn't answer but, when she didn't leave, Sakamura said, 'We'll start from the very basics. Stand so.'

Sakamura stepped forwards with his right side and Michelle stepped back with her left. Next, she moved forwards. One led; one followed, as in a dance.

The movements grew more complex. By one hand only, Sakamura seized Michelle's wrist with such grace and skill that she was lifted off the ground. Michelle felt herself caught in a swirl of power that she did not resist. She was flying, diving, rolling across the mat in a somersault. She sprang to her feet and threw Sakamura when he swept towards her so smoothly he seemed to glide on ice. She could not copy his advanced techniques, but she was exhilarated by the complexity of his movements. He swept her left, reversed to right then sent her rolling backwards with a force that seemed beyond muscular strength. She was not defeated by Sakamura's throws: he imparted his strength to her. When she faced him again, she realised her eyes were afire, not with desire for victory, but with anticipation of receiving his power.

'Final technique,' Sakamura said.

Michelle rushed him and was lifted in an arc over his head. She somersaulted in the air and landed in a crouch on her feet.

'We've worked up quite a sweat.'

Sakamura gave only a hint of a smile then walked to the front of the class and called a halt to the lesson. The students knelt and bowed, touching their foreheads to the mat. As they filed away, Michelle remained kneeling. Sakamura knelt in front of her. Michelle wiped her fingers across his full lips, which were damp with perspiration.

'We might need a bath, mightn't we?' she said.

'Wait here.' Sakamura returned with *yukata* and towels. 'There is a small pool farther from the one you were in yesterday, and the water is a bit hotter. Is that OK?'

'That was you, yesterday. Did you –'

'Did I what?'

'Nothing.'

They walked in silence uphill through dense forest until they came to a small pool. Thick clouds of mist rose from it.

Sakamura turned to face Michelle as he untied his *obi* and removed his jacket. His skin was nearly hairless and his musculature was sleek without the hard definition of Joe's, but nonetheless powerful.

'To answer your question,' he said, 'yes.'

'What question?'

'The one you wanted to ask at the *dojo*. You said it was nothing, but the answer is that I did look at you. When I met you at the door, I looked at your eyes and saw a fighter. At the bath, I looked at you in the light of a fiery red sun and saw a goddess, a champion.'

Michelle removed her belt and held his gaze with hers as she pulled her jacket open. She loosened the knots in the strings at either side of her trousers. Heat welled in the core of her body. She felt the speeding beat of her own heart fill her breast as she pushed the trousers down the gentle curve of her lower belly to the tuft of her mound. Her mouth was dry when she spoke. 'What do you see now, Yoshi?'

Sakamura's gaze followed the descent of Michelle's trousers before he lifted his eyes to hers. 'I see a woman.'

Together, they stepped out of their trousers and embraced. Michelle felt like she would sink for ever into his lush lips. They were the only thing soft about him. Her hands gripped his hard arse. Her lips parted to receive the warm inquisitive tongue that explored her

THE TAMING OF THE TIGRESS **17**

mouth as though seeking knowledge of her soul. His fingers, tracing the back of her neck, sparked an electric tingle through her spine. A craving roiled within her that she either had never known with such intensity or had forgotten. She wrapped her arms around his back, gripped her hands together and crushed him to her until she heard him moan in surrender.

'What do you feel now?' She squeezed harder still.

An animal fire burnt in his eye. 'I feel a tigress who ought to purr as well as growl.' Sakamura drew his hands away from Michelle. As he did, he easily broke her grip. Like a matador feinting from a charging bull, he turned smoothly so he stood behind her and pinned her arms at her back. He stepped close, pushing his cock into her hand. With his lips to her ear, he whispered, 'Never fighting, Michelle –' his hand slid over the sumptuous curve of her breast and teased its tip '– means never defeated.' He traced down her firm belly and combed his fingers through the tight curls at its base.

'I do fight. It is what I am.' She squeezed his staff hard.

'I know. But there is another part of you that is neglected. You can let it grow strong without diminishing the competitor within you.' He released his hold on her arms, but she kept her hands behind her back to knead his staff and balls. 'Face me, Michelle. Show me your other side, pliant and giving.'

She turned, and felt his hand slide down the curve of her belly and cup her sex. 'You've found the pliant part of me, haven't you?' Michelle put her hand over his and squeezed, then she gripped the base of Sakamura's cock and pushed lower to his balls.

Sakamura's finger caressed her tiny pearl and pushed towards her sheath. Michelle responded with a gentle squeeze to his sac. A sharp gasp sounded in her throat as his finger entered her. 'Am I giving, or are you taking?'

'It's the same.' His finger slid rapidly back and forth inside her.

Michelle pressed her forehead against his shoulder and her mouth found the cusp of his left chest. His hand was in her hair pushing her face against him as she teased the brown pip with her tongue and teeth. She felt a quiver run through his back.

'Not many women know men enjoy that,' he said.

Michelle merely hummed in reply and nipped his skin. Before she realised what was happening, Sakamura had lifted her and walked into the pool. As he lowered her slowly, her bottom and sex lips were the first parts of her body to feel the water.

She sighed as the water rose around her. On her knees before Sakamura, she cupped water in her hands and poured it over his iron prick. She had seen few men so large and had felt none so hard. She ran both hands along his cock, nuzzled its tip with her cheek and played her lips down its underside.

Sakamura pressed his fingers into pleasure points on the back and top of her head, massaging her scalp as she took his cushy tip between her lips. He bent forwards and cupped her breast in one hand.

Michelle stayed with him, taking him as deeply as she could, but her lips could not reach the base.

Sakamura groaned and, as his stomach tensed, his grip on her hair and breast tightened.

She released him quickly. 'Not yet, Yoshi. It's your turn.'

The water was dense with dissolved minerals and easily supported her weight as she lay back floating. Sakamura sat in the pool, brought his face to the juncture of her legs and with one hand lifted her higher in the water. Michelle felt as though she were weightless in a heavenly ether.

Sakamura's tongue lapped the length of her pussy before he stabbed it against her clitoris. He went lower, pushing inside her. 'You're delicious.' He looked into her eyes, watching an erotic glow envelop her as his tongue continued its play until it induced an orgasmic shudder through Michelle's body.

'It's good to be a woman.' She smiled. 'I'm still ready for the second act.'

Sakamura stood so that his loins were at her hips and put his hands under the small of her back. 'You do it, Michelle. Take me inside you.' His eyes glistened as Michelle grasped his prick.

She used the staff to part her lips, slippery with her own oil. She wrapped her legs around Sakamura's hips and he pulled her towards him, spreading her sex with his girth, driving his full length into her. She slid along his steel flesh at her own languid pace with the water caressing her back in easy warmth.

Sakamura swayed on his feet, letting Michelle control the rhythm. She moved faster, but slowed again when she felt him tense. 'Stay with me, Yoshi.'

His eyes narrowed, and she sensed a partial ejaculation. He put his head back and breathed slow and deep. He regained control, but his need was building. He lifted Michelle out of the water and held her against his chest. His hips quickened with long, sharp thrusts as a keening welled from his chest.

Michelle bit into his shoulder. Her belly clinched with each stab and she slammed her hips against him, savaging his prick. She gripped his hair, forced her tongue into his mouth and received the full rush of his white heat.

He held her and sank into the bath. The water soothed them as they kissed and stroked each other in silence. After the sun had set, they stood to leave.

Michelle held Sakamura's cock. 'Once for you.' She

took his hand and pressed it to her cleft. 'Twice for me.' She winked like a pixie. 'I win.'

Sakamura laughed and touched his finger to her lips. 'No, Michelle, *we* win. And as for "once", well, we've only just begun.'

The Game of Kings Maya Hess

Tessa drove her sweating horse down the field for the final time that day and clipped the ball with her mallet, sending it at an acute angle into the goal. The handful of onlookers sent a few casual claps her way before ambling back to the clubhouse, most of the other players and spectators having already retired to the veranda for pre-dinner drinks and talk of the impending matches.

Tessa was the last player left on the field and, as she guided her horse back to the stable yard, she again noticed that strangely familiar figure leaning against the perimeter fence, one foot cocked on the railings, both hands gripping the top bar. Tessa knew he'd been watching her throughout the afternoon's practice sessions. In fact, he hadn't taken his eyes off her from the moment she'd arrived at the club earlier. She didn't understand the man's interest in her, especially as she was caked in sweat and dust. Tessa had an uncertain feeling that she knew him from somewhere and guessed that he recognised her too.

'Last off the field. Does this mean that you're dedicated or apprehensive about tomorrow's play?' The man stepped away from the fence and positioned himself in front of Tessa's exhausted horse. The creature threw back its head and snorted indignantly.

Tessa brought her leg across the rear of the saddle and slipped lightly off her mount. Mandarin-coloured dust erupted around her black leather boots. She raised her eyebrows, allowing herself a beat to study his face, to harvest any recollections about the man before she spoke.

'Dedicated, of course. Apprehensive, never. My entire team is honed and ready.' Tessa offered a terse smile but wasn't sure why her voice hardened and her jaw clenched. She found herself tipping back her head and bringing her knees together in almost military style. She clicked her mouth and walked on, holding her horse's bridle.

The man remained by her side. 'Jack Wentworth,' he said, again positioning himself in the horse's path and this time sending it into a series of frustrated whinnies.

Tessa patted its shoulder and gripped the bridle. His name was vaguely recognisable but Tessa's impatience of the man's rudeness outweighed her desire to know who he was. Doubtless she'd heard his name mentioned at another match. He was evidently a Polo player, dressed in jodhpurs and team shirt and cap.

'I have to get Nitro back to the groom. He needs water and rest. Excuse me.' Again, Tessa urged her horse on and headed across the arid yard to the stable block. Even though the sun was teetering on the horizon, the temperature was still in the high eighties and the humidity was unbearable – quite different to the tepid English summer she had left a couple of days earlier. Orange and gold fingers spread from the sunset and stretched over the distant hills, illuminating the far-away clouds like brightly coloured saris. Tessa was aware that the man was following her and, as she gave Nitro to the stable boy, she felt a hand in the small of her back steering her towards the clubhouse.

'You look thirsty. Come and have a drink with me.'

Tessa was annoyed. She was exhausted, dirty and needed to collect her thoughts in readiness for tomorrow's game but nevertheless allowed herself to be guided to the clubhouse veranda, driven simply by intrigue.

Seated at a table underneath a gently ticking fan, Tessa enjoyed the feeling of sweat evaporating from her face. She allowed her head to drop back on to the soft padding of the cane chair and let her eyes fall shut. All she could hear was the pounding of her horse's feet through the dust and the thwack of mallet on ball in the day's relentless heat. The practice sessions had gone well and she was sure that her all-female team would easily hold their own in the initial games of the tournament.

Jack Wentworth soon returned with two tall gin and tonics and unexpectedly seated himself directly next to Tessa on the small Colonial-style chair.

'You don't remember me, do you?' He took a long draft of the icy drink and plucked out the chunk of lime. Jack was sitting with his elbows resting on his knees, his upper body angled round to confront Tessa.

She stared hard at his sun-browned face and noticed his southern-hemisphere accent. She drew upon all her remaining resources to place him but simply couldn't. The way his face broke into a series of laughter lines around his white teeth stirred something within Tessa but she finally convinced herself that she was merely responding to his fierce good looks. She shrugged and picked up her drink. 'Sorry, I don't.' She didn't want to flatter the stranger with too much interest and so gave more thought to sipping her drink and admiring the sunset.

Jaipur was certainly a stunning place and, as if he had read her mind, Jack Wentworth interrupted her thoughts. 'Indian sunsets are like no other in the world.' He gestured towards the west and the accumulating cirrus clouds hanging over the distant hills. 'There's a storm brewing. Tomorrow, maybe the day after.'

'I don't think so,' Tessa said, thankful for the change in conversation. 'I've heard that the –'

'Melbourne 2001. Our team won, yours lost. We got the prize.' Jack Wentworth's clipped tone coupled with the look of absolute triumph and smugness he now wore as he sipped his gin and tonic shattered any feelings of tranquillity or enjoyment the sunset held for Tessa. The man was clearly trying to suppress his laughter.

'Melbourne ... prize?' Tessa stammered. How could she ever forget *that* match? Simply the worst game of Polo her team had ever played; totally and utterly the most humiliating three days of her life. After leading her team to defeat on the field during the mixed-team match, she then had to lead three of her best players to the beds of the opposition. Having made the bet with the cocky, self-assured captain of the all-male over-35s team, it would have been dishonourable not to keep to their side of the bargain.

Tessa wasn't sure if it was shame or an involuntary reaction to the memory that caused her top lip to curl into a smile as she sipped her gin. The memories filtered back like the gathering clouds on the horizon. She recalled agreeing to such outlandish sexual frolics because she hadn't known any of the men in the room and had convinced herself and her teammates that they would never encounter any of them ever again. It was an anonymous orgy – a sweating mass of nameless bodies hungry for their prize and never to be seen again. But here he was, Jack Wentworth, veteran Polo player, veteran gambler and, if it was truly him four years ago in that hotel room, then expert lover too.

'I barely remember it,' she said, almost choking on her drink.

As if sent by the gods, an Indian boy interrupted the pair with a tray of fresh drinks and a dish of spiced nuts. Tessa took a large mouthful of her drink and closed her eyes for a second. Suddenly, she felt something fiddling with the top of her breast and recoiled, sloshing gin and tonic on her jodhpurs.

'A mosquito was about to crawl down your shirt.' Jack held up the insect and burst it between his finger and thumb.

'Gosh, you're brave,' Tessa said, reaching for a handful of nuts.

Jack gripped her arm and pulled her even closer. 'You were the best,' he whispered in her ear, his breath hot and spicy from the snack. 'I had a go with the other girls but, if you remember, we finished up together for hours.' Jack continued to crunch in her ear. 'Look, you're all wet.' He made to wipe the spilt gin from Tessa's inner thigh but she swatted his hand away.

'It was nothing to me. A casual fuck with a bunch of strangers. We were simply honouring our bet. And no, I don't remember you especially. It's all long forgotten.'

'Really?' Jack smirked. His pupils dilated and his breathing deepened.

Tessa noticed the dew of sweat across his forehead and top lip, somehow magnifying the roughness of his face and similarly the country from which he came. This lot were a tough team and Tessa knew they were in for a hard ride when they played the mixed games tomorrow.

'Hold still again.' Without considering the tenderness of her breast or even that her nipple had drawn up into an angry peak, Jack flicked the back of his hand across the front of Tessa's grimy shirt. 'Little bugger was after your tit.' A flash of white teeth again as, instead of plucking off the insect, Jack firmly took hold of Tessa's upturned nipple and refused to let go, even when she shifted uncomfortably.

'I'd like to make another bet with you.' He kept a firm grip on Tessa through her shirt. 'And given that you're so confident about your team's ability you needn't be worried. But if you should lose to us then, well, we'll see.' Jack smirked at Tessa's near inability to speak. But words weren't necessary. There was an unspoken agreement between them as palpable as the looming storm.

'Like I said, my team is –' Tessa grimaced and fought the sudden stab of heat that rocketed through her lower belly and between her legs.

'Your team is what?' Jack laughed as he rotated the nipple between his fingers. His body concealed Tessa's increased writhing from any onlookers, although he wouldn't have cared if anyone had seen him tormenting the woman's sensibilities.

'My team is up for any hollow bet you may toss our way, Mr Wentworth.' Tessa begged her body to be still because, with every uncomfortable twist that she made, the wretched man pinched her further. Shamefully and unable to suppress a large moan, her back suddenly arched and her head dropped back on to the cushion. She simply did not know if this was nice or not. The fire between her legs told her one thing and the pain in her breast told her quite another. She had an enormous desire to touch each end of her body, thrusting her flattened hand between her legs to build up the tiny pulsing waves as her unfolding lips blossomed from within her tight jodhpurs and also an infuriating desire to press Jack Wentworth's gin-drenched mouth firmly around her burning nipple. She did neither.

'It's not the rest of your team that we want. It's *you*. Tell me it's game on.' Jack was serious, his face reflecting the pleasure that only one half of Tessa was enjoying.

She abruptly swung her head away and took an eyeful of the bulging disc of fire as it finally dismissed the day and dropped out of sight below the horizon, turning the Polo field, the site of tomorrow's battle, into nothing more than a dull patch of brown wasteland.

Mustering all her inner strength and pride, Tessa wrenched herself free from Jack's grip and stood up, convinced that every other person seated on the veranda could feel the heat radiating from between her legs. 'Oh, definitely game on, Mr Wentworth. Prepare your team-mates for a thrashing.' Tessa added a satisfying whine to the end of her speech, mimicking Jack's heavy accent. 'When we win, I will take pleasure in flaunting what you can't have. Melbourne was a one-off. It can never happen again.'

Tessa left the table and heard Jack laughing as she walked away. She felt his stare burning her arse as she pressed through the crowded clubhouse and vowed that, despite the now incessant tingling in her knickers, she would fight to win tomorrow.

She'd hoped that she'd be alone in the hotel room. God knows, she *needed* the room to herself and was overcome by a wave of disappointment as she saw her teammate step out of the shower as she entered the small suite. Any privacy was out of the question.

'Boy, was I ready for that.' Sophie winked as she allowed her towel to drop to the floor. Judging by the pink glow on her skin and the skim of silver juice on the tip of her clit, Tessa figured that she'd done more than wash in there. 'It's those damned Australian players.' Sophie wiped her hand across her brow in a dramatic display of approval. 'I'm going to have to disappear to the loos after each chukka tomorrow. What with this heat, being in the saddle all day and those horny buggers from Down Under.' Again, she swiped her brow but stopped when she saw her filthy and worn-out captain. 'Hey, what's up with you?'

Before Tessa replied, she suddenly felt relieved. Sophie was right. It wasn't Jack Wentworth who had made her feel so horny, causing all rational thought to frazzle with the desire for sex. As usual, a day in the saddle, the relentless pounding from the well-worn leather had sent her level of desire and need for immediate relief spiralling out of control. Coupled with the heat and humidity, the exotic colours and smells of India, Tessa's senses were on fire. She couldn't wait to delve beneath her jodhpurs and find what awaited her. She just wasn't sure what to do about Sophie.

Tessa fixed a drink for them both from the mini-bar and settled on top of her bed, trying to gather the energy to shower. She watched as her unabashed and naked friend stood in the full-length window of their first-floor room and stared out at the twilight city beyond. Sophie sipped her drink, the only barrier between her and passers-by being the thin whiff of voile that billowed in the evening breeze, occasionally offering a glimpse of European breast or thigh to anyone lucky enough to be looking up.

Tessa took her chance. She couldn't wait any longer. Trying hard to obliterate her encounter with Jack Wentworth and the undeniably tough Polo she and her team would face the next day, Tessa raised her hips from the bed and slid her jodhpurs down her legs like she was peeling off skin. She knew she didn't have much time while her friend's back was turned and so, after hooking her panties aside, she drove two fingers up inside herself while her thumb beat against her saddle-ravaged clit. She was thankful when Sophie continued to gaze out of the window and began to talk about the day's events. It covered the mess of sound that came from her drenched pussy, literally like the floodgates had been opened now her jodhpurs were removed.

Tessa was only able to answer her friend in broken sentences and breathy gasps. She could hardly stand her fingers on her juiced-up lips, let alone when she caught the blossoming tip of her clit with her thumb. The temperature between her legs was surely a good ten degrees higher than the rest of her body, and as she worked on herself she caught a whiff of her own sweet musk mingled with saddle soap plus the reek of night-time Jaipur flooding in through the open window.

Another few seconds and Tessa was unable to prevent the hot rod of orgasm from choking her sex in strong waves of contraction, surging up into her belly, her breasts, her shoulders and throat. And it was only another second or two before Sophie finally turned from the window and saw her friend lying supine, several fingers still resting between her swollen lips, virtually passed out on the bed.

'Those Aussies get you all hot too, huh?' Sophie giggled and began to dress for the evening's social events. Slowly, Tessa pulled out of her delirious and exhausted state and realised that Sophie was staring at her sodden panties. 'I said, did that delicious team from Down Under do that to you, too?'

Tessa shook her head a little before pulling up her jodhpurs. She knocked back her drink, a frown creasing her brow. 'No, of course not. In my experience, they're uncouth convicts without any morals, on or off the Polo field.'

Shortly afterwards, when Sophie had dressed and vacated the hotel room, Tessa pondered just how serious Jack Wentworth had been about his wager. With the consequences of a defeat firmly in mind, Tessa stepped into the shower and began to work herself up all over again.

The heat was more intense than the previous day, despite the absence of sun. The distant cirrus clouds had matted to form a rosy-grey blanket of steamy cumulus that swelled and churned overhead. The conditions cast an eerie light over the Jaipur Polo Club as team captains from around the world gathered in the clubhouse. The afternoon's sport was set to include four games of mixed-team play, which was until recently a relatively unheard-of occurrence in the traditional and ancient game.

When Jack Wentworth tipped his cap and grinned in her direction from across the clubhouse, Tessa ignored him and ushered the rest of the Ashlea Ladies Team outside to the veranda. She wondered if Jack had been right yesterday about the impending storm. Certainly the sky was fleshed with layers of dense cloud and the air itself seemed to be saturated with anticipation. Tessa briefly looked to the skies and prayed for the rain to hold off. A downpour and a sodden pitch would certainly thwart the game against the Australian team, and in turn would scupper the result Tessa desired.

'Right, girls,' she announced, gathering them around her. 'Here are our tactics for today's play...'

The Ashlea Ladies won their first game against the female team from the USA six goals to four. Tessa urged her horse back to the stable yard, her expression a tight knot of anticipation and excitement. Tides of sweat and salt decorated the horse's black coat and, instead of allowing the stable boy to attend to the animal, Tessa set about cleaning him up and feeding him herself. She found the action therapeutic, despite the perspiration that poured off her own body as she worked hard to groom him. He would need several hours' rest and a big feed before the afternoon's game against Jack Wentworth's team. Tessa filled up Nitro's feeding trough to the brim and left him to rest.

The first chukka of the game against the Australian male team was a resounding victory for the Ashlea Ladies. Tessa scored a goal within three minutes of play, her mallet dangerously skimming the kneepads of Jack Wentworth as he thundered past trying to block her shot. She smirked as he pulled his horse around, a patina of sweat already visible underneath his faceguard. Tessa spoke softly to her horse as she steered him centre field again, patting his shoulder. Nitro was nervous and filled with untamed energy, fuelled and eager like his owner.

Sophie and the other two women supported their captain as the game continued but, within minutes of play resuming, Tessa could see that a win against the male team would be near impossible. Nitro was behaving devilishly, not at all like the highly trained animal she knew. Before she could think further about tactics, the Australian team scored a goal and when Tessa protested that there had been a foul she was slammed into silence by the umpire. The horn sounded and the teams swapped ends and during the next chukka two more goals were scored against the Ashlea Ladies.

Within three more chukkas, Tessa could see that the game had become virtually irretrievable and, in under an hour of play, the Australians rode off the field in victory seven goals to one. Tessa led her frenzied horse back to the stable yard, a dangerous glow decorating her cheeks.

'You girls go back to the clubhouse for refreshments. I'll settle the horses.' She patted her team on the backs as they trudged by, saddened by defeat. 'Tomorrow's another day and another match,' she offered as consolation.

Instead of attending to the horses immediately, Tessa tethered them and dropped down into a pile of fresh straw. She was exhausted and closed her eyes, allowing the straw to engulf her aching body. She wrapped her arms across her chest and was considering the delicious consequences of losing to Jack's team when she was suddenly startled by his resounding voice. She sat upright and took a moment to focus on the sight before her. Standing against the bruise-coloured sky in the stable doorway were the four members of the Melbourne squad. Each wore full uniform, including their boots and spurs, and firmly gripped their Polo whips. They formed an indomitable barrier, the sight of which sent Tessa's heart into arrhythmia.

'Prize-giving ceremony,' Jack announced with a smirk, stepping forwards from the group. Tessa made to stand but Jack easily lowered her back into the straw with one hand. 'Uh, uh. You're not going anywhere until we get what's ours.' Jack tapped his crop against the side of his boot.

Tessa hung her head, showing her shame for having lost and, in spite of her humility, she felt all her peripheral muscles tighten, sending a surge of heat and tension to the pit of her belly and beyond. 'I understand,' she said. 'You deserve your prize.' She sat limply and waited, while adrenalin seared her veins.

'Take off your shirt,' Jack ordered, distracting Tessa's gaze with a sharp thwack of his riding crop against the dusty leather of his boot.

Tessa swallowed and did as she was told. She crossed her arms and pulled the hem of her red and blue team shirt over her head. Instantly, she felt a breeze on her sticky skin but this was overshadowed by the heat coming from four pairs of eyes. Her full breasts, choked within her sports bra, were being studied from all angles by the other three players. Jack seemed untouched by the sight of her bare skin and sent the tip of his crop flicking across the sweat-soaked patch of white cotton between her breasts.

'Get that off too,' he said, disdain lacing his words, although Tessa detected a shudder in his voice.

She fumbled with the catch behind her back and allowed her bra straps to fall forwards. Before she could remove it completely, Jack had the leather end of his crop hooked under a strap and pulled the plain garment off completely. Tessa's shoulders instinctively drew inwards as her large breasts fell free but, when she saw three looks of approval from the others, she leant back on her hands and sank into the deep straw in order to better display her naked breasts. Her raspberry-coloured nipples had contracted to tight pink discs and her pale English skin was shimmering with sweat. Tessa waited with both fear and excitement as the other three Australians drew up by Jack's side. The men were clearly straining beneath their jodhpurs, the combined amount of eager cock a both frightening and delicious prospect for Tessa, who had now dropped completely back into the scratchy straw. She was surrounded by the team, with Jack very much in control of his players as he told them to flick and tease her with their crops.

'Take everything else off too,' Jack ordered.

Tessa could barely co-ordinate her fingers as the whips messed with her nipples and mouth. She managed to slide off her sturdy boots before lowering her jodhpurs to her ankles. It was always a relief to get them off, like shedding skin. The new layer of virgin flesh underneath was ultra-sensitive, maddened by every touch or breath of air.

Before she knew what was happening, Tessa was aware of Jack's riding boot easing her body back down into the straw. He deftly pulled the jodhpurs from her ankles and took a moment to appraise what had been revealed. He stood at her feet and looked back up her lean body, his gaze delayed by the tiny white triangle of thong at the top of her thighs.

Judging by the growing bulges in the team's tight-fitting uniforms, Tessa knew they approved of what they saw. Her lips and cheeks flushed with excitement and she felt like she'd pee herself if they didn't take her soon. But Tessa wasn't going to let them know how she felt.

No, that was her secret and, while she lay meekly in the straw, she felt her skin explode into a thousand tiny prickles at the thought of shoving her neat little mound towards the nearest mouth.

Fighting back her powerful desires, wanting to make the game last for ever, Tessa watched timidly as Jack and his three friends stripped off their team uniforms. Like an aphrodisiac weather front, Tessa was overcome by the powerful but sexy stench of pheromones and sweat as clothes were discarded. One by one, sheets of tanned skin stretched over hard-working muscle were revealed to her disbelieving eyes. The other three team players were fairer than Jack, their naked chests dappled with autumn-coloured hair over sun-bronzed skin, and they were so similar in their good looks that they could have passed for brothers. Tessa was suddenly faced with three stiff cocks bursting from their prisons and the thrill that they were all hers nearly caused her to orgasm immediately. She raised her hands out of the straw in an eager attempt to pull the nearest one to her but Jack swiped her arms away with his crop.

'Not yet,' he barked and then turned to the player who had taken first defence on the Polo field. 'Lick her out but don't allow her to come.'

'You're the boss,' he replied, his face breaking into a grin.

Unable to protest even if she wanted to, Tessa felt her ankles being gripped and drawn apart as she lay in the straw. The nameless Australian glanced at her briefly before getting to work. With his face close and his breath moist on her skin, he hooked a dusty finger inside Tessa's panties and drew them aside. The half-growl, half-moan he emitted assured Tessa that he approved of her neat and trimmed mound. She was certain that her clit would be straining between her swollen lips as if begging to be licked first. She hoped that he noticed and didn't waste any time. Maintaining the timid charade was becoming increasingly harder as her lust grew more urgent. She struggled violently against her body's needs as the first velvet stroke of tongue slowly drew up the entire length of her creamy pussy, sending her mind cascading into oblivion. All her senses merged together and battered her brain with unreliable signals. Overhead, she could see Jack looming, waiting, his stiffness growing ever bigger, keen to claim his prize.

The Australian's tongue felt huge and invading, like an independent creature set loose as it worked deftly on Tessa's sex. The fire that raged between her legs was somehow linked to the thoughts in her mind, and while she had often fantasised about sex with many men since the time in Melbourne, she never thought it would happen again. Tessa let out a wistful whimper as the realisation nearly drowned her. She lifted her hips from the straw and ground her sex into the man's face, like her swollen lips were a drooling mouth suffocating him with kissing.

'Get her to suck you off,' Tessa heard Jack say, although in her delirious state she was unable to put meaning to the words until she felt something warm and smooth and meat-like brushing against her mouth.

'Come on, sweetie. Open wide.' The voice seemed detached from the hard lines of his perspiring body as the Australian teased her mouth with his straining erection. It was the salty bead oozing from the tip that caused her to part her lips in order to taste it, leaving just enough space for the cock to push and ease itself between her teeth. The silent stranger held up Tessa's head and slowly manoeuvred his statuesque erection into her mouth, almost immediately having to fight against ejaculating down her throat.

'Steady, steady,' he growled, digging his nails into her shoulders.

Instinctively, Tessa pushed her fingers into the space behind his balls and began to circle the tacky patch of hairless flesh, causing the Australian to moan and sway as he levered his cock skilfully. He was sitting astride her chest, his buttocks brushing against the pale rise of her breasts, blocking any view of whatever was going on between Tessa's legs. But she was aware that something was happening, a changeover perhaps because the pattern of licking slowed and became firmer, and whoever it was down there was nibbling and biting at her clit with their teeth. She strained sideways, peering out over the top of the wide prick that was a millimetre away from choking her and saw the top of Jack's dark head between her legs. The other teammate, who had got her so wet initially, was now standing and looking a little lost alongside the fourth player. Jack must have sensed this also because he snapped a command at them.

'Don't just stand around. Make yourselves useful.' Jack beckoned them over. 'Get to work on her tits.' The lower half of Jack's face was smeared with Tessa's juices as he spoke and a low snarl could be heard as he buried himself once more between her engorged lips.

'You take that side and I'll have this one.' The raised clipped tones of the Australian's accent preceded the burning sensation that suddenly surrounded each nipple. Two unfamiliar mouths sucked and chewed noisily on her breasts, which somehow seemed to complete the electric circuit that was sparking throughout her body.

Moments later, Jack hauled himself upright as if he had surfaced from a long swim under water. His eyes were half-closed, perhaps because he was drunk on the juice drooling from Tessa's little pink sex, and he barely managed to give out further orders to the team through a gravelled voice.

One by one, the men dragged themselves away from their positions and rearranged according to Jack's wishes.

Tessa had no say in matters as she was roughly lifted and repositioned in the straw. She felt something warm beneath her back and when she sent her hands to investigate she realised that she had been put on top of Jack, her back covering his front so that she could feel his searing hot prick straining between her buttocks.

She felt his breath on her neck as he spoke. 'Ever had it up the arse before?' Jack was barely in control of his voice and the words came out as urgent staccato. Tessa shook her head as someone lifted her legs at a right angle to her hips and held them up high by the ankles. 'Ever had it up both before?' Jack let out an irrepressible laugh and took each of Tessa's breasts in his hands like they were handles for the impending ride. Tessa suddenly felt another mouth eating her sex and quickly working its way down to her exposed arse.

'No, of course not!' she insisted, her whole body now a mass of trembles and anticipation. The fear of what she knew was coming coupled with the pleasure of having her tight little arse exposed and prepared by a stranger was nearly enough to send her unconscious but she held on to the remaining shred of reality as her hips were lifted and her buttocks separated further by the remaining team player. Jack's thick cock nudged her little wet hole from underneath, while the other three Australians guided and pressed her down. She gasped as the tip probed her by a centimetre. Once Jack had found his target, he instinctively moved in mini-thrusts to gradually work the rest of his hungry shaft inside Tessa, lowering her on to his stiffness by pushing down on her hips. Eventually, it went in completely, causing Tessa to emit sharp moans as he moved.

'I want more,' Tessa wailed, surprising even herself as Jack powered home. 'You –' she pointed at one of the players '– fuck me now!' She already had her fingers pulling on her needy clit simply because she couldn't wait. Gone were her reservations and fake coyness. Tessa wanted them all in every part of her.

'I'll never fit in,' he said, eyeing Tessa's neat little sex with adoration. But he lowered himself on top of her anyway, jamming Tessa in between the two men like a sandwich filling. His cock soon found her swollen lips and gradually sank into her extra-tight pussy. With Jack pounding from behind, there wasn't much space left within her slim hips so the two men vied for space, eventually finding a rhythm that quickly brought each of them to the brink of orgasm and drove their shared lover to that critical peak of ecstasy.

Tessa stiffened, unable to comprehend anything at all except for the extreme feeling of fullness radiating from between her legs. As she was gasping for breath, turning her head both to the left and right, she was suddenly met by the remaining men's veined pricks competing for her mouth. Excited by the two different smells, Tessa lavished equal attention on each, offering a few slow and deep sucks to one before doing the same to the other.

The man on top of Tessa pumped her diligently, the stem of his cock grinding against her clit, before finally sending her catapulting inescapably into cascades of pleasure as her orgasm gripped and kneaded the men inside her. Pinwheels of ecstasy shot throughout her body to the very tips of her fingers as her sex contracted time and time again. Seconds later, both men were unable to prevent themselves from coming deep within Tessa's soft pink flesh. Their bodies went rigid above and below her as they were lost in their own feelings for the few seconds it took to empty their balls.

Tessa began to laugh. Aftershocks rippled within as her heart steadied and her open mouth suddenly became the receptacle for the other two men's hot and curdled ejaculation as they frantically pumped their cocks above her face. She was almost choking on the stuff as the tepid, salty liquid erupted over her in irregular bursts. Her tongue whipped around her lips to lap up the delicious mess, while the sensitive and softening pricks bobbed together mere millimetres away from her searching tongue.

'Allow me to help you,' said the Australian above Tessa, his semi-hardness still inside her. He dropped forwards and kissed her sopping face, cleaning up the milky puddles. Tessa was drenched and exhausted; she had been filled up to bursting point but was simply the happiest she'd ever been at losing a game of Polo.

As five exhausted bodies gradually relaxed and peeled off one another into the straw, Tessa heard thunder resonating in the distance. Moments later, fat bulbs of rain pelted the dusty ground outside the stable, slow at first but then with the urgency of a land that hadn't seen rain in months. The relief in the atmosphere was obvious. Jack had been right about the looming storm.

'So what went wrong with your game?' Jack asked above the noise, hoisting up his jodhpurs. 'You played like you were riding an unbroken colt.'

Tessa paused before replying, a girlish grin emerging beneath the sticky residue around her mouth. 'That'll be the oats I fed to Nitro earlier. They're guaranteed to drive him wild, making him virtually impossible to control.' She shrugged and picked up a crop, tapping it gently against her thigh. 'But it got me the ride I wanted.' She smirked naughtily and lay back in the straw to watch the lightning.

On His Honour Sophie Mouette

On the dark-panelled, high-ceilinged room, I heard the *tick-tick-tick* of fencing swords glancing off each other, accompanied by the occasional metallic swish. Once I entered from the locker room, I could also hear steady breathing behind the anonymous fencing masks and the slap of booted feet against the strip mats.

As I stretched, I watched Cameron, the club's top-seeded male fencer, winning point after point on his hapless opponent. Something about Cameron captivated me – and aroused me.

He was talented and cocky. It's not always a great combination, but there's a level at which I like cocky. I like seeing how deep it goes, if the outer display of bravado hides an inner desire to be bested.

Once suited up for fencing, most people looked sexless. The loose white canvas pants disguised curved hips or rounded asses, and the jackets did their best to make chests look flat – and for women sports bras rarely accented the figure. The strap on the jacket that went between the legs muted telltale bulges.

Yet for a few the outfits couldn't hide their shapes. Cameron was one. His rangy graceful body, piercing dark eyes and long dark ponytail hanging out from below his mask made him look like Musketeer material. It wasn't hard to imagine him in the plumed hat, fighting for the honour of Queen and Cardinal.

I leant my hands against the padded wall and pointed my right leg back, pressing my heel into the floor and feeling the glorious stretch in my calf muscle.

Honour. It seems like an archaic concept to some, but in fencing it's paramount. Competitions now require electronic scoring, with your sword wired to sense when the tip touches your opponent. But that's mostly for hard-to-call shots when there's less than a second between each *epée* touching the other person.

We practise here without electronics, which is one of the reasons I chose this club, chose Giulio Santorini as the fencing master who could push me to the limits of my abilities. Giulio demands honour and anyone without it is summarily dismissed from his presence and the club.

Cameron had honour. I'd been watching him closely and, although he was a lightning-fast, ruthless fencer, he never called a shot he didn't think was valid, never failed to accept a shot he knew was a solid hit.

I grabbed my *epée* and went to work on point control. Standing before the wall, I chose a spot and lunged. The tip hit the exact spot, the whippy blade bending before I snapped back to a standing position.

In a competition, if you miss the shot during that lunge, you'd better be sure you can get back out of the way in less than a heartbeat. Kind of like relationships: it pays to have a fast retreat, just in case.

I hadn't decided how Cameron felt about women. Oh, he wasn't gay. He strutted and preened around the ladies. He even had groupies, who came to competitions and fluttered from the sidelines. I was less clear on his attitude about women fencers. Competitions are segregated by gender, but practises can go either way.

The other fencers in the club had welcomed me and knew that I was damn good. But so far Cameron hadn't made any move to spar against me. Or any other kind of move. So, as usual, I took it upon myself to make the moves. That's why I was here on a Saturday evening. Giulio took weekends off, but we were free to come in and practise. I knew that Cameron did and tended to be the last one to leave.

I kept stretching until his opponent, sweaty and exhausted, headed to the locker room and I waited for Cameron to approach, a magpie after a shiny toy. I crossed my legs, then bent from the waist. I was limber enough to plant my hands flat on the floor. The bulky fencing outfit couldn't disguise my figure, either.

'Abby, isn't it?'

I'd been fencing here for almost a month, practising up to five times a week. I suspected that he did know my name. I bit back the smile that threatened to break free. He was like a teenage boy, trying to act cool in front of the girl he fancied. He had no idea that I saw right through him.

I straightened. 'That's right,' I said. 'And you're Cameron, I believe.'

When he saw that I wasn't going to swoon under his gaze, he changed his tack. Smart move. Never assume you can use the same successful attack over and over. Each opponent is different.

'I've been watching you,' he said. (As if I didn't know. So far, he thought I was prey and he the predator.) 'You show a great deal of promise.'

'I hope so,' I said evenly. 'I was the top seeded member of my last club.' I named it, and saw the flicker of respect in his dark eyes.

'Perhaps we can spar sometime,' he said.

Did he mean on the strip, or in the bedroom? Which begged the question, did I want to fence him until we dropped from exhaustion or fuck him until we dropped from exhaustion? The only issue was both had to be on my own terms. Cameron might not like that.

If my *proclivities* didn't interest him, then we'd go no further. I had a feeling that he wasn't used to acquiescing, and the challenge intrigued me. Aroused me. He didn't know that I was the predator and he the prey. I the spider and he the fly. And I could weave a very sticky web.

'I could give you a few pointers,' he went on.

I smiled then. 'Or I could give you a few.'

His nostrils flared at the challenge. I held my breath, waiting to see whether he'd pass this first test.

'You seem sure of yourself,' he said.

'I am sure of myself,' I said. 'I'm not saying there isn't room for learning but, rather than a teaching session, I'm interested in a challenge.'

He balanced the point of the *epée* on the toe of his soft boot and pressed down. The blade curved, twanged back into shape. 'A challenge?'

'I enjoy fighting against the best,' I said. 'It brings out my best.'

'You think you can beat me?' he asked.

Oh, I had him. He was intrigued. His ego was on the line. I homed in on the kill. 'Maybe,' I said. 'But to make it interesting, let's wager on the outcome.'

'Dinner?' His espresso eyes watched me with the same intensity he'd watch an opponent during a match. Good – he recognised that our match had already begun.

'I was thinking of something different.' I watched his reaction as I spoke. 'If I win, I get to do what I want with you for half an hour and you have to go along with it. If I lose, you get the same privilege. Could be cleaning my kitchen.' I moved closer, where I'd be inside his guard if we were fencing. 'Could be something more . . . personal.'

Cameron's smile looked, if anything, a little cockier, but his eyes lost their focus briefly and his pupils widened, black overtaking the brown. I love that expression, a bit of panic and a whole lot of lust mixing together. It's amusing as well as hot when the guy has the illusion he's still in control.

Cameron's answer showed he imagined he was. 'The

kitchen's the least interesting room in my house. We'll find someplace else for me to take advantage of my half-hour.'

Actually, my kitchen could be very interesting, but 'creative uses for wooden spoons' was a discussion for later.

'We should set ground rules,' I said, more for his benefit than my own. 'Nothing that could be truly harmful. And if the winner manages to pick the other person's worst nightmare that counts as harm.'

'Honour system that neither of us will invent phobias to get out of stuff.' Cameron said it as a statement, not a question. 'It has to really bother you to count. Otherwise you stick it out.'

'Of course!' I forced myself to look away from Cameron for a second, back to the strip mats. The place was starting to clear out. 'So, shall we?'

He bowed, an elegant courtier's gesture. I matched it, and we headed for the mats.

Beginners often think fencing is about speed or reach or grace. They're wrong. All of those are important, but the two key things are absolute control over your weapon and the ability to figure out your opponent's psychology. Rather like sex, at least *my* kind of sex.

You can't really watch your opponent's eyes when you fence. The masks interfere. Instead, you learn to read other things. It wasn't hard to tell what Cameron hoped I would do. Ideally that unspoken communication happens in sex, too. Of course, in sex, unlike fencing, sooner or later you try to give the other person what he wants.

For a while the world narrowed to the two of us and our *epées*. I could feel sweat clinging to me, soaking into my jacket and hair, but most of my attention was on Cameron's gorgeous body, which was simultaneously attacking and evading me just as skilfully as I'd expected, and on our efforts to symbolically kill each other. Some might consider that an odd seduction, but those people aren't fencers. At least we could get the stabbing each other in the heart bit out of the way right up front.

In the heart, actually, was where I got him. He went for a head shot, which I parried, but he didn't snap back into his defence fast enough. He left me a lightning-fast opening. A touch to the chest. Would it be enough? Some might claim it was too light.

He stopped in his tracks, lowered his blade with theatrical flair. 'Very impressive, Abby. Thank you for such a challenging match.'

There was a smattering of applause from the couple of people who were left, watching in their street clothes. After our bout ended they picked up their gear and headed out. I locked the door behind them, then turned and winked at Cameron, who was gratefully stripping off his sweaty jacket.

'So, am I cleaning your kitchen?'

I laughed. 'Do I look that dumb? Go take a shower and meet me out here.' I went off to follow my own advice.

I knew he could run out on me as soon as my back was turned. I also knew he wouldn't.

By the time I emerged from the locker room, Cameron was waiting for me. I found myself strutting as I crossed the room. Tight black jeans, high-heeled Goth boots, a form-fitting forest-green stretch-velvet turtleneck and an appreciate audience put a little feline in my walk.

'I didn't know if I should get dressed or not, so I compromised.' He gestured down his bare torso, where a few stray water drops gleamed. As if I hadn't already noticed the lovely view.

His lower body in snug faded Levis and bare feet was a nice view, too, but I had plans for improving it.

'You're not going to need those jeans,' I said casually. 'Take them off.' I could have softened it with a 'please', but I wanted to see how he reacted.

A look of confusion, then a catch in the breath and his pupils widening. This time he had no illusion he was in charge, but I couldn't tell how he felt about it. His hands fumbled for his zipper but his eyes stayed locked into mine as if he were scared to look away. No argument, though, just one gorgeous lanky boy slithering his jeans out of the way.

I'd anticipated the muscled legs, the sculpted ass and they were just as fine as I'd pictured them. He hadn't bothered putting underwear on – or maybe he never wore it.

'Now that's a pleasant surprise,' I said, circling my prey.

His cock twitched as if acknowledging the compliment.

The *salle* used to be a dance studio and a *barre* had been left on one wall for stretching. 'Hold on to that *barre* with one hand,' I ordered, 'and don't let go until I tell you. And hold still unless I tell you it's all right to move.'

I was glad I'd worn heels. I wouldn't have to use rappelling gear to kiss him. I took advantage of that immediately, pressing my clothed body against his naked one. It made his status clear: the naked one is the toy. I emphasised it by running my hands over his body, paying special attention to his perfect buns, like warm velveted marble. I felt him fighting the instinct to wrap his arms around me. I hadn't figured out what I'd do to him if he broke position, but I'd come up with something. I always did, because boys would break until they really accepted I was in charge. So far, though, Cameron was obeying.

Honour-bound.

Not being able to hold me wasn't keeping him from kissing me back. He used his tongue almost as skilfully as his sword. I could get to like that. Too much, in fact. I could spend my half-hour just kissing and touching him.

It would be fun for both of us, but it wouldn't answer certain crucial questions. I let go.

I went to my fencing bag, put my leather gloves back on, picked up my *epée* and returned to him. 'The name of today's game is Don't Come. I'm going to do things to you that I hope you'll enjoy. But you're not to come until I say it's OK.' I placed the *epée*'s guarded tip at the hollow of his throat, barely touching skin. I knew he could feel it, though. That's one of the most vulnerable points on the body, one that's usually protected by the mask and a gorget. 'Do you understand?' I asked.

Small shivers darted over his skin. He licked his lips. 'Yes, Abby,' he whispered, his normally firm voice barely audible. Something else, on the other hand, was looking damn firm.

'Yes, *my lady*,' I said.

He nodded and mouthed the words after me. His eyes were dark as Starbuck's finest and blank as a blind man's. He was gone, losing himself in a place where he wasn't in control and that was just fine. Cameron didn't telegraph a lot when he was fencing, but he was doing so now, and what he was telling me was that he was getting way into this. Perfect.

I let the blade trail, making sure he could feel the cold metal against his chest, down his belly, snaking down his thigh. Cameron had been fencing at least as long as I had. He knew an *epée* was dull, but knowing that doesn't fend off that stubborn part of your brain that only registers a sword on your naked skin and wants to panic. Or the nerve endings that feel the cold caress of metal and turn it into fire. Some people find those warring impulses distinctly non-erotic. Cameron, on the other hand, squirmed and sighed. My kind of guy.

I ran the *epée* up his leg, let it rest briefly against his balls. This elicited a little moan.

I glanced up at the clock. Fifteen minutes left and I

was just getting started. Damn, I should have asked for more time. Reluctantly, I set the sword down.

Warm leather on hot skin. I've always thought there's nothing like it. I started on his nipples, a light touch to see if they were sensitive. They were. I pinched gently.

'Please,' he hissed.

'Please no or please yes?'

'Please yes.' And as I complied he breathed, 'Harder.'

Oh yes. My kind of guy. But I couldn't let him get away with that almost-demand. 'Didn't you forget something?' I slapped his ass lightly, an application of warm leather on bare skin he hadn't been expecting. When he didn't answer immediately, I did it again, although I figured he wasn't answering because he'd momentarily lost higher brain function.

He figured it out on the third slap. 'Please yes, my lady.'

'Good boy.' I gave him what he wanted: one nipple pinched and twisted and the other captured in my hot mouth. My free hand reached between his legs, cupped his balls. One leather-clad finger teased that exquisitely sensitive spot at their base. He was making the most interesting noises now, so I kept it up for a few minutes. Then I kissed my way down his body.

Some women with my tastes won't suck cock. Think it spoils a boy or something. I enjoy it way too much to pass it up: that first chance to smell that intimate flesh, to taste it, to feel that iron-peach sensation in my mouth. The power of feeling him quiver, wanting so badly to explode down my throat. Then stopping and pulling back until he cooled down. Repeat as needed, until he was in a sweaty panic.

He never stirred from the position I'd told him to hold. Once I thought I saw his hand twitch as if he wanted to put it on the back of my head, but he didn't.

My time was almost up. The obvious choices were to

finish him off or to order him to attend to the growing puddle in my panties.

I chose a third path. 'Doing OK?' I asked, rising and lightly stroking his face.

'Oh yeah!' His voice was far away but not lost. Found, even.

'Ready to come?'

'Yes, my lady.' It seemed to fall so naturally from his lips. 'Please? That's in your hands now, I guess.'

I smiled. No, I smirked. 'I'm putting it into your hands. Make yourself come for me, Cameron.'

His free hand closed around his cock and began pumping. The hand on the *barre* never let go. He looked towards the wall, trying to hide in his own shoulder.

I turned his face forwards. 'Look at me, Cameron. Look in my eyes while you're coming for me.'

His face flared red, but he obeyed. And seconds later, he grunted out a string of curses as he came all over the floor. At which point, I echoed him – a mini-gasm, but not bad for no hands.

'How about a rematch later in the week, my lady?' he asked as soon as he caught his breath.

'Half-hour's up. You can call me Abby again.'

'Abby,' he repeated as dutifully as he'd called me 'my lady'. He wouldn't forget my name now. I thought he looked a little disappointed. Better and better.

We made a date for Wednesday evening. He offered to carry my fencing bag to the car, but I declined.

'You should clean that up before you leave,' I called over my shoulder as I walked away. I had no doubt that he would.

By Wednesday evening, I was buzzing with the combination of adrenalin and arousal.

We'd already agreed on the terms. A full half-hour of fighting, with the person winning the most points winning the match. Winner took the loser home and kept them 'til midnight.

As I changed into my gear, the question in my mind was: What did he truly want, deep down? Did he want to win so he could turn the tables on me? Or did he want me to win, because he craved finding out how much farther I would take him? If the latter, would he let me win? I hoped not. I respected honour more than anything.

As I walked into the *salle*, I took a deep, steadying breath. It would do me no good to let my imagination distract me from the bout. My own honour demanded I give him my best, too.

Cameron emerged from the men's locker room as I was stretching. He gave me a lazy salute, and I nodded. I warmed up with a few of my regular sparring partners, and then we were ready to begin.

We had an audience again – five or six people who abandoned their own practise and settled on to the bleachers to watch. News of our previous match had made its way through the club. We hadn't advertised this one, but as soon as people figured out we were going to spar they wanted to watch. The nice thing was that we were able to ask someone to keep score for us. As it turned out, we needed it.

We were both in rare form. I don't know if I'd ever seen Cameron move so swiftly, so gracefully. Even if he wanted me to win, he wasn't going to make it easy for me. Good.

Again, the world narrowed to my opponent and me, to the strip, to the sound of my own heart pounding and the feel of the slender blade I controlled. I lunged a hair too far and didn't pull back as fast as I normally could, and he made a solid hit. We stepped apart, saluted again and started over. This time I went for a strong attack, pressing him back. His retreat along the strip was graceful, his parries solid, not letting me in for a winning shot.

The next bout, we saluted, then neither of us moved. Fencing is often compared to chess: you have to gauge your opponent, see many moves ahead of them. Sometimes it's a stand-off. If you move first, you've already left yourself open. This time I outlasted him. Maybe he got to thinking about what was at stake. But when he changed stance and thrust I was already moving. My *epée* shot out and connected squarely on his chest.

And on it went. I was so intent on the match that I almost didn't hear the call announcing that the half-hour was up. The voice sounded distant, muffled. We stripped off our masks and waited for the tally. I was breathing heavily, the sweat trickling down my face. It had been a good match, either way. But I hoped I'd won. My stomach tightened and I couldn't look at him.

The tally was announced: I'd beaten him by one point.

'Well fought,' he said, shaking my hand. Although his face remained impassive, I saw the look in his eyes, one I liked very much.

'See you outside in twenty minutes,' I murmured just to him. 'You'll follow me home.'

When we got to my home, I pointed to the teak coffee table. 'There's a questionnaire on there for you,' I said. 'I know you'll be honest in your answers. Fill it out – neatly.'

'Yes, my lady,' he said promptly.

I didn't let him see my eyebrow raise. I was impressed: he was falling into the role quite nicely.

I had a basic idea of how the evening would go, but I'd wait to make final plans until I'd seen his responses to the questionnaire. First on the schedule, in any case, was a little fun for myself.

I'd discovered how talented his tongue was for kissing.

The first order of business was to put it to use elsewhere. To that end, I put on a simple teal-blue satin camisole that brushed the tops of my thighs. While there's something to be said for leather and spiked heels, I'd rather reinforce my status with actions and words than outfits that teeter on the brink of cliché. Sometimes an unexpected look keeps my prey nicely off-balance. Besides, I wanted to be comfortable. I was hoping for a long night of carnal inventiveness.

I took my time, giving him ample chance to finish the questionnaire. I'd included every variation and kink I could think of; no doubt some of them would intrigue him, while some would be a definite turn-off and some would give him pause for consideration.

When I entered the living room, he was sitting on the floor by the coffee table, chewing on the end of the pencil. He hadn't even sat on the sofa, as if he knew he'd have to ask permission for that. Oh my, this boy was a natural. I was amazed nobody had snapped him up yet, and thrilled that I'd been the first to tap into his submissive tendencies. I felt that thrill all the way down to my clit.

He looked up as I walked in. His nostrils flared at the sight of me. 'I'm sorry, my lady, but I'm not quite finished.'

'Take your time,' I said. 'It's important, and there's no penalty for taking too long.'

I poured myself a glass of crisp Chardonnay. I wouldn't drink much, but it could serve as a nice prop. I had settled myself into an armchair and taken a few sips when he rose to his knees and presented the questionnaire to me like a royal coronet on a pillow.

'Thank you, Cameron.' I set the wine down and accepted the pages. 'I'm going to take my time reading this, so for starters ... strip.'

I didn't look up until I sensed he was kneeling in front

of me again. Then I slowly raised my eyes over the paper and regarded him. Oh, he was lovely. That slender but muscular chest, the whipcord arms, firm thighs. He was approaching hardness, not quite fully erect.

'While I'm reading, we'll start with your massaging my feet. You may lick them if you want, but since I don't know if you're interested in that, you have the option not to. If you have a question, you may say, "my lady?"; otherwise, don't talk. Understood?'

'Yes, my lady.'

'Carry on, then.'

I perused his answers. He showed strong interest in bondage and pain play, with some reservations. Fair enough. I might be able to push those boundaries later, but I'd pay attention.

His hands worked magic on my feet, pressing on the right places with strokes firm enough not to tickle. When his tongue snaked in between my toes, I hid my smile behind the questionnaire. God, it felt so good!

I turned a page.

'You may lick my calves and work your way up my thighs.'

According to the survey, he wasn't sure about anal play. Fine, we could discuss that later, too.

I spread my legs, allowing him access farther up between my legs. I knew he could smell my musky scent now and goodness knows I was wet. He started to get close, then hesitated.

'Very good, Cameron,' I said. 'You knew you didn't have permission yet.'

His tongue trailed spirals high up on my inner thighs. 'My lady?'

'Yes, Cameron?'

'May I?'

'Yes, Cameron, you may.'

I'm sure the papers rattled a little when his tongue

swiped across my clit. Like his hands, his tongue moved in firm strokes. He spent some time lapping at my pussy, tasting me, using his tongue like a tiny cock to press inside me.

I skimmed the last page of the questionnaire, which listed some hardcore stuff we wouldn't do tonight anyway, then dropped the pages. It was time to enjoy myself. I grabbed his long dark ponytail, running my fingers between it and dividing into two, like reins. When I tugged, I heard him let loose with a breathy moan that vibrated into my sex, and he redoubled his efforts. So, he liked that? Good.

I used his hair to direct him and, when I finally pushed his head harder against me, he picked up the cue perfectly. His tongue whipped across my clit like a sword, faster and harder. Dimly I was aware that he'd kept his hands on his knees, as if knowing I hadn't given him permission to touch me except with his mouth. That realisation helped tumble me over the edge.

I kept his face pressed against me for a moment, then released some of the pressure. He responded by laving gently with the flat of his tongue, tasting my juices. My thighs quivered and I held him there until I'd recovered my composure.

Then, my hands still entwined in his hair, I pulled him so he was kneeling up. I think it surprised him when I pulled him close and kissed him. Hell, it surprised me a little, not so much the kiss itself as the wave of sweet possessiveness that washed over me as I devoured his mouth. I've had my share of play partners. Most of them probably figured I was the least romantic woman on earth. I didn't 'date' those guys. I topped them. I fucked them. We had a hot, sweaty time together and it never got more complicated than that.

Deep down, though, I *am* a romantic. Except I'm not looking for a white knight. I want to be the knight – or perhaps the queen – who protects, controls and cares for my beloved vassal, and punishes him in my dungeon when need be. (Which would be whenever we both thought it would be fun.)

It had never happened, though. The right 'vassal' had to be more than hot and submissive: I wanted strength, intelligence, shared interests outside the bedroom and, most of all, shared values. Archaic ones like *honour* and the importance of one's word.

Damn if I wasn't picturing Cameron in that role. Not a slave, but a knight in his own right, sworn to my service. I was jumping the gun badly. Tonight I only had until midnight, and then he was free to go. Unless he decided he didn't want to.

I put my hand on his chest, pushed him away and stood. 'I think we'll be more comfortable in the bedroom now.'

'My lady?'

'Yes.'

'Do I walk? Or –'

The question zinged right to my groin. I hadn't planned to tell him to crawl, but the tone of Cameron's voice, his lowered eyes and most of all his quivering cock told me he craved it. And he'd look so charming doing it, with his cat's grace.

I smiled, trying to put all the evil and tenderness I was feeling into it. 'Hands and knees.'

He took a deep breath, closed his eyes, flushed. Then he sank to all fours and for a second rested his head against my calf.

'Follow me.' I led him into the bedroom, glancing back frequently to enjoy the view.

My bedroom's nothing that unusual, although I do have restraint points attached to the bed. What made him whistle was the collection of whips and floggers hung artistically on the wall. They ranged from the merest caress of fur and light suede to a singletail I didn't have room to use indoors. An antique umbrella stand held canes of varying weights.

'Yes?' I said. 'What do you think?'

'I'm impressed, my lady. And nervous.'

And, I noted, hard enough to pound nails.

'Anything especially exciting? Or scary?'

He pointed to the singletail as scary. Smart boy. Someone skilled can flick the petals off a rose without bruising them but, used carelessly, a singletail is a weapon.

Somewhat to my surprise, he mentioned canes as something that intrigued him. 'I read a collection of Victorian porn back in college,' he confessed. 'Someone's getting caned – and loving it – every five pages. I've been fantasising ever since, my lady.'

Honesty compelled me to say, 'Canes can leave marks.'

'I know, my lady. But a couple of stripes ... would be worth it.'

I could have tied him up. Instead, I bent him over the foot of the bed and told him, on his honour, not to move.

Not moving when your butt is on fire takes fortitude. Even if the pain transmutes to pleasure almost immediately, instinct tells you to flinch away. This time, however, I wanted him to choose with each stroke to obey and stay put, choose to ride the pain through to pleasure.

I put my leather gloves on and ran my hands along his body letting him feel the leather against his skin. Then I began to spank.

I started softly: a sensuous rhythm of light taps brought a flush to his skin. He relaxed into it quickly, making noises of pleasure with each impact. As his ass flushed pink, I put more snap into the blows, syncopated the rhythm so he didn't know what to expect.

So far, Cameron was showing every sign of enjoying himself. Some of his noises were clearly gasps of pain, but most sounded like pure pleasure and his cock glistened with pre-come.

'Ready for something more intense?' I asked.

He nodded.

I buried my fingers in the hair on the back of his neck. 'Answer me, Cameron. Say it or you won't get it.'

Making an obvious effort to remember English, he whispered, 'Yes, my lady. I am.' Then, not as an afterthought, but as if he needed a pause for breath, he added, 'Please.'

I kissed his shoulder and whispered, 'You're doing great.'

Then I reached for a medium-weight deerskin flogger, one with both thud and sting, and let it snap.

I was rewarded by a sharply indrawn breath, a gasp and a barely audible, 'Thank you.'

He should have said, 'Thank you, my lady,' but I wasn't going to quibble. Not when the sound of his thanks left me with juices dripping down my leg.

Ten more strikes with that flogger, and a thanks drawn from his lips by each one. I stopped after that. Cupping his buns in my gloved hands, I could feel their throbbing heat even through the leather. Keeping my hand in contact with his skin, I walked up so I could see his face. The Cameron of the *salle* was gone, all the cockiness missing. He looked younger and curiously innocent with his flushed face, but at the same time Pan-like, timeless and ecstatic and filled with dark wisdom.

'More?'

'Please, my lady. Thank you.' I had to strain to hear him, but his face answered the question better than any words could.

Something harsher this time, braided falls with small, stinging knots on some of them. He keened with each stroke, a litany of 'yes' and 'thank you' and 'my lady'. Not much sense, just music that fit the dance of the lash.

I like inflicting pain, but only when someone embraces it. Cameron did more than embrace it. He was letting it take him on a journey to a place he'd never been before. And he was taking me along for the ride.

I was almost scared myself to take the next step. Basically it was a caning, something I'd done many times to other men, but this seemed more intimate, less like play and more like a ritual. I'd imagined the act, or something like it, from the first time I caught a glimpse of something receptive behind Cameron's strength. I hadn't imagined what would be going through my mind in the moment – a courtly scene, the liege striking her knight with a sword to bind him to her service. When I'd imagined it, I hadn't really imagined Cameron, just his body. Now that I knew more about him, it was irresistible.

I set down the whip, caressed his ass again, went to my fencing bag. Took out the *epée*. I brought it over so he could get a good look at it. 'Do you know why I have this?'

'You're going to cane me with it, my lady.'

'Very good. Do you know why?'

'Because you'll enjoy it.'

'Because *we'll* enjoy it,' I corrected. 'But that's not the only reason. I'm going to hit you with this because the *epée* brought you to me. The *epée* and your honour and your skill, because I wouldn't have been interested in you if you weren't who you are.'

I moved the blade closer to his lips. He knew what to do.

I positioned myself behind him, pulled it back, whipped it down hard on to the bed next to him. He jumped, laughed nervously. While he was still twitching, I struck him for real. He muffled a scream as a red welt blossomed.

If I'd wanted to be cruel, I'd have repeated it immediately. Instead, I waited for the sharp pain to shift to pleasure. I leant forwards, watching as his face transformed, the tight determination to endure changing to a dazzled smile.

'Again?' I asked.

I didn't correct him this time when he only nodded. There are times you can't expect someone to speak.

'I'm going to mark you with this, Cameron,' I crooned. 'I'm going to leave you something so you'll remember that, while you may win sometimes in the *salle*, you will yield to me when I ask it in private.' I didn't really know where the words were coming from. They just poured out.

'Yes, my lady, I will. I swear.'

Twice more, I pulled the blade back and brought it down like a cane across his ass. By the third blow, his breath was coming in sobbing gasps. He wasn't using a safe word or begging for mercy – if anything, his little gasps of 'Please' sounded like 'Please go on.' But I judged he'd had enough.

I set the *epée* down, crawled on to the bed and pulled Cameron down next to me. I folded him in my arms while he floated on his endorphin high. *Mine*, I thought contentedly, possessively.

I didn't realise I'd said it aloud until he responded, almost soundlessly, 'Yours.'

'Until midnight,' I corrected, glancing at the clock. Almost eleven. I hoped to end the night with a fuck, a pleasure we both deserved, but the first order of business was talking with him a little to make sure he was really all right. 'Then you're free to go.'

'But am I free to stay? Please, my lady?'

My heart clenched. 'Do you know what you might be getting yourself into?'

I propped myself up on one elbow so I could watch his face as he thought about how to answer.

'Not exactly, my lady,' he finally admitted. 'For tonight, anything you'd like, and then omelettes for breakfast. Or eggs Benedict if you prefer. After that, I'm sure you'll tell me.'

'For one thing,' I said, 'you did this unusual parry in the second bout. I'd like you to show me how you did it.'

'As you wish, my lady. As long as you don't use it against me in the future.'

I grabbed his hair again, pulled his head back so he was looking into my eyes. 'Silly boy,' I whispered. 'Of course I will. If you're not out of here by midnight, I'll use everything you have against you. And you'll love it.'

'Yes, my lady,' was all he managed to say before I stopped his foolish talking with a kiss.

Perfect Score Mae Nixon

People think it's exciting being a professional gymnast – glamorous even. But, boy, are they wrong. I spend all day training, persuading my unwilling body into shapes so unnatural that they'd earn a normal person a visit to the osteopath. My trainer is a sadist with a personality bypass who I'm convinced was a torturer in a labour camp before he started working in sport. I've got no social life and I'm on a permanent diet. I can't remember the last time I sat down to a meal that I really enjoyed but I'm pretty sure it came out of a bottle and my mother burped me afterwards. I don't drink and I'm not allowed to take so much as a Lemsip if I get a cold, so I'm a barrel of laughs at parties.

I spend all my time with a bunch of self-obsessed girls whose two topics of conversations are whether they'll still be able to fit into their leotards if they eat a fun-size Mars Bar and their dismount from the vault after the double twisting pike. When I get home at night I just have time to soak my abused limbs in Radox before I fall asleep in front of the telly. I haven't seen the ten o'clock news for years.

Before you ask, yes, there are male gymnasts, but they're almost as shallow as the girls, flexing their muscles as if they're God's gift while trying to look up our leotards without us noticing. All in all, sex is pretty thin on the ground. Last time I had an orgasm with someone else in the room Olga Korbutt still had pigtails.

Sometimes I wonder if I'll ever get my leg over again (or do women get theirs under? I'm never sure). It's not that I don't want to; believe me I wank myself to sleep every night fantasising about it. But what with the exhaustion, the training schedule and the limited social life I don't know when I'd ever find the time. And just where would I meet a willing bloke anyway? I never go out in the evening, so unless he knocks on the door and volunteers I haven't got a hope. I did consider chancing it with the washing-machine repair-man a while back, but it just seemed too much like a porn movie.

It's been so long I sometimes wonder if I'll even remember how to do it. Fortunately, I've made sure that my clit gets regular exercise – well, I am an athlete, after all – so if I ever get laid again at least I don't have to worry about having lost the knack. In fact, if there were an orgasm Olympics, I'm pretty sure I'd get the gold medal every time. I'm an expert on floor exercises and a positive virtuoso on the apparatus. I've got vibrators to suit every mood and I've even been known to raid the salad drawer when I want a bit of variety. I've done it in the bath, in the kitchen while waiting for the kettle to boil, in front of the TV while trying to solve the anagram on *Countdown* and first thing in the morning when I'm still half-asleep.

I can come in a couple of minutes if I'm pushed for time, but my favourite way of doing it is in bed after a bath when I'm all warm and relaxed. I light some scented candles and put something smooth and sexy on the CD player to get me in the mood. Then I climb under the covers with my favourite vibrator and let nature take its course.

Let me just say a word about vibrators. I've got several: fat ones, thin ones, short ones, long ones. I've got dual speed, high powered and some that work by remote control. There are battery vibes, mains-powered vibes, loud ones and quiet ones. Then there are phallic vibes designed for insertion (front or back, it's up to you) and butterfly vibes which you strap against your clit. It all depends on mood. Some days you want to be filled by something fat, throbbing and phallic; others you might want the gentle stimulation of a butterfly which keeps you at a peak for ages before tipping you over the edge.

My personal favourite is a Hitachi Magic Wand. It looks like a tennis ball on a stick and isn't designed for insertion – though I'd take my hat off to anyone brave enough to attempt it. I bought it in America, when I spent a summer training there. They call it the Cadillac of vibrators and I can understand why: it's powerful, relentless and reliable. The trouble with battery ones is that, sooner or later, their motors burn out. And – sod's law, I suppose – it always happens right at the decisive moment. There's nothing worse than almost getting there, making it right up to the winning post and then stopping dead unable to go any further. Close, but no cigar.

But my Hitachi never tires. It goes on and on, buzzing away against my button as long as I need it. I like to press its head against myself then close my legs tight. This way, the body – the stick part – is squashed between my thighs holding the head right where I want it. Once I turn it on, if I rock my hips, the working end rubs its way backwards and forwards across my clit. And the best part is that this leaves me with both of my hands free: I can play with my nipples or slide one round the back and finger my holes, if I want to.

I close my eyes and breathe in the delicate scent of the candle, sandalwood with a hint of vanilla. Music from the CD fills the room: a deep sultry saxophone solo which seems to hit me straight in the groin. I brush the flat of my hands against my nipples, persuading them to harden, and in seconds they stiffen and contract, sending the first shivers of arousal through my body like a badly needed blood transfusion.

I rub my swollen nipples with my thumbs, coaxing them to stiffen even more, and soon they look like two ripe raspberries, ready to be plucked and eaten. I'm beginning to pant now, my heaving chest falling into rhythm with my growing arousal. I pinch my nipples, pulling on them a little, and instantly I'm all goosepimply.

With my eyes closed, I concentrate on the feelings I am creating. I turn inwards, listening to my body, allowing sensation to overwhelm me, and my heart pounds. My hips rock steadily, rubbing my vibrator's throbbing head against my sensitive clit. At first, I keep my movements shallow, confining the vibe's tip to the area just above my sensitive nub. As every girl knows, it's just too sensitive to touch directly at first and you have to coax it, persuade it, reassure it that it will have a good time if it comes out to play. Just because there's only me on the bed, there's still no reason to skimp on the foreplay.

I pinch and pull my hardened nipples as my electric friend does its work between my legs, while I imagine a lover's mouth against my nips, instead of my fingers; his hot wet tongue teasing, tasting me. The sudden – always surprising – rush of wet heat as he takes it into his mouth and sucks.

My body's filmed with sweat. Damp hair sticks to my face. I push the quilt aside. My hips rock rhythmically. It's hot and slippery between my legs. I'm thrusting deep now and the vibrator slides across my clit and back with every stroke.

My nipples are alive with pleasure: I run my fingernail across one delicate tip, causing a delicious, electric tingle. I do the same to the other nipple and soon my whole chest is burning. It's itchy, prickly and almost unbearable, but it's wonderful. I moan, softly.

The tingle seems to spread through my veins. I feel it trickling down my arms and legs, rushing down to my groin. I shiver. It creeps up my neck, millimetre by millimetre. My skin feels warm and hypersensitive. The heat moves into my face, trailing up my cheeks like a lover's fingertips. It rushes into my head and I feel instantly drunk.

My breathing is shallow and rapid. My chest heaves. My excited moaning mingles with the gently wailing saxophone as the heady scent of the candle fills my nostrils.

A coil of warmth spreads out from my groin. I can feel my pulse beating in my throat. I'm on the edge now, riding the line between arousal and orgasm, knowing that at any moment I'll topple over the edge into ecstasy.

I brush wet hair away from my face. I rub my thumbs across my sensitive nipples. My moaning is louder now, drowning out the music with its own, more urgent, note. My body begins to shudder. My thighs quiver. I arch my back and bring my knees up towards my chest. The vibrator's head slides hard across my excited clit. I let out a sharp cry. I rock my hips the other way and the vibe slides back.

'Yes!'

My orgasm bursts inside me like a bomb. I'm trembling all over. I'm moaning. I'm shuddering. I'm gasping. My hips move like pistons, rubbing the toy against me as I come.

When it's all over, the sheets are damp and tangled and I'm lying in a wet spot. I slide over to the clean side of the bed and curl up against the cool, soft cotton. I'm asleep in minutes, as you can imagine.

When it comes to self-pleasure, I'm in a class of my own. I never fail to deliver and I get a perfect score every time. Until recently, I didn't even care if I seldom got a chance to compete in the team event. In fact, it had been so long I was beginning to forget what all the fuss was about anyway. But that all changed last summer when the hamstring injury that had kept me out of the Olympics healed just in time for me to qualify for the Atlas Games in Barcelona.

The Atlas Games might not be as famous as the Olympics, but the world's major athletes were all there. Marching round behind the Union Jack at the opening ceremony must have been the proudest moment of my life. And, let's face it, I was never going to make it to the medal podium, was I? The Yanks and former Soviet bloc countries were more or less guaranteed to get them all. It was an honour to be selected and being among the top fifty gymnasts in the world is still pretty impressive.

As I marched in my blazer, the Spanish sun beating down on me, I couldn't help noticing that the bloke carrying the British flag looked pretty hot. His shoulders positively rippled under his jacket. He was tall and well built and his neat dark hair had a lovely little curl at the nape of the neck. Something about that exuberant little curl which refused to be tamed made me want to kiss it and I could imagine the warmth of his skin against my soft lips and the scent of his hair in my nostrils.

He was so cute from behind that I practically fell in love with him there and then. Even though I had no idea who he was and hadn't even seen his face, something about the confidence and ease of his movement made me instantly warm to him. I just had to know who he was. As we left the stadium I quickened my pace, intending to catch him up. He headed towards the changing area and I followed behind, weaving between the crowds to keep up. We turned a corner and I collided with a German athlete. I spent a couple of minutes enquiring about injuries and attempting to apologise, which isn't easy when your only knowledge of the German language comes from watching *The Great Escape* at Christmas.

By the time I'd managed to extricate myself, he'd disappeared. I was disappointed but not downhearted.

After all, we were both on the same team and I was bound to bump into him again in the Atlas village. But first I needed to find out who he was.

Half an hour later, I'd managed to track down Georgia, the team's physiotherapist whose trusted position gave her access to the most juicy gossip, and I quickly established that the flag carrier was Jim Mann, Britain's decathlon champion. I should have known it was him, really, but that's the funny thing about athletes – you never see them with their clothes on. Unless they're dressed in shorts or a leotard and have a number on their chests, you haven't got a hope in hell of recognising them. I bumped into Kelly Holmes in the launderette once, and I was convinced she was the women who works behind the counter in my local newsagents, even though I'd sat beside her on the plane to the Commonwealth Games.

Anyway, I was pleasantly surprised to discover that the object of my lust was Jim Mann. For one thing, his front view was every bit as appealing as his rear. He was tall and ruggedly handsome and, what's more, a terrific athlete. Famously modest about both his looks and his sporting prowess, Jim was popular with men and women alike. At 34, he was older than most athletes. He'd won bronze at the games in Auckland and Paris but, like me, had missed Athens due to injury. The Atlas was his last hope of winning a gold at a major competition and he was at the top of his form.

Jim Mann had no shortage of admirers on the team but, according to Georgia, he kept himself to himself. Flings were common among athletes at big competitions like the Atlas, as all that adrenalin and nervous energy has to go somewhere when the competition ends. The winners are keen to celebrate and relax and the losers seek solace in the only physical activity that none of us really minds getting sweaty for. It's human nature. Even

I've indulged from time to time. Yet Georgie assured me that Jim went home alone every night, even though he could have had his pick of any woman on the team. I was intrigued.

I didn't bump into him again for a couple of days, even though I made a point of hanging about in the places Georgia assured me he frequented. I was disappointed and frustrated. I'd worked myself up into a frenzy fantasising about finding myself in the queue behind him in the cafeteria then wanking myself stupid about what we'd do for dessert. By the third day I was tense and exhausted and I had to give myself a stiff talking to. It would never do to waste all my energy on fantasising: I was due to compete in a few days, so I needed to take myself in hand. I headed down to the competitors' sports club for a swim and sauna. The swim, I reasoned, would use up my nervous energy and the sauna would relax me and send me off to sleep nice and peacefully.

Though I'd never be able to give Sharon Davies a run for her money, I love swimming. Slipping through the water, weightless and supple, is liberating and relaxing. The rhythm and the repetition of swimming somehow remind me of meditation. And there's something strange and soothing about the way the water and high ceilings absorb and transform sound: voices are swallowed and subdued and echoes are absorbed and softened into a soft, liquid blur. The muffled lapping of the water and my body's repetitive movements gradually take me to a place of peace and warmth.

When I came out of the changing rooms, I was pleased to notice that the pool was quite empty, with only half a dozen people swimming lengths and a couple standing by the steps, chatting. They stepped aside as I climbed in. I bobbed down into the water for a second, wetting my hair before pushing off from the side to set off on my first length. The water was pleasantly cool, especially after how uncomfortably warm it was outside, even though it was evening. I slid through the water, submerging my head with each stroke. I soon fell into a familiar rhythm and I felt myself relaxing. I'd trained hard all day, in preparation for the competition that began the day after tomorrow, and the water soothed my aching muscles and the repetitive, automatic movements, soothed my mind.

I swam backwards and forwards, completing length after length. The water cooled and soothed me and a comforting, welcome tiredness washed over me. Two more lengths and I'd dry off and head for the sauna. As I turned for my final length I saw a dark shape pass over my head and slip in the water in front of me. I paused, disorientated for a moment, then I saw a man's bottom, clad only in skimpy dark Speedos, swimming away from me. I slowed my pace a little to let him get ahead and, if I'm honest, to get a better view of his cute arse. I swam under water for a few strokes, watching him move through the water. He was fit: his muscles positively rippled as he swam. A swimmer's cap and goggles obscured his face, but I was willing to bet he was cute as well. I swam along behind, enjoying the view.

At the end of the pool I stood up and pulled off my goggles. I was breathless but happy.

'I hope I didn't land on your head. I didn't see you until I'd dived in. I do hope you can forgive my bad manners.'

I wiped water out of my eyes, squinting as the chlorine stung. I was about to launch into a lecture on pool etiquette when my vision finally cleared. The owner of the voice was indeed as cute as his Speedo-clad arse. It was Jim Mann. As I'd spent days trying to engineer an 'accidental' meeting with him, you might think I'd be grateful. But nature has her own way of reminding us what fools we are. I was dumbstruck. I stared at him, clutching my goggles so tightly that my knuckles went white. At the same time, I felt my face redden. The longer I stood there staring at him, the more I blushed. I could only hope that he'd think it was from exertion.

Finally, I realised that if I didn't speak soon he'd be totally convinced of what he must already be beginning to suspect – that I was a complete idiot. I had to say something, anything.

'Oh, no, it was my fault. I was in your way. I shouldn't have been ... swimming.' I should have kept my mouth shut. In one short sentence I'd removed all doubt about my stupidity. I shouldn't have been swimming? What else would I have been doing? Hang gliding? 'Anyway, I've got to go and have a sauna before I take my clothes off.' I dug my grave even deeper.

'Yes, good idea.' He looked amused. 'I always enjoy a good sweat at the end of the day.' He winked at me then disappeared into the water.

The next day the gymnastic competition began. The team event took place in the first week and the individual the week after. I put in a lifetime's best on the beam, but fluffed my dismount from the asymmetric bars. The coach was delighted with me, however, and Team GB went through to the second day with a respectable score.

At the end of the day I was exhausted but elated. I ate a late meal in the cafeteria and was standing in the corridor outside trying to decide whether I had enough energy for a swim and a sauna before bed. I'd just about decided to turn in for the night when Jim came through the doors and almost collided with me. He smiled and my legs turned to water and my nipples to granite.

'We must stop meeting like this. Otherwise people will think I'm stalking you.'

Chance would be a fine thing, I thought. My tongue felt like a rock in my mouth and I couldn't speak. I knew

I was blushing: my face felt so hot I was in danger of being mistaken for the Atlas torch. I forced myself to smile, hoping it might distract Jim's attention from my glowing cheeks.

'I was just going to do a few lengths before turning in.' He touched me on the shoulder and I felt as though I'd been struck by lightning. 'Are you coming?'

'I'm not sure.' God, I was a silver-tongued devil.

'Oh, come on. I'm dying for another chance to see you without your clothes on.'

The man must be a mind-reader.

'OK.' I tried to sound as though I got invitations to strip from handsome international athletes every day of my life and nothing bored me more. 'I'll see you there.' I strode away, hoping he'd think my sudden departure was motivated by eagerness to meet him in the pool rather than fear that my red face might give him a nasty case of sunburn.

I changed into my cossie faster than Superman in a phone booth and headed for the pool. I slid into the water at the shallow end and looked around for Jim. He wasn't hard to spot: he was about halfway down the pool, swimming away from me. He was doing the butterfly stroke, his powerful arms arcing over his head then swooping down into the water. His body rippled along its length and his perfect, lycra-clad buttocks peeked through the surface for a second and disappeared. I couldn't take my eyes off him. At the far end, he turned and swam breaststroke towards me, moving through the water like an eel. His dark hair was slicked against his head and shining in the light.

I knelt up to my neck in the shallow end, my eyes focused on Jim. He grew ever closer, his shoulders and arms rearing through the water as he swam. The pool scarcely rippled as he slid through it. He reached the end, stretching out one hand to touch the tile beside me. He stood up, and water cascaded down his muscular body. I looked up at him. He seemed enormous: his chest was as broad and welcoming as a mattress and his stomach was flat, his six pack clearly visible. A little trail of hair peeked over the top of his Speedo and crept up towards his navel. My eyes followed that trail all the way down to the bulge in the front of his trunks. I looked up at his face and he was smiling at me.

'Do you like what you see?'

'You're huge, aren't you?'

Jim laughed out loud. He sat down in the water beside me, his back against the tile. 'You're direct, aren't you? I mean, I did notice you checking out the front of my trunks, but I didn't expect marks out of ten.'

'I, um, I mean, I didn't mean, um, oh God ... I might as well give up.' I took a deep breath. 'I'm sorry.' I began again. 'I feel as though I've made an enormous fool of myself and everything I say just seems to confirm it. I really am quite sane, I assure you.'

'I'm glad to hear it.' He leant close and whispered right into my ear. 'To tell you the truth, I was beginning to think you might be the Atlas Village idiot.'

He smiled at me and his eyes twinkled with warmth. I felt suddenly at my ease. I smiled back.

'When I said you were enormous, what I actually meant was that you are very tall.'

'And here was me thinking you were curious about the contents of my Speedos. I suppose I shouldn't have flattered myself that such a beautiful, elegant girl would be interested in a big dumb beast like me.'

'Oh, I'm curious, all right.' I felt suddenly bold.

'Curiosity is like temptation, I always say. The only way to get rid of it is to yield to it.' He took my hand and brought it to his face, kissing the palm. His skin was soft and wet and I felt his hot breath on me. Still holding my hand, he slid it under the water and pressed it against the front of his trunks. He exhaled loudly as my hand made contact. He gripped my wrist, moving his hand so that mine slid over his lycra-covered crotch. I could just about make out the fat tube of his cock. He was smiling as his eyes gazed into mine.

He leant in close, his mouth right against my ear. 'You're making me hard.'

I could hear the arousal in his voice. Under my hand, I felt him stiffen and swell. I used my fingers to stroke him through the wet fabric and his cock grew solid and thick under my hand. He held my wrist and rocked his hips, rubbing himself against my hand. With his free hand he pulled me close and kissed me, softly on the lips. It was more than a peck, but it wasn't quite a lover's kiss, no tongue. Before I had time to respond he was gone. He swam the length of the pool and back while I sat at the edge, stunned.

When he reached my end again he swam to a stop beside me and smiled. 'I'm going to do another length before I call it a night. See you tomorrow?'

I nodded.

'Good, I'll look forward to it. Maybe I'll get to find out what you keep in your swimsuit. Shall we say seven o'clock? Goodnight, beautiful.' He waved and dived off through the water.

After Jim had gone I swam ten lengths, then had a quick sauna before turning in for the night. Needless to say, our watery encounter and the prospect of taking things further the next day fuelled more than a few fantasies before I finally managed to get to sleep.

The next day's competition went well. I was focused and energised and my flexibility and execution had never been better. The floor had always been my favourite exercise. On the beam and the bars, you've got no choice about the way you move and though you can be original to some extent the apparatus dictates the range of movements available to you. But on the floor I feel I am free to express myself however I want. I can dance, tumble and fly. I sometimes think I feel most alive – most *myself*, if that makes sense – during a good floor routine. Well, apart from sex, of course, but I don't usually invite a panel of judges to give me marks out of ten for that. I was in top form. The crowd whooped and cheered when I completed a difficult aerial successfully. I didn't get any deductions in the compulsories and was on target for a personal-best score.

In the evening, most of the team were going out for a meal to celebrate someone's birthday, but my plans for the night were rather more intimate. I sent my apologies and headed off for the pool. By seven I'd already done half a dozen lengths and I was swimming back towards the shallow end when I spotted Jim coming out of the changing rooms.

He was looking particularly gorgeous. The solid muscle in his belly seemed to slide under his skin as he walked to the edge of the pool. He bent down to dip his goggles into the water and his outstretched arm was so perfectly formed that it reminded me of Adam's on the ceiling of the Sistine Chapel. He stood up and fitted his goggles in place.

'Hey! Look where you're going.'

I stopped swimming. 'Sorry, I was distracted.'

I swam around the woman I had nearly collided with. When I looked at the poolside again, Jim was gone. At the shallow end I sat down in the water and lifted my goggles onto my forehead. I scanned the pool, looking for Jim. There he was, swimming towards the deep end, moving through the water as sleek and efficiently as a seal. When he reached the edge, he executed a perfect swimmer's turn and headed back towards me. I watched him swim. His wet body seemed to shine. I was captivated.

Jim swam directly towards me, coming to rest with one arm either side of me. He knelt down. 'Well, you're a sight for sore eyes, beautiful. But are you cold?' He nodded towards the front of my costume.

I looked down. My nipples were hard and protruding through the thin material of my swimsuit. I slid down into the water, covering them. 'Perhaps I'm just pleased to see you.'

'I hope so. Slide down a bit more, that's right.'

I slid down into the pool, up to my shoulders. Jim extended his hands and cupped my breasts. I gasped. He located my nipples with his thumbs and stroked them.

'Mmm, lovely. I'd say you were very pleased to see me. Either that or you've got a terrible case of hypothermia.' He smiled at me. 'Which is it?'

'If you'd like to put your hand between my legs, you'll find out for sure.' I took his left hand in both of mine and pressed it against the crotch of my swimsuit. Jim looked into my eyes. His fingers found the edge of the lycra and snaked inside.

'You're shaved. I suppose you've got no choice in those skimpy leotards. I've often wondered.'

'Waxed, actually. It lasts longer and you don't get a rash.'

His fingers ran along the length of my slit, brushing my clit, and I moaned softly.

'You're wet.'

I nodded.

'You want me?'

The way Jim said it, it sounded more like a statement of fact than a question, yet it didn't come across as arrogant. It was more like he was saying out loud what we both knew to be true.

'Yes, I want you.'

He smiled. His hand slid away from my crotch and I felt bereft. He must have been able to see the disappointment on his face because he smiled at me and said, 'Good things come to those who wait.'

'Why wait? I want you; you want me. We're both young, free and single. There's no time like the present.'

'You see, beautiful, I have a problem...'

My stomach turned a double salto. 'Don't tell me you're married?'

He smiled and shook his head.

'Or gay? You're not gay?'

He laughed out loud. He leant in close and whispered in my ear. 'Did my cock feel gay to you yesterday when you felt it grow in your hand? If you're still confused about my sexuality put your hand back down my trunks and you'll find the answer.' He gripped the front of his trunks and held them open. I stuck out my hand but, before I had the chance to slip it inside, he caught my wrist. 'Sorry, I know I offered, but I don't think I could bear it.'

'What's wrong, Jim? One minute you're all over me like a rash and the next you're pushing me away. Just what is your problem?'

'You're my problem. I've been lying awake every night since I met you. I just can't get you out of my head. I'm desperate to get you between the sheets, to see if what you've got inside that swimsuit looks as lovely as it feels, but I can't.'

'What do you mean, you can't? Your cock was hard yesterday when I felt it. I can't imagine you've got any problems in that department.'

He laughed. 'No, everything's in perfect working order. In fact, I sometimes wish it wasn't. It's pretty difficult getting off to sleep when you're trying to ignore a raging erection. The fact is I can't have sex until after the competition.'

'Why not? You can't believe it saps your strength – that's an old wives' tale surely?'

'Maybe, but I've always done it. Call it superstition, if you like, but it works for me. I feel as though my pent-up sexual energy helps me to compete better. It gives me an edge. I hope you don't mind. I know it's frustrating.'

'You're right there. Thank goodness for masturbation, eh?'

He shook his head slowly.

'Don't tell me that isn't allowed either?'

'Nope.'

'Wow. You must be pretty horny, then.'

'Oh yes. And it's all your fault.'

'So what happens now? The way I feel about you I could do it right here.'

'Me too.' He squeezed my hand. 'If you're prepared to wait, I'd really love to go to bed with you after the competition.'

'How long?'

'Eight inches, but you won't be able to verify that for a while yet.'

I laughed. 'I mean how long do I have to wait?'

'The twenty-fourth.'

'That's a week away!'

He nodded. 'But you'll wait?'

'If I have to, I suppose.'

'Great. I promise you, I'm worth waiting for. And you know what they say, patience is a virtue.'

'No, patience is a virtual impossibility.'

Jim and I met every evening in the pool after that. At the weekend we explored Barcelona together but, apart from a few kisses, our meetings were completely chaste. In the second week, I did well in the individual competitions and finished in the top twenty in each event. I came a respectable fifteenth in the all-round competition, the highest-placed British competitor. The women's gymnastics finished on 22 September and the decathlon began the next day, so I was able to watch Jim compete.

The decathlon is made up of ten events spread over two days. Points are awarded for each event and the competitor with the highest points wins the competition as a whole. The first day was bakingly hot, something athletes never like. Those of us who are used to the cooler climate of Britain find it particularly difficult. The air feels arid and its hard to breathe and all too easy to get dehydrated.

Jim was a good all-rounder but he excelled at the track events. He had to be placed in the top three in the 100 and 400 metres if he was to go through to the second day with a high enough score. He easily won the 100 metres and I knew that the resulting adrenalin high would help carry him through the next event, the long jump, where he came third. He managed to achieve fourth place in the shot put, followed by another third in the high jump. The last event of the day was the 400 metres, in which Jim was considered a hot favourite.

I sat at the edge of my seat, willing him to win. At the final turn he was shoulder to shoulder with Clay from the USA, with Karpov of Kazakstan a length behind. Jim edged his way forwards and breasted the tape just ahead of Clay. I was on my feet, clapping and cheering like a lunatic. As Jim slowed to a halt he turned to me and gave me the thumbs-up sign.

That night we shared a quick meal before heading off to our single beds. Naturally, I couldn't sleep. I'd waited more than a week to get naked with the sexiest bloke in the universe and tomorrow was the big day. Even better, Jim looked likely to win a medal, so our long-awaited shagging would also be a celebration. I was so horny I didn't think I'd even be able to wait until he'd finished his victory lap. I might wrestle him to the ground and rip off his running strip right there on the track. At least there would be some interesting photos in the next day's papers.

The next morning was a little cooler. I was sure it was a good omen. Jim came first in the hurdles, but did less well in the throwing events. He and Bryan Clay had equal points. If he was to win, he had to come first in the final event, the 1500 metres. Though Jim excelled on the track, he was a sprinter rather than a long-distance runner, as he was far too powerful and muscled to be naturally suited to endurance events. And he'd never been placed higher than second in the 1500 metres before. The crowd was behind him, which helped, but it could go either way.

I could hardly breathe as I sat in the stands. When the starter's gun went off I stood up and leant against the barrier, willing him forwards. He led the field from the start, while Clay, Karpov and a couple of others shadowed him, with the rest of the competitors straggling way behind. When the bell sounded for the final lap, he picked up speed. Jim was known for his sprint finish; he streaked forwards, losing everyone but Clay. His powerful legs thundered along the track. The gap between the two leaders grew steadily, as Jim sped along and Clay struggled to keep up. At the final turn Jim's lead was unbeatable. The crowd was wild and I was gripping the barrier, clapping and shouting at the top of my lungs.

Jim crossed the line yards ahead of Clay and Karpov was third. He'd won. And with a personal best score of 8950. I was leaping up and down clapping and I cheered so loud that it hurt my throat. Jim trotted over to me and we hugged. He was covered in sweat but I didn't care. He kissed me hard, sliding his tongue into my mouth and pulling me close.

'See you later.' He smiled at me and trotted away, pursued by the press.

The hours until I got to see him again were unbearably long. On the TV in my room I watched Jim receiving his medal and taking part in interview after interview. Finally, there was a tap on my door and I rushed over to answer it. He stood in the corridor holding a bunch of flowers. He looked me up and down let out a long low whistle. 'You're naked. I hope you haven't started without me?' He stepped inside.

'I just thought it would save time.' I started pulling off his clothes off.

'Can I put the flowers down first?'

I took the flowers and put them on the dressing table. I pulled up his T-shirt and he lifted up his arms to help me get it over his head. He toed off his trainers and slid out of his tracksuit bottoms. Underneath he was naked, except for the gold medal round his neck. And he was hard. His long, thick cock, stood out proudly from its mat of dark hairs. I got on my knees, to take a closer look. 'I'd say that was seven inches, not eight.' I looked up at him.

He shook his head. 'Put it in your mouth: I think you'll find it will measure up.'

I wrapped my hand around his cock and my fingers barely met. Slowly, I slid back his foreskin, revealing his glistening helmet. It was mauve and shiny. I stuck out my tongue and licked away a bead of moisture from its eye.

He moaned softly. I wanked him slowly a couple of times, licking the tip of his helmet every time it came in view. I swallowed him all the way down to the root and his skin felt silky and warm. He reached down and stroked my cheek. I looked up at him and he winked at me. He was smiling a little half-smile, sort of mysterious and secret, as if he was amused by some private joke.

'You really are beautiful,' he said, his voice soft and husky with lust. 'Come up here and kiss me.' He held out his hands and I took them and stood up. Jim put one hand on the back of my neck, under my hair. He bent his head to kiss me and I closed my eyes. His mouth was hot and wet. He smelt of expensive aftershave, lime with a deeper woody note and, underneath it all, his own masculine aroma.

He pulled me close, wrapping his free hand round my waist. My nipples rubbed against his hairy chest and grew hard. He ran his hands up and down my back, making me shiver. He trailed his fingertips down my spine and over my buttocks. I trembled.

'My legs have gone all quivery.' I kissed his ear.

'Then we'd better lie down.' He knelt down. 'Here –' he patted the carpet '– lie on your back. That's right.'

I lay on the floor. The carpet was rough and itchy and I didn't even want to think about the dirt, but I didn't care. I'd have laid in a muddy puddle in the middle of Oxford Street if he wanted me to. Jim got between my legs and stretched down on his front. He pressed my thighs apart with his strong hands. I put one foot on each of his shoulders and let my legs fall open. His fingers spread my lips. I watched him dip his head and cover my pussy with his hot mouth and I gasped as his tongue made contact with my hot little bead.

I could feel his warm breath against my skin. He licked me with his eyes closed and the expression on his face was pure bliss. I was covered in goosepimples; my nipples were swollen and red and I was tingling all over. I closed my eyes.

Jim's mouth worked its magic on me. Sometimes he licked, sometimes he sucked, taking my whole bud into his mouth. It was delicious, unbearable almost, yet I never wanted it to stop. The warm little tingle in the base of my belly became a flame. I rocked my hips, establishing a rhythm. The sound of my ragged breathing seemed to fill the room.

My back rubbed against the carpet. Jim wrapped his arms round my thighs, pulling me closer. His mouth was never still, sucking, licking and probing. I used my thumbs on my nipples, which hardened and grew under my touch.

The flame into my belly grew into an inferno, consuming me. My body was slick with sweat. Damp hair clung to my face. My chest heaved. I gasped and moaned. I braced my feet against his shoulders and moved my hips, rubbing Jim's face against my excited pussy.

The carpet chafed my skin and matted my hair. I was groaning and sobbing now, my thumbs teasing my swollen nipples, my hips pumping wildly. I pressed my feet down against his strong shoulders, raising my bottom off the carpet. Jim held on tight, his talented mouth working its magic.

I could hear myself moaning, wailing almost. I knew it was my voice, but I wasn't consciously making the sounds. I rubbed my crotch against Jim, pressing against him with my feet. I was close. The heat in my belly focused and broke. Jim pushed two fingers deep inside me and I cried out, a long, low animal moan of pleasure and fulfilment.

'Jim!' I was coming at last. I ground my crotch against his face. His invading fingers circled inside me. He held on tight, his mouth fastened over my sex. He was sucking the orgasm out of me, feeding on it, while I was panting, gasping. My legs quivered amd my whole body was trembling.

I reached down and laced my fingers through his hair. I lifted my head off the carpet and looked at his face. His eyes were still closed. He was beautiful. I stroked his cheek with my thumb.

'Was that good?'

I nodded.

'Good. Now I'm going to fuck you.' He got up onto his knees. 'Open wide.'

I spread my legs into the full splits position.

Jim's eyes widened. He smiled. 'All my life I've dreamt about a girl who could do that.' He lay down on top of me, supporting his weight on his hands.

'You look as though you're about to do fifty press-ups.'

'Oh no. I've got something far more pleasurable in mind.' He reached down with one hand and positioned his cock, then slid into me in one long movement. He circled his hips. 'Feel good, beautiful?'

I nodded.

His cock slid inside me teasingly slowly. Jim bent his head and we kissed. I cupped his face with both hands and explored his hot, wet mouth with my tongue.

Jim was thrusting deeper now, faster. My back rubbed against the floor.

'Do you mind if we change position? Only I think this carpet has taken all the skin off my back.'

'Of course. What do you have in mind?' Jim rolled off me and helped me up

I took him by the hand and raised my left leg in a high kick. I pulled him close. My leg was now trapped between our bodies, my foot over his shoulder. 'Now put it in.' My voice was urgent with lust.

He reached down and slid his prick home. 'Aren't you going to fall over, standing on one leg?'

I shook my head. 'That's where you come in. If you can hold on to me I'll be fine. That's assuming you can stay upright. Personally, my legs go all wobbly when I come.'

'I'll be fine.' He kissed my neck. 'Years of practice wanking in the shower as a teenager.'

I wrapped my arms round Jim's neck. He put both hands on my bottom and pulled me close. 'This is a bit like dancing. I like it.'

Jim rocked his hips slowly and his prick began to move inside me. He slid it in and out achingly slowly. I held on tight, moving my own hips, making sure that my clit rubbed against Jim's pubes with every thrust. I could feel his heart beating against mine. My sweat-slicked body slid against his. His mouth was against my neck and his breath felt hot and moist on my skin. His strong arms held me tight as he moved inside me.

I held on to his neck, tilting my hips as he fucked me, making sure that he went in at just the right angle. If I tilted my pelvis down and then back on his in stroke, my crotch mashed itself against his pubes with every thrust. Eventually it would make me come. I could already feel the heat building. I leant back a little, rubbing the tips of my nipples against his chest.

Jim was kissing my neck, nibbling on my ear lobe. He kissed the sensitive spot where neck, ear and jaw meet and I shivered all over. My nipples were tingly and hot. A sort of liquid tremor ran down the length of my spine and settled at the base of my belly.

My mouth found Jim's. I kissed him, holding his face in both hands. Excited breath snorted loudly out of his nostrils as he nibbled on my lower lip. The heat of his mouth seemed to seep into my bloodstream and make me glow. His sweat dripped into my face, but I didn't care.

I rubbed myself against his curly hairs. He fucked me deep and hard. He held me tight, his fingers digging into my flesh. I was breathing hard. I tossed my damp hair away from my eyes. Jim was half-groaning, half-breath-ing, a husky, masculine sound that somehow got inside my brain and turned my own arousal up a notch.

He was pounding me now. His hairy crotch provided delicious friction for my sensitive clit as he moved inside me. My legs were trembling and I wobbled dangerously on my single foot. If Jim hadn't been holding me up I would have collapsed in a heap. My nipples brushed against his chest. I arched my back.

Jim picked up speed. I sobbed loudly as I came. Jim's

deeper moans harmonised with mine. He pulled me in close, thrusting one last time, deep inside me. I felt him tremble and, for a moment, I though we both might fall. But he held on tight as he rode out his orgasm. I looked up at his face as we came and he gazed into my eyes, his lips formed into that cute little half-smile. Finally he kissed me and held me steady while I lowered my leg.

'That's pretty impressive, I must say. There seem to be some advantages of sex with a gymnast that I'd just never considered.' He kissed me again.

'Mark out of ten?'

'Twelve. In fact, I can do better than that.' He took off his gold medal and put it round my neck. 'You deserve this more than me: you're unbeatable.'

Jim and I have been having regular workouts ever since we got back. Thanks to him, I'm fitter than I ever have been and I've drastically reduced my battery expenditure. In fact, he'll be moving in with me next year, when he moves to London to take up a training post. His gold medal still sits on my mantelpiece to remind us of that summer when we both achieved our personal best score.

Tighthead Nuala Deuel

I've heard them all, all those so-called jokes. About how we like to play with odd-shaped balls. And what exactly does the hooker get up to during a match? I wouldn't mind mauling with you, love. Fancy a ruck? Don't get me started on the scrum down. The only thing I wondered about was that business regarding repressed homosexuality. All that testosterone buzzing around, slamming into each other: an eighty-minute bump and grind that would drop jaws all round if it were happening anywhere else but on a rugby pitch. I doubted I'd ever nail that particular rumour.

Especially as I'm a girl, the only woman in an all-male fifteen.

You might have read about me in the papers. There was a big froth from the sport's governing body when they found out and I was banned from turning out for my team, The Rope & Anchor, a pub outfit playing in a minor league, but rules is rules. The local press pricked up their ears and mounted a big campaign to let me play rugby again and the suits, under pressure from equal-rights campaigners and big names from the sport (I had my picture taken with, among others, Will Carling, Rob Andrew and Jeremy Guscott), stepped down. I was back in my hooped top and shorts, taping up my fingers and ears before matches on drizzly weekends, matching the guys pint for pint in the Rope afterwards. I loved my teammates and I loved the game. I didn't think anything could ruin things after that. But that was before Jamie Garland came to play for us.

It was Steamo, our captain, an uncompromising sec-
ond-row monolith of a man, who brought Jamie along to
training one night. And I knew I was done for. It wasn't
because Jamie played in my position – he was a tighthead prop and I was blindside flanker – or that we took
an instant dislike to each other that would have meant
disrupting the harmony of our team: it was the opposite.
The moment I saw him – his shorn head, the taut bulk
of his shoulders, the solid meat of his thighs as they
moved beneath the lycra shorts he was running in – I
knew I would give anything to have him.

I avoided the showers and deflected the invitations to
join the team for a post-training beer and decided to go
home, a headache building behind my eyes. Headaches
are what I get when I'm so high on desire that I think I'll
pass out. It's been a long time since I've had to reach for
the Nurofen. Being surrounded by a bunch of men seep-
ing the subtle smell of hot seed from every pore is not
necessarily the thrill you might think it to be. I treat
these boys like my brothers, and they are as protective
and supportive of me as if I were their kid sister. Sex
doesn't come into it. I even shower with these bruisers; I
soap their backs for them. The nearest I ever came to
fancying one of them was Steamo himself, but he's so
professional, so dedicated to his sport that I would have
had to accompany him on five-mile runs three times a
week to be in with a chance of ever sharing his bed. So
no, if there were going to be any dressing room fucka-
thons with me at the bottom of a pile of sweating limbs,
it would have happened by now, I can promise you.

But Jamie Garland . . .

I drifted for what seems like hours. I was like Sigour-
ney Weaver in *The Year of Living Dangerously* in the
scene where she leaves her room, in a trance it would
seem, driven by her need to make love to Mel Gibson. I
understood that impulse now as I meandered along the

streets, feeling a fist of heat unclench in my belly, its fingers reaching out to touch me, drag slow fingers over my puckered breasts, test the heat building between my legs. If I'd known where Jamie lived ... well, I don't know what I might have done. We hadn't exchanged more than two words: hello and goodbye.

I got home, poured myself a stiff drink and sipped it while I soaked away the mud and the aches in a hot, deep bath. I couldn't get the image of Jamie's legs from my mind or the curve of his iron buttocks as he burrowed into another practice scrum, his shoulders, the way they arched and rolled as he worked to gain purchase in the turf. There wasn't a shred of fat on his body.

The glass made a soft, clinking sound as I set it down uncertainly on the side of the bath. I was too absorbed by my daydreams to care if I spilt any. Candlelight flickered and surged against the wall like the play of muscle in a body filled with drive and purpose. My heartbeat was sending out steady tremors through the water; my breath provided a rhythmic background. I always drew baths that were way too hot. I could feel sweat spiking my forehead but I didn't wipe it away; I liked the feeling of gathering tensions, minor discomforts. Grit shifted on the foot of the bathtub. It prickled my arse and I liked that too. Jamie's feet might have disturbed some of that soil.

I stretched in the bath and saw through satisfied, half-shut eyes the swells of my breasts break the surface of the water. I have smallish breasts – a good thing, really, if you're playing a high-contact sport like rugby – but my nipples tend to become erect very easily when I play so I usually cover them up with a few criss-crosses of black gaffer tape. This also helps to prevent any more smart mouthing from opposition players, especially on cold days. Now I traced my own fingers over those soft nubs and felt the twinge in my loins as my body answered a familiar call. I enclosed one breast with my palm and imagined Jamie's lips doing the same job, softly sucking my entire tit – almost inhaling it – into his mouth. My other hand strayed south. I felt my fingers reach my soft, unruly bush and bump against my clit.

Such a hard body, he had. I wondered what his cock looked like. I reached further and felt the folds of my lips, the way they felt slightly more viscous than the water that sloshed around them. I arched my back and began to softly strum myself . . . and the telephone rang.

The moment passed. I was a slightly stocky girl again, sitting in a muddy bath, the hot smell of scotch rising from the towels on the floor. I pulled on my tatty bathrobe and picked up the phone in the hall. It was Steamo.

'What happened tonight?' he asked.

In the background I could hear his blender working full throttle: another batch of his renowned protein smoothies. He probably had a piece of fish steaming and a large plateful of iron-rich greens. He was a dedicated man where fitness was concerned.

'Nothing, why?' My voice carried a tweak of petulance about it.

Steamo wasn't stupid. He knew his players. Precious little slipped by the captain's attention and trying to bluff him wasn't going to wash, but it didn't stop me trying. I couldn't just bleat my feelings to him, not after one stupid, smitten evening. It was my problem. I had to get a grip of myself. I had to deal with it.

'You were playing like you'd tied your boots together.'

'We all have off days,' I said.

'Is there something you're hiding from me? About Jamie?'

Unusually perceptive, our captain. I caught my reflection in the hallway mirror and snapped my mouth shut.

'Loz? Loz? You there?'

'I'm here,' I said.

'So? What is it? Do you know him or something? Have you two got some history?'

If only ... 'No. No. It's nothing to do with Jamie. I don't know why you even mention him.'

'Because you were staring at him half the night as if he was playing with a third leg. I mean it, Loz, if there's some back story you're not telling me about then –'

'There's nothing. I swear. I don't know the guy.' I bit my lip. 'Where's he from, anyway? What's *his* back story? I mean, where does he live?'

The blender cut out. There was silence at the end of the phone. And then, very quietly, with a tone in his voice that told me he was smiling, he said, 'You fancy him, that's it, isn't it?'

'Oh go to hell!' I slammed the phone down. How dare he? How dare he reduce what he saw as my failings on the training ground to some girly crush? I had half a mind to call him back and tell him to stick his team. And then I saw my reflection in the mirror again. I was smiling too.

We had a match that weekend away to Cherry Wood Lions, the league leaders. Steamo wanted us to convene at a pub in the town centre for a light pre-match lunch where he would run through a few tactics and plays that we might deploy during the game. I picked at my salad while the other boys tucked into their pasta. I watched the way Jamie ate and imagined his jaws moving like that as he tongued my sex. I squeezed my thighs together and forced myself to concentrate on what Steamo was saying.

When the plates had been cleared away Steamo clapped his hands together and said: 'Right, let's get on the road. Everyone know the way?'

I was driving Munny, our fly-half, and Goose, the full-back, down to the ground in my old Citroën. We were in the car park when Steamo called to me. 'Loz? Jamie's got a flat. Can you squeeze him in?'

I gabbled some affirmative reply while I hurried myself into the driving seat and prayed the blush away from my cheeks. Munny got into the back with Goose before I could ask one of them to sit up front with me. There was a forced smile on my lips as Jamie eased his monster frame into the seat beside mine.

'Tight fit,' he said.

'Oh yeah,' I replied lightly, feeling the heat come back to my face.

I don't remember the drive to the ground. I recall the smell of Jamie's skin and the dull pain building up in my head to a point where I thought I would either black out or crash the car. I dared not look at him while I steered. All I saw was his smooth strong right hand resting on the crease-free expanse of his right thigh. Clean fingernails, square cut. I could see that hand cupping me, rubbing me, becoming wet with my juices as I bucked and writhed against his fingers. I wanted that hand clamped over my mouth as I came. I wanted it turned hot with my breath and oaths. I wanted to be able to smell myself on it long hours later.

I parked the car and he got out. I had almost forgotten that Munny and Goose were in the back. We unloaded our sports bags and traipsed across gravel and grass to the Portakabins that were Cherry Wood Lions' dressing rooms. The pitch beyond them was pale with a thin wintry mist. There were maybe a dozen spectators spread out around the touchline and a couple of dogs. The sun was trying its best to make itself known through the high blanket of cloud but only a vague bright patch hinted at its location. The cold hung in the air like something that could be touched. I followed the others into the cabin, hoping I'd remembered to pack my tape.

I tried my best not to watch Jamie while he pulled on his shorts and shirt. Only the thought of Steamo's smug expression prevented me from glancing at Jamie's body, though I sorely wanted to. I allowed myself a brief glimpse as he was bent over his boots, tying his laces. I saw his muscles flexing in his arm and that was enough to be going on with. I taped up my boobs, hoping he might be watching me, and pulled on my number-six shirt.

The match itself was a scrappy affair, mired for the most part in midfield, where the recycled ball was never used to as good effect as it might. The kicking was awry, the tackles mistimed and there were an unusual number of knock-ons; it didn't help that the pitch started cutting up after twenty minutes. We went into half time 26–10 down. All of our points had been from converted penalties whereas the Cherries had scored two tries. It always bothered Steamo if we hadn't been able to impose ourselves try-wise. We decided at the break to run the ball more. If we were going to lose then at least we would do so in style.

'Quick hands,' Steamo said as we trotted back to our positions. 'Pass, move, support.'

Almost as soon as we won possession we scored a try, the ball fumbled by their full-back when a simple kick into touch seemed the likely outcome. It was Steamo himself, true to his name, powering through to block the clearance and dive for the line. The try converted, we were a changed outfit. We swung the ball left and right, the team's line unbending, unbroken, like something impelled by arcane mathematics. Ten minutes to go, the score 26–24 in their favour, I intercepted a pass and took off, my eyes fast on the posts. I'm quick when I get going and I could hear the laboured breathing of their backs as they tried to bring me down. One of them managed to trip me, a last-ditch tap of my foot that cause me to overbalance. Bodies piled in. I tried to keep possession without incurring a penalty and forced the ball back under my body, waiting for it to be recycled.

In the melee I felt a hand squirm under my top and squeeze my left breast. I jerked away, ready to unleash a great torrent of abuse, when I saw the square-cut fingernails of the hand that had groped me. The bodies were getting off. The referee was peering in, trying to make sense of the pile-up. I took hold of the hand before it disappeared and sucked the forefinger into my mouth, squirmed my tongue against it, gave it a little nip.

We scored another try, a scrappy push for the line, with a couple of minutes to go. The conversion was sliced wide of the posts but it didn't matter. We'd beaten the league leaders 26–29. The excitement of the win was enough to keep my mind off what had happened between me and Jamie. When I remembered, as I tugged my knickers free, I felt a jolt of electricity jag up through my pelvis as if his fingers had done the job for me. Naked, I brushed past him on my way to the showers. He was still in his shorts, trading bellows of triumph with Steamo and Goose, but he noticed the smear of my thigh against his arse. I know he did. I spent ten minutes longer in the shower than was necessary but he didn't appear out of the mist to stand under the spigot next to mine. Disgruntled I wrapped myself in towels and left, just as he was stepping by me. I smiled at him, desperate to look down at his cock, but I couldn't. Not until I was sure about him.

The boys were almost dressed. I took my time towelling my hair and then made a show of looking for my shampoo. Stomach churning, I headed back to the showers. He was still there, on his own. I stopped. It felt as though my tongue had grown too thick for my mouth. I looked around because I heard someone knocking on the door but it was me: it was my heart.

Oh God. He was standing under a jet of water, his hand wrapped around the shaft of his cock, and he was soaping himself slowly, thoroughly, and turning his head this way and that to watch how his prick shifted as he stroked. He didn't have a full erection, not yet, but his prick was swollen and heavy. It gleamed under the wet lights. I heard its soft sucking sounds and the light slap of his hand's edge as it bounced against his lathered balls. I reached inside the towel skirt I had fashioned and my fingers confirmed what I thought. I was sopping. I was ready for him. Was he waiting here for me?

But I couldn't go to him. Something was holding me back. Not just the arresting sight of him lazily tossing himself off, although deliciously that would have been reason enough. It was the fear that I had got it wrong, that it wasn't his hand that had squeezed my tit. It was the fear that Steamo would walk in on us and decide that inter-team fucking was not the best preparation for a league campaign.

I chewed my lip, began to edge away from the steam. There would be plenty of opportunities. There would be dozens of dressing rooms, showers and –

'Don't go.' He looked up at me, his hand still working himself, a thick tide of soap dripping from the head of his cock, his tight, swollen balls.

He asked me to wash his back.

I did so, all my fears evaporating, dissolving into the steam. I no longer cared who might stumble upon us. His skin was creamy and tight against the muscles beneath. Freckles were scattered across his back in random patterns, like constellations. I found myself studying them, as if trying to unpack their meaning. He turned towards me and said thank you. His face was filled with colour, his lips ruddy. He looked as though he was going to say something else but he simply turned his attention back to his dick. He was hard now. The flesh of his cock tight, his slit like a small mouth shaping an O of ecstasy.

'Your hand must be getting tired,' I said, my voice thick in my throat.

He didn't say anything but released his grip. His prick swung lazily upright and bobbed at me as I reached out for him.

'Do you want me to help you with that tape?' he asked. His soft, brown eyes never blinked. They were staring hard into mine, searching me, testing my limit. The only way I could have given him more encouragement would have been if my eyes were green. I focused on his cock and nodded, unable to speak. I thought that if I opened my mouth I might scream.

I held him and even under the heat of the water powering from the shower his heat was greater. I felt the soft outer sheath of his dick move against its rock-hard core. I ran my thumb over the glistening tip and wondered how he would taste, how he could fill every vacuum in my body. His fingers teased back the shiny black crosses of tape and I heard his breath turn ragged, whether at the pressure I was exerting with my fingers or the sight of my breasts I'm not sure. I'd like to think it was down to a little of both. He leant over and ran his tongue over my nipples. Water crashed against the back of his neck, making his shoulders gleam. I wanted to say something, wanted to warn him that someone might come in, but none of that mattered. I pressed him back against the wall and the torrent disfigured his face: all I could tell was that his eyes were shut and his mouth open.

I sank to my knees and let the moment spin out before me, his cock twitching above me now, my fingers at its base, gently pressing against his balls, peeling his foreskin back to reveal his sensitive inner, making him sleek and long. I paused with my mouth a millimetre away from it, needles of hot water pricking me all over my face. I dabbed at him with my tongue then, unable to wait any longer, let his entire length slide between my lips until my nose mashed against his pubes. I sucked at him greedily, loving the feel of his steely thighs under my fingers and the dense, filling sensation of his cock in my mouth. I kneaded at his buttocks, wanting him to come in my mouth, but he gently pushed me away and whispered that he wanted to fuck. The drumming of the water, the thrum of pain in my head, matched with the pulse of desire between my legs – if he didn't fill me up there I was going to have to rub myself – it was all becoming too much. I thought I might faint.

I turned around and pressed the side of my face against the floor, presented myself to him, slipped my forearms through the inverted V created by my legs and gently teased apart the sodden lips of my sex. Not the most ladylike of offerings, I know, but I'm a rugby player. I know what I want and how to get it. I wanted him to pound me into the ground. I wanted him deep.

I felt the head of his cock widen me as he pushed in. Then slowly, deliriously, he began pumping and I could feel every wonderful inch of him as my pussy drew him in. I touched myself and felt him too, where our bodies were joined, where a perfect seal was formed. His balls drummed against me. I felt a soapy finger stroke the super-sensitive flesh of my anus. Suds and water sluiced around my face and I felt the textured tiles beneath me scrape my nipples as I jiggled against them. The slap of his hard stomach against my arse. It was all too much. Building, it was building within so intensely I thought I would burst. I felt the first powerful surge of an orgasm plough through me and as I began to moan felt him increase his pace. I came again and ground myself against him. His hands grabbed hold of me roughly by the hips. I was vaguely aware of a presence at the shower entrance watching us through the clouds of steam but by then I didn't care. I let myself be fucked as though it were the last time for both of us. I felt him begin to tense and, although I wanted to feel him spray all that heat inside me, I wanted to see it happen even more. I wriggled off him and turned around, and I got hold of his cock just as he was beginning to come. I guided the head of his prick against my chest and felt his impossibly hot spunk draw a glorious route across the map of my body. Jamie's face was nothing but the clenched bar of his teeth and tightly screwed eyes. I kneaded his balls as another jet of come sizzled out of him, whipping across my cheek. I coaxed another few drops from him and then, spent, he came back to the real world. The person at the entrance was gone.

I leant over and kissed the tip of his cock clean as he dwindled. He tasted fresh and spicy, like the marine tang of the sea. Neither of us could say much. We showered, soaping each other clean, then meekly tiptoed back to the changing rooms. Happily, the other players had decamped to the bar. We dressed quickly and, before leaving, he pulled me close. 'I haven't even kissed you yet,' he said.

We both laughed, embarrassed by the strength of our carnality. I kissed him now, pressing my body fully against his, and broke away when things started to get too heated again.

'Come home with me tonight?' he said.

'Yes,' I said. I felt I could go through my whole life with him and say no other word. 'Steamo's not going to be happy about this,' I said. 'I mean, it isn't good form to have your tighthead and your flanker getting up close and personal, is it?'

'Steamo can go and drop-kick himself through the posts for all I care,' Jamie said.

'He could have done that to me too, after what you did to me out on that pitch. I wouldn't have noticed.'

Jamie's expression faltered. 'What do you mean?'

I punched his arm gently. 'You know exactly what I mean. When you copped a feel of my puppies.'

He blinked and the smile died from his face.

'Oh dear,' I said. 'That wasn't you?'

He shook his head.

In the bar we got a few suspicious glances from the other players, but nobody said anything. Neither of us could enjoy those drinks, despite what had happened in the changing rooms. We inspected the faces of our opponents, wondering which one of them could have committed such an odious act. I felt like going to each one in turn and shaking them by the hand, just so I could inspect their fingernails.

'Forget it,' Jamie said, and winked at me. 'I'll buy you dinner.'

'We're not leaving together, are we?'

'Of course. You gave me a lift, didn't you? I'll need a lift back.'

Goose and Munny came too, which saved us from being grist for the gossip mill, and I contrived a route that meant they would have to get out of the car first. When we were alone again, I asked Jamie what he wanted to eat.

'You,' he said. 'In the back of the car.'

I laughed, but his hand was already worming its way between my legs. I shifted in my seat, feeling hot colour bloom on my cheeks for the second time in as many hours.

'Jamie,' I started to protest but, even as I said his name, I was clambering into the back seat, only pausing to hitch up my skirt and hook a finger in my gusset to draw it to one side, 'we're on a main road.'

'Don't worry,' he said. 'It's too late in the day to get a parking ticket.'

And then he dropped his head between my legs and I felt his tongue and lips probing me. I could feel my juices and his saliva dribbling down the soft skin of my inner thigh. The car filled with the smell of my sex and the windows misted over. He kissed and sucked my clit while he drove the tips of his fingers under my bra, cupped and stroked my breasts with a pleasing roughness that stayed just the right side of pain.

I lifted my legs and planted the soles of my feet on the ceiling of the car. I felt his tongue lick around my anus and I gasped when he jabbed it in, his other finger now alternating between rubbing my mons and exploring my creases. I came suddenly, with a force that twisted my knee and caused me to almost put my foot through the window.

I wanted to return the favour but a police car had parked across the road from us. We surreptitiously straightened our clothes and I tidied up my hair in the rear-view mirror. My knee had flared up quite badly by now but I didn't give it much thought. Before pulling away from the kerb I leant over and licked away the drying juices on his chin and cheeks.

We got back to his place and he cooked dinner. Then we went to bed and I didn't get any sleep until the colour of the night was draining away from the rooftops. I was going to have to buy a family pack of headache tablets after all this.

We had training the following evening, a light session of stretching and swimming, to help our bodies repair after the rigours of the match. I should have cried off; my knee was quite badly swollen, but I didn't want to give Steamo any more ammunition to have a go at me. I could tell something wasn't quite right when I started a series of stretches to benefit the thigh muscles. I heard something pop and greyed out for a while. When I came to, Jamie was leaning over me. I looked down. A cold compress was positioned over my knee.

'Ouch,' I said.

'Looks like you've bust your cruciates from where I'm standing,' he said.

'What's that mean in English?'

'No more rugby,' Steamo said. He sat down by my side. 'Sorry, kiddo. You've had it.'

He reached out and patted my hand. The shock of the moment seemed too great. It was only a game. A game I loved but, still, it wasn't the be all and end all of my life. And then I realised why my shock felt so profound. Steamo's fingernails were clean and square cut.

So I left the team. The injury put paid to my rugby future, but I would have turned my back on them anyway, after what our skipper had done to me that day. I was furious. Jamie was ample compensation, however, and I let him know how much I appreciated him every night, to the point where we were both collecting bags under our eyes and I was beginning to get saddle sore.

Then, one night, there was a knock at the door.

'Leave it,' I said. We'd just uncorked the wine and sat down to eat. I didn't want any distractions.

He got up, a trifle sheepishly. 'I can't,' he said. 'I invited him.'

'Who?' But, as I asked the question, I knew exactly. 'Jamie!'

To his credit, Steamo was very contrite. He had bought me a bottle of wine to aid the apology and said it was totally out of character, which was true enough, I suppose. And he was man enough to admit, in front of Jamie, that the only reason he did it was out of desperation: he was jealous of my obvious attraction to the new boy which had forced his hand.

'It was stupid of me. Ill thought out. But, I hope, not unforgivable.'

'Oh, come here, you,' I said, and hugged him. I glimpsed Jamie licking his lips.

'I saw you in the shower,' Steamo said. 'I was coming in after you ... I thought you'd given me the come-on when you, you know, sucked my finger out on the pitch. I just got the wrong end of the stick.'

Jamie's eyes were glittering. I couldn't believe what I was seeing. He was getting off on me hugging Steamo, my tiny hands flat against his powerful back. I have to admit, Steamo's mouth was very close to my throat and the vibration of his words gave me a little tickle. I held him for longer than seemed correct.

'I used to fancy you,' I said. 'But you were too high maintenance. I wouldn't have been able to keep up with you.'

'Pity,' Steamo said. 'I think we could have been great together. You've got a beautiful body.'

'So have you,' I said. My heart was thudding so hard I thought Steamo might get a bruised chest.

'Me and Jamie,' Steamo said, 'we go way back.'

'Yeah,' Jamie said, unfastening the top button of his shirt. 'We share everything.'

I pushed Steamo away and smiled. I was too thrilled by what was happening to be angry. But I wasn't going to let them get their own way so easily. It was time to find out, once and for all.

'Remember, I've got a dodgy knee, boys,' I said. 'But I'll think about letting you share me ... if you share each other first.'

Whatever Floats Your Boat
Primula Bond

The kitchen window was really a small hatch – the sort that snaps shut in the door of a prison cell. A porthole in the galley of a ship. A few measly inches of space. Just enough room to either shove your nose and mouth through it to gulp in the fresh air or squint your eyes sideways to see the river.

We weren't supposed to take time off, let alone clamber on to the draining board to look through the window, even if we were about to pass out from the ghastly heat. Chef would kill you. Or so they told me when I started dishwashing at The Water Rats Boat Club.

I can't believe I was so law-abiding back then. Say jump and I used to ask how high. And I think those rules and threats even turned me on. I've always liked masterful types who looked as if they'd put me across their knees for impudence. But the main reason I had picked the job was because I needed money while I studied, pittance though it was, and I wanted it to be pretty mindless in my chores, saving my brain power for swotting up on Latin poetry. And I figured a riverside club in a posh part of the county would be a fun place to work. There would be roaring log fires in the winter, if I stuck it until then, and in the summer smart people in blazers swigging Pimm's and swarming on to the club's famous terraces to watch the regattas.

'If you get a chance, look out of the window before

the lunchtime rush,' Claire, the barmaid, told me, as she was chopping lemons on my worktop. Something else forbidden. The juice would mingle with the bleach, and then guess who would have my guts for garters if someone's G&T tasted of Zamo? I felt as if I'd known no other life for the past two months and, as for opening my books, forget it. I was way too knackered.

Claire pointed at the square of blue sky above our heads. 'It's time to give the frustrated old tart a little thrill,' she jested.

'Hey!' I warned her. 'Less of the old!' My fingers were red raw from the industrial Brillo which had already grated through my Marigolds. I ripped them off. 'What about chef? He's bound to catch me,' I said, twisting my damp hair back into its knot. 'So why should I risk my high-powered job?'

'He's always out at lunchtime. Haven't you noticed? He's only been here since the new owner took over, and already he reckons he's far too important to do any real work.'

Claire turned me round and started massaging my neck. Her pert breasts under her apron nudged softly against my aching spine. 'It'll be worth it, I promise,' she went on. 'It'll take you away from all this drudgery, at least for a few seconds. Just fix your eyes on that bend in the river. Feast them. Around noon.'

It was springtime at its chilliest, but the kitchen was still a hell-hole of heat. Vast pans bubbled and spat; piles of meat dripped blood on white plates and people red with puffing and blowing hunched and stirred, squatted and swore, ducking whenever chef appeared. He'd stalk and stare his way from oven to cold store to sink, bark some orders, then disappear again.

But that day, come noon, chef's hat and apron, even the blue and white chequered trousers, were hanging by the back door. So I dropped my knives, vegetable peelers and scrubbing brushes into some boiling water and hauled myself up to the window sill.

'Fancy a leg-up, Ellie?' shouted Ron the sous chef, grabbing at my ankles while the others, all blokes, laughed laddishly. 'Great pins you've got. You should wear skirts more often. Go on, hitch it up that bit higher. God knows we could all do with a thrill!'

I tugged about with the frayed hem of my denim skirt, making it worse. I was about to jump down again, my face burning, when outside the window I saw what looked like the tip of an arrow slicing across the surface of the river. Ron pushed me up and I hooked my elbows on the window sill and wriggled my shoulders through so that I was half in, half out of the hatch. Now they'd all see my knickers, for sure. Sod it. Let them. They were hardly going to gang-bang me on chef's pristine surfaces, were they?

The arrow elongated into the prow of a boat, skimming across the surface of the water, and now I could see stretching forwards, as if reaching for something, a pair of muscled arms. Oh, man. Or rather, men. As the first one disappeared through the frame of my window, the second appeared, leaning back, the oar lying across his stomach, and below the massive oar a pair of big thighs tightened up from the knees as they took the strain.

The third guy followed swiftly, leaning forwards again. Like the others, all he wore on this cool day was a loose white vest, sticking to every ridge of his spine and shoulder blades with sweat. A fourth man. My eyes were dry with staring. How many to a rowing boat? Eight, wasn't it? The fourth man pulled backwards, his mouth slightly open, as if he wasn't in a boat at all, but in a bed about to orgasm. I was focusing on that absent look men get when they're exerting themselves – which led my eyes down to his groin and the tight black shorts bulging there.

Not eight. That was it. They'd flashed past, out of the frame of my window, a silvery wake frothing up behind them. Four men in a boat.

The window remained empty. Claire was right: it had been worth it. All that brawn and beauty, sweating and straining to glide through the water. It was enough to gladden a skivvy's heart. Then, as if to mock my situation even more, the sun came out, licking the settling water into zig-zags of yellow and, as I half-turned to go back below, a tiny motorboat zoomed past as if chasing the rowers. The driver, dressed in a dark coat, face shadowed by a peaked cap, stood holding the steering wheel with one hand and, in the other, he held a megaphone.

I peered harder. He was yelling something. I had to lip-read from where I was standing, and it made no sense. It looked and sounded like, 'Easy on the slide!'

'Down, girl!' said Claire, laughing and making me jump so that I stepped right into the basin, scalding the bare skin past my ankle. 'Told you it would be worth an ogle, didn't I? Aren't they just to die for, those great hunks?'

I hopped about holding my reddening leg. I remembered the look on the last oarsman's face, eyes staring into space, totally lost in the struggle, so vulnerable somehow, yet all that power! I nodded. 'Greek gods, the lot of them!'

'Whatever.' Claire shrugged blankly. I thought of my pile of classical love poetry gathering dust at home. Catullus, Ovid, they were all horny as hell. But how pretentious would that be, standing in this horrible kitchen translating a poem about a thousand kisses rained down on a lover's muff? What was the Latin for muff, anyway?

'Well, they did win a gold at Athens, didn't they?' quipped Colin, tossing me an ice-cold towel to wrap round my foot. 'Wake up, girls. I'm talking about the

Olympic rowers? The coxless fours! Talk about sex on legs.'

He flicked his ponytail, hand on hip, and I grinned, realising that it would never be my knickers he was after.

'Think again, Col. Nothing cockless about those guys,' Claire said, picking up a tray of glasses and flouncing out of the kitchen. The hubbub out in the bar was already rising. 'They are all one hundred per cent red-blooded hetero man, I'm afraid.'

'And you know that *how*, exactly?'

Claire imitated Colin's hand on hip stance, balancing the loaded glasses tray with her other hand. 'Because I get in to work just when they're about to start training in their gym, downstairs in the boathouse. We've been, you know, talking about the regatta at the end of the month. Chef says it'll be great for business. And apparently their new coach is working them ever so hard, but Bruno, the stroke, that's the important one at the front of the boat for your information –'

'Ooh, he can stroke me any time!' Colin butted in, camp as Christmas.

'He's asked me to come as his guest to the party afterwards, so I'll be off duty that night, folks.' She kicked open the door, then looked at us all over her bare shoulder. 'Oh, and you can keep those dirty mitts off, Ellie, because I'll be having a pop at all his horny teammates, too, before the summer's out.'

'You go, girl!' trilled Colin, turning back to the souffles.

A week or so later Claire banged through the swing door just as chef had left for his daily skive. I had kept out of his way until my burnt leg healed. As it was, we'd never actually spoken. He barely knew I existed, but if I hobbled about too obviously he'd certainly give me a rocket and my marching orders.

'Guess what!' Claire cried, spinning me round from where I was peeling onions. 'They're coming into the bar at lunchtime, and you're going to meet them. Roster says Eleanor due an afternoon off. How about that? Claire due an afternoon off, too!'

'Who's coming into the bar?' I took the dishcloth off my shoulder and wiped my watering eyes.

'You look a right mess,' she said, laughing and dragging me across the floor. 'The rowers, of course! I got chatting to them again this morning. They're off the leash for the day. Apparently their coach gives them a break a couple of days before the big event, and I've persuaded them to come and have a beer.'

I glanced over at the square of window, my stomach tightening. I'd managed to sneak a look each day at those golden straining bodies zipping past on their sliver of wood, each day a little faster than before. The way they strained, back and forth, was a sight for sore eyes when I spent all my time staring at onions and carrots. 'Oh, I don't think so. Look at me.' I wiped my streaming nose. 'Don't forget I'm a lot older than you, Claire. I'm not really into public schoolboys –'

Claire was busy unwinding my apron strings, and tossed it over the taps. 'You're not even thirty yet, unless you've lied on your CV. Oh, yeah, I took a look. Now, listen up, girl –' she lowered her voice '– these are no chinless wonders, I assure you. They're mature students. Just like you, really. They're grown-ups.'

'Still younger than me, though.' I fluffed my hair up as best I could, and slid some lipstick on to my parched lips in the broken mirror by the door. She was dancing with impatience. 'But I thought you wanted me to keep my dirty mitts off?' I enquired.

'Well, sort of, but I thought it was only fair you had a little fun.' Claire suddenly ripped down the zip of my tiny, sawn-off jogging top so that my cleavage was surprised into view. 'Because I'm going to need a favour from you later.'

I followed her and we crept behind the bar. I couldn't relax now that I was out of my natural habitat. A row of four identical guys, anatomically perfect, were standing by the bar. Their identical neat heads nearly scraped the ceiling, and their enormous hands came down with one accord to pick up their pints.

'Chief would go mad if he saw us in here,' one of them said in a deep public-school accent. 'Lucky he's out on his own, sculling today.' He lowered his pint and studied Claire as she wiped an imaginary spillage on the bar. 'He's a real slave-driver.'

'Ooh.' Claire smiled, nudging me in the ribs but batting her eyelashes over the bar at him. 'He sounds just my type! I'd make a good slave!'

The rower smiled back at her. His eyes were the clear, bright blue of a healthy child. All four of them had the same eyes. The same chiselled jaws. The same narrow noses with flared, sensitive nostrils, the same sunglasses resting on their foreheads, even though the sunshine outside was still weak. And, of course, the same clean, mint-green tracksuit tops with the Water Rats logo, designed to cover their muscled, sporty torsos. Not a shrunk purple fashion number like mine with the word 'Please' ripped apart when the zip was undone, designed to barely cover a body whose sole exercise was dashing up the fire escape to get into the kitchen each morning before clocking on, on time.

'He sounds just like chef,' I muttered, glancing behind me. 'All *he* needs is a whip.'

The four men turned to me politely, and I blushed, still hot from the kitchen, sweat trickling down my back. I fiddled with the zip. My top felt too tight. It had been cold when I left home this morning. How stupid was I to wear nothing underneath but a lacy bra? What would those fine young men make of that? The scullery maid, showing her tits? Normally it didn't matter what I wore. I was hardly front of house, was I?

'It'll be worth all the aggro when you're the next Nigella Lawson,' remarked the oarsman standing next to Claire, peering at me over the top of his glass, and the others nodded, licking their lips in unison, their eyes aimed at my nipples. 'You're halfway there already.'

'Ellie's not cooking. She's scrubbing.' Claire followed the jibe with a merry laugh and pushed firmly in front of me. 'So, come on, boys. What would your "chief" do if he caught you here with us girls?'

'Well, there are three rules,' said the third rower, still looking at me. I noticed that his eyes were green, not blue, but they were still as clear as glass. He held up three fingers. 'No smoking. No soaking. So you've already made us break that one –'

'Oh, a harmless beer.' Claire wagged her finger, turning to include me again. 'We won't let that affect your performance!'

'And no poking.' The green-eyed rower finished, lowering his third finger slowly.

'Horrible way of putting it!' Claire pursed her lips and smoothed her hand down her dress. 'He's obviously very crude.'

'Just practical. He wants the rules to rhyme,' said the fourth rower, tapping the side of his head. 'Easier to remember.'

All four of them were still looking at me. I was beginning to enjoy it. But then Claire turned, too, and zipped me up crossly.

'I'll get back to the grindstone, then.' I shrugged, backing through the swing doors.

'Not noon yet,' Colin said, blocking my way back to the sink. 'Why don't you let your hair down a bit with those love dogs out there?'

'Chef will be back –'

'He's not such an ogre, you know.' Colin lovingly laid out several pieces of beef then raised the steak hammer. 'Quite different without his big hat on. Actually a bit of a sweetie, when you get to know him, even if he is another elusive hetero.' Colin sighed. 'Go on. One of us has to play Cinderella, and the clock hasn't struck twelve yet.'

I stepped out on to the fire escape. The sun was stronger now. Summer wasn't far off. There was no one about. I could hear Claire and her merry men laughing in the bar. Defiantly, I unzipped my top again and let the breeze lick my neck.

A few of the old gents who frequented the bar (old sporting heroes, Colin had told me) were sitting out on the balcony. They waved at me, pointing over to my right. 'Have a look at this one. Champion sculls.'

I had no idea what they were talking about, but I ran down to the riverbank and flopped down on to the grass to see what the fuss was about.

This time it was one man. One boat. A sharp speck in the distance, like a bird with thin black wings rising and falling into the water. As he approached I heard the gentle dip and plash of the blades (Colin had told me they weren't called oars) as they sent up silver droplets, but he still seemed to be flying.

The solitary rower wore a dark-blue baseball cap, and his vest and shorts were also dark. It must be the same guy who'd looked so cool driving the motorboat. This must be their slave-driving coach, I thought. The old boys were watching him, nodding, but the four naughty rowers were inside, being led astray by Claire.

I glanced back at the rower. She could keep them. Whatever Claire thought, those four were boys. This champion scull was a *man*. His arms and legs were even bulkier than theirs, but it was still the long, trimmed bulk of the rower, the big shoulders and slim waist, as opposed to the brutish, all-over bulk of the rugby player. That much I had learnt from a month's fantasising.

For a couple of seconds, as he skimmed the surface of the river, this one was mine. I'd watched him steering his motorboat, the jacket abandoned now the weather was warmer, teaching those boys all he knew, bellowing through his megaphone. And now he was doing it for himself. For me.

I was experiencing lust, pure and simple. It was brewing, coming luxuriously to the boil, a tight ball of hungry desire rolling from the pit of my stomach down to the source of the trouble. I lay back on the grass and let my thighs flop sideways to relieve the heat building between my legs. What *was* the Latin for muff? I watched him through my eyelashes. A few more strokes and he'd be right in front of me.

He can stroke me any time. A bubble of laughter blocked my throat as I pulled open my top, hooked aside the pink lace of my bra, and thrust my red nipples out just as he drew opposite me. He'd never see. He'd be focused, concentrating, the pure sportsman. But it gave me a cheap thrill, pretending to distract him. As he guided his boat so effortlessly past, I thought I heard the faintest of grunts. Not so effortless, after all.

The silvery wake trailed behind him, gradually flattening back into the water as if he'd never been there. I tipped my head back, my chest warming gently in the sun, and closed my eyes. I imagined it again. I wanted to hear that sexy grunt in my ear. But all I heard was the sound of muted clapping. My champion scull had vanished. But up on the balcony, those distinguished old men reckoned I'd made their day.

'Hey, not so fast, girl.'

I'd only been dozing for a few minutes, but my head was spinning with exhaustion as I staggered across the grass towards the car park.

'I'm hanging up my rubber gloves. The roster told me I had the afternoon off, remember?'

'Yeah, but I need that favour now.' Claire was sitting on the bottom step of the fire escape, pulling her shoes off. 'Bruno and I are going to break another of his chief's little rules, and we need you to look out in case he comes back.'

'I need to get home. I've got so much study to do –'

'You can get right off your high horse, lady, or I'll tell chef about your stripping in front of the punters just now on the riverbank.'

What could I say? Before I could protest, Bruno appeared from the boathouse, already naked to the waist, and Claire and I both gasped. The mint-green track top was off and you could river dance on that rock-hard stomach. He beckoned to Claire. The slapper didn't need telling twice. She ran across the concrete landing stage towards him and he scooped her over his massive shoulder in a fireman's lift. My God, she'd already yanked her knickers off, I noticed. Her little pink pussy flashed as she pretended to kick and struggle and he hoisted her inside his cave.

The boathouse was huge and dark and smelt of varnish, rubber and wet concrete. Wooden and fibreglass boats rested like beached fish on racks along the walls, but I could hardly see them after the glare of the unseasonal sunshine. I groped my way further inside, and heard Claire giggling somewhere at the far end.

A shiver of envy went through me. She was about to get the shafting of her life and all I'd managed in months was a little self-inflicted moist excitement on the riverbank. I crept closer, nearly tripping over a rowing machine.

Through a door I could see a gym with rows of exercise bikes, more rowing machines and weights and on the far side of that were the showers, and in the showers Claire's clothes were already off and Bruno was squeezing her breasts and burying his face between them. His buttocks tightened as he bent to lift her up so she could wrap her legs round him. He looked as if he couldn't hold back a second longer. How long had their coach forbidden sex, for goodness sake?

Now Bruno was about to give Claire a right good stroking, his strong legs slightly bent as he thrust into her, slamming her against the wall of the shower as he wasted no time and her fingers clawed at his wet back to get a grip as the water cascaded over them both.

I watched. She'd called me a frustrated old tart, and she was spot on. I ached for some action, some great big hands fondling me like that, huge strong thighs supporting my weight while an impossibly enormous dick impaled me. Watching Claire being thoroughly fucked by such a beautiful specimen only made me burn with longing. I was still hot from watching my champion sculler on the river. I had to let it all go somehow.

Bruno was grunting now, a little like the lone oarsman had done as he passed me. I wanted to climb the walls with frustration. With the rutting noises of Claire and Bruno in my ears I couldn't even retreat into my own fantasy. They could probably be heard up in the bar. Didn't they realise that the shower tiles only amplified the sound?

I glanced outside the boathouse. I could leave them to it, let the coach find them and mete out whatever punishment he had in mind. But then Claire would tell chef what I'd been up to, and then all hell would break loose below deck.

I pulled my skirt up and sat down on the hard little seat of the rowing machine. My knickers were damp. I trailed my fingers inside them, felt the moisture tangling my bush, and squirmed against my own touch. My tiny muscles all pulled tight, frantic to suck at my fingers.

I ripped the knickers off, the hot sweet female aroma stinging the air as I tossed them on to the floor. I straddled the rowing machine. Some strenuous exercise – that should help relieve the frustration. This was a boat club, after all. A place for getting fit. I decided to set myself a target on the machine until they'd stopped shagging, although by the sound of it that Bruno had the stamina of an ox. Claire would be delighted. But would his chief approve? The rowing machine was facing the entrance to the boathouse, so I could see if anyone came in.

I grabbed the handles, and started to pull. I could barely get the pulley towards my stomach. But there was a great side-effect. A sharp twinge of excitement as my bare cleft rubbed on the hard little seat. The way I was leaning touched my clit instantly against the slightly rough surface, sending sparks shooting up my belly. I half-closed my eyes, licking my lips, still pulling. The little seat slid forwards until my knees practically banged my chin, then I forced myself backwards, taking the handles as far back with me as I could. My legs were straight now, my thighs tightly closed over to squeeze the sensation between my legs. I held it for a moment, that position and the melting sensation, before I was flung back to the front again.

I braced my knees, determined to try again and, after a couple of pathetic pulls, I managed to get a laborious rhythm going. The more I moved, the harder I rubbed myself to ferocious excitement, the delicious opening and teasing closing of my sex with each sliding action; the whirring of the machine and my own gasping drowned everything out, including the riotous moaning from Bruno and Claire. I was aching with dissatisfaction, but at least I was exerting myself in the next best way.

Behind me their noises were building to a crescendo. In front of me, as I lunged backwards for the tenth time, an enormous figure wearing a cap loomed in the doorway. The handles of the rowing machine flung me forwards. My fingers were clamped on. I couldn't stop. I couldn't call out a warning. I was too out of breath. Claire and Bruno banged away regardless, and the figure in the doorway, just a black silhouette against the blinding sunlight, walked slowly inside the boathouse.

'Claire!' I croaked, robotically pulling myself backwards again.

The coach hung his blades up carefully on the wall then continued to walk towards me. I could now see the outline of those incredible muscles; the way his torso tapered to the waist and the tensing of his knees. His feet were bare. I stared hungrily all the way up his divine body. I couldn't help it – he may as well have been naked. I lingered on the jutting shape in his groin. Didn't they have some sort of jockstrap inside those tight shorts to protect their cocks from all that sliding up and down? Well, it must be too big for that because it looked as if there were another 'blade' wedged right there in his shorts.

'You can't come in!' I let the handles of the machine spin crookedly back into their cradle.

'I can do whatever I like, Eleanor, this is my boathouse,' was the reply. His face had been hidden by the dark cap, but now he took it off and ran a large hand through his hair so that it stood up in thick tufts. A pair of dark-brown eyes glared at me. I'd never seen him without a hat. He looked totally different. Totally gorgeous.

My neck creaked painfully as I covered my mouth. Only one person in this place ever called me Eleanor.

'*Your* boathouse?'

'I own The Water Rats. The club. Everything.'

I tried to stand up, but I was too aware of the juicy sensation going on under me, and what marks it may have left on the hard little seat. As I wriggled, the aroma of excited female wafted up again. He was looking straight at my crotch.

'It's my afternoon off,' I managed to croak.

He hooked his cap over the display panel and arranged the handles properly in their cradle. 'That rowing machine's broken. The tension is far too heavy. That's why it's outside the gym. Even I can barely pull it.'

He was talking macho boat things. Was he going to acknowledge my state? Had he been aware of my arousal, or had I imagined it? He was standing right over me and my eyes were on a level with his groin. The familiar way he was standing, questioning, accusing, with his hands on his hips meant that he was thrust slightly forwards. That left nothing to the imagination. He may as well have been wearing ballet dancer's tights. I could see the outline of his cock clearly, and he had a thumping great hard-on.

'And you should never, ever, do it wearing a skirt. It could catch under the seat. And God knows what the friction's doing to you. You really should wear knickers if you're going to work out. But it's a mouth-watering sight.'

My little pink pussy, like Claire's earlier, flashed in response. I tried to close my knees, but I couldn't move my legs. He started to laugh, a lovely low laugh right down in his chest. I'd certainly never heard him laugh before. It was lovely, rumbling in my ears.

'I've seen it all, now, haven't I? Your amazing tits – oh, yes, Eleanor, your trick worked. A man's got eyes, you know, even when he's rowing. Do you have anything else for me while you're here, or is it time to throw you out?'

'I thought you'd be far too disciplined to look,' I threw back. 'What about your rules?'

'I haven't had a drink for weeks.'

I smiled. There was just a whisper of lycra between me and him. I lifted my hand, measured the length of his erection with my fingers. Then I rubbed it. His prick jerked against the palm of my hand, straining at the fabric. I rubbed again, up, down, mercilessly, seeing the way his stomach caved in with surprise or pleasure, I wasn't sure. Rubbing harder now, making him bigger, so that it threatened to burst out of the top of his shorts.

He took hold of my arms, and started to lift me. 'The rules are for the crew. Not for me,' he said.

I'd never been this close to him. I could see how white his teeth were. Prickles of dark stubble on his chin. A full lower lip, glistening, which he was biting.

'They all said you'd kill me,' I quipped.

My skirt was still rucked up round my waist. I was about to tug it down when my sex ground up against him, and his long hard shape jabbed up between my legs. I pushed harder, moist again, wanting my moisture all over him.

'Oh, I don't want to kill you, Eleanor.' He planted his big hands on my bare buttocks and lifted me up. 'I'm not such an ogre, you know.'

These rowers, so strong! I felt light as a chicken fillet. I wrapped my knees round his slim waist, my arms round his neck. From now on I'd call this position The Oarsman. Now I could touch the muscles and sinews I'd seen heaving in the little boat. I started to rock against him, my pussy aching to be filled now.

'Will you sack me, then?'

'I want to fuck you, Eleanor. I've wanted to fuck you since you started scrubbing for me.'

He laughed again, backing round the rack of resting boats, and collapsed backwards onto an old sofa hidden in the corner of the boathouse. I fell on top of him. That simple, crude word, coming from him of all people, sheared through me. I was restless with urgent desire. I got up on to my knees and pulled his tight shorts down over his hips. The glorious cock bounced out and I took it in my hand again, dipped my head and circled its beading tip with my tongue, then trailed down the shaft and sucked on it, my head spinning with the excitement of doing this to him.

His head fell back. I saw his throat tighten. There was a dip of disappointment in me, and I pulled him out of my mouth before he came. His eyes were still closed – those incredibly long black eyelashes flickering slightly – but he smiled, shifted further down beneath me and his big hands were on my thighs again, lifting me lightly, his fingers briefly tickling the edges of my sex lips. And then the tip of his cock was there, teasing my burning clit. I was writhing on it for a moment, but enough waiting, I slid down as the smooth length filled me up. Thick, pulsing, nearly filling me, so that I forced myself to hold back before the real, deep plunge, and now it was my turn to row, row, row the boat, bending over him so that my hair fell on his face, licking his open mouth. His head came up to kiss me, but I pushed him back down, the great man in his dark-blue singlet, his warm hands on my butt, spreading the cheeks as I bucked harder, happy to do the work, squeezing him hard inside me, feeling him swelling in response, thrusting hard as I rode him, losing the will to keep it slow, riding faster and faster.

'Easy on the slide,' he whispered, and that flicked the switch for me, ripples turning into a powerful surge of ecstasy as he thrust and pumped and then burst his load, half-sitting up to meet my mouth and grunting softly in my ear as I came, too, shuddering to a halt on top of him then lying on his broad chest as our breathing slowed.

There was a scrape of feet on the concrete. Claire and Bruno, gleaming, wet, satisfied and fully dressed, were standing by the broken rowing machine, failing to stifle their amazement. As I rolled sideways on to the sofa, stretching my arms lazily above my head and waggling my fingers in greeting, they caught sight of my lover.

'Chef!' shrieked Claire.

Sports Widow Bonnie Dee

I sat, eyes glazed over, watching the asses in their tight white pants move back and forth in front of me. One of the asses turned around and I looked hard at the package in front but it was well shielded by an athletic cup. I yawned. Of all the sporting events to which my husband dragged me football was the most boring; too much padding and uniform and helmets covering up those healthy young bodies. You couldn't catch a glimpse of *anything*! Not even in the prime seats right behind the bench.

I am a sports widow. The sad thing is I knew when I married Todd he was a fanatic. Football, baseball, basketball, soccer, auto racing, hockey – he managed to watch a little bit of all of them. I used to think it was cute and sexy that he was a he-man sports guy but that was when I was 24, young and stupid. I didn't understand that his sex drive was secondary to his sports obsession and that after less than a year of marriage his fascination with bedding me would take a back seat to his fascination with scores and averages and watching a lot of men in uniforms play gladiator games.

I tried everything to get his attention back but his libido was nil. Sexy lingerie, striptease, kinky sex toys – none of them could distract him from sports and focus his attention back on me. Sometimes I even attended games with him hoping I could learn to share in his passion but I usually ended up as bored as I was today watching the playoff game between Kentworth College and Gurney University, my husband's alma mater.

'Take him down! Take him down!' Todd screamed, jumping to his feet and spilling his popcorn on my lap. 'Five yards, yeah, baby!'

I brushed the kernels off my black spandex skirt and reached down the front of my white halter-top to rescue a piece of popcorn that was trapped in my cleavage. When I looked up at the players again, popping the errant kernel in my mouth, I noticed one of the defensive linemen staring up into the stands straight at me. I cut my eyes to the right and left to make sure there wasn't someone else he was contacting then I gave him a seductive smile and a wink. He grinned back.

This guy was a second stringer and hadn't been sent into the game the whole afternoon. He had dark unruly hair and deep-brown eyes. At least I thought they were brown. It was hard to tell from up in the stands and I'd been looking more at the bodies than the faces up until now.

Todd was seated again and still glowing with excitement about that last play. 'Damn, did you see that? They held him to five yards.'

'Uh-huh. That was exciting,' I murmured as I continued to flirt with the bench warmer. I tossed back my hair and cocked my head then I gave him a provocative look from beneath half-lowered lashes and slowly licked my lips.

The young athlete's smile deepened and he pursed his lips and gave me an air kiss before turning his attention back to the game. Evidently our little flirtation was over and I settled in with a sigh to endure another hour of football.

I was deep into a hedonistic daydream of naked athletes in the locker room taking me every which way I could imagine, when Todd nudged me. 'Game's over, hon,' he said. 'Let's go.'

I pressed my thighs together and willed my aching

sex to settle down. I was surprised Todd or the fan on the other side of me hadn't noticed my shifting around in my seat as I repeatedly brought myself to the brink from my fantasy. I had even taken advantage of touchdowns when the crowd roared and jumped collectively to its feet to let out moans of delight at my private diversion.

Following the football game there was a mixer with a meet and greet, during which alumni Broncos reliving their glory days could schmooze with the new generation of star players. The college wasn't my alma mater and I was bored to tears until I discovered the buffet table and dug in.

As we mingled with the crowd I munched on a baby quiche and listened to former ball players like my husband regale anyone who would listen with stories of magical fall days when they made the perfect play or scored the winning touchdown. Ho-hum.

Then I caught sight of the hottie who'd been giving me the eye during the game. He smiled and nodded at me from across the room and I sashayed over, swinging my hips to set my tight little skirt swinging. My legs had been cold as hell all afternoon, but now I was glad I'd worn it.

'Great game,' I purred when I reached him.

'Yeah, I guess.' He shrugged. 'You looked as bored as I was riding the bench.'

'Now, aren't you supposed to be all gung-ho and supporting the rest of the team?' I asked, resting my hand on his well-muscled arm.

'Not after eight straight games where you're never sent in once.' He glanced lasciviously at my chest. 'And not when the view of the stands is so much more interesting.'

I leant in close and whispered, 'Don't you think this mixer is kind of a drag too? I've got something better than a bench that you could be riding.' I kneaded his arm a little to drive my point home. 'My husband is Class of '93 but I've never toured the campus before. Maybe you could show me around.'

The young athlete looked shocked, as though he hadn't expected more than a diverting flirtation, but he quickly recovered his composure and said, 'Sure.'

I found my husband and told him I was being given a personal tour of the campus by one of the players. I've always found it's best to stick to the truth as much as possible. Then I took the stud muffin's arm and he led me from the room.

'What's your name?' I asked as we strolled across the green grass of the quad. 'I'm Delia.'

'Mark.' His reply was short and his tone nervous and I suddenly realised how young he was. The idea of playing Mrs Robinson to a hot, hunky boy-man was extremely appealing and his shyness empowered me.

'Well, what do you want to show me ... Mark?' I enquired suggestively. 'Are there any spots on campus that are scenic and secluded?'

'Um.' His nervousness was so appealing. 'There's the chapel. Nobody goes there except Sundays. And there's the locker room. I have a key.'

Well, I might not get my complete locker-room orgy fantasy come true, but one player was better than none. 'The locker room it is,' I replied, taking his hand and letting him lead the way.

The smell of sweat hit me as we entered the dark room. Mark switched on the lights and I looked around at the inner sanctum of the ball players. Although most of the jerseys and towels had made it into a huge hamper in one corner, there were still a number of uniform bits scattered around the floor and on the benches. The place reeked of man – perhaps a little too much – and my beautiful fantasy of testosterone-fuelled ballplayers fucking me like Vikings had neglected to include the sense of smell that would accompany it.

'Uh, perhaps the chapel or a janitor closet would be better,' I began.

But somewhere after 'Uh', Mark interrupted by tackling me, pushing me up against the wall and covering my mouth with his. I immediately forgot the smell and the mess and responded to his ardent fumbling. His lips were soft and warm and his tongue wet and slippery as a seal. He plumbed the depths of my mouth and lifted me off the ground in his strong arms. Pressed between the hard wall at my back and the hard body in front of me, I felt his rigid erection already grinding at my crotch. I had evidently misjudged the boy's 'aw shucks' demeanour. He now seemed to know exactly what he was doing and what he wanted.

Mark's body was so toned and muscular and huge I felt like a doll in his embrace. I could feel his biceps bulging under my hands as I gripped him and I was entranced by the idea of so much power under my control.

His mouth moved to my jaw and neck, licking and nibbling his way down to my collarbone. I gasped and twisted in his arms as the tickling kisses sent shocks of lust like a lightning bolt straight to my crotch. He reached to untie my halter-top with one hand while still supporting my ass with the other. I was sliding down the wall a little so I wrapped my legs around his waist and grappled him to me.

Mark was having trouble releasing my boobs from my shirt so I reached behind my neck with both hands and unfastened the halter. My heavy breasts fell free of the binding material and he dipped his head to lick one dark nipple while grasping the other full globe in his big fist. I ran my hands through his soft hair and gripped his head, encouraging his suckling with my soft moans of pleasure.

He turned his attention to my other breast, licking, teasing and gently biting at the nipple while my ardent cries grew louder. I clutched a handful of his shirt and tugged at it, needing to feel the hot skin underneath.

'I want to feel all of you,' I said. 'Take your clothes off.'

Mark obliged, setting me on my feet and quickly shucking his shirt, shoes and pants. In moments he stood before me, a young Adonis with perfectly toned chest, ridged abs and an angelic face. And the light which had been hidden under the bushel of an athletic cup was glorious. His penis was thick, long and straining towards me as if it had a mind of its own. It pulsed with vitality and youth. Balls to body, Mark was gorgeous and he was all mine for the afternoon.

'Now you,' he said, unable to drag his eyes from my bounteous chest.

'All right.' I unfastened the bottom of my halter and stood topless before him, then quickly unzipped my skirt and let it drop to the floor around my feet. I stepped out of both my shoes and the circle of skirt and stood there in only my silky blue thong. I knew I was fucking gorgeous too. Men's eyes told me that all the time, even if my husband was too sports obsessed to notice.

I pushed my hand through my shoulder-length black hair and smiled at him provocatively. 'So, what next?'

His eyes moved from my breasts to my face and he looked suddenly uncertain. 'Can I – Can I ask you to do something for me?'

'How kinky is it?' I teased with a grin. 'I'm a pretty adventurous sort.'

It was charming. He was actually blushing as he said, 'Will you put on a team jersey while we do it?'

The connotations underlying that request didn't

escape me, but it was a pretty mild kink so I said, 'Sure. Whatever turns you on.'

He grinned like teacher had just given him a big gold star and walked to the hamper from which he pulled a grass-stained, sweat-drenched jersey.

'Oh.' I was taken aback. I had assumed he meant for me to wear a nice, freshly laundered shirt. But he looked so excited and the request was so sweet, I took the shirt. The heady odour of man-sweat surrounded me as the jersey slipped over my head and arms. It was slippery polyester mesh in white and green, with the number 54 and the name Carrington emblazoned on the back. I had to wonder if Mark had chosen a shirt at random or if he had special feelings for this Carrington dude.

'You like?' I asked, twitching the shirt into place. It was so big that it hung loosely, exposing my shoulders and most of my breasts and ending at my knees. 'That Carrington's some big guy, eh?' I grabbed the shirt as if it were a dress and flounced it back and forth.

'You look so hot!' The shirt obviously rang his bell. 'Can I ask you to do one more thing?'

'Um . . .' I had thought his first request odd enough. I wasn't quite sure I wanted to know what other secret fantasies the boy had.

'Could you wear a helmet too?'

I raised an eyebrow but shrugged my assent. 'Sure. Why not?'

'Thanks so much. You don't know what a turn-on this is for me.' He hurried to get a helmet. Watching his cock bob before him like a divining rod, I could see ample evidence of what a turn-on it was.

I was proud of myself for being such a good sport as I lowered the helmet over my head and blinked at Mark from the depths of it. 'Good?' I asked.

'Oh, hell yeah! Lean over the bench and spread your legs,' he commanded, and I wondered what had happened to the shy, pleading boy of two seconds ago. But my pussy was still aching from my long hours of mental masturbation in the bleachers. I had done all the foreplay in my head; now I was ready for the main event. As was Mark, evidently.

'Condom,' I reminded him, as I stripped off my thong, spread my legs, leant over the bench and braced my hands on it. I could hear him rip open a foil packet and was amazed at his preparedness. What a boy scout. But before I had time to think about where the hell he had produced the thing from, I felt the long shirt dragged up to reveal my bare ass and Mark's hands were running over my skin almost reverently.

'This is so fucking hot,' he said again, and his hand moved between my legs, two fingers thrusting into me again. I pushed back against them. He snaked his other hand around my waist and began rotating my clit with a nimble finger. Sparks of fire shot out from the sensitive nerve bundle and I was already on the edge of coming. He removed his wet, thrusting fingers and began working them around and inside my anus. I had never been penetrated there, and tensed up as he pushed one slick finger then two inside, but it actually felt good coupled with the insistent circling on my clit, so I relaxed and let him work his fingers carefully in an out.

'Oh jeez,' he groaned as he spread my cheeks and began to slowly press into my ass. The condom must have been a pre-lubed brand because it pushed in with surprisingly little resistance.

There was an odd, stretching, burning sensation and I thought, That's never going to fit. Yet it did. Half-inch by half-inch he slowly sheathed himself inside me, never halting in his ministrations to my clit. By now I was arching into his hand and didn't care if he stuck a whole baseball bat up my rear as long as he made me come with that talented hand.

A bright flash of light went off in my head as I reached orgasm, bucking wildly and impaling myself hard on to Mark's cock without being aware of any pain at all. I just wanted him inside me. Didn't care where. Didn't care how.

'Oh yeah! Fuck me, baby! Fuck me hard!' I screamed like a porn star with a bad script. But I really meant it.

Meanwhile, Mark was finding his own pleasure. He sped up, thrusting in and out with harder strokes, while his hands clutched my hips and held me steady. My arms were still braced on the bench and my spread legs were shaking from the aftershocks of my orgasm. I felt myself coming down from the high and became more aware of the feeling of Mark's ample length plunging in and out of my tight channel. It was a little sore, but in a really good way.

'That's right. Do it,' I encouraged. 'You're so big and hard and –'

'Sh,' he gasped, as he continued to thrust. 'Don't ... talk.'

It didn't take a rocket scientist to figure out that I was a stand-in for the ubiquitous Carrington. I went with Mark's private fantasy and kept silent to preserve the illusion that I was one of his teammates. It seemed that the boy might need to book some counselling soon to come out of that closet.

After a minute or two's silence he let out a wild cry and pushed into me one last time, then collapsed against my back. My arms were crying out at supporting both our weight and I had to tell him to pull out after a second. He did and, as I straightened up and turned, I became aware that there was someone else in the locker room, near the door, watching us.

I removed the helmet, my hair sweaty and matted from the cushioned lining, and saw that the voyeur was Todd. He looked from me to the panting Mark and back again like he was trying to fit a square peg in a round hole.

'Todd, er . . . it's not like it looks,' I said lamely.

'Really? Cos it looks like that guy just finished fucking you doggy style,' he said. 'And was it actually in the ass?'

Glancing from poor dismayed Mark to my husband, I gave in and decided to take the offensive. 'Why shouldn't he fuck me? You certainly aren't interested in doing it these days.'

Then Todd said the totally unexpected: 'Maybe because you've never looked as hot as you do right now wearing that jersey.'

Ah hah. I knew it. It had to be more than the game that gave Todd his fascination for athletes. There were some definite issues of sexual orientation here but, maybe if we could incorporate a willing partner like Mark into our sex play, it would all work out.

'You think I'm hot?' I asked, adopting a teasing tone. 'Why don't you show me *how* hot? I'm up for another go – without the helmet this time.'

Mark gaped at me and Todd gaped at Mark's naked young body and I gaped in amazement at the total cluelessness of these two guys about their own erotic desires.

'Look. Here's the play,' I said. 'Mark, sit on the bench. Todd, go around from behind. I'll suck Mark, Todd can fuck me and everybody wins.'

As the two men continued to assimilate the idea, I tossed off the sweaty jersey then moved to Todd and began peeling his Broncos sweatshirt off over his head. 'Helps if you get naked,' I reminded him.

Evidently Mark had a short refraction time, especially when the opportunity for being involved in a threesome arose. So, for the second time that day, Mark sat on the bench. I went down in front of him. I wrapped one hand around his half-hard dick and my lips stretched around the head. Meanwhile, I felt Todd kneel, straddling my legs and reaching between them in search of my bud. Even though I'd already been through one torrid session, I hadn't been satisfied in the usual way, and my pussy was clamouring to be filled. I waited impatiently while Todd guided himself to it and pushed inside.

As I worked into a rhythm of sucking and stroking Mark, Todd matched the movement with his thrusts into me. Both men were gasping and moaning already, excited by the forbidden nature of having a woman simultaneously. I was overwhelmed by the reality of being the focus of two men at once. There seemed to be hands everywhere on my body. Todd's were stroking up and down my sides, reaching around to fondle my breasts and then sliding down to grip my hips firmly. Mark's were tangled in my hair, cradling my skull and guiding the pace of my mouth on him.

I then became aware that Mark was leaning over me. I stopped the blowjob long enough to look up and see what he was doing. Above my head, Todd and Mark were leaning towards each other and kissing! It was a deep soul kiss with mouths wide open and a lot of tongue action. Hmm. Interesting. Evidently I was the conduit they needed to complete their connection.

I turned my attention back to sucking Mark and was rewarded shortly by an increase in pace and a constant groaning as he neared climax. The two men had stopped kissing, and behind me Todd's efforts were redoubled as he too approached orgasm. With one man pumping in my sex and one in my mouth, I had if not my hands then my orifices full. My knees were sore from contact with the hard, cement floor and my jaw was beginning to ache from being open so long. I was in a decidedly submissive position and I revelled in the naughty sensation of being the sex object of the day. It might not be politically correct, but it fulfilled my fantasies to feel used for pleasure like this. It also thrilled me to witness something as unusual as my husband tongueing another man.

Finally – and within seconds of each other – both men came. I could taste the warm spunk spurting from Mark's cock against my tongue and I swallowed each spasm as it erupted. And I could feel Todd pulsing inside me, expanding and contracting as he released his load and gripping my hips almost painfully as he rammed home one last time. Both men were crying out in atonal synchronicity. The primitive sound of their hoarse, ecstatic cries gave me the extra nudge I needed to crest the wave.

I let Mark's still rigid penis fall from my mouth as I let out my own primal scream and, for the second time that afternoon, experienced the fireworks display of orgasm popping and sparkling against the dark screen of my tightly closed eyelids. I cried out as I scored a personal touchdown and heard the invisible crowd roar in my ears.

Afterwards I collapsed on the floor in a boneless heap, gasping, panting and trying to remember why earlier today I had been mentally bitching and moaning about coming to the ballgame with Todd. If every sporting event ended like this, I could become a fan too.

Mark the bench-warmer was the first to break from our huddle. He rose stiffly and stepped over me to go in search of his discarded clothing. I heard Todd get up and the rustling of clothes as he too dressed himself. Finally I stretched and pushed up off the floor. Every part of me felt drugged and dreamy. My whole nether regions were sore from being ploughed with wild abandon, but these body aches were those of muscles which have been well exercised. I felt like a star athlete after a tough challenge.

Todd reached a hand down and helped me to my feet. Mark handed me my skirt and top but said he couldn't find the thong. I wondered if he had pocketed it as a memento.

I saw Todd glancing at Mark and blushing. He couldn't deny that kiss had happened, no matter how much he might like to chalk it up to the heat of the moment. I saw Mark meet his glance and then look quickly away. It was going to take some time and effort to teach these two to play nicely together but if the young athlete and my husband were willing to put themselves in my hands I was sure I could coach them to greatness.

I reached in Todd's trouser pocket, fished out his wallet and withdrew one of his business cards, which I presented to Mark. 'Any time you want to get in the game again, give us a call. Our home phone number is on the bottom,' I informed him.

'Thanks.' He took it with a shy grin and ambled sheepishly from the room.

'You gave him our number! And he knows our names! What were you thinking? This could cause so much trouble. I can't believe we did this!' Todd suddenly looked frantic – not at all like a guy who had just had a sweaty threesome in a sweaty locker room.

'Sweetie, relax,' I told him. 'It was all in good fun, just a Saturday-afternoon game. No harm, no foul. You enjoyed it didn't you? *All* of it?'

He shrugged, not meeting my eyes, toeing the ground and generally looking like a third-grader caught cheating on a test.

Todd might take additional workouts and training at Camp Delia, but I was sure that given time I could help him release his repressed erotic fantasies. As for me, now that I'd found out how much fun athletes could be I was ready to try out a number of different players on the home team before making a final draft pick.

Glove Story Elizabeth Coldwell

The first thing I saw was his arse. It was pretty much all I could see of him as we walked along the side of the training pitch towards the goalmouth. He was lying on his back, legs off the ground and bent at the knees and, as his coach kicked the ball towards him, he sprang to his feet and made the save. Impressive, I thought. And then I took in the muscular build of his body, the boyish face beneath a spiky blond fringe and, most gloriously, the thick honey-tanned thighs and decided that, at last, I had been handed an assignment which was worth covering.

I had been working as assistant photographer on the *Leader* for all of three days, having transferred from its sister paper in Nottingham. I had finally grown tired of being passed over for promotion in favour of blokes who had been working in the department for a fraction of the time I had and, when I had been offered the post, I had agreed without hesitation, even though it meant moving thirty-odd miles up the M1. After all, it wasn't as though I had anyone to uproot but myself. Now, I was beginning to wish I had given it a little more thought. So far, I had been sent to cover two tree-planting ceremonies, prize-giving day at the local college of art and technology and a protest against the proposed building of industrial units on a site where rare lizards were breeding. Already I was beginning to miss the fast pace of the big city. When I had been summoned by the sports desk and told I would be going to photograph the local football team's latest signing, my heart had sank. Though my dad and kid brother were both mad-keen Forest fans, I had somehow managed to avoid developing an interest in the sport. Saturday afternoons, when I had them free, were for shopping and going for coffee and a gossip with the girls, not for sitting in a freezing-cold stand watching blokes kicking a ball about. But a job was a job, and I would just have to grit my teeth and get on with it. It couldn't be any less boring than the prize-giving.

The paper's football reporter, Pete, had filled me in on the background to the story as he drove us up to the club's training ground. Danny Wolf was a promising young goalkeeper who had been signed from Darlington. His predecessor had put in a string of performances the previous season which had been impressive enough to earn him a call-up to the England squad. Though he had only sat on the subs' bench, bigger teams had noticed him and Charlton had put in a bid which was too much for the club's chairman to turn down. Pete also told me all I needed to know about the club's performances over the last few seasons; basically, it seemed they were overachieving given their resources, but they had a manager who was well liked by the fans and had the knack of getting good performances out of run-of-the-mill players. He also had an eye for a bargain in the transfer market, and Pete reckoned Danny Wolf was a brilliant signing.

I had been listening to all of this with half an ear, as I had been busy casting surreptitious glances at Pete as he drove. He was the first shaggable man I'd come across on the *Leader*; everyone else I had worked with since I'd arrived had been in their fifties and pretty much fossilised. Pete was closer to my own age, thirty, and was fit in a slightly scruffy way. He had a day's growth of stubble on his chin, sleepy brown eyes and was dressed in a battered biker's jacket, dark jeans and a Motorhead T-shirt which had been washed so often it had faded from black to charcoal grey. He looked as though he would be happier working for *Q* or the *NME*, rather than some provincial weekly paper, but I suppose in my summer plumage of white ribbed vest, denim miniskirt and calf-length caramel leather boots I gave pretty much the same impression. I wondered if he had caught me admiring the way the tight crotch of his jeans clearly outlined the bulge of his cock and balls, and what he would think if he knew I had been having idle daydreams in which I got him to stop the car and give me a swift one on the back seat. And then I'd seen Danny, and Pete had suddenly been relegated to the second division of my fantasies.

At that moment, Pete's mobile rang. 'Excuse me a second,' he said, and wandered a couple of feet away to take the call. I heard the muttered phrases, 'See what I can do' and 'Soon as I can, I promise,' before he cut the connection.

'Sorry about that, Naomi,' he said as he walked back to me, 'but there's been a change of plan. That was Clare, my wife. She's supposed to pick up our son from the childminder but something's come up at work and she needs me to do it. Would you mind if I did the interview first, and then left you with Danny to take the photos?'

Did I mind? Not only was I being given the opportunity to spend some time alone with this gorgeous goalkeeper, but also Pete had said the magic words which were guaranteed to send him plummeting into the non-league as far as my lecherous intentions towards him were concerned – 'wife' and 'son'. I didn't chase married men, even for a quickie in the back of a Vauxhall Corsa; it wasn't worth the grief.

'Yeah, sure,' I told him. 'The only problem is you're my lift out of here.'

'Don't worry,' Pete said, flashing me a grin which

suddenly seemed less roguish than it had now I knew it had domestic responsibilities attached to it. 'I'll sort something out. Either I'll come back up here and fetch you once I've collected Jack, or I'll get you a taxi on my expenses. I won't leave you stranded here, I promise. Now come on, and I'll introduce you to Danny.'

We wandered on to the pitch; Danny's coach picked up the ball he had been about to launch in the young goalkeeper's direction and came over to meet us. He obviously knew Pete already, and the two men shook hands briskly before Pete said, 'Don, this is Naomi, the *Leader*'s new photographer. Naomi, this is Don Henry, United's goalkeeping coach.'

Don gripped my hand in his big paw. 'Very nice to meet you, Naomi.'

'And this is Danny Wolf, the club's new star,' Pete added.

Danny, not at all fazed by Pete's extravagant praise, slipped his hand out of his glove, took mine and gave me a wink which hit me right between the legs. 'Hi there,' he said, a definite North-eastern edge to his accent.

When he let go of my hand it was as though he'd just pulled his cock out of me, leaving me wanting, so strong had been the physical connection between the two of us.

'Danny, I just want to ask you a few questions about how you're getting on at the club, what you feel about the challenge of stepping up to this level after playing in the bottom division, that kind of thing,' Pete explained, 'then I've got to shoot off and leave you in Naomi's capable hands.'

'No problem,' Danny replied, sounding as though there was nowhere he would rather have been than in my hands – though that could just have been my rapidly overheating imagination talking.

'Well, if you don't mind,' Don said, 'I'm going to call it

a day. Training finished about forty minutes before you got here, and I've been giving Wolfie a good workout while we were waiting for you, but Leicester are playing a friendly tonight and we've got them the first match of the season. I've got to get off down there to check them out, so –'

'Are you going to want any shots of Danny in action?' I asked Pete. 'You know, making a save or anything like that? It's just that, if you do, I'll need Don to kick the ball to Danny like he was doing when we arrived.'

Pete shook his head. 'No, that can look a bit cheesy, and I'm trying to make the football pages a cheese-free zone. A couple of decent portrait shots will be fine.' He turned to Don, clapping him on the shoulder. 'Thanks for your help, mate. Don't worry, we won't wear your boy out.'

Much as I could think of a few ways to, I thought. While Pete fiddled about setting up his tape recorder, I grabbed the bottle of water I kept in my camera bag and went to sit on an upturned bucket, out of the way. There was still plenty of heat in the August afternoon, and I basked in the strong sunshine, watching Pete conduct the interview through half-closed eyes as I swigged from the bottle. My already short skirt had ridden up a fair way as I sat down, and I suspected that if Danny glanced over he might well catch a glimpse of the tight triangle of scarlet lace between my thighs. Modesty should have compelled me to sit in a more ladylike fashion, but something about this whole situation was making me feel very far from modest. I wanted to flaunt myself, and I wanted Danny to watch me doing it.

I shut my eyes and imagined myself lifting up my top as I sat there, to reveal my pert, braless breasts to Danny's gaze. Pete, his back to me, would be oblivious to my action as I casually stroked my nipples with my fingers, deliberately distracting Danny as he tried to answer Pete's carefully thought-out questions. And if that didn't work, then I would simply open my legs a little and slip a couple of fingers into my dampening knickers ...

'OK, Naomi, he's all yours.' Pete's words would have fitted so perfectly into my filthy little fantasy that I was genuinely startled to realise the interview had come to an end and it was time for me to take over. 'I'll be back as soon as I can,' he told me, and headed back to where he had parked the car, jacket slung over one shoulder, rebel without a babysitter.

'Is everything OK?' Danny asked, watching Pete's retreating figure.

'Family emergency,' I said. 'He's got to help his missus out with something.'

'Ah, right. That's not a problem I have any more. I split up with my girlfriend when she found out I was leaving Darlington. Said she didn't fancy the move south.'

'So are you trying to make me feel sorry for you, or are you trying to let me know you're available?'

'Both.' Danny grinned, and this time I realised it wasn't my imagination – he was flirting with me.

Lust gripped my pussy and gave it a good, hard squeeze. I did my best to ignore what my body was suggesting, though: I had work to do. I rooted in my bag, and pulled out my camera, checking the settings and the battery levels.

'How do you want me?' Danny asked.

On your back with me straddling those amazing thighs would be nice, I thought. 'Let's have you leaning up against the goalpost to start off with,' I said.

Danny went to stand where I asked, holding the pose as I moved round him, taking the shot from various angles. 'OK, now I want you to crouch down and hold your hands up by your face.' Apart from the fact that my subject was more handsome than usual, this was all bread-and-butter stuff. I wished I could be more creative in my choice of pose, but Pete had given me the narrowest of briefs. No doubt he would consider these pictures, designed to show off Danny's prime assets – his hands – to be cheesy, but I was sure the *Leader*'s art editor would approve.

Suddenly, my mobile rang. I snatched it up, glanced at the display: Pete. 'Hi, Naomi,' he said as I answered. 'All sorted, you'll be glad to know. I'm just dropping Jack off at the house and I'll be with you in half an hour, tops. And when we get back into town, I'm going to take you for a pint. It's the least I can do after messing you around like this.'

No, I thought, the least you can do is leave me here with Danny for long enough to see if things as going to get as down and dirty as I hope they are. 'OK, see you,' I said. 'That was Pete,' I explained to Danny. 'He's on his way back to collect me. If you want to go and get changed, I think we're just about done.'

'Actually,' he said, 'this is probably going to sound daft, but can I ask you a favour?'

'Anything,' I assured him. Peel you out of your jock-strap, I thought. Scrub your back in the shower. You only have to ask.

'When I was at Darlo, the lads posed naked for a calendar for charity. I was going to take part, but then I had to go for some treatment on my knee and couldn't do it. They said it was a real laugh, and I always felt like I'd missed out. Would you mind taking some photos like that of me?' He blushed slightly, charmingly. 'I'll pay you for them.'

'That's not necessary,' I told him. 'I'll enjoy it.' Now it was my turn to blush. 'I mean, I very rarely get to do much arty stuff, and I could take some great black-and-white shots of you.'

This was my opportunity to get creative. I had submitted some nude portraits of a long-ago boyfriend as part of the portfolio for my degree course, and I still counted them as among the best photographs I had ever taken. No other man had been willing to pose naked for my lens – until now. So what if Danny's request sounded suspiciously like a come-on? In the back of my mind, I was hoping that was exactly what it was.

I quickly changed the memory card in the camera; these were definitely not going to be shots that could be kept on file in the *Leader* office.

'Right,' I said. 'Let's start off much as we did before, with you against the goalpost, only this time with your top off.'

I watched as Danny shrugged off his sweat-soaked grey training top, exposing a torso which was nicely defined but not too bulky, with a sprinkling of blond hair across his pecs. This time, I got him to raise his arms above his head and hold on to the post, in a pose which was vaguely submissive and deeply suggestive.

Next, I had him peering through the mesh of the goal net. All the time I was observing him through my viewfinder, taking a voyeuristic delight in capturing the planes and hollows of his upper body as he moved. The atmosphere between us, which until now had been nothing more than mildly flirtatious, had changed, as though Danny had shed some of his inhibitions along with his top. We were no longer two professionals doing our jobs; we had moved, almost without being aware of it, to a more intimate level. As I got down on my haunches to photograph Danny from below, I felt the gusset of my skimpy knickers settling into the cleft of my sex, and realised just how wet and turned on I was.

'Right, it's about time the rest came off,' I told him, 'but we'll go in the changing rooms for that.' The thought of asking Danny to strip off completely then and there had crossed my mind: I would have loved to take a shot of him lying in the goalmouth using only the ball to preserve his modesty, but I didn't know how Pete would react if he turned up and saw what we were doing in his absence.

I waited for Danny to pick up his discarded top and gloves, then we made our way to the low L-shaped brick building which turned out to house a small canteen, a gym and the changing facilities.

The changing room itself could have done with a lick of paint, and there were damp patches on the floor and the wooden benches from where the rest of the players had dried off following their showers, but there was something about the slightly run-down surroundings which just added to the sleaziness of the shots I was about to take, as though I was intruding on a private moment.

'The light isn't brilliant in here,' I said, as I set my camera bag down on one of the benches, 'but I think we'll get away with it. After all, it's not as though these photos are for public consumption.'

'OK, let's go for it.' Danny sat and began to unfasten his football boots.

I tried to remain detached as he removed his socks, short and jockstrap, but it was difficult. For a moment he prevented me from seeing what I was desperate to see by holding his hand in front of his groin, but then he stood up and revealed himself in all his glory. Half-dressed, he had been handsome; naked, he was stunning. His cock, already beginning to get hard, rose from a mat of sandy hair, and when he turned away from me he revealed a taut and very biteable pair of buttocks.

'Very nice,' I managed to murmur, wanting nothing more than to put down the camera and let Danny fuck my brains out. Instead, at my request, he put his gloves back on and I took a few shots of him using them to conceal his cock. Under my guidance, he lay back on the bench, drawing one leg up and bending it at the knee to hide what was rapidly becoming a conspicuous erection. All the time I could feel my nipples pressing against my vest, hard and needing the touch of Danny's gloved fingers.

The tension between us was almost unbearable but, much as I longed to make a move, I knew we had very little time before Pete returned. Danny, however, was clearly not worrying about that.

He threw down his gloves and strode into the showers. 'Why don't you take a couple of photos of me under the shower?' he asked. 'Oh, and you might want to take your boots off – it's a bit slippery in here.'

I did as he suggested and followed him in. The shower was already running, and Danny stepped into it. I framed the shot on automatic pilot, watching the water beat down on his body in shimmering droplets. He threw his head back, revelling in the feel of the steamy spray, then caught hold of his cock and began to pump it languidly in his big fist. Any pretence that this was still just about making up for a missed photo opportunity had been forgotten: this was about sex, pure and simple.

'Put the camera down,' Danny urged. Then he grabbed my hand and pulled me into the shower.

I squealed as the water hit me. I was still fully dressed, apart from my boots, but I managed to unzip my skirt and throw it to safety before it got too wet. My vest, however, was another matter: it was soon sticking to me, outlining the hard points of my nipples. Danny's hands burrowed swiftly underneath it, his thumbs settling on the sensitive buds. I gasped, then his lips came down on mine and he kissed me, hard.

'God, Naomi, you're gorgeous,' he groaned when he finally broke away. 'I've been dying to fuck you from the moment I saw you, but I only thought I had a chance when I realised you and Pete weren't an item.'

'I can see how you might think that,' I said, as Danny began to ease my saturated knickers down my legs, 'but, speaking of Pete, what if he comes in and finds us like this?'

'He can watch. He can even join in, if he wants. Would you like that?'

'I don't know,' I replied, and at that moment I honestly didn't. Despite all my rules about not getting involved with married men, what Danny was doing to me was making me feel so downright horny that if Pete walked in right now and caught me in the young keeper's embrace, soaking wet and wearing nothing but a revealingly clinging vest, I wouldn't attempt to stop him if he decided he just had to slip into me from behind.

Suddenly, it was Danny's thick fingers, made even bigger by the strapping he had used to protect them during training, filling me up, stretching me in a way I had never known before. I moaned as his thumb settled on my clit and started to rub, brief discomfort giving way to glorious pleasure. I thought he had proved he was good with his hands when Don was putting him through his paces out on the pitch, but now I realised just how skilful his handling really was. Even though what he was doing to me was taking me rapidly to the brink, it was his cock I really wanted inside me, and I heard myself begging Danny to fuck me.

Given that he was a good foot taller than me, I expected Danny to haul me out of the shower and take me on the wet, tiled floor, but I hadn't counted on him being strong enough to hoist me up till my legs were around his waist and he could slot himself home, impaling me on his hot, hard prick.

I clung on to him for dear life as he pounded into me,

the water still beating down on our bodies. I was completely lost in the feel of him, loving the way he was lodged so snugly in me. His hands were gripping my bum cheeks, forcing me further on to him, and the pressure as he ground his pelvis against me was pushing me close to an unstoppable climax. When he pulled up my vest so he could find my nipple with his mouth and begin to suck, that was all it took. I shrieked with pleasure, the noise ringing off the changing room walls as I came and came. With a groan, Danny began to let himself go, still holding me in place despite a sudden weakness in his knees.

At last, we broke apart and I slithered down his body to the floor, exhausted but with the smuggest of smiles on my face. Danny helped me to my feet and handed me a towel. As I was beginning to dry myself, I heard Pete's voice call out, 'Hello? Anyone in there?'

'We'll be out in a couple of minutes,' I called out, looking down at my soaking wet vest where it lay balled up on the floor and wondering quite how I was going to bluff my way out of this. What Pete really thought when I finally appeared, wearing Danny's training top, which was way too big for me, and with the excuse that I'd managed to spill a cup of tea down myself while we were waiting for him to return, I never found out. I kept the truth of the situation quiet from him even when he was quizzing me over the pint he'd promised me in the Duke of Canklow, the pub round the corner from the *Leader* building, just as I neglected to mention the direction the photo shoot had taken in his absence, or the fact I had Danny's number safely stored in my mobile. I just made some comment to the effect that I now thoroughly agreed with his assessment of Danny as a rising star, though I'm sure my irritatingly satisfied expression must have given the game away.

* * *

The team played their first match of the season the following Saturday, and Danny put in a performance which earned him the *Leader*'s man of the match award. I liked to think I had played my own small part in helping him settle into his new surroundings so quickly. And I couldn't help smiling when I looked at Pete's match report and read how Danny had 'made himself big' in order to pull off a vital last-minute save. After all, I knew from experience exactly how big he could get . . .

The Yoga Teacher Angel Blake

I've always been a bit apprehensive before going to anything new and this yoga class was no different. For a start it was a student class and I haven't been a student for ten years. I'd called up the organisers first to check that it was OK to go, and they'd told me it would be fine, but still I felt conspicuous as I walked up the Union-building steps. It was the beginning of the university term and I'd thought the bitter January weather would put people off, but it looked like a few students had New Year's resolutions they were keen to keep. Almost everyone else I could see seemed to be heading in the same direction, if the bundled towels and roll-mats they carried were any indication, and they were all younger than me and sleeker, more petite.

A couple of the girls gave me strange looks when I joined the crowd outside the doors to the practice room, and I almost bolted – it wasn't too late, not until I'd paid and gone in – but I stood my ground. What was the worst that could happen?

As we waited, I couldn't help overhearing what a couple of the fresh-faced girls next to me were saying. 'I haven't done any exercise for – ooh – weeks, now.' The girl, skinny and blonde, patted her stomach thoughtfully. 'I can't believe how much weight I put on over Christmas!'

The other girl, an equally scrawny specimen with tawny hair and a nose that looked like Daddy had poured thousands into it – not entirely successfully – leant over to whisper something in her ear, and the pair dissolved into fits of giggles. I caught the hurried near-whisper 'but seventy per cent cocoa solids, yeah', before they returned to their normal voices.

'So what's the teacher like? What's his name? Merlin?' asked the tawny-haired one.

I stifled a laugh. What the fuck was this? The round table? Maybe he'd do a couple of magic tricks for us.

'Oh, he's cute,' the blonde replied breathlessly. I stole a glance at her, and saw that her eyes were wide. Then there was a commotion behind them, and the blonde jumped and grabbed hold of her friend's shoulders. 'Oh my God – he's coming!'

A silver-haired man of about forty swung into view at the top of the stairs, and the students pressed to either side of the corridor to let him through. He smiled vaguely around, swept a hand through his hair and let himself into the room, oblivious to the cries of 'Hi, Merlin' around him. The blonde was one of the girls trying to catch his attention, and I got a strange feeling of satisfaction as I watched her face crumple when he completely ignored her. He might have been a cheeseball – nobody called themselves Merlin in my book without taking some stick – but at least he had a bit of taste.

I peered through the wire-veined window on the door. Merlin had taken pole position at the head of the room and just sat there on his roll-mat, ommm-ing quietly to himself with his eyes closed. He didn't budge when a student opened the door and started taking money or even when everyone started to move in and arrange themselves around him.

He looked good, I had to admit. His hair was long and thick, and he carried it well, and he was wearing a sleeveless T-shirt and a pair of black joggers. He was slim, but he looked strong: you could see the ropes of veins on his arms, which shone with a light golden down. Far more attractive than the other men in the room, anyway. There were only two others, one a gawky, angular student with glasses and a shock of woolly hair and the other a slightly tubby freckled boy who looked like he'd wandered into the wrong room. Perhaps he was after a role-playing session or the scrabble society, I thought, and stifled a giggle, then abruptly stopped smiling when I saw a couple of the girls look at me. I was at least as much an outsider as this boy here, far curvier than the other girls, raven-haired in contrast to their almost universally blonde locks, and long since graduated and employed as an art therapist.

The thought made me relax. At least I was working and had a real job. These girls were probably going to end up in some rehab clinic having snorted their trust funds up their cosmetically enhanced nostrils while chasing a job in TV; the best they could hope for was to marry some hooray banker and witter through an endless round of dinner parties and cocktail dos. Then I remembered what I was here for.

The job had been stressing me out. I'd had an aching back after dealing with the resentment and hostility of one damaged individual after another. The students were annoying in their own way, right at the other end of the spectrum, with their unattractive mixture of arrogance and naivety, but I'd come here for solace. Peace. To de-stress myself. Being hostile to my environment wasn't going to help. Sighing, I rolled my head to one side. It cracked loudly. As if on cue, the teacher opened his eyes, beamed broadly and looked around the room.

'Hello, people.' He clasped his hands in front of his chest, as though in prayer. 'Peace and kindness to you all.'

What a cretin, I thought, then inwardly kicked myself. Being a cynic wasn't going to get me anywhere here.

'My name's Merlin and I've been teaching Ashtanga yoga for ten years now. I studied under Sri Aurobindo, in

Pune in India –' he let his eyes roll back slightly, and returned his hands to his knees, making circles with his thumbs and forefingers '– until I reached this advanced stage.'

He smiled, then reached for one foot and stretched it up towards him until it was hooked around his neck; then he did the other. A gasp ran through the room. Even I had to admit it was impressive, but it seemed to have had more of an impact on some of the other girls. I glanced at my neighbour, who was staring at him, adoration in her wide glistening eyes, and felt my hostility rise again. With an effort I turned back to what Merlin was saying, his legs now in the lotus position before him.

'Before we start, I'd like to know if anyone's suffering from back problems or if anyone's pregnant. No? OK, we'll go into sun salute.'

He took us through the steps, one by one. I'd learnt the sequence by heart years ago, and when he told us to start practising I demonstrated my expertise, going through the set of moves quickly and methodically. But when I finished everyone was staring at me. I was red in the face after the exercise anyway and flushed further at the attention.

'We're just doing the first half of the sequence, people, OK? Please try to pay attention, yeah?' Merlin nodded to me, then carried on walking round.

My face burning, I tried to concentrate on the moves. Better not let myself get carried away next time. But my attention was soon distracted by what Merlin was doing. He'd been wandering around the room, repositioning students – like all the yoga teachers I'd ever known – but he'd stopped near me now, and I noticed that there was something incredibly suspect about the way he was doing it.

I'd noticed the girl earlier – she was definitely one of

the prettiest in the class. It looked like he'd noticed her too, as he was standing behind her with his hands on her thighs, pushing them apart and stroking the backs of her legs as her arms shook with the strain of holding the position, pushing her bottom further up into the air. So far, so normal, except that his hands were going right up to the top of her thighs, and I could have sworn that he actually brushed against her crotch once or twice.

I could only see it because I'd come out of the position, and I don't think anyone else had picked up on it. The girl's face was flushed, as were most people's after doing the move, but the blush had moved down on to her chest, leaving it blotchy and mottled, and her pupils looked huge.

At first I thought I'd just imagined it; yoga and sleaze just didn't fit together in my mind, and what I'd imagined was definitely sleazy. In any case, I soon had other things on my mind.

Merlin told the class to split up into those who'd done shoulder stands before and those who 'knew what they were doing', who could go ahead and do headstands. I counted myself with some pride among the latter group, but I had to wait for the students who'd grabbed the best places to move on. By the time I'd got myself into position, teetering with my legs in the air, the blood roaring in my ears and my face swollen to what seemed like twice its normal size, I was in my own world. Which is why it took me a while to register that Merlin was talking to me as he repeated, 'Excuse me?' I must have responded on the third attempt, and came down out of the stance, dizzy, the blood draining from my head. All of the students were sitting around him in a circle.

'Don't do headstands when I'm not watching, yeah?' he asked.

'I'm – I'm sorry,' I stammered.

'Just don't do things you're not ready for in my class,

OK? There's no point in trying to show off. Anyway, your posture was all wrong.'

At this a couple of the students tittered. I felt a wave of rage and humiliation well up inside me and just nodded, not trusting my voice to stay steady if I tried to answer back.

Why was he picking on me? I considered bolting, but decided it would be too much of an admission of defeat. I'd already vowed to salve my wounded pride in beer – defeating the purpose of the yoga, maybe, but I was past caring now – when I saw him getting hands-on again with the student. This time there was no mistaking it – there was definitely something inappropriate going on.

He was kneeling in front of her, positioning her hands to arch her back better. But he was right in front of her, his crotch almost touching her face, and as she shifted into the pose, stretching her face out towards him, he slipped a hand under the waistband of his joggers and curled it under, as though he was cradling something.

And later, towards the end of the session, he was helping the same girl get into the lotus position. By now some of the other students seemed to have noticed that he was spending a lot of time with one of them, but the only effect it had was to make them try to get his attention. One or two wobbled and fell and a couple squealed; but it seemed that nothing could distract him from his chosen favourite for the session. She had her back to me in the lotus and I couldn't see exactly what he was doing, but his arms were working and he was staring into her eyes. Despite myself, despite the way he'd treated me, there was something about it that turned me on. I couldn't help imagining his strong hands clutching her thighs, his thumbs pressed against the groove of her sex, pushing slowly up and down, opening her, making her bite her lip as she tried to stop herself from greasing inside ...

When the session ended I felt light-headed and unsure of my emotions. Merlin was definitely a sleaze, but he was a damned attractive one and, while I was annoyed with him for the way he'd shown me up, if I was being totally honest with myself I was cross because that was pretty much the only attention he'd paid me. Maybe I wasn't so different from the other girls here: it looked like everyone wanted a piece of him, from the way they all crowded around after the final relaxation.

As I put my shoes and socks back on I kept an eye on what he was doing. He was smiling at the other girls, but still saving most of his attention for his special friend and I overheard some of what he was saying to her: 'Blocked chakras ... groin-stretching exercises ... happy to help ... private session.' Then he handed her a slip of paper and sauntered out, ignoring the other girls trying to get his attention. The girl he'd given the paper to was staring after him, her eyes wide and the flush starting again on her chest.

It was only after I'd already cycled halfway home, my fingers numb on the handlebars and my head scrunched close to my chest to avoid getting any of the icy air on my neck, that I realised I'd left my bag behind. With a groan, I swung the bike around.

The Union seemed fuller now and there was someone on the door checking student passes, no doubt trying to dissuade chancers from trying to neck subsidised booze. He listened to my slightly flustered explanation with a slight smile on his face, then looked at the yoga mat I'd taken off the bike panniers, nodded and let me in.

There was another session happening in the room now – karate, it looked like, and I knocked, already feeling myself redden with embarrassment. The thuds and groans from inside died down and a short man came to the door. 'You've missed the yoga,' he told me, after taking in the mat and the way I was dressed.

'Oh, no, I went to it. It's just that I left my bag behind. Can I come in and look for it?' I stammered.

He moved away from the door and, with a sweep of his arm, invited me in. 'Be my guest.'

I could already see the bag in the corner of the room and rushed over to pick it up and rifle quickly through the contents. Nothing had been touched. I thanked the man, who'd already clapped his hands and got the students working again, and left the room.

As I walked back down the corridor towards the lift, relieved to have found my belongings intact but also mentally kicking myself for being such a loser – my wallet, my keys, in fact pretty much everything I needed was in there – I heard a long low moan from one of the rooms. Intrigued by the thought of even more activities going on here – the karate room had been packed out – I followed the sound and soon found myself in an adjacent corridor. It was unlit, but there was a light on in one of the rooms, and the sound was louder now. It was definitely coming from there.

I've never thought of myself as a nosy person, but I had to look. How was I meant to know what was going on in there? So I had a quick peek, then swung away from the door, shocked and holding my breath, petrified that they'd hear me. It was obviously the room that Merlin had chosen for his 'private session' with the girl and he'd evidently been able to talk her into something that didn't look very yogic to me at all. Unsure that I'd seen it properly, I moved back to the grille in the door and looked again, confident that they wouldn't be able to see me in the darkness.

It was just as I'd thought. The girl was lying back on a mat, still clad in her joggers, with Merlin kneeling in front of her outstretched legs. His hands were on her inner thighs, and his thumbs were slowly massaging her crease. I heard the girl moan again. She looked flushed and her eyes were closed. There was the beginning of a dark stain on the front of her joggers, which grew as Merlin rubbed her. I listened closely and could hear Merlin muttering some tosh about 'this will help you release the energy you have trapped here. I can feel that your chakras are blocked and with this massage I can free the power. Can you feel it coursing through you?' With that he stroked her between the legs with renewed vigour.

I couldn't believe the girl was falling for this. Surely she could see that he was only trying to get his sexual kicks out of her? He should be reported. But my mind was in a whirl. I knew it wasn't right, but I was breathing heavily and, after a quick check down the corridor either side, I burrowed a hand down into my pants. It was just as I thought – I was oozing down there, more than just damp.

I guiltily took my hand away. This wasn't supposed to happen! But I couldn't take my eyes off what was going on in the room. Merlin's hands were faster now and the girl's legs were trembling. Biting my lip, terrified of what might happen if I got caught but unable to resist the temptation, excited by the wrongness of what I was watching, by the way I was responding to it, I began to stroke myself.

As Merlin's hands moved faster, the girl's moans grew louder, until he clamped a hand over her mouth and gripped her sex hard. Suddenly she bucked, her whole body writhing under him, and let out a high-pitched squeal, while Merlin's voice, louder now, encouraged her to 'feel the energy release, feel it flow through your body, feel the power, the yin and the yang, the masculine and the feminine', and he grabbed one of her hands and put it on his crotch.

The hand jerked away at first and the girl opened her eyes to look at him, confused, but Merlin carried on talking to her, smoothing her forehead with the hand that had just brought her off, while he pulled the other back to his crotch. This time the girl grabbed his stiff cock through the joggers and held it, and she didn't need much encouragement to start pumping.

Merlin threw his head back, shook his silvery mane and let out a long groan, then pushed the girl's hand away for a second and released his cock. It caught for a second on the waistband of his pants, then bobbed up again, hard and angry-looking, the balls large and tight against the base.

The girl grabbed it again, her small white hand barely circling its girth, and started to pump it, harder now. At the sight of his prick I'd flooded juice over my fingers and was starting to tease my clit now, flicking over it again and again as I stared at the unexpected show being performed in front of me.

Merlin was still speaking to the girl, his level relaxed voice intoning, 'Feel my masculine power. Feel it as a gift from me to you; and from you to me, to release the energy I feel trapped here.' He gave his balls a squeeze, and thrust his hips against the girl's hand a couple of times. Her eyes were open now, and wide, and she was licking her lips as she stared at his cock, giving it long, hard tugs.

'Massage me harder, faster,' groaned Merlin. 'I can feel the release of energy, it's going to happen, your beautiful feminine energy and my male power, it's –'

And with that he bucked his hips once, twice, and his prick jetted over the girl's face, long streamers of come spraying her from forehead to chin. I felt my pussy twinge at the sight, the sheer amount of it stunning, and could feel my own orgasm building up, impossibly fast. But the girl had opened her mouth in shock and clearly hadn't been able to close her eyes in time, and she was blinking and choking, even as Merlin, moaning, squeezed the last few drops out over her.

Then she screamed, pushing him away and clawing at the thick ropes dripping from her face, then flicking her fingers in a desperate attempt to get it off her. Even as Merlin made soothing sounds, she was up and stumbling, half-blind, to the door. I pulled my hand, my fingertips wet with my own juices, out of my pants and, weak-legged, started to half-jog down the corridor. I managed to make it to the first turn-off when the door opened, and I waited there until she passed, unable to resist the temptation to look at the girl properly.

She was in tears now, rubbing at the gloopy come with her top but only succeeding in smearing it into her red face, until she looked like she'd been glazed. Some of it had gone in her hair, too, and it was drying fast, looking like a hapless teen's first go at using gel. There was a bathroom nearby – I knew, I'd passed it on the way – and a second after the door closed behind her, I heard a muffled wail.

I left before Merlin came out.

I didn't really know what to do when I left. Half of me was tempted to report him, sure that the girl whose face he'd covered wouldn't do it; but half of me was still turned on, excited by the sheer inappropriateness of it. I was ashamed by the way my body had responded: it went against everything I'd learnt about solidarity with other women. But if I couldn't control the way I was turned on it didn't mean I had to fall for the guy – he was cute, and I wanted to use him, but I didn't want him to use me in the same way. This had to be different.

The question was, how did I get his attention? I was older than the other girls and it was possible that their fresh-faced youth and inexperience were exactly what he went for. If I couldn't provide those, perhaps he'd go for their opposite: sexual knowledge and tartiness. That I could do in spades.

I was wet hours before the next session, a week later, my stomach turning with the thought of what I was going to do. I'd prepared for the class, wearing clothes that weren't exactly suitable: rather than the baggy, shapeless tracksuit I'd worn the first time, I had a cropped T-shirt, with no bra underneath, in the hope of catching his eye with my firm, full breasts; a tighter, lower-cut pair of joggers, ones with the 'Juicy' logo on the back, which might raise an eyebrow; and a high-cut thong, pulled right up into my crease, so that the sides of it were visible above the hipster waistband.

I was feeling a little self-conscious as I climbed the steps to the Union building again, my nervousness almost making me turn tail and flee, but I knew I wouldn't be going to the class again after this, and my coat would cover everything up until I was actually up there.

The room was half-full when I arrived, and Merlin was talking to one of the girls who took the money. At least he wasn't omming, I was relieved to discover: I'd been wondering how to get his attention as I took my coat off. This way it was easy – I dropped my bag on the floor, making an almighty clatter over the hushed voices of the students, and pretty much every head turned as I dropped my coat to the floor too.

My nipples were already stiff and there was a kind of gurgling sound from one of the boys, who busied himself trying to hide a lump in his crotch when I turned to look at him. Merlin was looking at me too, unguardedly checking me out with an expression of surprised appreciation on his face, and I could have sworn he went a little pink when I winked at him.

The lesson went exactly as I'd thought it would. Merlin paid me the same attentions he'd paid the other girl the week before, kind attentiveness soon turning into lecherous fondling when he saw that I wasn't about to complain. And to be fair I probably wouldn't have done even if I hadn't had my plan: it seemed so deliciously rude to have him pawing me in a yoga class, his hands stretching my thighs out, his palms grazing the hard points of my nipples, his strong, supple fingers moulding my skin. He even had the decency to look embarrassed when he asked me not to do the headstand – my top would have fallen down, and everyone would have seen my tits – but arranged a different pose instead, one that would give him the best view of my bum, neatly bisected by the slender thong.

When the class ended, a few of the other girls tried to talk to him, but he approached me, just as I'd expected, and started on his spiel. As I listened to him, I saw one of the girls snort out of the corner of my eye, flicking her hair to the side and flouncing out of the room to slam the door behind her. Merlin didn't flinch.

'You did really well in class today, I'm very happy with you.' He beamed, and seemed to be expecting a response.

'Thanks, Merlin. It's easy when you're getting so much special attention.' And with this I leered at him, giving him my best truck-driver saucy expression, and was delighted to see a shadow of confusion flicker over his eyes.

'There were just one or two poses I thought you might need help with. Your groin –' he patted my inner thigh '– needs to be stretched more. I know some excellent massage techniques and wondered if you'd like a special lesson? I can give you one free of charge; it will help to clear any blockages in your chakras, and I love to see the release of energy. That is the only reward I need.' He beamed again.

'OK, Merlin. Special groin massage? Sounds good to me.' I looked down at his crotch, sure that there was already a swelling down there, then returned my gaze to his face and slowly licked my lips.

Now he looked even more confused, but pressed bravely on. Maybe he was so used to his routine by now that he ignored anything that didn't fit into it; and maybe he just couldn't believe his luck. Whatever the case, he still couldn't take his eyes off my chest, and I thrust out my tits, bouncing a little on my feet to make them wobble. He gulped.

'I was thinking – I know a private room we could go to?' he offered in an uncertain voice.

I looked around. The last student had left, and the room suddenly felt very empty. 'Why don't we do it here?' I asked.

He looked slightly nervous, and I knew it was now or never. Leaning forwards, I made a sudden grab for his cock and felt it twitch in my hand through his joggers. He tried to take a step back, his eyes widening. 'What are you doing?'

'Tonight, Merlin, it's your turn for the groin massage.' I licked my lips then sank down in front of him to squat on my heels, pulling his joggers down as I went so his impressive semi was bumping against my face. None of the men I'd known could ever resist a blowjob, and Merlin was no exception, his prick pulsing into full erection as he realised what I was going to do.

As I started to pump the shaft and opened my mouth to lick the drop of pre-come off the end of his cock, he started to talk, his eyes darting nervously towards the door. 'I can feel my chakras opening. The kundalini serpent is awakening within me. I make you an offering of my male energy.' And he pushed his dick into my mouth.

I made a noisy job of it, slurping and drooling, and not only for his benefit. I loved sucking cock and his was a beauty, the head the size of a plum in my mouth and his balls just as big, tightening now against the base of his prick. I felt my pussy twinge with the thought of how his cock would feel in there, and couldn't resist the temptation to run a palm over his balls, feeling them contract in response. He let out a groan and I pulled my mouth off his prick. I didn't want it to end this way.

He was still babbling some nonsense about chakras as I stood up and pulled my joggers down, but he stopped when I pulled the thong up into my oily crease, shimmying from hip to hip, then gasped as I tugged the gusset, already soaked through, to the side to give him a flash of pink.

'The sacred yoni!' His voice was breathless, and his pupils dilated.

He couldn't take his eyes off it as I trailed a finger down to coat my clit with oil and give it a few hard flicks, feeling the pulses of pleasure shoot through me. 'You want some of this, then?'

'The lingam meets the yoni. The sacred male energy entwined with the sacred female energy; the kundalini serpent joining the two together. The energy flow from the conjoined chakras should be truly something to see.' But there was an expression of pure lust on his face, a goatish leer at odds with his Eastern blather as he made a lunge for me.

'Ah ah, Merlin! If you want that, you'll have to let me do this.' I reached for one of the yoga belts lying on the floor. 'Maybe this'll let your chakras release energy better.' I could barely keep the giggle out of my voice. But he was standing still, waiting to see what I'd do with it, and I moved behind him to wrap the belt around his wrists.

'Ah, restriction. Useful in some meditation practice, but I'm not –' He was eyeing me suspiciously, although he made no effort to free his wrists.

'Just relax and trust me, Merlin. You're going to love this. Sit down.'

He did as he was told and crossed his legs. His joggers were still bunched up around his ankles and I wrapped another belt around them, tying it until he was held firm and giving his cockhead little nibbles as I worked. It looked angry now, purple and huge, even bigger than before, straining with the need for attention.

I tugged my thong well to the side, turned to face away from Merlin then bent back until my slit was in front of his face.

'The yoni! I can sense the energy in your – glmph.' His steady burble was abruptly cut off as I sat myself on his face. After a short pause, I could feel his tongue take tentative stabs at the swollen crease, then long, slow laps up and down before circling the clit. I shuddered and cupped my tits. I'd never known the nipples to be so long, and I rolled them between my fingers as I ground my pussy against Merlin's face.

He was nibbling me now, sucking my bud into his mouth and flicking it hard, and I could feel the tension building up in me, everything that had built up as I'd thought about this moment, prepared for it – but I didn't want to come yet and I lifted my sex off his face and crouched down.

The tip of his penis bumped against me, grazing my bottom hole. I giggled, my mind reeling at the thought of what it might do there, then took it in one hand and guided it into the other hole. Both of us groaned as I sank on to it, inch by inch, tight and hot.

I started to rock back and forth, feeling it huge and stiff, grinding deep inside me, and reached a hand down to feel the base of it stretching me, his balls so tight I couldn't tell where one ended and the other began. Then I started to rub my clit, slowly at first, not wanting to waste the moment, then harder, losing control as I bucked up and down on his cock, dimly aware that Merlin was still rambling about chakras even as the first bolts of ecstasy began to course through me, hot spirals of pleasure radiating from my burning clit, pinched between my fingers. I knew my sex was spasming, milking his cock, but I didn't want him to come inside me – that would ruin it – and before my orgasm had properly finished, still shivering with the force of it, I pulled myself reluctantly off his prick, even the lifting off delicious to me now, and looked at him as he groaned, this time in disappointment.

His face was slick with girl grease, with a whitish residue coating his nose and chin, and he was chanting something like 'the sacred release of yoni energy' to himself, even as his hips were twitching in an effort to bring his cock, on the verge of shooting his load, into something – anything.

I complied, taking it in one hand and giving it a few hard, fast strokes, making sure it was pointing in the right direction, while squeezing his balls hard in the other hand.

He let out a groan, started to say, 'The sacred release of lingam – I'm going to –', then his whole body quivered, and I felt the cock thicken still further in my hand as I pumped it, before it spurted long white jets of come, straight into Merlin's face. One streamer landed in his mouth, and even as he was still coming he was trying to spit it out, groaning, shuddering and spitting all at the same time, come rolling down his cheeks and dripping off his chin. One spurt had gone in an eye too, and he looked ludicrous as he squashed it closed, blinking in an attempt to clean it while he looked wildly around with the other one. His dick was still oozing, and I wiped the glutinous pool that had landed on my hand on his hair, then quickly checked the clock. Just in time.

I pulled my joggers back on and walked to the door, looking back once again to take in the sight of Merlin, his face dripping come. It was only then that he seemed to return to his senses. 'What?'

I flashed him my best shit-eating grin and walked out of the door. On my way to the lift I passed the stocky karate teacher, who gave me a nod and a curious look as he went past, followed by about ten of his students.

The doors to the lift were just closing when I heard the first shocked exclamation.

Gift Horse Mathilde Madden

You give yourself away, you know. You ask too many questions. How much do I love you? How much can I take? How far would I go?

Well, you know, they're all really the same question. And if you really want to know, let me tell you – it's scary how far you will go – how much you can take when you love someone as much as I love you. Really, really scary.

And if you really want to know . . .

We're in the bedroom of your tiny box of a flat. You're lying on the bed wearing grey jogging bottoms and a grey T-shirt. And, even though I'm only feet away by the wardrobe, I can barely look at you because you just look so sexy.

While you're relaxing in your supersoft lounge wear, I, on the other hand, am being granted no such comfort-based favours. I'm wearing a pair of very tight black lace knickers. In fact, the extreme tightness of this garment in particular is one of the reasons I don't want to look at you too much and get too turned on. Lacy knickers are just not built for such things.

I'm also wearing a matching black camisole, black stockings and a black suspender belt, topped – or rather bottomed – off with a rather uncomfortable pair of black patent ankle boots. (What can I say? I like black. I think it's elegant and, like most cross-dressers, I need all the elegance I can get.)

By the way, the not looking at you to avoid getting too turned on – so not working. Because I'm just getting off so much just on being dressed like this, despite the discomfort and how exposed I feel, that alone is making me ridiculously hard. I'm sure you've noticed.

Anyway, you seem rather pleased with my outfit so far. At least you're smiling rather indulgently, which is always a good sign. I'm kind of expecting the usual next stage, which is for you to secure me to the bed using the cuffs I'm wearing on my wrists and ankles (which are, incidentally, also black), so you can take me with your strap-on, but you don't do that today.

Instead you say, 'Simon, I think you need something else on.'

And I'm a bit stuck there because so far in our relationship my cross-dressing has been limited to underwear. You don't usually want me to wear much clothing. So, I don't actually have anything else to put on – nothing that fits with what I'm wearing so far anyway.

But you're way ahead of me, because you say, 'Choose something of mine, from the wardrobe.'

And that's how I come to be rifling through the very back of your wardrobe – which is startlingly big, considering the size of the rest of your flat. And that's how I found it.

Right at the back of your wardrobe I feel a rather nice velvety texture, I spy a blackness of fabric, and – convinced I have struck gold – I pull a wonderful soft something from so far back in the depths it's practically in Narnia.

'Oh no,' you say quickly, 'not that one.' But I already have it out in the open. And I look down to see that I'm holding in my hand a beautiful black velvet riding coat, with a pair of butter-soft, cream-coloured jodhpurs dangling off the same hanger. (And when I look down at the floor of the wardrobe I notice – yes – nestling in the back corner a pair of oil-sleek riding boots.)

I can't stop looking at the clothes. They are so beautiful. I ignore the fact you asked me not to get them out and say, 'I didn't know you rode?' And I can't help being vaguely aroused by the idea of – I'm not sure quite what – the idea of you in these clothes, I guess.

'I don't,' you say, 'I don't have a horse.' And although you hide it quite well, I can hear the tiniest scrap of sadness in your voice.

And it's that little exchange, not the rather excellent sex that the evening quickly develops into, that occupies my thoughts late into the night. Because, call me soft hearted if you like, I hate the idea of you being sad about anything – I really do. And I decide right then that you are not going to be, not if I can do something about it.

My first, and strikingly obvious, idea is to buy you some riding lessons or pony trekking or something like that. Sliding out of your embrace in the warm bed and creeping around while you sleep, I trawl through the Yellow Pages and find a couple of places that I think I could easily take you. Places where you could trot around to your heart's content. But deep down I know a few hours on a borrowed horse isn't really going to cut it with you. You want a horse of your own – I know that for sure – you're a pretty all or nothing sort of person. But there's no way I can afford to buy you a pony, let alone deal with the logistics of horse-keeping in the middle of a city. I end up filing the idea away, disappointed that I can't make it work for you.

But then, a few days later, I'm walking home from the supermarket and I realise how I can make you happy. I realise exactly what I need to do.

It's not going to be easy. There a lot of factors. A lot of imponderables. But as soon as I hit on the plan I know I have to make it work. No matter what.

And that's how much I love you.

* * *

First of all I need a few essential items: an outfit, some equipment and a venue, mainly. A, B and C. Now the venue could be tricky, really tricky actually. But I figure I can deal with that later. I might as well start with the simplest part of the equation. And that's the outfit. And that's where Jeremy comes in.

I'm so bloody excited as I work things through in my head that I don't even go home with my shopping. I go straight to Jeremy's and dump my carriers of groceries on the floor of his shabby rented workshop.

Jeremy is a professional leather worker. I met him at art school. And I have to say, he's a bloody useful friend to have if you have, let's say, 'alternative' tastes. After all, leather equipment is pricey – most of my collection would normally have been beyond my limited means – but Jeremy and I have a special arrangement. See, Jeremy has a little kink all of his own.

I've always been a reasonably proficient cartoonist – just pen and ink stuff. And what I've always drawn, ever since I discovered my talent, are little bondage cartoons. Pictures of myself, basically, in situations I'd like to be in: cross-dressed, tied up, caged, you know the sort of stuff I like – the stuff that makes me squirm and pant. I've been drawing them for years.

I'll show you some time – I'm pretty sure you'd like them.

Anyway, this one time, back when we were at art school, Jeremy somehow got his hands on a rather saucy picture I'd done of myself, naked, hog-tied and gagged. And, in short, he liked the picture. He liked it a lot. Enough to suggest that in return for me letting him keep it he'd make me a little present.

The present was a leather gag; the rest is sort of history.

So, to get to the point, we now have a simple deal, I buy all kinds of leather gear from Jeremy with my cartoons (plus material costs). He tells me what he wants me to draw (kinky stuff) and I tell him what I want him to make (more kinky stuff). It's the perfect deal.

Or, it was.

Because things don't go quite that smoothly when I ask for what I want this time. To be fair, it is the most complex thing I've ever asked for. For example, it's the first time I've ever had to do a series of drawings up front to show exactly what I want. And it's the first time that Jeremy has asked for more than a few bondage cartoons plus the cost of the leather as payment.

'You know I've always liked you, Simon,' is how he puts it. And what he wants is really no surprise. He's always been more than a little tactile with me. So I know he likes me. That part of it isn't the shock. The shock is that he expects something rather more 3-D than my usual doodles as payment for my latest kinky specifications.

I've never sucked a man's cock before. And you'll have noticed that I had to use the word 'man's' in that sentence, because you don't just fuck my arse with your strap-on. In fact, sometimes, we never even get to that point. You know I like the way it looks – jutting out from your crotch, powerful, hard and ever-ready. It makes my mouth dry to see you wearing it, whether you're naked and predatory or just have it on casually, peeping out from your pyjamas. I've licked my lips and begged to suck it more times than I could possibly remember.

So that's what I do right now, when Jeremy drops his trousers and reveals his hard glistening cock right in front of my mouth. I suck greedily, thinking of you and your big silicone phallus, and how happy I'm going to make you by doing this.

And when Jeremy grabs my hair so he can force himself deeper into my mouth, jerks hard and comes down my throat, the deal is struck. My outfit is taken care of.

And that's how much I love you.

But that's not quite all. I stay for a cup of tea and, when I mention that I'm not sure about how I'm going to deal with the other stuff I need for your surprise, Jeremy smiles and says, 'You know what, I think I might be able to help you with that too.'

Keeping Jeremy sweet, it turns out, was a bloody good move on my part. First of all, he has a friend, Eloise, who's a bit nifty with metal work. He's certain she can make the piece of equipment I need, and he pockets my design with a leave-it-to-me grin. Even more jaw dropping, though, is Jeremy's second friend: Sebastian.

Sebastian, apparently, has a beautiful country estate in Berkshire. It has everything I could possibly want, including private woodland, a pretty secluded paddock and, very importantly, stables. It's more than I could have asked for. It's way beyond lucky. Or it will be, as soon as I can find a way of persuading him to let me use it.

But that's not going to be such a big problem. Sebastian isn't quite as willing to do something for nothing as Eloise, but, like Jeremy himself, Sebastian has his soft spots. Which is where the party comes in. Apparently Jeremy's friend holds a lot of rather wild parties, and the ever helpful Jeremy is willing to do a little bit of string-pulling. I'm going to be a party guest. Well, maybe that's not really the right phrase. I'm going to be a party favour.

And that's how much I love you.

When party time arrives, Jeremy helps me with my outfit, after a rather strongly worded warning that this is not the place for any of 'that trannie shit you waste your time with' (Jeremy isn't a big fan of my cross-dressing). So I'm wearing a combination of my leather body harness and leather collar – all originally the work of dear Jeremy – and a borrowed pair of leather trousers, which are a touch too tight. I take a deep, nervous breath and think of you, as Jeremy's little Hyundai scrunches its way up a majestic drive. In front of the house flaming torches are dancing. And my heart is banging.

As we climb the steps up to the main doors a beautifully dressed middle-aged man strides forwards to greet us and Jeremy hisses in my ear that this is Sebastian, our host for the evening and the person who I need to impress if I want use of his facilities.

I watch him hopefully. His feet are light and elegant on the beautiful sweeping stone steps and, when he gets to where we are standing, he stops just a shade too close than feels really right for me.

He eyes me up and down, looking a little like he's planning on eating me. 'So,' he says after a good deal of this blatant eyeing, 'this is the one who wants to borrow the stables for a little bit of horseplay?'

'Oh yes,' says Jeremy, answering for me in a way that implies that I am not going to be talking very much in this little exchange.

'Hmm,' says Sebastian, 'well, he must be a very dirty boy.' And he gives me an eyebrow flash as he lasciviously over pronounces the word 'dirty'.

In response to this, Jeremy pulls a piece of paper from his pocket. A piece of paper that I know contains my drawing of the exotic leather outfit that Jeremy is making for me. I shift a little in uncomfortable embarrassment and look at the ornate stonework beneath my feet.

The middle-aged man makes a very appreciative noise. And then says, 'Oh, how could I refuse?'

I'm still looking at the paving and he reaches out and

lifts my chin, bringing my eyes to meet his. 'I can't think of anything I'd like trotting about my grounds more,' he says, all softly indulgent.

And that sort of puts me at my ease a bit. I end up grinning right back. It can't really be that simple, can it?

My job at the party is pretty simple: I'm top-up-boy. I'm given a bottle of champagne, wrapped in the obligatory snowy napkin and sent to waft around the effortlessly tasteful surrounds of this country house, looking cute and smiling serenely at the other guests, who range from middle-aged care-worn types, like my host, to semi-naked pretty boys like, well, like me. OK, I have to put up with the odd – uninvited – hand on my arse and one or two tongues in my ear, but hey – big deal, my venue is secured.

And that's how much I love you.

Ten days later. Everything is set, planned to within an inch of its life. Jeremy has come good on everything he promised and his and Eloise's creations are ready and waiting for me inside Sebastian's wonderland.

Of course, you're sitting in the passenger seat beside me, as we scrunch up a familiar driveway and pull up outside a familiar huge country pile.

'Simon,' you say, puzzled, as I bring the car to a crunchy halt, 'what is going on?'

I jerk the handbrake and turn to look at you, grinning like a schoolboy. 'Just wait. I swear it will be worth it.'

I leave you in a lovely, if rather chintzy, bedroom to get changed into the outfit I've brought along for you. Your jacket, jodhpurs and boots, naturally. I've also left you some instructions on the dressing table. It's just directions down to the paddock and a request to wait for me there. Just that and a few words about how much I love you, but that's a given really.

And while you're slipping into your outfit in one of the great house's infinite number of swishy bedrooms, I'm in another, where I'm supposed to be doing likewise.

But actually, I'm feeling a little panicky. My made-to-measure design is laid out on the bed, but my hands are shaking so much I can barely fasten the buckles. What's more there are parts of this outfit that I know I couldn't fasten myself, even if my fingers were steady as a surgeon's. I swallow and think of you, probably dressed already and making your way down to the grounds, wondering what on earth is taking me so long.

So, I'm about to venture into the house and look for someone to help me – not a request I really relish making – when there is a soft knock at the door.

I might have known: Jeremy.

'Hi,' he says, breezing in without being asked and taking in a good eyeful of my semi-naked body. 'You're never going to get into that outfit on your own, you know. I made it, and I understand better than anyone all its more fiddly parts.'

I simultaneously sigh and smile at him, helplessly agreeing to his implicit offer, partly because he is so relentlessly incorrigible, but mostly because I don't have any choice.

And it's with a surprisingly brisk and workmanlike air that Jeremy begins to strap me into a close-fitting body harness that forms the main part of my outfit.

The harness has anchor points on the back for my wrist cuffs, which secure my arms high and tight out of the way, somewhere in the middle of my upper back. I yelp slightly when he fixes them in place, but can't help liking the way the position pushes my chest out and makes me stand just as straight and proud as a real thoroughbred.

But I don't get much of a chance to enjoy my new

posture, as Jeremy is already brandishing the next part of my transformation – the bridle.

Cold straps quickly encase my head, holding blinkers and an icy metal bit, which feels alien and clunky in my mouth. In fact, the bit makes me start to drool a little, and I have to hold my head up very high to stop this little humiliation. I'm happy to drool in front of you – if that's what you want to see – but somehow I don't really like drooling in front of Jeremy.

I know you really like gags. You like to strap things into my mouth and watch my mortified face as my saliva pools in my mouth and then eventually escapes my invaded lips and runs down my chin. You love the noises I make when I'm gagged. You love it when I try to beg. You'll strap a too tight, too big, red rubber ball into my mouth and tell me to beg to have it removed, laughing when the only sounds I can make are muffled gibberish. That's why I knew, right from the start, that you would love the bit. Which I guess is why I made it so real, hard metal, big and uncomfortable. All to make it more enjoyable for you – and far more uncomfortable for me.

But I don't have to worry about holding my head up to stop the drool factor for long, because a second later I don't have a choice about it. Jeremy fixes in the short strap that connects my head harness to my confined wrists, forcing me to stand proud and high, with my head pulled back, whether I'm worried about drooling or not.

Right then I'm so focused on the sensations I'm feeling, being strapped and pulled and made helpless, that for a moment I don't notice when Jeremy pauses, standing square in front of me and staring into my eyes.

'Simon,' he says gently, 'I know this is taking a terrible liberty, and I know you blew me, and everything, which was great, but I'm greedy. I couldn't stop thinking about doing this all the time I was making this outfit for you, and I know you appreciate all my hard work.'

I stare at him, which is practically all I can do. I have no idea where this is going, but the bit in my mouth is stopping me from asking. In fact, what with the blinkers and the head strap tightly in place I can't even look away from his earnest face.

'So, this is just between us, OK.' And then – sudden and quick – Jeremy kisses me, right on my bitted mouth. He presses his soft lips against my tortured ones, flickering his tongue around the tide-line of my lips and then pushing his way inside. I'm helpless to resist – I can't even close my mouth properly.

He kisses me for a long time, his hands tight on my upper arms. And when he pulls away, I moan and crane my neck to try and follow his lips.

Jeremy just laughs. 'And now,' he says, deliberately ignoring my whimpers, 'the final stages.'

I let Jeremy pull down my underpants – not that I really have a lot of choice at this stage. My cock jumps out, already eager and hard, partly from my current delicious bondage predicament and partly from Jeremy's eloquent kissing. Jeremy laughs again, and sets about replacing my underwear with an arrangement of straps to match the ones encasing my torso and head. I can't actually see what he's doing but it does feel rather wonderful as he encases me in tight, soft leather.

I decide to try to squirm a little, just to test how well held I am, and when I can barely twitch my whole body starts to fizz with excitement. I realise how helpless I really am. My eyes close and I think of you. I'm so convinced you're going to love every aspect of this just as much as I – so obviously – do.

And I'd probably have disappeared into an oblivious rapture about you right then if I hadn't felt something pressing up against my arsehole at that very moment. Because, in my diagram, the horse had a tail, and Jeremy hasn't failed to deliver.

With a little pressure, he slides the butt plug home. I've worn them before, with you of course, but this time it is slightly different, because I can feel the long leather strands of the 'tail' brushing the backs of my legs. I gasp and jerk, but I don't think it is actually possible for my cock to get any harder unless it were suddenly made of adamantium.

And with my tail in place, which I give a few practice swishes, I'm fully dressed. Fully dressed in nothing but an arrangement of leather straps and a pair of sturdy boots. And all I can think about is how much I know you're going to love it.

With a sly grin Jeremy takes hold of the reins that are attached to either side of my bridle and leads me out of the bedroom and down the stairs.

And that's how much I love you.

Eloise's beautiful handiwork is all ready and waiting for us behind the stable block. A pretty little cart. Small and light as it can be, with a padded chair (which is for you, of course), and elegantly curving struts emerging from the front, designed to attached to the heavy D-rings which jingle at my sides.

Jeremy raises his eyebrows. 'Nice, huh?' he says in a sort of half-whistle.

And I say nothing, because I can't.

Once I'm hitched to the cart Jeremy bids me goodbye, with a sharp pat on my bare backside, and I trot around the side of the stable block with the cart trundling behind me to where you stand in the paddock, looking just amazing.

And when you see me, you try to be cool about it, but from the way you smile, the way your feet sort of leave the ground for the tiniest, tiniest moment, I know I've made you happy.

And that's how much I love you.

I bet I look pretty strange as I pick my way across the muddy earth to where you are standing. I'm grinning like an idiot, but with the bit in my mouth it probably looks more like a deranged grimace. You're so cool, though. As you watch me coming you're all ice princess, wryly amused by this latest little whimsy of mine.

But you play your part so well. Once I'm stood in front of you, you give me a cursory inspection – all uninterested surface, but with real excitement burning somewhere behind your eyes.

I'm helplessly straight and erect (actually, I'm sure you've noticed, erect everywhere!) while you circle me, checking the straps of my harness, taking up the slack here, allowing a little extra movement here. It's so intimate, so special, letting you play with my body like this – teasing me with how easy it is for you to give my already sore muscles a little extra comfort or, of course, restrict them even more tightly.

I shiver slightly when you take your touch away. It's cool in the paddock. But I don't think the breezes whirling around my limbs are going to be bothering me soon, because, with a creak and a jingle, you settle yourself into the carriage.

At first you go easy on me. You let me find my own pace, learning the patterns of the ground, the hidden dangers in the terrain. I quickly find out which parts of the paddock are boggy, which are pitted, which are ridged. I walk and I trot. I even try a little run once I feel confident that I'm not going to fall – a real worry with my arms bound and my sight impaired by the blinkers. But soon, sooner than I would have thought possible, I start to feel less vulnerable, more confident, strong. Oh, and the cold? Really not a problem any more, not now I'm more concerned about the sweat running into my eyes as I work for you.

That's when you stop me, of course. You sense my growing confidence easily; you're so perfectly tuned in sometimes. Sometimes, to me, when I'm feeling so helpless, just a piece of flotsam, buffeted around on a sort of sea of your whims, your instinct seems kind of magical. But I suppose that's what you do.

In a soft voice you tell me how you want me to move. How you want me to lift my knees high when I trot, how you want me to respond to your voice commands, how you are going to tap me with the crop on my shoulder when I don't. For a moment I wonder where the crop has appeared from, and the delicate piece of sugar that you push into my mouth, but only for a moment. A second later you are back in the driving seat, the last crystals of sugar are just a gossamer memory on my tongue, and we're off again.

This time you train me harder. You want faster, slower, this way, that way, stop, start, stop again. I race up and down the paddock, until my lungs and my shoulders are burning. It's so exhilarating I could fly. And then, when I am starting to feel quite exhausted and my mouth is dusty dry, I hear a familiar jingling noise, and manage to turn far enough around that I can see another horse and carriage trundling into the paddock. I'm so lost in my horsey world I find it hard to understand for a minute what is happening. But then the mist clears.

I might have known: Jeremy.

Or, to be precise, Jeremy and Sebastian. Jeremy is the one in the harness and Sebastian is in the carriage – all smiles and waves. I double take.

Sebastian hails us as soon as he is within braying distance. Or, at least, he hails you. 'Hello, my dear, how is he handling?'

'Like a dream,' you call back. (I love the way your voice sounds so proud.)

'I knew it. So, would you care for a race?' Sebastian sounds so ridiculously matter of fact, like he's offering you a cup of tea. 'It's so much more fun with a little element of competition.'

Jeremy has been pulling Sebastian's carriage closer and closer during this little exchange and now he is alongside me. I can see he is wearing exactly the same harness as I am – my design. The carriage is exactly the same too. I can't stop looking at him. He looks wonderful. He looks obscene. I never realised I looked like that. A human made into a horse, a pony, pulling a little carriage. I feel myself get a little harder just at the thought of how I must look right now – strapped and bound like Jeremy, displayed and tortured, and – in my case certainly – flushed and sweaty from trotting and jumping.

You are talking to Sebastian, agreeing to his suggested race. What was once my own little scheme is now twisting and dancing out of my hands. I'm left with no choice but to give up control of this project to you. But I'm cool.

And that's how much I love you.

It's all agreed. The race is on. It's you and me against Jeremy and Sebastian. Once around the paddock on a route Sebastian has suggested that involves us racketing around a very narrow track at close quarters. It almost feels like it's going to be some kind of Roman chariot race. And I really like the idea of that. I wonder if next time we do this – and there really is no doubt in my mind that there will be a next time – we could get hold of Roman-style carriages, so you could be standing up as you drive me on, ever harder, ever faster. But that's not happening now. This is a rather simpler proposition.

'Would you like to make a wager?' Sebastian is saying

to you. 'It would certainly add to the excitement, give you a reason not to spare the rod on your lovely boy.'

Sebastian's voice sounds ridiculously filthy when he says that. I sort of know he's playing a part right now, but he really does play it well.

And, although his wager idea is fair enough, you have a better one. 'Silly for us to have a bet,' you say, 'when we could make things far more interesting than that. Why play for boring old money, when we both know what we'd really like to win?'

Suddenly Sebastian's eyes are on stalks. I get the distinct impression that this is what he was really after all along. 'Really?' he gasps. 'You'd really bet your boy?'

'My pony, yes. My pony against yours. If you win, you can take both of them for the evening. If I win, I get them. What do you say?'

'You know I couldn't say no, but, really, are you sure? You'd risk losing him?'

And in my head I can see your smile as you say. 'I don't think it's much of a risk, really.'

I think you have a point. After all why drive me on with a shout and a crop when you can use something far more potent: the thought of not being with you this evening. The thought of not getting to share the end of this amazing day with you. Of course I'm going to give this race everything I've got.

There's just one problem, which becomes very apparent, very quickly, as soon as the race begins: I've been training with you for over an hour, where Jeremy is fresh and perky. I might be running on sheer adrenalin, but he still takes an early lead with his newer legs. And Sebastian is frantic to win, screaming and shouting at Jeremy as we crash around the course.

My feet pound the dirt as I skirt pot holes that might upturn the carriage and brace my calves in the muddier soil. And there's my advantage right there, I might be more worn but I know the ground much better, having already completed several circuits of the paddock today. Jeremy isn't so lucky, running at full pelt he manages to miss one of the paddock's biggest pits, but the carriage doesn't and it topples, ending up in an easily overtaken heap and we lope to victory.

And that's how much I love you.

While Jeremy and Sebastian recover from their tumble with a few small dents to their carriage and a few much larger ones to their egos, by the time they are upright, I'm standing leaning on the fence by the gate, giving myself time to recover after my crazed exertion. You've dismounted and you're standing next to me, stroking my side. I can tell you're pleased. But I'm not, not entirely.

You see, during the race I was totally focused on the winning. Not winning meant spending the night with Jeremy and Sebastian rather than you, and that was unthinkable. But now we have won, I realise the flipside: winning means you've won Jeremy, which means, at a rough guess, you're going to forgo a romantic evening á deux, for getting your two pony boys to put on a little floorshow for you. And, although I'm trying to feel OK about that, I'm really quite disappointed at missing the one-on-one afterglow. And then you lean in close to me, and I can feel the warmth of your body against the chill of my sweat-cooled skin. And you whisper, 'Don't worry about it, baby.'

So I don't.

And that's how much I love you.

Much later, after warm blankets, warm showers, hot dinners and hot sex, we are up in one of the bedrooms – the one you used to change in, just lying on the bed together.

Jeremy is there too. He turned up as soon as we retired, all fresh faced and ready to perform his duties as prize. But you are so many steps ahead of him I doubt he can even see you. Which is why he's spent the evening tied to a chair in the corner, with one of the pony bridles on to keep him quiet. It's worked too. I've almost forgotten he's there. I certainly didn't notice him when you pinned me down on the bed and straddled me, showing me how much you enjoyed your day. And that you really do know how to ride.

And that's how much I love you.

Terra Firma Severin Rossetti

'I'm stuck! I can't move!' Angela cried, her voice shrill with panic.

Thirty feet below, arms crossed and one foot tapping, Kathy looked up at her friend, seeing limbs splayed, a body pressed to the rock face like a bug squashed flat against a car windscreen and thought, You conniving bitch.

'Let go! I'll lower you down!' called Andrew, their instructor, tightening his grip on the safety rope.

'I can't! I'll fall!' Angela felt sure, clinging on all the more fiercely, her legs locked rigid, her knuckles white.

Andrew exchanged a wry grin with the rest of the class, some of whom grinned and shook their heads at Angela's panic. Only Kathy recognised the panic for what it was, more a ploy than a genuine fear. She had known Angela since school, seen her shin up trees and walls and wrought-iron gates with never a hint of hesitation.

'Here, take this and hold tight,' said Andrew, passing the rope to another of the class, then dusted his hands with chalk as he called up to Angela, 'Hold on there! I'm coming up for you!'

Which is exactly what the scheming cow wants, Kathy thought, containing a grin as she watched Andrew begin to scale the wall.

Naked but for his shorts, and the climbing tackle he wore strapped about his waist, he quickly clambered up the first dozen feet or so, fingers stretched to a quiver, bare toes digging into the tiniest of crevices to boost him up. In repose he could seem quite slim, slender, but once in action his body rippled, all sinew and muscle, as Kathy knew only too well. She admired the tension in his thighs as he climbed, recalled them locking about her waist on many an occasion, the dimpled spine and the straining shoulders which she had so often caressed or raked with her sharp nails.

There was a slight sheen of perspiration which gave his tanned back a soft glow, like the tarnished armour of some ancient hero; his blond hair was damp against the back of his neck and she licked her lips as she imagined what Angela must be feeling.

Angela tensed as she heard Andrew draw closer, the rhythmic rattle of the buckles on his harness, the soft creak of supple leather and then the regular rhythm of his breathing. It was as if he was a predator approaching, she his prey, and though the tension in her body was more the result of excitement than fear it could only serve to make her seem more helpless, more vulnerable.

His hot breath caught the back of her legs as he reached her, and she was aware of his fragrance, a fruity cologne not quite masking his sweat, and then saw his strong hands to either side of her, fingers digging, climbing, pulling his body higher.

'I have you, you're safe,' he said, his body now enclosing hers, surrounding her, pressing lightly against her to make her feel a little more secure. 'You can ease up on the rope now!' he called down, and then more softly to her, an encouraging whisper in her ear, 'One foot at a time, Angela, match your step with mine. We'll go down together and I won't let you fall.'

Angela nodded, her cheek brushing his shoulder as she did so, and reached down with her right foot as she felt him reach down with his, finding the next foothold. Her left foot following his, her hands fumbling for a grip, she trembled a little and he pressed his body against hers, holding her fast, squashing her against the rough surface of the rock face so that her breasts were flattened deliciously against it. His groin against her buttocks felt hot, with a hardness there which she felt sure had nothing to do with climbing tackle.

'OK, again, there's not far left,' he told her, encouraging her to go on.

'Thank you, Andrew,' she said, her voice a sigh, a soft sibilance to it which spoke of eternal gratitude.

And now she didn't cling quite so closely to the rock face but let her body fall back from it a little, rubbing against his, her back to his chest, her buttocks to his groin.

'There we are, terra firma, you're safe,' he told her, as their feet touched the floor together, and she turned in his arms, smiling up at him as he snapped the safety rope free and unbuckled her harness.

'Thank you, Andrew, you saved my life,' she said, sliding from his embrace before he could break it, her breast brushing his arm as she turned from him.

'I wouldn't quite say that,' he said, calling the class to a close.

'Still, I'm very grateful,' Angela told him, walking away.

'Well, that was quite some performance,' remarked Kathy at her side, as they went to shower and change.

'But isn't it why I came, why you invited me? To sample some bulging biceps and perfect pecs?'

'The invitation was to prove to you that you can have your own sport, just as Mark does.'

'And sport it was, sport it is.' Angela grinned, stripping before soaping her body beneath the steaming shower, her hands caressing as much as cleaning, palms circling her full breasts, slipping down her belly, working between her thighs as if for the benefit of some third party. 'Mm! His body pressed against mine, soft words of reassurance like kisses against my ear, his arms around me, and I'll swear I could feel him grow hard against my bum.'

'For God's sake!' said Kathy, finding it hard to take her eyes from her friend's slick body. 'Mark really does have you in a state, doesn't he? Are things really that bad?'

'You could say so.' Angela nodded. 'He's more like a husband than a boyfriend, middle-aged before his time, him working hard and playing hard and sleeping so deeply that I think the only thing he needs me for is a pillow. All he needs is the comfort of a woman, but I need more from a man,' she said. 'I need – what I need is –'

'A good shafting?' Kathy suggested bluntly, when her friend hesitated.

'Eh?' asked Angela, surprised.

'A good shafting,' Kathy repeated, and Angela let out a snort of a laugh.

'Yes! If you want to put it so crudely, a bloody good shafting is exactly what I need!' she agreed, tossing her head, ringing out her hair as she stepped from the shower and began to towel herself dry.

'And there was me thinking you and Mark had the perfect relationship,' Kathy sympathised, following her out of the shower. 'Of all my friends you two seem the happiest.'

'In most respects we are happy,' Angela conceded. 'Mark is loving, faithful, attentive, he gives me every-thing I could ask for ... except passion.'

Kathy nodded her understanding and said, 'You've asked him for passion?'

'Well, not in so many words,' Angela confessed. 'I mean, it's not like asking for a new car or a new kitchen.'

'It isn't?' Kathy grinned slyly.

'No, Kathy!' Angela insisted, again taken aback by the unexpected response. 'Passion isn't a commodity, so I haven't asked him for it. I've dropped hints enough though, there's the body language there if only he'd read it. But he's content just to kiss and cuddle and fall asleep in my arms.'

'And that's it?' asked Kathy.

'Oh, there's some lovemaking,' Angela admitted, 'and love is involved, I can feel it in him. I just wish that sometimes it could be a little more like fucking than making love.'

'Poor Angela.' Kathy smiled, taking her hand and giving it a squeeze. 'But men like Mark, hard working, successful ... these things happen, they thrive more on the comfort of a woman than her passion.'

'But Derek is no different to Mark,' Angela pointed out, citing Kathy's own boyfriend as an example, 'just as industrious, just as motivated by his career. How do you two cope?'

'Who says we do?'

'Oh come on, Kathy!' Angela exclaimed. 'We've known each other since schooldays, we know each other only too well. If anyone couldn't survive without passion in her life then it's you.'

'Should I be flattered by that remark?' Kathy laughed.

'It's true and you know it,' Angela insisted. 'So, come on, what's your secret? Where does the passion come from? Give me a clue so I might find it for myself.'

'My secret?' said Kathy, a glint in her eye. 'Let me tell you over a drink in the bar.'

'Andrew's there!' said Angela, holding back at the entrance to the bar.

'So? Were you hoping he wouldn't be?' asked Kathy, gripping her wrist and holding her fast.

'Yes ... no ... I don't know!' Angela dithered, as Kathy drew her forwards, waving to Andrew and pointing to the bottle of beer on the table before him.

He raised it to show it was still full and shook his

head; Kathy got two glasses of chilled wine from the bar, then led Angela across to the table to join him.

'My secret? You really want to know?' she whispered to Kathy, as they crossed the room.

'Please,' said Angela. 'I really am getting quite desperate.'

'Very well then.' Kathy nodded and, as they sat with Andrew, Angela almost choked to see her friend reach out, grasp the instructor by the front of his shirt and pull his face across the table to hers.

'Kathy?' she gasped, but Kathy seemed not to hear, had fastened her mouth to Andrew's and was kissing him, long and deep, with unmistakable passion. 'Kathy!'

Slowly Kathy broke the kiss, and as their mouths parted Angela saw both wet with saliva, tongues flicking against each other a last time before withdrawing. Then they both turned to grin at her.

'Erm? What was that about?' she asked.

'Rather dishy, eh?' Kathy smiled, her hand caressing Andrew's knee.

'Explain yourselves,' Angela insisted.

'Well, Derek's job does take him away from home a lot, and like Mark he has his own sports and hobbies.' Kathy smirked.

'And Kathy is much too passionate a woman to spend all that time alone,' said Andrew, his hand on hers, encouraging her to caress his thigh.

'You mean? The two of you?' asked Angela. 'And this is a regular thing? How long has it been going on? How did it start?'

Kathy laughed at the profusion of questions and said, 'What does any of that matter?'

'It matters!' said Angela in exasperation. 'And it matters that you kept it secret from me!'

'OK then, what matters is that I had a problem,' said

Kathy. 'One not unlike yours. I needed passion. Derek was away so often and so I addressed the problem. Yes, it is a regular thing, but how long it's been going on and how it came about really isn't important. I have my passion, I'm happy, and when Derek finds the time to come back to me he comes back to a happy woman.'

'Well Kathy, I'm –' Angela shook her head and took a long drink of wine before she tried again. 'I'm –'

'Gob-smacked?' Kathy offered.

'Utterly! So smacked in the gob I am positively reeling! And I always thought you and Derek were such a contented couple!'

Kathy set down her glass on the table before her, took both Angela's hands in hers and said, 'But we are, perfectly contented! And now perhaps you can see the reason why?'

'I need another drink,' said Angela, and immediately Andrew was on his feet, striding across to the bar.

Kathy waited until he was out of earshot, then said, 'Now, what about you?'

'Eh?

'Your own problem, your own personal need. What shall we do about it?'

'Find me someone like your instructor friend?' Angela giggled, casting a glance in his direction.

'No sooner said than done,' Kathy told her, getting up from her seat, and before Angela could question her she was at the bar, whispering into Andrew's ear, and he was cancelling the order with the barman.

He made for the exit as Kathy came back towards her.

'OK, what gives? What're you up to?' demanded Angela suspiciously.

'You're coming with us,' Kathy told her, scooping up their sports bags.

'Coming? Us?' Angela echoed. 'Andrew is coming too?'

'Oh yes, he'll be coming soon, though not coming too

soon, if you understand my meaning.' Kathy grinned, taking her by the arm and leading her from the bar. 'Come, try it; trust me.' Kathy's voice was coaxing and cajoling.

Angela tried to resist the hands which drew her forwards but was too weak-willed. In the car park Andrew was waiting for them, a rucksack slung over his shoulder, his tight denim-clad backside resting against Kathy's car.

'You've flirted with him, you've attracted him, and now it's time to enjoy him,' Kathy told her, and though the prospect was thrilling the doubts were returning by the time they reached Kathy's place.

'But in your bed?' Angela said, as they entered the house and went directly to the foot of the stairs.

'The guest room,' Kathy countered.

'I'll be seeing Mark, too much guilt,' Angela tried, as they climbed the stairs.

'Then we will blindfold you, you will see who you choose – there will be no guilt.'

And then her final protest, as they entered the guest room and she saw the double bed: 'I know every contour of Mark's body, I'll recognise him even if I can't see him.'

'Then you won't touch,' Andrew said, sitting her on the bed, persuading her to lie back.

'Kathy, I really don't think I want to do this,' she said.

'Yes you do,' Kathy insisted, as Andrew rummaged in his rucksack and took out two lengths of rope.

'Soft, silk,' he told her, snapping them taut between his hands. 'Not much use for climbing, but –' He winked at Kathy and said, 'If you could see to the blindfold?'

'Relax and enjoy,' Kathy said, taking a scarf from the bedside table and wrapping it around Angela's eyes, then knotting it tightly so that she could see nothing. 'After tonight your life will no longer lack passion.'

'Kathy, I really don't want to do this. Please, let me go.'

'Nonsense, you'll thank me for it.' Kathy laughed.

'And me too, I hope,' said Andrew.

'Kathy!' Angela cried. 'Kathy!'

'Ssh,' said Andrew, and she felt the edge of the mattress dip under his weight, the soft touch of a fingertip to her lips. 'Ssh.'

Instinctively Angela turned towards the voice and there was a light kiss on her cheek, the sort of goodnight peck a child might receive from a parent, the lips warm and dry, the breath of the kiss slightly perfumed, or perhaps it was the nearness of his cologne, so subtle that it was only now that she noticed it. Unable to see, she could almost forget the unfamiliar bedroom, imagine herself in some fragrant glade, the scent of herbs and flowers all around her.

'Calmer now?' he asked, but before she could answer a wave of panic was washing over her again as she felt fingers at the buttons of her blouse.

Her hands came up, but were caught – by Kathy, she thought – and then she felt the soft silk cords wrapping around her wrists, her skirt lifted and her hands drawn down to be tied to her thighs, holding them fast to her sides.

'Stop this!' Angela said, twisting her body but unable to prevent the fingers from parting her blouse, revealing her bra.

'I would if you wanted me to, but I don't really think you want me to,' said Andrew, moving his hands to her breasts then resting his palms lightly on them. 'See? Your nipples are getting hard already, Angela. You can't deny that, can you?'

No, to her shame, to her delight, Angela could not deny that beneath the white lace her nipples were pricking and tingling.

'So?' said Andrew, as if asking whether he should

continue, and they both knew that she would say nothing.

Angela's hair spilt about her face as her head tossed, a wayward strand irritating her but she was unable to raise a hand to move it, so Andrew brushed it aside, rested a hand against her cheek, where his finger had brushed it, then bowed over her, bringing his face closer to her. His other hand slipped inside her bra to free one breast, his mouth only inches away, and he pursed his lips as her body tensed to feel his closeness, but then simply breathed on the nipple.

It hardened immediately, as if his breath was scalding. He smiled to see the reaction and sat back, and he brought his hand from her cheek, along her neck, around her breasts and then between them. Her body shifted and she wanted to bring her breast beneath his hand but already it was gone, running across her belly and away.

His hands ran all over her, down her neck, across her breasts, now baring the other, the short nails nicely manicured, not chewed to the quick like her husband's, lightly grazing her skin. The hands, too, were softer than Mark's, their touch more gentle, and they moved back up to cup her cheeks, to hold her face still while he kissed her on the lips.

Or could they have been Kathy's hands she felt. Angela could no longer tell, no longer cared, she had to respond now. Her mouth opened to admit Andrew's tongue and felt it wash against her own, and then felt him suck at it to draw a deep breath from her. His kiss lingered, his tongue probed; though it was not as fervent as Mark's it seemed to have something more – more of the passion which had been missing for so long.

Feeling a fire build inside, Angela began to lap hungrily at Andrew's mouth, but the moment she did this he drew back, leaving her gasping. Blindly searching for his lips, her head tossing from side to side, she felt them touch the top of her breasts, then skip down to kiss her belly.

'Lift a little,' Andrew told her, his fingers at the waist of her skirt as his tongue licked at her navel, and she raised her hips.

In an instant her skirt was bunched beneath her, her knickers tugged down just enough to bare her groin, and Andrew had taken a scarf of such fine silk that it was almost transparent and was running it up the length of her body from her toes to her thighs, stroking it between her legs for a moment and then draping it across her chest, so that she could feel her own wetness against her breasts. Through the diaphanous material he could sense her nipples burn and ache; if he moved the scarf they might hurt, while if it just lay there it was a teasing irritation.

He lowered his head again and this time touched his lips to a nipple, drew it into his mouth and sucked it through the silk, licking his tongue around it. Through the silk it felt as though his tongue was as rough as a cat's and Angela squirmed with delight, trying to raise her shoulders from the pillow.

'Keep still,' he told her, nipping her nipple lightly between his teeth. Then he took his mouth away and watched her head fall back on to the pillow, her face turned away for the moment, a brief grimace of pain dissolving into a grin.

She might have dozed for a moment, slipped into a dream, but then behind her blindfold her eyes fluttered as she felt something light and tickling between her thighs. She cocked her head to one side curiously, as if to ask: What?

'A feather,' Andrew told her, softly stroking it along the inside of one thigh, from knee to groin.

She gasped as he switched to the other thigh and did

the same there, her hands straining against the cords which held them, wanting to plunge them between her legs where the feather now rested.

Lightly Andrew moved it backwards and forwards across the lips of her pussy, which began to swell and part and soak the feather with her juices. In no time it was sodden. Andrew tossed it aside and took the scarf from her breasts, trailed it down her body and bunched it between her thighs. With a finger he pushed it deep inside her while he kissed her hip and belly, dipped his tongue into her navel and then licked her breasts. While the scarf went deeper inside her, and his finger with it, he sucked hard on her nipple, so hot and firm that it seemed to burn his lips.

The whole of the scarf was inside Angela now, and Andrew rested his hand over her sex to keep it there. He could feel her wetness dripping over his fingers, took his hand away to taste it, then ran his fingers across her mouth and let her suck on them to taste herself.

Her whole body was flushed, burning, and he felt her swollen clitoris, rubbing the scarf around and around it. She was straining more than ever and he wondered if he was hurting her. He asked if she really wanted to continue with this.

'Kathy promised me passion,' Angela said, her voice coming in ragged gasps, and though she was experiencing more than ever before she was not yet satisfied. 'Screw me, Andrew.'

'Make love to you?' he asked, his fingers now slipping inside her, taking up where his tongue had left off.

'No! Screw me! Screw me senseless!' insisted Angela, her body bucking beneath him, knowing what she wanted, aware of the distinction more than ever before.

Smiling, Andrew withdrew the scarf so slowly that to Angela it felt as if he was removing a part of her, as if her soul might be tugged out with it. It stroked the walls of her sex as it came and unwound itself around her clitoris so that her body bucked uncontrollably.

Andrew, resting a hand on her belly to hold her still, saw spasms shiver beneath her skin as the scarf was finally pulled free. He moistened the lips of her pussy with the scarf, even though they were already wet, and then draped it across her face. The silk was soaking and moulded itself to her features; he saw her eyes, her cheekbones, her lips all perfectly formed beneath it.

As his mouth moved lower again, his tongue washing over her bush, Angela remembered a crude barroom trick of Mark's: a stick figure of a woman made from twisted pieces of paper, and the merest drop of liquid would make its legs part lewdly. She was that helpless automaton now: as Andrew's tongue burrowed into the mat of hair her legs spread wider and wider, needing him deeper, into the very core of her.

His fingers caressed the inside of her thighs, found the wet lips of her sex and parted them, holding them obscenely wide to make way for his tongue. Even her own fingers playing with herself had never delighted her more: as if his tongue was a part of herself, and driven by her, it went to the very places she wanted.

As Andrew's hands began to climb slowly back up her belly so Angela sank down the bed, pressing her groin harder against his face. She heard a low sound escape, not the soft snort of disgust which she sometimes guessed was Mark's response but more a growl of satisfaction, and she understood that Andrew was enjoying this as much as she was.

Stretched to her limit, Angela shifted her hips from side to side, gyrating against his face, and eventually he had to pull back.

Then she felt his mouth fasten on her breast; he sucked the nipple into his mouth and then a greedy portion of the flesh. She had never had children but she knew this is what it must be like, this is what she had missed, to be suckled with such urgent fervour that her whole body tingled.

She grew wetter and she was sure she must have been drenching his fingers, but where Mark would surely have responded with revulsion, if he had ever brought her this far, it only seemed to spur Andrew on. As his fingers worked faster inside her, his mouth worked harder on her breast, and he drove her body into unaccustomed paroxysms of delight. And when his fingers withdrawing from her made a wet 'plop' of a sound they both giggled.

'And now the passion,' he told her, taking his mouth from her breast, running his sopping fingers across her lips so that she could suck them and taste herself.

Slowly he rose on his knees, leaving her body burning and aching for his, and she felt his fingertips trail down her body and the mattress give as he adjusted his position.

'Yes, now,' she pleaded. 'Now.' After so many years of waiting for real, intense passion it had to be now.

Andrew laid himself between her thighs now, let his body rest on hers and kissed her on the mouth. When his tongue slipped between her lips she could taste herself, as could he and they both shared the flavour of her excitement. His hands cupping her cheeks, he held her face still while he drank her in.

His cock was hard, and, as it rested against her belly, she felt it burning into her and her hands fought against their bonds, wanting to touch it.

Andrew lifted his hips, drew back slightly, his mouth not leaving hers as he let his cock run along her thighs. The tip of it was weeping and it left a sticky smear across her skin, adding his wetness to hers. Both their bodies were becoming slick with sex and perspiration.

Pushing forwards, he let the head of his cock nudge

against the mouth of her sex. Then a little more, and he was in her, but only the tip. He asked her if she wanted him inside her. He whispered his question in her ear, and when he recognised the answer in the slight parting of the lips his whisper became a kiss, his tongue licked across her ear and then inside.

Angela sighed, and it was the soft intake of breath which drew him into her, her hands were tied but still she was able to draw him inside her. He slid deep into her and felt the warm wetness surround him, slipped in so deeply that he thought ... no, I can't have tugged out her soul, for now it seems as though I am touching it.

He pulled back, lifted his body and arched his back. Once he was out of her, the head of his cock just resting against her lips once more, the air chilled his erection and he drove in again, and again, each time deeper, each time with more force. He had to bite his lips to keep from coming now. If he released Angela's hands and let her embrace him he knew he would orgasm for sure and so he kept her tied, immobilised beneath him.

'I will only come when you come,' he told her, whispering again, asking her, commanding her, 'Come for me, Angela, now.'

With slow steady strokes Andrew moved into her, against her, a measured progression, as if he needed to gradually coat his prick with her juices and make it slick before that promised passion.

'You will come,' he said, knowing her need. 'As will the passion.'

'Promise?' she sobbed, her body rising to his. 'Promise?'

'I promise,' he said, as he was finally deep enough inside her for their groins to meet, flesh slapping flesh, bone bumping bone.

Now he pulled out quickly and pushed back hard, no

cautious inch-by-inch intrusion this time but a driving thrust which forced her body deep into the soft mattress.

His hands were to either side of her head, supporting his body; his thighs were between hers to keep them apart; there was no tender caress of his hands or soft touch of his lips, just the increasing rhythm of his cock inside her, moving faster, working deeper.

From a part of her that no other man had ever managed to touch, Angela felt her orgasm build, and she actually screamed out loud, out of fear that she might ultimately be denied it, out of fear that it might be too much for her to bear.

'Come!' Andrew said, his pounding movements making the whole bed shake. 'Give in. Come!'

OK, the orgasm didn't last for ever, but after waiting so long for such passion it maybe seemed that way. Angela's body shuddered and trembled as if with a series of aftershocks, only slowly subsiding.

Remembering how it usually was with Mark, his greatest joy being to have her arms enfolding him, a fragrant breast to cushion his cheek, she now felt the same need, wanting to wrap this newest lover in her arms, or be wrapped in his. Her hands were still tied though, so all she could say was, 'Oh, Andrew! Andrew! Andrew!'

'Oh, Angela! Angela! Angela!' he responded, with a soft laugh.

'How I ache to take you in my arms now,' she sighed.

'Not quite possible at the moment, is it?' he said, that mischievous hint of humour in his voice again. 'But maybe instead –?'

'Yes?' she said, then sensed the weight of his body settling on the bed beside her and felt an arm work its way between her body and the mattress, taking her in a half-embrace. 'Oh yes,' she sighed.

'Yes?'

'Yes!' She hoped that after such passion there had to be tenderness.

'Very well,' he agreed, and she felt fingers at her right hand untying the scarf which had fastened it to her thigh.

Angela flexed her fingers, brought some feeling back to them, was able to roll into the loving embrace she needed and felt the arms enfold her, the smooth touch of flesh against her lips, the . . .?

The soft fragrant breast which cushioned her cheek?

She blinked in the harsh light of the bedroom as the blindfold was removed and had to accustom herself to its glare before she could make out the figures: Andrew naked on one side of her, Kathy to the other, holding her in a tender embrace.

'Sometimes it really is the comfort of a woman that a man wants, the passion of a man that a woman needs,' her friend told her, lowering her face to kiss her. 'And now, will you two offer me some comfort and passion in return?'

Number 1 Candy Wong

There was a sharp vegetable tang to the room: dirt-caked boots, she thought, and damp clothes crushed to the bottom of nylon kit-bags and left to fester for another week. It was always the same, the smell, and yet for ever strange to her, unpleasant and yet attractive in some way she couldn't put her finger on, arousing something primal in her. Kneeling forwards, she tied her laces with two brisk tugs, then clutched her stick across her chest and left the room.

The cold spanked her across the face, but the contrast with the overheated changing room was invigorating. She inhaled deeply and set off for the patch of green behind the line of trees to the right of the building. On the field she could see a few figures already limbering up, smudges of black against the blank white sky.

She was almost level with the shed when the girls appeared at her shoulders, like dark angels. One of them – she wasn't sure if it was pin-thin Julie with her lank tawny hair or the more rounded Jane with her frizzy halo of strawberry-blonde curls – shot out an elbow that caught her in the ribs and made her yell out.

'Oi! Goalie,' quipped Jane with a sardonic smile. 'Seen lover boy yet? He in there?'

Tamara hazarded a glance at the shed. The door swung open on its hinges but no one was inside among the massed ranks of gardening tools and little pots of seedlings.

But Jane had barely paused for a reply before adding, 'Oh no, you won't have, will you? He'll be out there already, waiting for you.' She turned to Julie triumphantly, and the pair snickered conspiratorially.

Tamara chewed her lip and looked back towards the playing field. She hoped her college-mate was wrong, but feared that too. His presence embarrassed her, and more so the longer it went on, but if he wasn't there today then something would have changed in some obscure way that she wouldn't be able to fathom because she didn't know why he was there to begin with, and why he looked at her the way he did.

At first she'd tried to tell herself that it wasn't her, that he was watching all of them. But then the others – and not just spite-filled Jane and Julie – had started to make remarks, and she'd had to admit to herself that she was why he came, drove his spade hard into the earth and folded his arm over the handle as he followed her about the pitch with his small black eyes.

They were almost at the field now and she could hear the other girls tittering behind her as they made him out at the other end of the field, immobile, taking deep drags on a cigarette and blowing smoke out into the freezing air.

'What would dear old Trissy say,' called Julie, 'if he knew about your secret admirer? Your bit of rough? He wouldn't be too thrilled about it, I'm sure.'

Tamara ignored the tacit threat; she'd long since concluded that to rise to Jane and Julie would only encourage them, let them think they had some kind of hold over her. Which they didn't. She didn't give a stuff what they said to her or about her. Or what they said to other people, least of all Tristan. She reached the halfway line and began to bend and stretch.

Gradually the remaining players filtered on to the pitch and Mrs Wass blew her whistle for the two centres to bully off. There followed an hour of fairly uninspired play, with lots of dribbling up and down the field by the wings but few shots at either end. Tamara far preferred the cut and thrust of real games to these practice sessions, which lacked any feeling of aggression or risk, especially as the last game of the campaign had been played. This training session had a pointless, empty feeling to it. *A bit like Tristan*, she thought, and giggled quietly at her own cruelty.

Her position in the team meant that, when she wasn't required to actively defend her goal, there really wasn't much for her to do, and that in turn increased her self-consciousness. Throughout the game she was aware of the man at the limits of her vision, always there, like a fault on her retina, and she was haunted by the danger of inadvertently meeting his gaze. So she was glad whenever she did see a little action, when she got the chance to hurl her body at oncoming balls, savouring the feel of the cold mud as it slicked across her knees and thighs.

Afterwards, as she peeled off her kit in the changing room with its misted-up windows, its radiators steaming with sweaty socks and its almost cloacal smell, she found herself thinking about him, really thinking, for the first time. She didn't know what he looked like, not from close up, or even how old he was, not to mention what was going through his mind as he watched her leap and dive, brandishing her stick like some kind of weapon. His scrutiny had affected her though. She felt dizzy, thickened in the throat as if she had been embarrassed in front of her fellow players. She was warm and tingling in places that she really ought not to be, especially on such a chilly day.

Pulling her sports bra up over her head, enjoying the brief chafe of rough cotton against her nipples, she became aware that stick-insect Julie, with her slightly bulging, reptilian eyes and her small tight mean mouth, was staring at her across the room. They'd been mates once, the three of them, and then, out of the blue, the other two had turned on her. She'd never understood why. Now, as she saw how Julie's gaze flickered over her planes and curves, lingering for one barely perceptible moment on her breasts with their mocha areolae, she thought she knew why. The gardener wasn't the only one who thought Tamara had a beautiful body. Well, let them admire her. She arched her body as she reached into her locker for the shampoo, aware of how her breasts would rise and separate, her tummy become taut, perhaps even bring a little of her bush into view above the waistband of her shorts. She pretended to be distracted by some minuscule piece of grit on her chest and swept it away, careful to brush her fingers over the stiffened flesh of her left breast, which jiggled in just the way she wanted.

She glanced at Julie as she made her way to the showers. Her erstwhile friend was red in the face, trying to keep a towel around her own nudity, which wasn't as bad as her clumsy attempts at modesty suggested. She was thin, sure, and her ribs were painfully visible, but she had perky boobs with generous, rude pink nipples and a good curve to her hips. Her bum was firm and round. Tamara almost laughed out loud. Being leched over on a hockey pitch seemed to be all she needed to get her in a froth to the extent that she could begin having fantasies about her teammates.

In the shower, camouflaged by steam, she soaped her breasts for a long time, paying more attention than was necessary to the nipples, which felt so hard under her fingers that she thought they would never again turn soft. But as much as she wanted to she couldn't bring herself to rub her pussy. Not yet. Not when so many things about her body, about sex, about Tristan, were still so uncertain. She noticed other girls spending inordinate amounts of time with loofahs or flannels or bare fingers, bent over, mashing them against the soft flesh of their pussies. She heard the squishing of thick lather and the low sighs barely audible above the hissing showerheads. She wished for some of their daring. As she stepped from the shower she smelt the unmistake-able aroma of female sex and wondered why it was that, no matter how much she dabbed the towel against her sex, she could not get it dry.

Back home, alone in the house, she tried to finish some coursework as she waited for Tristan to arrive. But her thoughts kept returning to the figure lurking at the end of the hockey pitch, to that face barely visible beneath the hood of his ample jacket, pulled up against the wind and rain, to those eyes trained on her. When the doorbell rang, she started as if from a trance.

'Hi Tam,' said Tristan, blustering in in his tracksuit.

She returned his kiss briefly, then led him into the kitchen, where a pot of pasta and sauce spat and bubbled on the hob. After ladling some into two large white bowls, she sprinkled them with grated Parmesan from a packet and set them down on the breakfast bar, at which Tristan was by now seated.

She barely spoke, mechanically taking in forkfuls of pasta and letting his talk of student-union politics and rowing victories wash over her. She looked at his smooth face, at his skin, unblemished, almost supernaturally clean, at his ash-blond hair and thought again of those words of her mother – 'If I were twenty years younger, God almighty ...' The look on her face as she had said it – Tamara would never forget that. Tristan was, by any-one's standards, the university catch. The face of an angel with the physique of a Greek god. The golden boy. Who could resist?

He needed to be gone by seven, he told her as he rejected the brownie she offered him. That gave them an hour to kill. His perfect white teeth flashed at her as he grinned. She let the dishes clatter into the sink, wiped her hands on some kitchen roll and followed him into her bedroom.

He was bare-chested on the bed before she had even crossed the threshold, hands behind his head, a knowing smile on his lips. She stopped, looked at his hairless chest, at his flat brown stomach with its encroaching mesh of curls the colour of burned sugar. Lowering herself on to the bed, she placed her hand on his belly and brought her face down to him, inhaling the mint and tea-tree aromas of his deodorant. He encircled her upper arm with his hand, quite tightly, and pulled her up towards him, his lips seeking hers.

'I'm still hungry,' he said when she finally pulled her head away.

'Tris,' she began. Already she hated the whiney tone in her voice.

'Oh, Christ, Tam.' His chest rose and fell heavily. 'Not a-bloody-gain.'

'I'm just not sure –'

'Not sure I'm ready.' His voice rose a few octaves in imitation of hers.

'Tris, please. Just –'

He sat up, threw his shoulders back and looked at her with those baby-blue eyes of his, a look that said, 'They all want me, I could have any girl I want, and you dare to refuse me. Who the hell do you think you are?'

'OK,' she conceded, tearing her gaze away from his, bending forward to undo her shoes.

At once he was upon her, dragging her back on to the bed by her shoulders, then rolling her over and pushing her skirt up over her thighs. All the while his mouth was on hers, his tongue probing her. She struggled to breathe, felt suffocated. She felt his hands tugging at her knickers, felt the give of the elastic over her buttocks as they were yanked down. Then he sat up, and she watched appalled as he slipped his tracksuit bottoms down over his hips, revealing a flawless cock that looked polished as a pebble, scrubbed and pink as a mollusc emerged from its shell. A clean velvety cock that demanded to be held and to be worshipped. He was holding it in his hand, as if proffering it to her. She took it gently in her fist and watched as its little gummy eye wept a clear tear for her. She leant forwards, hesitantly, and flicked it away with her tongue. It tasted salty and warm, like jellied sea water. Tristan's lips pulled back from his teeth and a hiss of satisfaction escaped between them. His face was darkening. She watched, amazed by the simple power she was wielding over him, as the tip of his cock pulsed and reddened. He was trying to thrust against her grip, to roll his foreskin back under her fingers, but she wasn't moving against his motion.

'Please,' he said.

She dipped her hand beneath his balls and ran a fingernail along along the seam of his sac. He trembled, threatening to fall against her. Another tear of pre-come dripped across her wrist. She opened her mouth and placed the throbbing bulb of his cock beneath her lips, without touching him. She breathed hot air over him, allowed her saliva to drizzle his head. He sounded as if he might start crying. But something felt wrong.

She released him and he fell back, his eyes open and shocked. 'What?' he managed.

She couldn't put it into words. But it was something to do with the way that it was suddenly more about the actual act than any intimacy between them. She felt that she could have been anyone and he would have been happy. He didn't pay her any heed, not like the gardener. She was invisible to Tristan; she was something hot and wet to deposit in when he wanted to. Well, not while she was in control of things.

She moved back over the bed, away from him, pulling her skirt down. 'I can't, Tris.'

He stared at her, then before she could say a word packed himself away, hastily, leaving his shirt untucked, and pulled on his tracksuit top. 'I've fucking had it with you, you frigid cow,' he shouted on his way out of the room.

She lay on the bed and listened to doors slamming as he made his way through the house and back out on to the street. Then she undressed fully, retrieved a pot of yogurt from the fridge and went to run a bath.

As the sweet scent of geranium oil permeated the air, she looked at herself in the mirror. Like Tristan, she had a kind of physical perfection that aroused lust in many, envy in some, not least Jane and Julie. Not that she cared about that. Who wanted to hang out with bitches like that anyway? She was glad to be rid of them. But something was bothering her and, as she looked at her long lean limbs and symmetrical curves, she realised what it was: no matter what everybody else said about him, not matter how much even her own mother wantonly lusted after him, she just couldn't find Tristan sexy. Did that mean there was something wrong with her?

For months now, ever since they started seeing each other, he'd been coming around after working out at the gym, rubbing her breasts, putting his hands further and further up her skirt. It didn't matter how often she'd protested, or what form that protest took – I'm only seventeen; I've got my period; my housemates are going to be home any minute – he was determined to get her between the sheets. She'd thought it was fear; now she realised his basic lack of respect for her – his reducing of her to a pair of tits and a tight pussy – revolted her.

Or was it sex itself that revolted her? Still looking at herself in the full-length mirror, she sank to the tiled floor. She pulled her long auburn hair back with one hand and studied her face. Perhaps she was just one of those non-physical people you heard about sometimes. People who just don't have any interest in sex, who can go a whole lifetime without. She opened her legs and stared between them in the mirror. Her lips, surrounded by downy fronds of copper-coloured hair, gaped a little, allowing her to see into the nest of pinks and reds. It was darker than she had imagined, meatier, more swollen. She thought of butcher's shop windows, of slabs of steak, but the image didn't disturb her. She licked her fingers and brought them to her pussy. She'd never even masturbated before. Did that mean she was asexual? Did all the other first-year girls wank?

She glanced down again. She was wet. She moved her fingers and began to explore her folds and creases, the delicate petals of herself. She closed her eyes. This was *good*. This was better than good. She reached for the towel beside her, slid it beneath her and lay back, spilling the yogurt as she did so. Fuck it, she thought. To her left she could hear water coursing from the taps and wondered vaguely if she should get up and turn them off before the bath overflowed, but before she could decide a jag of pleasure ripped through her loins. It was as if she'd touched some button. That must be my clit, then, she thought. She gasped, laughed, swore. Her free hand lashed out and smeared the slick of yogurt. She brought it back to its twin and slathered the cool, creamy stuff all over her hot pussy. Her fingers squelched and sucked inside her as she delved for a rare sensation that stayed tantalisingly out of reach. Everything she was seemed focused now on the hole at her core. She didn't recognise the creature in the mirror, hair plastered to her forehead, hands jammed between her legs, her breasts quivering as she hit a rhythm that she knew would bring her the climax she desired. Stars danced inside her.

'Tamara, are you in?' she heard from the hallway, and

she stifled a moan of frustration, jumped up and climbed into the bath, submerging herself completely.

She rose in the dark, dressed in silence and left the house. She hadn't worked out how she was going to get there, but when she saw Dave's bike leaning against the fence she figured he wouldn't notice if it went missing for an hour or two.

She rode through the streets, through the orange pools of light cast by the streetlamps, looking up at the dark windows she passed, wondering what people were dreaming of behind their closed curtains, or what they were doing to each other across the beds, up against the walls, on the stairs … She travelled slowly; she wasn't in a hurry. She'd dressed in her hockey shorts – they were to hand – and the night air was icy on her bare legs. She felt more alive than ever before.

The gate was locked, as she had known it would be, but the wall was easy to scale for someone as athletic as her. She paused as she hit the ground, looked around her at the strangeness of the deserted park laid out beneath the moon. It could just have been that she was spaced out from not sleeping and from the shock of the glacial air in her lungs as she pedalled, but she didn't think so. To see this public space, usually so full of activity – not just hockey players, but dog-walkers, joggers, gangs of schoolboys sneaking a cigarette in the lunch break, little old men napping on benches – devoid of all life and movement was bizarre. It was like entering an alien territory where none of the familiar rules applied.

She followed the main path towards the house, then continued to the right when it forked. The shed lay a few steps away, side on to the house and the door to the changing room. She hesitated. Part of her wanted to go into the changing room, to inhale its rich, earthy odours of sweat and mud and rot, of old forgotten things. But she was pretty sure that would be locked too. The shed, on the other hand, she could see from where she stood that the door to that was ajar, and that a faint light emanated from within. She stepped up and grasped the handle, her breath caught in her throat.

He was working by the light of a storm lamp, a cigarette crumbling to ash in an ashtray beside him. He was rapt in his work, easing his sturdy fingers down into the soil and moving them carefully until he had loosened the root system and could pull the seedling out. Beside him on the wooden workbench were a row of larger pots to hold the burgeoning plants.

He hadn't heard her pull the door open, and she was able to watch him a while. She could see his face clearly now, side on at least, and the first thought that came to her was that he was hairy, very hairy. He didn't have a beard, but his stubble was advanced, his eyebrows thick and unruly, and she could even make out a few hairs sprouting along the line of his cheekbone. His hair, now that it wasn't hidden by a hood, appeared bushy and tangled, with sprinklings of grey. His eyes were small, intent, inspecting every plant as he transferred it over to its new home. He seemed to stroke them as he did so, give them an encouraging or reassuring little rub with his fingertips.

She looked him up and down, noted that he was shorter than she had realised, probably a little shorter than herself, with a slight paunch. His clothes, corduroy trousers and a brown jumper, were worn and ill-fitting. But it was his hands to which her eyes kept returning, those weathered extremities with their mud-encrusted nails, their surfaces lined as road maps. It was as if dirt had worked its way into every pore and crevice, year on year, until it had become a part of his very being. Those hands, she thought, were this man's life. His contact with the universe. She imagined them on her, rough and

greedy, leaving grubby fingerprints on her clean innocent breasts.

He had stopped now, and stood expressionless, looking down at his workbench. He seemed lost in a reverie,
and suddenly she felt like an intruder. She had no right
to be watching him like this. At least when he watched
her, both parties knew about it, and all the other players
too. This was something else.

She walked away, out past the house and the door to
the changing room towards the pitch. She didn't know
what time it was, but thought that the sky seemed a
little paler now than when she had arrived. She hadn't
got far when she heard a noise behind her, and when
she looked over her shoulder she saw that the shed door
was closed. So he *had* been aware of her, she thought,
and now he was shutting her out. That was fair enough.
She had been spying on him and he'd been too polite or
too shy to tell her to go away. He was obviously a loner,
wasn't good at dealing with things like that. But she'd
overstepped the boundaries.

Then she heard the footsteps behind her on the path
and she realised she was wrong. She tried not to change
her rhythm lest it scare him off, keeping to a leisurely
pace as she veered off through the trees and on to the
hockey field. Despite the chill of the night, her blood
pulsed warmly inside her, fizzed in her ears in the
silence. She was having trouble not turning around.

What was he expecting of her, she wondered. She had
a dread feeling that she would make the wrong move
and lose him, kill the moment. She strode up towards
the goal, the goal that only yesterday she had been
defending as the man looked on. All that seemed like
light years away. When she had still been Tristan's girl.
The body that Tristan wanted to fuck. Another notch on
his bedpost.

She thought again of Tristan's dick, his smooth pale

dick like a swatch of silk in her hand. The way he'd presented himself to her. He thought he was sex on a stick, that guy. He didn't know the meaning of the word.

She shrugged off her coat and scarf, began to unbutton her shirt and then grew impatient and pulled it up over her head, tossing it to the ground beside her. Before she could tell herself otherwise, she had turned to face the man. He was only steps behind her now, his face contorted with longing. Full on, she could see now that he wasn't old enough to be her father, but must have had a good fifteen years on her. She held out her hand. He looked at it, and she could almost hear his brain ticking over.

'It's OK,' she whispered. 'I won't tell. It'll be our little secret.'

He scrunched his face up, as if weighing up her words, deciding whether he could trust her. 'Not here,' he whispered finally, glancing up at the moon, as if it were some all-seeing eye.

'Then where?'

He pointed back in the direction of his shed.

'No.' She stepped forwards and encircled his wrist with her hand, pulling him over towards a mass of bushes. Her coat and shirt remained on the grass behind her.

He took off his donkey jacket as they reached the flower bed and made to throw it down on the earth, but she pushed his hand away.

'No,' she said again, still more forcefully. And then she slipped off her remaining clothes and shoes and laid herself down.

He stood looking over her. 'Are you sure?' he said.

She nodded. 'Absolutely. Now just fucking get on with it, will you, I'm freezing my tits off.'

He snorted, repressing a laugh. 'Bossy little madam, aren't you?'

She smiled. 'Just take your clothes off. Or do I have to do it for you?' At this she sat up and lunged for him, pulling him back down on to her by his tired brown sweater and then pulling it up over his head. Beneath it was an equally worn navy T-shirt that she tore off him too. In the half-dark she could see the fur of his chest, of his shoulders. She pressed her hands against it, the fuzz of it. It felt comforting. There was a ripe smell about him: sweat and onions and nicotine and lust, and that comforted her too. There was something so irrepressibly male about it.

She lay back, spread her legs. 'Lick me,' she commanded.

He smiled, as if he still couldn't quite believe his luck, and then brought his face down to her. She arched her back as she felt his tongue jab inside her, once, twice, and then plunge right into her and stay there, exploring the walls of her. The melting feeling returned.

'Don't stop,' she murmured. 'Just don't fucking stop.'

He came up for air, and she saw the lower half of his face glistening. Straining upwards, she licked his chin and around his mouth, her tongue rasping against his beard growth, tasting her own slightly sour juices on his skin. Then she lowered herself to the ground again, and pulled his head back down. This time his tongue flicked at the nub of her clitoris, and she felt herself jerk like a puppet, at the mercy of new forces. It was uncomfortable, almost unbearable, and yet she didn't want it to end. Her hands opened and closed like avid claws, convulsively, tearing up the soil beneath her. Her legs spasmed peculiarly, almost comically. A couple of times she came close to pushing him away from her but realised she couldn't. She was on the verge of tears, even while she was shouting out with joy.

'I want you inside me,' she said, not knowing where she found it in herself to order this grown man about.

He raised his head, smiled down at her, then pulled her legs wide apart and placed his clenched fist up against her pussy.

'Relax,' he whispered.

She smiled. 'I am,' she said. 'Perfectly relaxed.'

He unfurled his hand, pushed three fingers inside her and waited, watching her face. She had half-closed her eyes now, and her head was pushed back, chin jutting up, in a swoon. 'More,' she whispered. 'Go further. Harder.'

Soon his entire hand was inside her, and he stopped again, reading her face for a signal. She looked up at him, remembering the care with which he handled his plants, the way he caressed their leaves with his finger-tips, urging them to trust him. She trusted him. She nodded.

He began to rock his hand gently inside her, moving slightly from one side and then to the other. She was still now, palms pressed down against the soil, breath stopped. And then a flood tide opened within her, and the contractions started, and for a time she lost all contact with the earth beneath her.

When she woke up he was gone, but he'd draped his coat over her, and her own. It was still only half-light, and sounds from the road were scant, so she guessed she'd only been asleep a matter of minutes, perhaps an hour at the most.

She sat up, pulled away the covering and looked at her bare legs, at her lips still glistening in the dawn, at the smearing of blood on her thighs, mingling with the crust of mud. She lay back, just for a moment, and felt the dewy soil against her skin.

'You dirty, dirty girl,' she said and laughed.

She stood up and got dressed. When she passed the shed, the door was closed and the storm lamp was out.

She folded his jacket and placed it on the ground outside, wondering whether he would be back to watch her the following week. Then she remembered the hockey season was over.

'Goodbye,' she shouted as she made for the gate, not waiting for a reply.

Playing a Round Amber Leigh

Emma almost shrieked when she saw them.

Blundering through the small copse that lurked beside the ninth hole, impatient to find Ricky's Dunlop Steelcore so they could hurry along with their game and catch up with Eric and Rhea, Emma clapped a hand over her mouth to contain the cry. Her heart lurched to the back of her throat; a gut-punch of arousal left her breathless; and she stood perfectly still among the green shadows and rustling gorse.

The couple were screwing.

Grinning, close to choking on a burst of mad laughter, Emma stepped discreetly back so that she didn't disturb the pair. She felt certain neither of them was aware of her – they hadn't heard her approach and they were clearly too involved to notice an intruder standing still – but she didn't want to look like some pervert who watched indiscreet couples screwing. And yet, despite that attitude of propriety, she couldn't tear her gaze from the pair as she backed away.

Oblivious to their audience they continued to buck, thrash and moan. His baritone voice mumbled grunts of appreciation and she responded with long drawn-out sighs. They were naked, pressed against the bark of a mature pine, and almost lost in the shadows of its dense, overhanging needles. He had his back to Emma and his head and shoulders covered the face of his partner. Emma could see the woman's slender legs wrapped around his hips and her hands were linked behind the back of his neck. Emma marked it as the classic 'knee-trembler' position but she couldn't see any of the lewder details of their union. She could hear the groans of each measured penetration: a long, slurping kiss that made her ill with lustful envy. She listened more intently to catch their wordless exchange of passion. He gasped; she sighed; and they both encouraged each other to do more with nods, grunts and growls.

Unable to see them clearly in the shadows of the copse – not able to work out if they were regulars she might know from the clubhouse – Emma was ready to give up on finding out who they were and return to finishing the hole. And then she saw the tartan trolley bag.

Parked beside the couple, with a pair of pink panties dangling from the head of a fairway wood that poked out of the top, Emma knew it wasn't just any tartan trolley bag. It was a Full Black Watch Tartan trolley bag: a one-of-a-kind trolley bag identical to the one she had bought for Eric.

The urge to shriek struck her again and this time she had to wrap both hands over her mouth to contain the sound. Unable to think of any other explanation, amazed that she hadn't seen this was bound to happen, Emma realised that Eric had made good on his promise of the previous evening: Eric was screwing Rhea.

Another body blow of arousal struck Emma hard in the stomach. It made her knees weak and left her close to collapsing. She grabbed at the branch of one of the dense pines close by, uncaring that the needles stabbed at her palm. Bewildered by what she was seeing, she took another step back.

She had intended giggling about the sight when she got back to Ricky, confiding that she had found an amorous couple, and maybe pointing out the location so he could have a quick glimpse at them. Those thoughts were banished as she backed away with stealthy haste.

Her cheeks had reddened. Her T-shirt suddenly felt too tight and it was now dank with perspiration. She came close to tripping on something in a thicket of gorse and, after glancing down, found Ricky's Dunlop Steelcore had nearly toppled her. With only a moment's hesitation to get her bearings, she kicked the ball out of the rough and sent it rolling back down the apron of the fairway.

The ninth was gloriously bright after the canopied gloom of the copse. With one nervous glance Emma saw Ricky stooped over a nearby bunker. His head was lowered and his concentration absorbed in the painstaking search for his ball.

Emma glanced back at the couple, no longer troubling herself with the details of Eric's blue and black golf trolley or the pink panties that dangled from the fairway wood. They remained hidden in shadows – surprisingly well-covered for a pair screwing on a golf course in broad daylight – and their shadowy bodies mesmerised her.

His back was hard and lean. The tension of holding his partner had made his buttocks spectacularly taut. The muscles quivered with each thrust and made Emma want to return to the shade of the copse and lovingly stroke her fingers against him. Touching Eric wouldn't provide the same thrill that Rhea was clearly enjoying but to be a part of what they were doing . . .

The unfinished thought made her tremble. She shook her head and discounted the idea of joining them as madness. But, although Emma repeatedly told herself she wasn't going to interrupt the scene, she didn't immediately step away. She watched him thrusting in and out, admired the way the muscles in his well-formed back rippled with each movement, and realised that was how Eric looked while riding her. The next time he took her against the bedroom wall or the bathroom wall – almost certainly the next time he was adventurous enough to take her against a pine tree on a golf course –

this was exactly how he would look from behind. It was a magnificent sight.

She squeezed her thighs together and became poignantly conscious of the friction that her bare legs made when they touched. Breathing heavily, she felt her T-shirt shrink against the swell of her stiffening nipples. Finally finding the courage to step away she escaped from the thicket and called to Ricky that she had found his Dunlop.

'That's yours, isn't it?' she asked, pointing.

'I looked there.'

'You didn't look hard enough.'

'Bloody thing,' he grumbled, trudging out of the bunker and wielding a cumbersome iron. 'How the hell did it get there?'

Watching him address the ball, Emma was struck by a rush of possibilities.

The previous evening, during foreplay, she and Eric had exchanged their usual thoughts about swapping with another couple. Because of their golf date with Ricky and Rhea the pair had seemed like natural fodder for the fantasy and she had suggested Eric could enjoy sliding his length into Rhea's tight pussy. The blonde was slender and petite – the perfect contrast to Emma's curvaceous brunette – and their excitement had grown as they discussed various scenarios. As she sucked, licked and teased him, Emma had asked Eric to think how it would feel to have the skinny blonde riding up and down his shaft.

His responding grunt had told her that the idea appealed to him. Enjoying the control she had over him, thrilling at the way she was able to manipulate him to the point of release, Emma used her coarsest phrases to suggest how Rhea might respond to his advances. She licked her tongue along his length, teasing the tip against the hole in his slit, and confided that Rhea had a passion for giving blowjobs.

It was enough to make him groan that he was on the verge of release. Because she didn't want to feel his climax in her mouth that evening, and wanted the same treatment he had said he would give to Rhea, Emma pulled her lips away from him and asked how he would feel if she were to have sex with Ricky. His enthusiasm had been unnerving.

At the time Emma had thought he was merely humouring her. He had waxed lyrical on the idea of Ricky's sliding into her and breathed with soft respect when he spoke about the idea of her kissing, holding and touching the other man. He had insisted she must do it, demanded she should let him watch and begged she would confess every detail if it ever happened. His kinky chatter had been stimulating; his crude suggestions had made her wet and hungry for him; and she had blithely given in to the thrill of the orgasm.

But she had never thought Eric would really turn the fantasy into a reality.

Even at the start of their round of golf, when he suggested they swap partners to play the club's shotgun rounds, Emma had never thought he was planning such a move. Such cunning was normally beyond him and she wondered what charms he had exercised to lead Rhea so willingly into the copse beside the ninth.

'You sly bastard,' she murmured, glancing back towards the thicket of pine trees. Her grin was so tight it made her mouth ache. A tickle of jealousy piqued her chest but it was overshadowed by the weight of a torturous arousal. Tugging at the neckline of her T-shirt, trying to encourage cool air to grace the slick, scalding skin of her breast and shoulders, she shook her head in disbelief and said again, 'You sly bastard.'

'Who's a sly bastard?'

She jumped as though Ricky had goosed her. Momentarily short of a response, she shook her head, tried to make her smile convincing, and toyed with the idea of telling him what she had seen. Unhappy with that way forwards, sure she could seduce Ricky without the visual aid of his girlfriend and her boyfriend locked in a passionate clinch, Emma said it was nothing.

Ricky wouldn't let the subject drop so easily. 'Have you seen Eric doing something devious?' he asked. 'Has he been dropping his balls to an advantageous position?'

She blushed, and hoped the sudden colouring didn't look too obvious. 'Have you seen Eric and Rhea since we teed off?'

Ricky shook his head. 'I guess he's playing a hole we can't see from here.'

Emma studied him warily, wondering if Ricky knew what was going on, or if it was simply the language of the game that lent itself to innuendo. She took a deep breath, remembered how she had thought of him the previous evening during her orgasm, and a heat of anticipation scorched through her loins. The decision came to her in that instant. If Eric was going to have Rhea today, then she was determined to have Ricky. Outraged by her own daring, and blushing more furiously than ever, she watched him strike his Dunlop and send it soaring up towards the green.

'Good stroke.'

'Thanks.'

They fell into step, side-by-side, walking easily alongside the fairway. Ricky shouldered his silver carry bag while Emma trailed a navy trolley behind her. The sky above was clear and free from clouds and the greens before them stretched to the far-away border of a tree-fringed horizon. Now that she had made her decision,

Emma felt torn between a euphoria of freedom and an oppressive weight of anticipation.

'It was good of Eric and Rhea to let us play together,' he told her.

'It made sense with us having the same handicap,' she agreed.

'I hope they're having as much fun as we are. If Rhea finds herself stuck in any hazard, she could hold Eric up for ages.'

From what she remembered seeing, Emma thought Eric looked like the one who was holding up Rhea, but she kept that remark to herself. Deciding it was time to lead the conversation in a specific direction, she drew a deep breath and said, 'I wasn't overly keen when Eric first suggested we should take up golf.' She lowered her voice so Ricky had to stay close to hear.

The summer sunlight warmed the day and made the scenery look miraculously cultivated and natural. The sounds of occasional birdsong chirruped lazily, broken only by the far-away cries of 'FORE!' from unseen players. The picturesque layout, peppered with golden bunkers, dazzling blue streams and verdant copses made the course look like a vast and beautiful garden.

'I don't think I would have taken to it,' Emma continued, 'if golf hadn't turned out to be such a sexy game.'

Ricky chuckled. 'Golf is sexy? Since when?'

She fanned her chest with her hand. The movement of air wasn't enough to bring any soothing chill but it drew Ricky's attention to the front of her T-shirt. The thrust of her nipples remained obvious and she was pleased to see his eyes widen. His smile glinted with appreciation and apprehension.

'Sure it's sexy,' she argued. 'Just look at the location.'

He glanced sceptically around the course. The groundskeeper's shed, laying east of the twelfth and designed to look like a Swiss chalet, was visible as they mounted a rise on their hole. Ricky's Dunlop and Emma's Nike had landed in the green and they exchanged approving smiles as they stepped towards them.

'It's pretty around here,' Ricky agreed. 'But that's not sexy, is it?'

'It's more than pretty: it's glorious.' She kept her voice low, this time making the tone soft and reverential. 'And because it's all at my disposal, that makes me feel like a goddess.' She turned to glance at him and asked, 'Doesn't it make you feel like a god? Able to possess everything you see?'

She fixed him with a meaningful glance and then fanned her chest again. Watching his eyes light on her breasts she struggled to suppress a grin at how easy it was to seduce some men. Not waiting to see how he responded, she hurried down the fairway towards her ball.

Ricky caught up with her as she levelled a putter against her Nike. Emma had her backside pushed out more than was usual but she wanted him to notice the swell of her buttocks and the way her coltish legs were revealed by the high hem of her short skirt. Heels would have helped emphasise their alluring curves but she had yet to find a golf course that allowed the female players to wear high heels on the fairways.

'What else is it about golf that makes you think it's sexy?'

She stiffened, delighted he had taken her bait so easily. Normally Ricky only talked business and politics on the course. It was a pleasure to hear him express an interest in her opinions on the sexiness of golf and she hoped she understood his motives for pressing the subject.

'There's so much that's sexy about the game,' she breathed. Keeping her concentration fixed on the ball, knowing his gaze was freely roving her legs and buttocks, she said, 'I love holding this length in my hands, controlling it perfectly, keeping the shaft firm and adjusting my hold so I've got just the right grip.' With a grin she added, 'I can't imagine why that makes me think sexy thoughts.'

Ricky coughed polite laughter.

From the corner of her eye she could see the front panel of his pants bulged noticeably. He pulled at his jumper, trying to conceal the symptoms of his arousal, but Emma had already seen enough to know he would be easy prey. The thought made her feel decidedly wicked and that added to her escalating excitement.

'I love the co-ordination that's necessary,' she continued. 'I find it sexy that I have to assume the correct position every time to achieve maximum effect. I admire the object of the game: the focus of being civilised and skilled as you aim to get inside that hole. As I said before: everything about golf is sexy. That's why I love the game.' As though she was punctuating the sentence, Emma sank her putt with one crisp chip.

Ricky made a note on the scorecard and addressed his Dunlop. 'I'd never looked on golf as being sexy before,' he told her. He padded his feet on either side of the ball, renewing his grip on his putter and switching his gaze apprehensively from the Dunlop to the hole.

'Those aren't the only things about golf that I find sexy,' she said quickly. 'Can I share a secret?'

He continued to contemplate the putt. His attention was so intense he could have been completing the final strokes in The Grand Slam. Without lifting his head he said, 'Of course you can share a secret. You can tell me anything.'

'Sometimes Eric and I reward each other for a well-played round.'

Ricky glanced up from his putt and raised an eyebrow. 'Reward each other?'

'If I win a hole, he might give me a kiss,' she explained. The inner muscles of her sex tightened as she continued to speak with a combination of allure and naivety. 'If he wins, I might do something to make him feel special.'

Ricky returned his concentration to the ball. He switched his gaze from the Dunlop to the hole and his entire body grew stiff as he prepared to match her score. Feigning nonchalance, he asked, 'What would you do to make him feel special?'

'I might give him a kiss,' Emma confided.

Ricky nodded and adjusted his posture.

'I might tell him how great a golfer he is ...'

Ricky raised his putter and stiffened on the brink of taking the shot.

'... or I might just suck his cock.'

The Dunlop sailed past the hole.

'That was a bastard's trick on the ninth,' Ricky muttered. 'I could have had myself an eagle.' He had positioned himself over the ball and the tenth hole looked like it would be a re-enactment of the ninth.

They were both on good form and one shot away from claiming a birdie each. The air between them had been thick with tension since Emma last spoke but she was pleased to see that her words were having the desired effect. Rather than shouldering his carry bag, Ricky now held the clubs in front of his groin, as though he was trying to conceal something. Instead of walking by her side he seemed to take every opportunity possible to fall behind. Each time that happened she could feel the weight of his gaze appraising her legs.

'You would have overshot the putt,' Emma assured him. 'You looked very stiff to me.'

A blush darkened his cheeks. 'The Royal and Ancient Golf Club rules state that no one should talk when a player is making a stroke. I could claim that round by default.'

She shrugged. 'If you can't play the game you shouldn't be on the course.'

'I can play the game. And I would have sunk that putt.'

'You feel confident you could beat me?'

'Yes.'

'Confident enough to make a wager?' He was still considering the shot and she stepped closer so that her legs were in the range of his vision. The golf shoes weren't flattering but she felt sure the glimpse of bare skin would be enough to capture his interest.

Ricky looked up. Because he had stooped over the ball his face was on the same level as her breasts. Her nipples remained hard and obvious against the flimsy cotton of her T-shirt. He swallowed and asked, 'What sort of wager?'

'If I win this hole, maybe you could give me a kiss?' Emma suggested. Hurrying to explain the reason, she added, 'Rhea tells me you're a great kisser.'

He beamed. 'Rhea says that about me? That's sweet.' Frowning briefly, struggling to lift his gaze up to her face, he asked, 'What if I won?'

Emma didn't hesitate. Meeting his eyes, she said simply, 'Win this hole and I'll give you my panties.'

She could still see the copse of trees that lay to the east of the ninth fairway – the copse where she had caught Eric and Rhea – and Emma wondered if they were still there. Admittedly Eric loved his golf but she knew that the chance to bury himself inside Rhea for another hour or more would easily override his interest in an amateur shotgun championship. Wishing she knew what he was up to, tempted to call him on his mobile and lewdly ask which hole he was currently playing, she tried to push

Eric and Rhea from her thoughts as she turned her attention back to Ricky.

'Is the wager agreed?'

He leant over his putter, concentrating heavily on the shot. 'Don't try and distract me again,' he complained. 'You know the wager is agreed.'

She lifted the flag from the hole and fell silent. It was only when he stiffened, ready to nudge the ball three yards and into the hole, that Emma turned around and lifted the hem of her skirt. Showing him the rear panel of her panties, wiggling her rear provocatively, she said, 'Make it a good one, Ricky. This is what you're playing for.'

The putt sailed past the tenth and he cursed.

She laughed and, with insouciant arrogance, Emma tapped the back of her own putter against the Nike. She was so confident of the shot she didn't bother to watch as it entered the pot through the back door. Running quickly over to him, presenting her lips in a full pout, she said, 'I claim my prize, Ricky. You owe me a kiss.'

His face was a hilarious mix of anger and arousal. Tossing his club to one side he glared at Emma as she continued to wait for her kiss. 'I've still got to finish the hole,' he said petulantly.

'It's a gimme,' she decided flippantly. 'Now gimme my prize.'

The kiss surprised her. His lips were soft and sensuous against hers. As she stood shocked on the green, amazed that he had finally succumbed to her teasing, she was stunned by the sensitivity he imbued into the exchange. Half expecting him to plunge his tongue into her mouth, she was mesmerised by the intimacy of having him lightly brush his lips against hers.

He stepped closer, their bodies touching, and one arm encircled her waist. One hand slipped over the curve of her bottom while his other went to the back of her neck. He gently massaged her nape and drew the kiss to a chaste conclusion.

When he stepped away, Emma whispered, 'Wow.'

'You cheated,' Ricky told her. 'You distracted me when I was taking my shot.'

She drew a ragged breath and wondered if he knew how much he had excited her with his simple kiss. Trying to remember that she was playing the role of the siren, Emma asked, 'Would it make you feel better if I gave you your prize?'

He started to stammer a response and then closed his mouth with a snap. His eyes grew wide as she stepped away from him and discreetly reached beneath the hem of her skirt. After teasing the elasticated waistband away from her hips and drawing the cotton slowly from her crotch, she kept herself modestly covered as she pulled the panties down her thighs.

The openness of her position wasn't something she could ignore. It was a furiously bright day; she was standing on the green of the tenth and slipping the panties from her hips. Although Ricky couldn't see anything untoward she felt exhilarated by the moment's exhibitionism. After stepping out of the white cotton underwear, she grinned as she handed them to him.

Ricky drew two deep breaths before speaking. He shuffled uncomfortably in front of her and she watched him tug at his jumper in a futile bid to conceal his excitement. 'What do I do with these?'

'Keep hold of them.' Her voice had lowered to a husky drawl. The temptation to hold his hand while he held the panties, then to lean close and extract another kiss, was almost unbearable. But Emma resisted. Smiling with an ease she didn't really feel, she said again, 'Keep hold of them. You might get lucky on the next fairway.'

* * *

The eleventh hole was a five-hundred-yard course besieged by bunkers and concluded by a shallow stream. Gorse surrounding the groundskeeper's ornamental shed lay to the west while the fairway's rough apron threatened to be another potential hazard. Because of its dog-leg layout the eleventh hole was a notoriously difficult par five. However, Ricky drove his Dunlop with a blend of accuracy and force that pitched the ball hurtling towards the green.

'Show me how you do that,' Emma insisted.

Needing little encouragement, Ricky came up behind her as she addressed the ball. He pressed himself against her back, putting his hands over her wrists and making her lower her left hand and raise her right so she had more control of her iron. His cheek brushed against hers and she was touched by the thrill of potential intimacy. Suspecting he was stung by the same thought, and wanting to capitalise on that response, she warned softly, 'You should be careful how you push against me. You haven't forgotten that I'm no longer wearing any panties, have you?'

He drew a deep breath. 'That detail hasn't slipped my mind.'

She wriggled her buttocks against him. 'Do you still have my panties safe?'

'They're in my pocket.'

'May I check?' Without waiting for a reply she slipped her hand from his grip and reached behind. After patting his hip pocket with one hand she slid her fingers over the front of his pants. The swollen bulge that lay there was as hard as she expected. The heat that radiated from him was enormous and she felt ill with her need for him. Stealing her fingers away from the bulge, Emma rubbed his other hip pocket. 'There they are,' she breathed softly. 'Thanks for keeping them safe.'

He shivered against her and resumed his grip on her

wrists. Guiding her hands back to the correct position on the iron, he pressed his groin against her and she was stung by the sensation of having his length rub between her buttocks. His trousers and her skirt prevented the contact from being flesh touching flesh but it gave Emma a promise of how good that moment would feel when it inevitably happened.

'What are we playing for on this round?'

'If I win, I might want my panties back.'

'And if I win?'

'I'll show you what was inside them.'

The tension between them remained unbearable as they walked along the course. With Ricky's help Emma had landed her first drive just a little way off the green and knew she could complete two strokes under par. Ricky's initial swing had landed him closer but, considering his weak putting skills, she didn't think he would fare better than an eagle. That thought was confirmed when he chipped his putt and sent his Dunlop hopping over the pot.

'You helped me improve my drive,' she reminded him. 'Can I help you with your putting?' Without waiting for a reply, she stepped behind him and grabbed his wrists. Curving her body against his, trembling with sudden need she mumbled, 'Perhaps I shouldn't be doing this. It makes me feel vulnerable.'

'You feel vulnerable?'

She held him more tightly. 'I'm pressing my body into the back of a sexy guy,' Emma explained. 'I'm holding your wrists and there's only this short skirt that's stopping my pussy from touching you. That certainly makes me feel something.' She lifted one hand from his wrist and daringly stroked her fingers over the front of his pants. 'Does it make you feel something too?'

He said nothing.

For an instant Emma thought she had taken things

too far and pushed Ricky beyond his limitations. It was only when he raised his putter and sank the Dunlop in one smooth shot that she realised he had been wilfully concentrating on the shot.

With a heavy sigh, Ricky said, 'It did make me feel something. It made me feel determined to win this hole.' He half-turned, facing Emma without breaking their embrace. The pressure of his erection pushed rudely against her stomach. His lips hovered precariously close to her mouth.

'You won the hole,' she said simply. 'Do you want your prize?'

'You wouldn't believe how much I want it.'

Easing herself from his grip, Emma strolled lazily towards the hole and bent down. Keeping her legs straight, knowing the hem of her skirt was going to raise as she tilted forwards, she heard Ricky gasp behind her. Making sure her legs were hip distance apart she reached one hand into the hole and held herself motionless.

'Wow.'

She heard his exclamation and struggled to suppress a grin. Bending over, she knew the split of her sex would be visible. The hem would have lifted and she didn't doubt he could see the dark curls that covered her cleft and every dewy fold. She held the position for a moment or two longer, wondering if he might step behind her and stroke his fingers against the febrile lips of her flesh.

Neither of them spoke as they began the twelfth.

As though they had both intuited what was coming next, Emma allowed Ricky the honour of teeing off. She followed his powerful drive with a shot that was equally forceful and direct. They strolled wordlessly along the side of the fairway, each lugging the weight of their own carry bag and Ricky no longer hiding the fact of his erection.

A par four, and only besieged by one potential hazard, Emma thought she should easily score a birdie. By pure good fortune she sank her Nike on the second shot.

Ricky slammed his clubs to the ground in frustration. 'Damn!' he growled. 'I wanted to win that one.'

'What was so important about that hole?'

'I wanted the prize at the end of it.'

She raised an eyebrow. 'What prize would that be?'

'I wanted another glimpse of your gorgeous little muff.'

She tested a wicked grin. Lewdly appraising him, Emma said, 'I might let you look while I'm claiming my prize from you.'

'What's your prize?'

She held out a hand and nodded towards the ground-skeeper's shed. 'Come in there with me, and I'll show you.'

He needed no further encouragement, hurrying with her to the trees that surrounded the Swiss-style chalet. Brushing aside her suggestion that they should break into the shed, Ricky led her around the back of the building until they were beneath the shade of a pine. 'Outdoors,' he gasped urgently, stroking her breasts through the film of her T-shirt. 'I love the outdoors but Rhea's a prude about the open air.'

Emma wondered if she should tell him she knew otherwise, but his caresses had made her in no mood for small talk. Pressing her mouth over his, melting beneath the power of his kiss, she moulded her body against him as he pushed her against the pine.

'What prize did you want?' he murmured.

She snaked a hand down to his groin and stroked him through his pants. After sliding the zip down and slipping her hand inside, her fingers found the scalding flesh of his erection. She briefly remembered the sight of Eric and Rhea at it in the bushes, and wondered if they had fallen together with such passion and enthusiasm. The idea made her squeeze tight around Ricky's shaft and they both groaned together. 'This is the prize I want. Are you going to give it to me?' Rather than waiting for his reply, she stood on tiptoe and guided his half-exposed length towards her sex. Stroking the swollen dome over her flushed sex, she shivered.

'Let me undress,' he insisted.

She nodded, not sure she could wait, but wanting to feel and see his naked flesh. After slipping the skirt from her hips and pulling the T-shirt over her head, she was stung again by her own daring as she stood naked in the small copse of trees.

Ricky stepped out of his trousers and jumper with unseemly haste. Taking her fully in his embrace, pressing a hungry kiss over her mouth, he pushed her back against the pine tree and thrust his length towards her.

For one instant she wondered if she should stop him. The concept of infidelity was a subject she seldom liked to brood on, but Emma felt certain that having sex with Ricky could fall under that description. Regardless of what she had seen before, and no matter what Rhea and Eric did as they played their rounds, Emma couldn't think of a way to rationalise her behaviour as anything other than infidelity.

The wickedness of that idea added fresh excitement to her mood. With renewed urgency, she struggled to ease Ricky's cock inside her. Wet from fetid need – so hot inside she feared her warmth could melt him – Emma slipped the head of his shaft against her pussy lips and then devoured his length.

He continued to kiss her. His mouth worked delicate miracles against her lips while his penis slid firmly inside her and, by this time, Emma no longer considered herself to be unfaithful: she was only in need of a climax.

He encouraged her to wrap her legs behind his back.

While the position felt precarious, it allowed him to slide deeper inside. Starbursts of raw delight fluttered through her loins and she struggled to find breath for the orgasm he was about to bestow. Wrapping her arms around his neck, melting into the furious ardour of his kiss, she bucked her hips back and forth and rode him, grazing her sensitive bud along his cock.

But it was only when she glanced over his shoulder – when she opened her eyes and saw the figure watching them from the fringes of the copse – that the climax finally soared through her body. A second wave of exquisite pleasure was inspired by Ricky's release: the pulse of his shaft trembled directly through her clitoris and made her squeal with satisfaction. And then he was helping her down from his erection and kissing her with a blend of giggles and gratitude.

'That was good,' she gasped. 'But it has to be better if I win the next hole.'

Instead of laughing, he regarded her seriously. 'Whether you win or lose,' he said solemnly, 'I guarantee it will be memorable.'

Three hours later, and following an unremarkable drink in the clubhouse, Emma and Eric drove away from the golf course. The radio played at a whisper and they travelled in a comfortable silence. Eventually deciding it was time her boyfriend confessed what he had been doing, Emma said, 'The twelfth was my favourite hole. I found it to be surprisingly satisfying.'

Eric said nothing. His gaze was fixed on the road ahead as he drove them away from the golf course towards a glorious sunset. In the back of the Range Rover his Full Black Watch Tartan trolley all but obscured the rear window.

'I thought I saw you and Rhea when we were on the ninth,' Emma continued. She was trying to sound casual and suspected she was failing abysmally. Determined to extricate a confession she asked, 'How did you fare there? Did you find it easy?'

He grinned but his concentration was fixed on the road ahead. 'I remember the ninth,' he admitted. 'I think that one's going to stay with me for a long time.'

'Really? What made the ninth so special for you?'

Eric laughed and snatched his gaze briefly from the road. 'It was on the ninth that I discovered my one-of-a-kind tartan trolley isn't as unique as I thought it was. I saw another couple dragging an identical bag into that thicket of pines that lies to the east of the fairway there.'

He turned his gaze back to the road and asked, 'So, what made the twelfth so remarkable for you?'

Emma opened her mouth and then closed it quickly. Whatever it was she had wanted to say, she somehow thought this was no longer the right time or place.

Doubles Heather Towne

When I scoped out Jenn at the tennis club, I knew for sure that I'd made the right decision in purchasing a membership. She was studying the tournament sign-up sheet on the club bulletin board in the pro shop, a tall, leggy girl in her early twenties, with small breasts and a taut bottom. With her lean tanned physique and long blonde hair, she was the drooling image of tennis supervixen Maria Sharapova, to my Mary Pierce, and I yearned to have East meet West as soon and as often as possible.

'Hi, I'm Linda Zale,' I said, hustling over to the hottie and extending a friendly hand.

'Jennifer Carmotti,' she replied, her pale blue eyes melting into mine.

We shook, and shook, till I finally released her warm hand when she gave me a queer look. Then I asked, 'You gonna sign up for the tourney?'

She bobbed her head. 'Yup.'

'Great. Maybe we'll play against each other.'

'Could be. You're pretty good, I hear.'

I was staring at the girl's slim honey-dipped legs, wonderfully showcased as they were in a pair of hot-pink shorty-shorts. 'Huh? Oh, uh ... I'm not too bad, I guess – unless I wanna be.' I joked. 'I really just joined the club to, you know, stay in shape.' That was partly true; I'd also joined to check out the action – and I don't mean of the fuzzy balls variety.

'Me too,' Jenn responded, flashing a smile. 'Hey, why don't we go in the doubles competition together? My usual partner just dumped me, and I'd love to teach her and her new playmate a lesson.'

'Great,' I gushed. I couldn't for the life of me understand how anyone could ever dump the golden girl but, then again, maybe her game didn't match her good looks. Tennis and beauty often don't mix, when it comes to on-court success.

A week before the club tournament, Jenn and I started playing against one another, practising. She was really pretty good – actually, pretty and good. And since no one at the club was going to be hoisting a silver platter at Wimbledon any time soon, it looked to me like either one of us had a decent shot at winning the under-40s singles title, and both of us at winning the doubles title.

We practised hard on the outdoor courts, challenging each other's weaknesses – my backhand and her drop-shot. But more important than tuning up for the tourney, to me, was the quality eye-popping time I was spending with the luscious babe.

It was wicked-hot all that week, which meant that Jenn sported a different skimpy outfit each and every day – skimpy even by teensy tennis standards. She donned an assortment of aquamarine, purple, peach and crimson tanks, all of which fit her like a second skin, her pert breasts straining against the stretchy, sweat-soaked fabric, bouncing deliciously whenever she chased down a ball. And she swaddled her hips and bum in the shortest white and pink and blue skirts and shorts available on the planet – short enough to make even Anna Kournikova blush. The girl's lightly muscled lower limbs flashed smooth and shiny under the glaring sun, under the tiny skirts, and her tight white cotton-clad bottom was on breathtaking display whenever she bent over to pick up a ball or a racquet or a water bottle I just happened to toss a tad too far.

But an even better opportunity for me to get an erotic eyeful, and handful, of the tennis tart was when we paired up on the same side of the net to work on our doubles game. We usually played against a couple of old ladies who were overjoyed just to return a serve, let alone score a point, so they weren't much help in building our game, but they sure were helpful in building – and building – my lust for lithesome Jenny C.

Whenever it was my turn to serve, I could barely muster the concentration necessary to connect with the airborne ball, because I was concentrating so hard on Jenn. She'd get into her tennis stance near the net – slightly bent over and forwards, legs wide apart, butt swaying from side-to-side – waiting for the 'pock' signalling racquet-ball connection, and my competitive juices would give way to other far more urgent juices.

I love the female form in all its varied sexy parts, but I guess I've had a special affinity for legs and ass ever since I was a little girl, since the dreamy-eyed days of Catherine Bach parading around in her daisy dukes, poster child Farrah Fawcett and a hot-panted Lynda Carter, aka Wonder Woman. And Jenn had the limbs and cheek to compete with any of those gals in their primetime. So, given my partner's physical distractions, half the time I ended up spraying the ball into the wrong court or the net or plunking one of the old ladies or Jenn right in the back. Thank God for second serves.

The absolute best part of playing doubles with Jenn, though, aside from the jaw-dropping view, was the point, set and match celebrations. Every time we scored, which was early and often, I scored. I'd high-five Jenn or give her a hug or, best of all, a lingering pat on the ass. I had a real good feel, so to speak, for the girl by the time our heated practice week was over. And, of course, the game wasn't truly over even when the on-court action ended, because there was still the blistering post-match locker and shower-room showcase to come.

I'd openly ogle Jenn as she stripped down in front of her locker, timing my movements with hers so that we'd pad, nude and attitudinal, into the communal shower room at the same time. Then I'd hide the soap or snap her bum with a towel or otherwise provoke the giggly girl in some gleefully innocent manner such that our slick bods would end up entangled together in a seemingly playful manner, under the hot coursing jets of the showerheads in the steamy confines of the shower room.

Jenn had a trimmed strip of golden fur covering her pussy, while I have a lightning bolt of dirty-blonde pubes of my own shaven creation, the business end of the bolt directing traffic to my otherwise bare pussy. It's a great conversation piece, and it drew Jenn's instant attention, like I'd hoped.

'That's wild,' she yelled above the pulsing water, pointing at my pussy.

'Thanks. I've got quite a few compliments on it,' I shouted back.

She moved in for a closer look, and I directed a stream of water in between my legs, clearing away the suds, adding to my buzz. Jenn bent over, hands on her knees, and stared at my shocking pubic design. I turned wet with something more than water, got downright squishy in the knees when the glistening girl reached out and touched my furry bolt. She traced the soft, jagged outline of it with her pink-painted fingertips, brushing the super-sensitive skin surrounding it. My body jerked like I'd taken a ball to the breadbasket and I had to grip a water spigot to keep from liquefying and spilling on to the floor.

'That sure is neat,' Jenn enthused, her breath steaming against my tingling lips.

I gulped some humid air and gazed through misty eyes at the girl's sun- and water-drenched body.

'Maybe you can do mine like that one day,' she said, laughing and straightening up.

'I'll do you – yours – any day,' I mumbled.

Jenn laughed again, then pivoted and pranced back to her nozzle to finish dousing her bod. I stared hungrily at her flexing butt cheeks, her supple legs.

The club tournament was played over the 4 July long weekend, and I got bounced like a fresh-from-the-tube Slazenger out of the singles competition in just my first game. Jenn didn't fare much better, losing her second match. So, we had only the doubles title to shoot for, and shoot for it we did, paddling our first two opponents in straight sets.

There weren't a ton of teams in the doubles competition, so, after only one more game, set and match, we advanced to the final. It was played late Monday afternoon, in front of a crowd of virtually no one. The singles title had been decided earlier in the day and, as this was the ugly sister to that event, there were maybe ten people watching from the air-conditioned comfort of the club building and not one in the stands, when Jenn and I strode on to the court to face our opponents, Lacey Leung and Preeya Dhillon.

Lacey and Preeya were a couple of cute little girls in their late-teens, with Lacey, as it turned out, being Jenn's former doubles partner. Jenn had extra incentive, therefore, to spank the firm bottoms of those girls, while all my incentive was provided, as usual, by my gorgeous partner.

It was a hundred degrees in the shade and Jenn and I

were attired in almost identical teeny tennis togs. I didn't quite have the legs or glutes to pull off the short-skirt, peek-a-boo-panties look like Jenn did, but my large boobs jostled nicely, I thought, under my tight-fitting turquoise tank. Jenn was wearing a pale-green top that got damper and damper and her breasts more defined with every hard-fought point and a white wrap-around tenny skirt which bulged dangerously with twitching butt flesh. Two little green fluffy tennis balls peeked out from the backs of the girl's white shoes, attached to her socks, marking the terminus of her sleek legs.

The match was hotly contested – hot, period. Back and forth it went, the four of us giving our all, me giving Jenn warmer and warmer celebratory embraces as the points grew in magnitude. Finally, after a see-saw affair, we had Lacey and Preeya down to match point in the third set.

Jenn and I huddled up briefly. It was my serve. 'Let's do it,' she exhorted, gripping my shoulder and pumping her racquet, getting into my face.

'Yes,' I shouted back, pressing my nose against hers. I stared excitedly into her blue-flame eyes, my lips so very close to hers, hard-breathing in the heady scent of the tennis vamp. My senses overloaded, and I would've flat-out smooched the girl right out there in the open if she hadn't suddenly broken away. I had to settle for a sharp slap on her butt, for encouragement, of course.

I toed the line, glancing briefly at the backs of Jenn's spring-loaded legs, her panty-clad bum, and then I gritted my teeth, flared my nostrils and tossed the ball in the air and jumped up after it. I whistled my racquet through in a speed-of-sound arc and smashed the ball – right into the net. I grinned sheepishly at Jenn when she looked back at me, then served up a powder-puff second serve.

Preeya smacked the ball back at me and I whipped a shot into Lacey's side of the court. Jenn stayed at the net, while I stayed back. Lacey got to the ball and cranked a screamer down the line, to my left. I chased it down, spanked it back where it belonged with a Jenn-strengthened, two-handed backhand and a grunt of exertion. Preeya returned the ball fast and hard, straight at Jenn, who coolly lifted her racquet and laid the ball down on the enemy side of the mesh, dropping it soft and spinning backwards right in the middle of the court, within two feet of the net. It was a perfect drop-shot – just the way I'd taught her – and Preeya and Lacey collided, Stooge-style, in their mad rush to dig the ball out of the asphalt. Not that they would've had any chance of legally returning it anyway, since the ball was already on its second dribble by the time they dove for it.

'Yes,' I hollered, tossing my racquet into the air and racing over to embrace the grinning Jenn.

We hugged and jumped around like we'd beaten the Williams sisters, my hot little hands roaming all over Jenn's slippery body. Then we shook hands with our defeated opponents and the President of the club handed us a tin-plated trophy that almost fell apart on contact. We paraded around the court with our bargain-bin prize, drinking in the lukewarm applause from the five or six tournament volunteers still remaining. And by the time we finally ran off the court and skipped down the steps into the locker room, I'd made a vow to the tennis gods to take our celebration to the next level.

I chased Jenn into the locker room, tracking her jiggling bum and limber legs with slightly glazed eyes. Then I cornered the giddy girl against a bank of cool metal lockers, and she waved the trophy around over her head, laughing deliriously. We wrestled for possession of our prize, Jenn's sun-kissed skin burning against mine. I quickly lost interest in securing the trophy, instead securing my hands on my partner's hips. I moved my hands down, over the giggling hottie's hips and skirt, on to her bare legs, then in behind her legs, at last cupping her bold bottom – the ultimate prize.

'Hey, the trophy's up here,' Jenn squealed.

I was not to be distracted, however, squeezing and kneading the babe's full buttocks while I stared at her heaving chest, the twin nipple indentations on her soaked-to-see-through top. She tried to wriggle away from me, but I clung to her, clung to her glorious glutes. And then she stopped wriggling, perhaps finally realising that I was making an out-of-bounds play for her. I looked up into her sky-blue eyes, willing her to see things my way.

'What's that?' she asked, looking over my head.

'What's what?' I breathed. My sun- and sex-heated body shivered with excitement, my sex wet, my nipples hard.

'Listen.'

I listened, heard the muffled sound of someone moaning – in the direction of the shower room. Jenn used the distraction to break free of my grasp and she disappeared around the bank of lockers to investigate the noise. I ran after her.

We heard the hiss of water, saw the billowing clouds of steam, even before we peeked around the corner and peered into the communal shower area. And what we beheld in there was a steamy scene straight out of one of my après-tennis jill-off fantasies. Lacey and Preeya, our on-court opponents, occupied the five-head shower room, Preeya on her knees with her face buried in between Lacey's legs.

I gripped Jenn's shoulder, my red, white and blue-painted nails digging into her flesh. She looked back at me and raised her eyebrows and grinned, then turned back to the sizzling shower scenario. Lacey was pinned in a corner of the tiled soak room, her back to the wall, drowning her sorrows in her partner's mouth. She had one hand on Preeya's head, gripping the girl's stringy black hair, while her other hand was on her left boob, squeezing it, fingering her nipple. Preeya had a hold of Lacey's bum and was rocking her head back and forth, lapping at Lacey's pussy.

I blinked my eyes, straining to keep them focused on the girl-girl sex game going on right before us, but the mist from the water and the lust for Jenn's heavy-breathing bod so close to me made it difficult. The hot and humid lez and Jenn-action made my legs noodle and my head spin.

'Looks like they're doubles partners on and off the court,' Jenn whispered.

'Y-yes,' I agreed, watching, wonder-struck, as Lacey gasped and clutched Preeya's hair with both of her hands, her tiny body, her small tits, spasming with what had to be orgasm. Preeya spread her partner's pussy lips and tongued the girl's clit, which set Lacey off wailing with joy, her body shaking with ecstasy. And it finally got me to realising that this was exactly the opening I'd been looking for to put my own do-I-dare game plan for me and Jenn into effect.

I tore my gaze away from the sopping sex match and stared at Jenn, at her sun-burnished neck and shoulders, at the straw-coloured ponytail that dangled down her back. Then I sucked a mouthful of 100 per cent humidity into my lungs and got down and dirty, planting my lips on the back of the babe's neck, my hands on her swelled bottom.

'Hey, whatcha doin'?' Jenn shrieked, twisting her head around.

I answered the startled honey with my warm, wet tongue, running it along her slender neck, all the way up to one of her cute, little ears. I massaged her butt cheeks as I tongued in behind her ear, my bold hands sliding under her panties and going skin-on-skin with her tanlines. I was determined to score with the tantalising tennis tease – like now.

'What's got into you, Linda?' Jenn exclaimed, swivelling around, facing me.

'Just rewarding my partner for a great game,' I murmured, readjusting my hands on the girl's bum, groping it some more. Then I pressed my lips against Jenn's lips, making no bones about the fact that I wanted to take her to the net.

She turned her head away, but I chased her with my mouth. I kissed her lips, her cheeks, her neck, always working her bottom with my hands, my overheated body pushing urgently against hers, my boobs smothering her boobs.

'I – I don't know ...' she began to protest, her voice trailing off when I went for the throat, bit into her neck. She moaned softly, and I knew then that I had the advantage, had the blonde bombshell exactly where I wanted her.

I mashed my lips against her lips, snaked my tongue into her mouth and swirled it around, still feeling up her rump. Jenn responded with her tongue, entwining it around mine, speaking to me of love and lust without saying a word. She wrapped her arms around my body and hugged me close, our slimy tongues flailing away, the two of us frenching with utter abandon.

I caught Jenn's tongue between my teeth and began sucking on it, moving my head back and forth, the girl's anxious moans filling my mouth, firing my body. I pulled my hands off her bottom and brought them up to her shoulders, hooking my fingers into the floss-thin straps of her top then yanking them down. Her soaked garment fell away, exposing her bare breasts.

'Suck my tits,' Jenn urged, retracting her tongue from my mouth.

I stared into her eyes. She looked both scared and

excited, eyes wide, mouth open. I gripped her small mounds and squeezed them. She closed her eyes and groaned, lolled her head back against the wall. Her breasts were tanned the same burnt-sugar as the rest of her, except for a pair of white triangles around her nipples, where her bikini top normally covered her up. Her nipples were obscenely pink against that white and brown background, and they flared long and hard between my fingers.

'Yeah,' Jenn breathed, her fingernails biting into my shoulders, her blonde head twisting against the wall.

I rolled her engorged nipples, then bent my head down and licked at them, teasing first one and then the other with the tip of my tongue. I lapped at the under-side of her blossomed buds, wet-stroking them even longer still, before swirling my tongue all around and over them. Then I inhaled one of her breasts and tugged on it, revelling in the taste of her hot sweet flesh, her jutting, rubbery nipple. I sucked hard on her tit, scouring her nipple with my tongue.

'Oh, God, yeah,' Jenn cried.

I disgorged her damp boob and sucked on her other tit, then pushed the two of them together and lashed at both of her nipples at once, over and over, whipping my head from side-to-side, exhilarating in the ecstatic reac-tion I was eliciting from my tenny girl. Until finally, with Jenn's spit-slick tits still cradled in my hands, I stole a glance around the wall at the two lovers who had provided me with the spontaneous combustion with which to ignite Jenn's passion and satisfy mine. Preeya was now the one on her feet, her back to the wall, Lacey on her knees, slurping at her girlfriend's pussy.

It looked like the two girls would be tied up for some time, so I unhanded Jenn's boobs, broke out of her grasp and took her hand and led her back into the locker room. When we were safely sheltered by the banks of metal storage compartments, I spread a towel out on the double-bench that bisected two rows of lockers, and told Jenn to lie down.

She complied, and I quickly straddled the bench and went to work on the babe's hot-caramel legs. I untied and jerked off her shoes, tugged off her socks. Then I scooped up a bottle of water and squirted the girl's dancing feet with the cool liquid, bathing the both of them in turn.

'Mmmm,' Jenn groaned, hands fondling her tits, fingers primping her nipples. She probably wasn't really sure what I was up to, but I was sure – darn sure.

I carefully lifted her naked right foot and felt its delicately arched beauty, then tilted it back and tongued its shapely bottom from heel to toes. Jenn shuddered and bit her lip and stared up at me, at her precious bronze ped in my covetous hands, my tongue stroking her bared sole.

I lapped and lapped at the sensitive underside of Jenn's foot, before gathering up her other ped and doing the same to its bottom, painting the soles of her feet with my tongue. Then I pushed her feet together, side by side, and opened my mouth up wide and swallowed all ten of her wiggling toes, began sucking on them, my mouth stretching to accommodate all of the girl's delightful piggies.

'Suck my toes, you kinky bitch,' Jenn hissed.

I tugged on all of her foot-digits for a good long while, then popped them, dripping wet, out of my mouth and latched my lips on to her twin big toes, sucked on them for a time. I slithered my tongue in between her toes, one by one, and Jenn writhed around on the wooden bench, tearing off her skirt and diving a hand down into her panties. She frantically rubbed her pussy and felt up her tits, as I tongue-lashed her toes.

But I didn't want the leggy peach-bottomed babe coming on her own terms, so I soon placed her feet back down on the bench and got her to scramble up on to her knees, so that her bum was facing me, her legs bent into the proper worshipping position. God, what a sight. I stared at the doggy-positioned hottie, at her bubble butt, her lush legs, her dainty feet. Then I crouched down over her legs and traced my fingernails over their luxurious length, over her golden haunches. I grabbed Jenn's panties and ripped them apart, flung them aside, baring the girl's pussy and ass.

I smacked her bottom, one cheek at a time, watching them ripple and blush, drinking in Jenn's gasps and groans. Then I covered their smooth, heated surfaces with my hands and caressed those glorious globes, groping them thoroughly, before hosing them down with some soothing water. I spread her butt cheeks and dipped my tongue into her hole, tickling her pucker.

'Yeah, lick me, you dirty slut,' Jenn hollered, head buried in her folded arms, bum and legs trembling.

I pulled the girl's ass apart and probed deep into her opening. Then I bent my head down lower and licked her pussy, tonguing her repeatedly. She was as wet as shower babes Lacey and Preeya and, after only a couple of frenzied minutes of lapping the tennis babe from clitty to bumhole, her body was quivering out of control.

'God almighty,' she wailed, orgasm shocking her from tip to toe. She came in a heated gush as I relentlessly licked at her pussy, almost drowning me in her tangy juices. Then she collapsed flat on to the bench, slowly and exhaustedly rolled over, and said, 'Guess the ball's in my court now, huh?'

I nodded eagerly, stood up and stripped off my skirt and panties. I restraddled the bench and positioned my sopping sex directly above Jenn's mouth, my legs on either side of her head. She quickly grabbed on to my bum and pulled my pussy down to her mouth, stuck out her tongue and started licking.

'That's the way,' I moaned, pulling off my top and popping open my bra. I cupped my boobs and played with them like I'd played with Jenn's boobs, a heavy heat washing through me as my golden girl lapped at my puss.

She pulled my pussy lips apart and formed her tongue into a hardened spear and drove it into my sex, again and again and again.

'Yes,' I shrieked, mashing my tits together and wildly fingering my nipples, my legs shaking and my pussy smouldering.

Jenn dug her tongue deep inside me and flailed it around, and then began lapping at my pussy again, her velvet sandpaper tongue stroking me, stoking me, to a fever pitch. And when the erotic angel sought out my clitty with her devilish tongue, tickled and teased it, I caught fire.

'I'm coming,' I screamed, white-hot orgasm blazing up from my tingling button and engulfing me. The room spun and my body burnt as I jetted juice into Jenn's mouth, all over her face.

'Wayta score, Jenny-girl,' someone shouted from somewhere.

I swivelled my dizzy head around, my body still flaring with ecstasy. Lacey and Preeya were standing in the opening between the two rows of lockers, hand in hand and naked as you please, watching Jenn bring me off.

Lacey padded closer, then bent down and kissed Jenn's come-smeared lips. 'Glad to see your game plan worked out,' she said.

'Yeah. Thanks for all your guys' help,' Jenn replied, from between my legs.

And as my foggy brain struggled to comprehend it all, Jenn took another swipe at my pussy with her tongue, then smiled a sticky, satisfied smile up at me.

Geek God Violet Parker

One of the good things about where I work, in fact the only good thing about where I work, is the fact we still have a proper tea break. At 4 p.m., everyone who fancies it wanders over to the staffroom and has a cup of tea (and maybe even cake, if it's someone's birthday). Some days, someone brings some entertainment, usually a stupid email to read out, or a saucy quiz, or something like that.

Today we have the best of both worlds: an email quiz.

'It's called the geek test, OK.' That's Mary talking. Mary is one of those people who like to be centre of attention. That's Mary's thing. I expect that's why Mary is always bringing stuff like this along to tea break. 'It's kind of like the purity test, you know that thing that tells you how much of a slag you are, but this one sees if you are a geek or not.'

In the corner, Chris, the fat IT guy laughs – half to himself – and then says, 'I bet I do pretty well.'

And then everyone laughs, because Chris is funny like that, and always sending up his blatant geekitude. That's Chris's thing.

Anyway, Mary starts reading out the questions on the geek test, and we all laugh and raise our hands if we are guilty of the various crimes of geekhood. No one actually keeps score, but it's clear that Chris is raising his hand on everything, from 'Have you ever been to a *Star Trek* convention?' to 'Can you program in machine code?'

The test is quite long and, by the time Mary's on to the last page, there aren't that many of us left in the staffroom; just me and Chris and Mary, and also Caroline – my opposite in the Press Office – who has been smirking knowingly to herself for the entire test.

The last page is all about role-playing games. 'You know, like Dungeons and Dragons,' Mary says, which makes Chris snort in loud derision.

It soon becomes clear that Chris is, again, going to be the victor here. I sit behind my teacup with an amused grin on my face as Chris cheerily admits to 'Have you ever painted miniatures?' and 'Have you ever spent more than six hours in a gaming shop?' And we all laugh at that last confession.

Then Mary says, 'OK, nearly on to the last few here. Have you ever Larped?' Mary frowns. 'Larped?'

'Live Action Role Play,' Chris offers. 'It's like, ahem, Dungeons and Dragons, but you run about outside and act it out for real.'

'Gosh,' says Mary, 'well that's a new one on me.'

Chris raises his hand and smirks. 'Guilty.'

And that's when we all notice that Caroline has her hand up in the air too. And that's when we all suddenly stop being interested in the geek test and start being interested in Caroline's murky past, because Caroline is one of those people who you can depend on for a really good murky-past story. That's Caroline's thing.

But Caroline is having none of our clamouring questioning about how a nice girl like her ended up doing a geeky thing like Live Action Role Play, because 'It's a long story,' and 'Tea break was over a quarter of an hour ago.' But we've got to know, and so Caroline suggests we meet in the pub over the road at 5.30.

Chris gets the first round in, making us swear that we won't bully Caroline into starting the story before he gets back. So we manage to contain ourselves, but the very second the drinks clink down on our sticky table, we make her begin.

She grins a saucy grin for a moment before she opens her mouth.

'Charlie Baker was fucking gorgeous. He had the body of an athlete, the face of a model and, as I was to discover, the brain of a geek,' she says, clearly relishing the looks of absolute concentration on our faces.

Caroline takes a sip of her drink and goes on. 'OK, so this was ten years ago, when I was at university in Sheffield. Charlie turned up in my psychology lectures in the second year. I knew he wasn't a psychology student so I asked around, and it turned out he was a computer science student and was sitting in on the lectures because he was into some kind of artificial intelligence stuff, or something dull like that. And that single boring fact seemed to be all anyone knew about him. Well, that and the fact that he had a smile that could melt knickers at twenty paces – not that he appeared to use it much.

'He always sat near the door for lectures and dashed straight off when they were done. I tried time and time again to sit next to him and get him in conversation, but he was having none of it. Always had to get back to the computer lab. Always so busy.

'He was like an iceberg. Not the nine-tenths under water thing, just, you know, the made of ice thing. And I'd basically all but resigned myself to admiring him from afar, when I suddenly got a lucky break.

'I was in the dark basement corridor of the student's union – a poky little rabbit warren, where all the clubs and societies have their little rooms – and I saw Charlie. He was right there – walking along the corridor in front of me. So I followed him, of course, straight down the rabbit hole. Or at least down the corridor, and I saw him disappear into a room, the door of which proclaimed it was the home of the "Gaming Soc".

'Now, I didn't quite have the guts to just follow him straight into the room. But luckily the student launderette was just across the hall. So I nipped in there instead, and staked it out.

'Well, I was waiting there, among the whirring and the sudsy smells, for bloody ages. It started to get late. I started to get hungry. It began to look as if Charlie had escaped once again. But then the door of the Gaming Soc room opened.

'But it wasn't Charlie who came out of the room. It was Tom.

'Now, I knew Tom – the year before he had been in the same corridor as me in halls. He was an über-geek, little and nerdy with big thick spectacles and a strange twitchy manner. Basically, he was creepy, and I'd normally avoid the likes of him, perhaps even denying all knowledge of our previous connection. But at that moment I loved that connection with all my heart, because a connection to Tom – it seemed – was a connection to Charlie.

'So, I feigned coming out of the launderette, acted all long-time-no-see and the next thing you know I was walking down one of the many hills of Sheffield with him, towards the area where he lived, and I was pretending I was heading there too. And, with very little prompting, Tom explained all about the various delights of the Gaming Soc. They were into role-playing games, i.e. Dungeons and Dragons sort of things, and these games could go on for hours and hours. That's why Charlie had been in that room so long. Because Charlie, as Tom explained, was a huge fan of all things role play.'

Caroline picks up her smeary glass. 'Course,' she says, 'this put me off him a bit. He might have been God's gift, but he was also a total geek.'

She sits back at this point and takes a little sip of her

vodka tonic, but clearly not wanting to pause for too long in case she loses the floor.

'Hey,' says Chris, grabbing his chance, 'this is such a sweet story: what will win out? Caroline's prejudice or Caroline's lust? It's like Shakespeare.'

Caroline sighs. 'OK, well, truth is, it didn't put me off him that much, not really. I was just, well, just saying … he *was* a geek, but he was also just far too sexy a geek to be ignored. I wanted Charlie. And the only way to get to Charlie was clearly through this role-play stuff. He didn't seem to be interested in anything else. But how to find out about role play? There was no internet back then in 1994. OK, there probably was, but I didn't know how to use it.

'I only had one source of information: Tom.

'Two days later I was grabbing lunch in the dingy union bar and there he was, my source of information, perched over a burger and chips. I wove my way through the studyers and the skivers and plonked my tray down on his table, sliding on to a stool and grabbing hold of the conversation straight away by demanding to know more about the world of role play.

'I have to say that most of what he told me went in one ear and out the other – loads of stuff about orcs and dice and goblins. But then he started talking about this thing called live combat, or Live Action Role Play, and my ears pricked up then, because I saw the possibilities straight away.

'"So you go away for four days?" I said, trying to sound as calm as possible. "Like on a mini holiday?"

'"Yeah. In fact we're going to Wales over the Easter vacation. I can't wait." Tom paused to pop a chip into his mouth.

'The very idea of Wales in April filled me with a soggy dread, but, well, Charlie! So I pushed on. "So, er, do you let beginners come along on these things?"

'Tom frowned at me as if he didn't exactly understand the question. Then he screwed up his face so he looked even more weasel-like than ever and said, "What? Do you want to come?"

'I nodded.

'And then he kind of blushed, but he looked really happy. "Wow," he said, "that's excellent. We always need more girls. You would make an excellent she-orc."

'My heart sank a bit at this; somehow, I didn't think seducing Charlie would be made any easier if I were dressed as a she-orc. "Do I have to be a she-orc? Couldn't I be an elvin maiden or something?"

'"Well, not really: this is kind of a battle – orcs versus barbarians. So you'd have to be an orc or a barbarian and there aren't really any female barbarians, so –"

'"I see," I interrupted, and then added casually, "is Charlie being an orc?" I said this while fiddling with my fork so it looked as if I didn't really care one way or the other.

'"Nah, Charlie'll be a barbarian. Charlie's always a barbarian. Got the build, see." Then Tom grinned knowingly at me. "I'm an orc though," he said with a certain relish. And then, I can't be sure – not sure-sure – but I think he winked at me.

'So that was that, it was all set. I told my housemates I wasn't coming on the planned holiday to the Lakes over Easter, because I had made plans for a little holiday of my own. And when I told them about it they tried, only half jokingly, to get me to go to casualty and get my brain checked out.

'And they might well have had a point because three weeks later I was in the back of a mini-bus rubbing damp thighs with the University of Sheffield's most spoddy ultra-geeks, and I wasn't even sitting next to Charlie.

'Not only that, I didn't even get to spend the four-hour-long journey to Wales staring at Charlie, who was looking particularly dreamy in tight jeans and a sort of furry gillet thingy over his cheesecloth shirt. I didn't get to gaze lovingly at Charlie because Tom decided I needed pointers and started giving me an impromptu tutorial on how to wield a sword in an orcish sort of a way.

'Something that included grunting, grunting in front of Charlie, which – however much he might be ignoring me – was so not fun.

'Somehow, though, I managed to grunt and snuffle my way through miles of drizzley motorway and into the heart of such breathtaking, crackly-fern-covered Welsh scenery. Brownish-grey hills rose up to meet greyish-brown sky in a way that was both beautiful and slightly depressing. I leant against the mini-bus to drink it in, inevitably picturing Charlie striding windswept across it like a lone stag. But I didn't get to enjoy this image for long, because I was quickly dragged off by Tom to help pitch the bloody orc tents.

'Standing in the rain, smashing tent pegs into boggy soil with a mallet, I was suddenly faced with the water-logged reality of life under canvas in Wales at this time of year. I found myself fantasising about all the drinking and partying and cosy log fires in the Lake District cottage that I had sacrificed for this weirdness. In all honesty it was probably raining there too, but at least they had some bricks and mortar between them and the elements.

'Bloody Charlie, he'd better be worth it. And my plan (oh yes, I had a plan) had better work.

'Although gorgeous barbarian Charlie was on the other side – he was the enemy, as it were – that could actually prove to be to my advantage. My oh-so-clever-idea was that once battle began and the fake swords started to clash, I would engineer getting myself taken prisoner by Charlie, who would then, no doubt, take me back to his tent and ravage me in a barbarian manner, as the game demanded. See, I'd figured out that the best way to get some Charlie-shaped action was to make the action itself part of his passion, make it part of a role play.

'By the time I was standing, shivering, in a line of orcs, clutching my padded fibreglass sword, I could think of nothing but the fantastic Charlie-ravaging that awaited me (despite the fact that I had been rather unsubtly made up as an orc, with disgusting green grease paint). I could see my beautiful quarry in the opposing line, across the scratchy grass. It had finally stopped raining, but the sky was still a heavy grey, and he shone against it like a blond beacon. He was so beautiful, dominating the majestic landscape with a majesty all of his own, with his tousled blond hair whipping about in the squally wind. The furry thing and cheesecloth shirt he had been wearing earlier remained, but the tight jeans had been replaced by even tighter brown leather trousers – it was almost as if he were deliberately trying to get me excited.

'With a sudden urgency, a whistle blew and then all hell broke loose as the two opposing sides hurtled towards each other, roaring. I crouched low in the long scratchy grass and darted around in the crowd.

'Avoiding the swords and pikes and clubs actually turned out to be quite exhilarating. I rolled and dived around, my tactic of keeping close to the ground working very well. And as soon as I got within striking distance of my quarry, my delicious barbarian prince, I feigned a tumble and rolled around in the mud yelping.

'But Charlie didn't even seem to notice.

'And then someone – someone else – grabbed me by the arm and bundled me up and over his shoulder.

'After some very uncomfortable travelling upside down across the grassland, I was dumped in a heap on the ground, behind enemy lines in the barbarian's encampment. Slightly stunned, I looked up into the face of my captor. He was a cute little thing. I was seriously surprised he had managed to run cross-country with the not insubstantial moi over his shoulder. He had rather floppy brown hair drifting into his eyes and, of course, he was wearing the standard barbarian uniform of leather and fur and bare biteable skin.

'"Hi," I said.

'"Don't talk," he hissed back, "you're meant to be a prisoner. I never got a prisoner before."

'"OK." And I know it sounds strange but just for a few tiny moments I must have forgotten all about wanting to be captured by Charlie, because I said, "Are you going to ravage me?"

'He laughed. "Doubt it. I probably have to give you to my commander."

'"Who's your commander?"

'"Charlie Baker."

'"Oh." Bingo!

'The downside of this great news was that I had to spend the next few hours in the prisoner-holding bay – which was actually just a large tent – until Charlie returned from the battlefield. I found myself a cosy spot near one of the paraffin heaters and settled in for the duration.

'In one corner, a large gang of the prisoners had begun playing a separate game-within-a-game, setting up an elaborate and entirely different role play on the table, battling with tiny figurines.

'I sulked in my cosy corner, excited, yet bored.

'It began to rain again, storm clouds ushering in the evening before it was really due. I didn't know the exact time because watches were a big old anachronism and hence banned but, shortly after the heavens reopened, a worrying rumour started to go around the tent. It seemed several high-powered barbarians had been captured by the orcs and a Berlin Wall-style prisoner exchange was going to take place – which meant all ravaging was off!

'Obviously, my heart sank. The last thing I wanted was to be traded back to the ruddy orcs and end up having to get captured all over again. When I heard that one of the high-up types captured was Charlie himself, my heart sank even lower.

'Now I really couldn't win. I was trapped on the barbarian side, Charlie was trapped with the orcs! I kicked an anachronistic lemonade can on the muddy tent floor.

'But, despite my despairing mood, the prisoner exchange itself turned out to be quite exhilarating, despite the rain slithering down the back of my neck. We were all comically roped together and herded into a small woody clearing in the fast-fading light. Various negotiations took place in orc-grunts and barbarian-grunts, while I scanned the other set of prisoners until I saw a distinctive mass of blond hair and furry waistcoat. So near, and yet so far. Dammit, I didn't even get to be on home turf while he was our prisoner.

'Making my way back into base camp, I found Tom was at my elbow, proffering a rather out of character orange cagoule. "Hi, Caroline, are you OK?"

'"Yeah, yeah," I said, grabbing his offering and pulling it over my orc clothes without breaking stride.

'"I'm sorry you got captured." He shrugged. "I meant to keep an eye out for you. Still, I got you back, didn't I?"

'By the time Tom was saying this we were already outside his tent. It was only then that I noticed that his tent was ever so slightly bigger than the others. I began to wonder about something. "Tom," I said slowly, "are you, like, in charge of the orcs?"

'"Um, not exactly," Tom said, looking slightly pleased

I had asked. "I'm one of five commanders. But the prisoner exchange trick was all my idea."

'"Oh," I said, "thanks." And then I thought for a moment and said, "What do you mean by trick?"

'Tom smiled. "Oh yeah, you wouldn't know. Well, we didn't want to hand over Charlie did we? After all, he's one of their commanders. It's like, you know, having taken their queen in chess or something. So we pulled a little trick, got one of our tallest barbarian prisoners to dress up in Charlie's clothes, tied him up and gagged him and in all the scuffle it –'

'"Oh my God," I interrupted.

'"I know," said Tom, clearly swelling with the pride at the thought of his excellent plan. "It shouldn't have worked really, but it did!"

'I brushed his boasting aside. "Yeah, yeah, never mind that now. Are you trying to tell me that Charlie is still here?"

'"Yeah."

'"And he's our prisoner?"

'"Yeah."

'"And he's naked?"

'Tom looked at me, very puzzled. "Well no, of course not. He has his underwear on." He cocked his head to one side. "Caroline? Caroline, are you OK?"

'"I'm just fine, Tom," I said, in a very odd-sounding voice. "Very fine indeed."

'Night had properly fallen now. The boggy campsite that I was currently calling home looked different in the dark. It twinkled prettily in torchlight, like a squelchy fairy land.

'"Er, Tom," I said as we headed across camp to the big sort of main tent right in the middle – apparently there was going to be some kind of feast and celebration of today's minor victory. "Do you need anyone to guard Charlie?"

'"Guard Charlie? Nah, I got someone on it. Anyway, you've got to come to the feast – you're a part of it, after all."

'I cursed under my breath, but followed Tom into the tent.

'But after just half an hour – and that was all I could take of ale swigging and weird singing – I slipped out, determined to find out where Charlie was. Most of the camp was in darkness now, but I could see torchlight coming from the front of one of the tents. Hunching myself up against the drizzle (having lost my precious cagoule at some point during the feast), I headed in that direction.

'As I approached, I saw that there was a young-looking guy sitting outside it, sheltered by a small awning. Even by torchlight I could tell he had really terrible skin, which probably wasn't being helped by the caked layer of green orc make-up he was wearing. "Hi," I said breezily, "not going to the feast?"

'"Nah," bad-skin replied grumpily, "got this bloody job, didn't I?"

'"Oh, well, you know, I don't really go in for feasts all that much. I'd be happy to stand in for you for half an hour," I said, with all the breeziness I could conjure up under the circumstances.

'Bad-skin looked sceptical. "I dunno," he said. "If anything happens to him I'll be in dreadful trouble. He's a big prize. A commander, you know. Tom said not to leave my post for anything. Look." And by way of a horrible demonstration he produced from the shadows a plastic bottle that clearly contained urine.

'"Ew." I said, then shrugged. "Well, it's up to you, but if you let me take over, I promise I'll keep a very close eye on him."

'Bad-skin put down his bottle and fixed me with a

glare, but I could tell he was wavering – how could he resist the ale and singing?

'"Well, OK then," he said eventually, "just for half an hour, but don't leave your post, whatever happens. And don't go in there either; apparently he has ways of talking to you to try to get you to let him go."

'And a few minutes later, once bad-skin had disappeared into the feast tent and I had gingerly kicked the horrific bottle into the dark grass, I was standing by the tent's entrance, heart banging with excitement.

'Charlie. Could I even go in?

'Could I not?

'I pushed one of the flaps aside with a fingertip and peeped inside. One of those camping gas lights sat on the floor, emitting a strange whitewashy light, and I could just about make out Charlie.

'He was sitting on the edge of a little camp bed, his big bare shoulders shiny in the odd light. A blanket was draped over his lap and he was holding his arms awkwardly behind his back. I had to look carefully before I realised, with a surge of lust, that his arms were actually tied behind him.

'He looked up. He looked right at me. Well, at the little sliver of me that must have been visible through the tent flaps, and he said, "Hello, Caroline." And I was totally shocked that he knew my name.

'"Hi," I said, stepping through the tent entrance. The rain seemed to get harder as I did so, drumming urgently on the canvas above me. Not that things like that were really making much impression on me at that moment. My world was so full of Charlie.

'He looked so sexy, sitting there in the half dark, all semi-naked and tied up, that it didn't twig for a moment or two, but then the penny dropped: the odd contrast between Charlie's experience of captivity and my own.

'"How come you're tied up?" I said. "I thought that if you got captured you got to come out of role and just hang out backstage?"

'Charlie snorted. "Because, Caroline, that bastard Tom knows full well that if I wasn't tied up I'd walk straight out of here and up to the game moderators and demand an enquiry into that tricky little fake exchange deal he pulled. It's totally against protocol and he knows it. What's more, tying people up without supervision is pretty dodgy behaviour too. He's going to be in serious trouble the minute I'm out of here. That's why."

'"Oh," I said, "so he's broken the rules?"

'"Yeah," said Charlie, as if I was an idiot. "I'd be surprised if he's allowed to play live combat anywhere in the country when this gets out."

'"Seriously?" That really surprised me. "Well then, why has he done it?"

'"Because, Caroline," Charlie said, very slowly, "he couldn't get his other commanders to agree to a straight swap of me for you. Obviously I'm worth a good deal more than you are, tactically –" he paused dramatically, "– but not to Tom, it would seem."

'I took a few minutes for this to sink in. I couldn't think of anything to say, so I said, "Oh God."

'Charlie shrugged his shoulders. "He does this every so often. Gets a girl he fancies, talks her into playing, gets her done up as a she-orc . . ." He tailed off into a sigh and then said, "Some of us are more interested in the actual game."

'I looked at the ground for a minute. "So your being here, like this, it's kind of all my fault then."

'"Well, kind of I suppose," said Charlie. "But you can easily make it right. How about you untie me and we both head off to the moderators' camp and sort this mess out."

'And I suppose that would have been the right thing

to do, but he looked so sexy all tied up and bristling with his righteous anger. How could I just let him go?

'I moved closer to him, across the tent. "I'll let you go, Charlie, if you do something for me first."

'Charlie looked up at me; I was standing over him at this point and I inched forward, straddling his bare legs.

'He wetted his lips. "What do you want me to do?"

'I didn't answer. There was no need. I bent down and I kissed him. And then I could hear the rain on the roof again, even over the roar of my blood pounding in my ears.

'For a little while he didn't kiss back. He held his mouth still, lips pressed firmly together. I found his reticence strangely arousing, and kept right on working on his mouth, easing and teasing until his lips parted, just a little and his head moved forward a tiny fraction. And he finally gave in and let me kiss him.

'I kissed him for quite a long time, making myself repeat over and over in my head: This is Charlie Baker! You are kissing Charlie Baker! Until I was so wound up and excited I couldn't wait any longer to see his cock.

'I began to work my way downwards. I kissed my way across his throat and down his bare chest. I slipped my hands under the blanket on his lap and found a pair of underpants, barely containing a very hard, very ready cock.

'Charlie inhaled. "Caroline," he said, "I'm not sure if this is a good idea ..."

'But it was too late. I had just slid his underpants down far enough to liberate his erection. I clapped my right hand over his mouth and smiled up at him. "Now, Charlie, I really don't think that's the kind of thing a barbarian would say."

'And I dipped my head and slid my mouth over his smooth, smooth cock.

'He was hot there. Every other part of his body had

been cool, chilled by the cold night air and his lack of clothing. But his cock was hot, so hot that I felt like the contrast was enough to sear my mouth as I sucked. He was delicious.

'When I looked up at him, I saw he had closed his eyes and tipped back his head, with my right hand still clamped over his mouth. His cheeks were gently flushed and his longish hair was drooping across his beautifully sculpted face. I pushed my left hand down between my legs. I wasn't surprised to find that I was very wet.

'Now, although sucking Charlie's cock was all very well – in fact it was a dream come true – I wanted more. I slid my mouth free.

'Charlie's eyes popped open, questioning. I smiled and finally took my hand away from his mouth, looping my arm around his neck instead and pulling him off the camp bed and down on to the groundsheet with me.

'Somehow I managed to get my muddy trousers and knickers off, squirming around Charlie as he knelt on the floor next to me. He looked at my crotch, which was glistening in the pale light. He didn't say anything.

'"I know you want to come, Charlie," I hissed softly, "but I think you should be a proper barbarian gentleman about it and sort me out first." And I stared meaningfully at his beautiful face, before flicking my gaze down.

'Charlie still didn't say anything, but he jerked at his bound wrists. He wanted to be untied first.

'I almost laughed out loud. "Oh no. Not yet, remember? I'm not stupid."

'And with a sigh that I'm sure turned into a smirk, Charlie dipped his head and buried his face between my legs. His tongue touched me almost at once, and I realised how close I was already. I gazed down at him, crouching on the ground with his bound hands poking up in the air, and I found I was bucking up into his mouth. I didn't want a slow build up or anything like that. I'd had enough build up – months of it, in fact! I just wanted Charlie's tongue against my clit right now, over and over until I was coming in his mouth. And in less time than it took to think it, that was what was happening. I clapped my hand over my own mouth then, muffling my cries as I saw tight little blue stars behind my eyes.

'And I didn't forget that I had promised Charlie an orgasm too. In fact, I pulled myself together as quickly as I could, remembering, as my own orgasm faded, that bad-skin had only reckoned on being gone for half an hour. Time was running short.

'I scrambled up into a sitting position and pushed Charlie down on to his back. His cock was harder than ever now, jutting out of his underpants and cherry red. I fell on it, sucking hard, and I couldn't resist working my own clit at the same time, bringing myself back to the peak in a few quick strokes. Charlie jerked hard and desperate as he came, thrusting himself deeper into my mouth, over and over, and his delicious orgasm was enough to make my clit start to spasm all over again – if anything harder and longer than before.

'Not long afterwards, Charlie and I sneaked carefully out of the tent. We raced across the sodden grass and into the woods, where I could see the lights of the barbarian camp not far away.

' "Where's the moderators' camp?" I asked in a whisper. "Aren't they somewhere in the middle?"

' "It's not far."

'We dashed on a little further and then something occurred to me. "Charlie," I hissed.

' "What?"

' "Well, you know that swap thing that Tom pulled? You said it was against protocol or something."

' "Yeah, that's right."

' "Well, surely your team would have reported it to the

moderators by now. I mean, they would have noticed pretty quickly that it wasn't you that was handed over."

'Before I'd even finished speaking, Charlie's hand suddenly appeared out of the darkness and grabbed one of my wrists. I tried to jerk it away, but he was far too strong and in a split-second he had tight hold of my other wrist too. Suddenly I was Charlie's prisoner.

'"Oh, Caroline, I'm so sorry," he said in a low voice, "I can't quite believe you fell for that."

'And, ignoring my screams of protest, Charlie whisked me up in the air and flung me over his shoulder. Just moments later I found myself on the damp ground, bathed in the flickering light from the barbarian's camp fire, as all around me Charlie's stunning escape was celebrated with manic whoops and cheers.'

Caroline stops talking. Last orders has come and gone and drinking up is now being urged. Our table is so covered in empty glasses now that there is scarcely room for us to rest our elbows as we all stare at her in awe.

Finally Chris says, 'God, Caroline. That Charlie was a bastard.'

'Not really,' says Caroline, finishing her last vodka tonic, 'he was just bloody good at playing the game.'

'Fuck,' says Mary, who is probably the drunkest of any of us, 'I can't believe you told us all that.'

Caroline laughs. 'Blame that last double you bought me. I was planning to gloss over the explicit stuff a bit more than that, but, well.' And she shrugs as we all stand up and sway our way into our coats.

As we totter out into the night I say, 'So what happened after that, After you were captured again?'

'Oh,' says Caroline, and then smiles a sort of secrety smile, 'I was finally Charlie's prisoner. There were no more exchanges after that.' And she turns and hails a cab, which chugs to a halt at the kerb.

'Was Tom pissed off?'

'Kind of,' she says as she climbs into the warmth, 'but it was only a role play.'

When I get home that night, my husband is sitting at the dining table, painting little miniature goblins with a tiny, tiny brush.

When he hears the door he looks up. 'Hi,' he says, 'good evening?'

'Interesting,' I say, as I slip into the seat opposite him and glance at the fantastical army spread across the table top.

'Good,' he says, going back to his painting.

I purse my lips and watch him for a minute. Then I say, 'Charlie, you went to Sheffield University, right? Ever meet a girl called Caroline?'

The Substitute
Francesca Brouillard

Thursday was leching day, or at least that's what Angie called it. Not that those sweaty five-a-siders with their stodgy legs and bulldog backsides did anything for me, but I'd sit with her anyway and eat my tuna mayo roll and crisps. Most days I'd have lunch on my own while Angie took care of reception and bookings but on Thursdays Karl, the manager, would 'service the public', as we called it. That was when the under-twenty-fives' netball matches took place. Leery old git.

I quite enjoyed my little lunchtime routine, up there in the spectator's gallery, gawping at the punters and listening to the hum of the junk food machines. On Mondays and Wednesdays there was badminton for the oldies. A right gas they were, tottering about the court in their tracky bottoms and Fred Perry shirts. They were all right, though; you could have a bit of a laugh and a joke with them. They didn't take their racquet sports as seriously as the suits. Stuck-up arseholes, they were.

Tuesday was when the lads from the local school came in to practise basketball, all lanky limbs and size fifteen feet. You could whiff those adolescent armpits from where I was sat but, fair dos, I had to admit they were neat to watch. Friday was young mums and tots and, as Ange used to say, they were the best warning against unprotected sex!

So I'd watch the punters while I had my roll, then I would sneak into the disabled toilet to have a wank before starting work again. I used the disabled toilet because it was down the far end of the corridor and more private than the others. You don't exactly want to get caught banging away against the partitions when you're staff. Anyway, those stupid cubicles were too small; you'd be catching your knees on the bog seat and knocking over the sanitary unit.

But the disabled loo was perfect; silenced by floor to ceiling walls, loads of room and a low mirror so you could watch yourself if you wanted – which I usually did. I'd hitch up my T-shirt and pull my boobs out and then watch my nipples harden while I indulged myself.

Actually, I've always quite fancied having my nips pierced but I'm too scared. A couple of gold rings or some of those bar things would look mint. I reckon I'm the sort of person nipple piercings were invented for.

I never washed my hands afterwards. Never. That's how I got my kicks in the afternoon, handing back change and plastic cards with my Marmite-y female smell on them. In all those pockets and wallets and handbags lurked the aromatic traces of my lunchbreak wank – my musky scent infiltrating offices and homes and cars and shops.

I'd daydream sometimes about being tracked down by someone who'd got turned on by the smell and recognised it. I could picture them sniffing their leisure passes as they took their wallets out, frowning, sniffing it again. Between their legs the blood would be rising. They'd turn the card over and sniff again, trying to remember when they'd last used it. There'd be a hardening in the groin as they held it to their noses and breathed in the subtle perfume of concentrated sex juice.

Then, cocks pointing the way, they'd hot-foot it back to the Sports Centre, lust mounting as they picked up the pheromone trail ... through the sliding doors, over to the reception desk where the scent was now hot and intense. Cocks would be straining at belts and zips; faces would be red with lust.

I'd smile my professional customer service smile and ask, 'What can I do for you?' or 'Can I be of any assistance, sir?' and they'd groan, inarticulate with desire, and reach over the counter to drag me out.

I'd got various scenarios worked out after that: the ravishing over the manager's desk using his mobile as a dildo; the shagging in the showers all slicked up with oil, and the full service from the entire hockey team making use of all orifices. Just depended how I was feeling, really.

I didn't usually do the late shift but Angie generally takes off to Tenerife with her old man in February and Karl always pulls rank when it looks like his drinking time might be jeopardised, so I didn't have much choice.

On Fridays last admission was normally 9.00p.m., so it was pretty dead after that. By 9.15 I'd done the till and checked Saturday's bookings, so I decided to while away the remaining time browsing through one of my dirty books. There was nothing else to do till the punters had finished in the changing rooms, anyway. I wasn't going to be some corporate jobsworth and come up with new brand initiatives or whatever. Late shift was my time for a bit of a doss.

I soon got on to one of my favourite stories about this couple who have met on the internet and decide to get it together in a hotel. There's a bit of build-up where he chooses which sexy underwear she puts on and then he ends up giving her one with some kind of truncheon thing 'cos she's begging for it and he turns out to be a copper.

Predictably it got me so slicked up that I had to retire to the disabled toilet to finish the job. I locked the door and shoved my jeans down to my knees, then leant back against the wall in front of the mirror. My pants, skimpy flimsy things, had already disappeared into my bum crease so, when I tugged them at the front, the crotch slipped easily into the damp slit. I watched myself in the mirror, gently pulling the fabric taut then releasing it. Each time I pulled up, my lips, all plump and juicy, closed around the fabric as if they were swallowing it and added to the friction on my clit.

Not so fast, not so fast! I pulled the sides of my pants up over my hips so the crotch cheesewired my muff and kept the pressure on. Then I yanked up my T-shirt and slipped my bra straps off my shoulders to wriggle my tits out. The nipples were soft and dozy like they'd just woken up and wanted to be slipped into some warm wet mouth. I imagined leaking milk out of them in little sweet spurts and having a man suckle on them – or better still, two men, one on each. I squeezed them till they puckered and clenched my thighs together, picturing a two-pronged dildo impaling me. A sizzling wetness flooded between my legs and my backside arched against the cold Formica.

I'd not made a sound, I was sure of it. Long practice had perfected the silent, deep throat orgasm. In the mirror my nipples peeped out from under the T-shirt like a voyeur's eyes; they'd lost that look of innocence. I extricated my pants from where they were buried in my crotch and pushed my fingers deep into the wetness till I could feel the pulsing of my sex. The stickiness coated my fingers conspiratorially and tried to suck them in. I twiddled them round a bit then reluctantly withdrew them and sorted out my clothing.

A quick check in the mirror revealed roughed-up hair, too-bright eyes and a pink patch at my throat. Still, the punters should be long gone. I unlocked the door and stepped out. Leaning against the wall opposite – as if waiting for me to vacate – was a young bloke in overalls.

Oh God, how long had he been there? My hand was still on the door and I was almost tempted to step back in but it would have looked ridiculous. Besides, who the hell was this creep and what was he doing there?

'Did you want something?' My embarrassment was immediately crushed by hostility and I gave him the icy glare I usually reserve for jerks that make menstrual jokes. He didn't reply, just shrugged and looked at me with a half-smile as if he knew exactly what I'd been up to.

'How long have you been stood there?' I demanded, though it was hardly the most pertinent question. It was gone 10.00p.m. and the doors should have been locked.

'Long enough.' He smiled broadly and I noticed he had nice teeth. It wasn't going to save him, though. I was feeling right pissed off.

'Long enough for what exactly?' My hands were on my hips and my chin thrust out. His smug self-assurance was really winding me up. Cocky prick!

He looked me up and down casually then stared me straight in the eye with a sort of lopsided smile.

'Long enough to know what you've been up to.'

He was bluffing. He had to be. He wasn't going to catch me out like that.

'I've just been freshening up actually.' Shit, why did I say that? No need to explain anything to him. Now it looked like a cover-up; like I'd known exactly what he was implying.

He started to laugh, slapping me on the shoulder like we were sharing some great joke.

'Don't you worry, gal, I admire you for it! Half the blokes out there don't know the difference between a clit and a clematis and the rest of them are dickheads. Know what I mean? I'm all for a feisty bird who can take care of herself in that area.'

I wanted to slap him, despite the cheeky smile and

the teasing eyes. I felt like he'd just shoved his hand down my knickers. I scowled and put on my most frosty official tone.

'I don't know what you're doing here but the Centre's closed, so you'd better leave.'

'Oh sorry, gal, I should've mentioned – I'm relieving for Mick. He's gone down with his back again.'

'Mick?'

He looked at me with his head on one side.

'You're not the regular, right? Mick. The cleaner – caretaker, whatever ... I'm covering for him. I'm the substitute.'

I shrugged, my authority dented. 'It's normally Angie on lates. She sees to all that stuff. You know where everything is?' I avoided looking at him.

'Sure.' He smiled again and I could see a glint of white teeth from the corner of my eye. 'I've covered for him when he's gone off before. I know the ropes.'

'I'll be off, then.' I started back to reception stiffly, knowing his eyes would be glued to my backside.

'Hang on, just run the security code by us again. It took me twenty minutes to get it set last night.'

I turned my head. 'Six three four o.'

I'd almost reached my desk when he called out again. 'By the way, if you need freshening up again...'

The blood rushed to my face. I snatched up my bag and stalked out.

He turned up the following evening, just as the last punters were leaving.

'Hi, sex bomb!'

'Fuck off,' I mouthed, screwing up my eyes and giving him my most hateful look. The embarrassment of the previous nights was still raw. He grinned at me over the counter and I noticed he had a roguish air about him, even if he was a bit on the thin side.

'Not forgiven me yet, then?' he asked.

'Piss off.' I didn't need to lower my voice this time.

'Really! I hope that's not how you speak to your customers.'

I turned away and pretended to be sorting out some files.

'I've got you a present.'

I looked up, despite myself. 'What for?' I snarled ungraciously.

'For taking the piss last night. It was cruel, but you gave me such a stuck-up look. Soz.' He put a box of liqueur chocolates on the counter.

'I don't eat chocolates.' I wasn't going to be bought off that easily.

He frowned. 'You drink though?'

I nodded.

'Good. I know what we'll do, then. Just lean over here a minute.'

Puzzled, I leant across the counter and, suddenly, his hand was on the back of my neck and his face was pushed right up to mine. I pulled away but he pressed his mouth against my lips and held me firmly by the neck. I braced my hands against the desk and tried to pull back but he moved with me as though our mouths were stuck together.

The tip of his tongue began to explore my lips, softly but insistently, and his other hand came up to stroke my cheek. A heat no longer due to anger surged up my body and down my legs; I started to open my lips. Then, just as suddenly, he released me.

A lump of disappointment blocked my throat.

'I'm sorry, gal, I just couldn't resist. Since I saw you step out of the bog last night with those fuck-me eyes and up-your-crotch jeans I've not been able to stop thinking about you.'

OK, I know it's not cool, but the fact is I can always be

seduced by a sweet talker. And, for that matter, by sexy strangers who talk dirty to me and touch me up across the desk. And by blokes who say I'm feisty and notice my jeans have ridden up my arse and think it's hot for birds to wank in the toilet.

Angie says I'm straight up too easy. I don't need to be wooed or seduced or admired. I'll fall into bed with virtually anyone who so much as holds the door open for me. So what? I say. Are we girls still expected to be dragged to bed screaming and kicking, even if we fancy the pants off a bloke?

To be honest, though, for all my talk I've not actually been seduced that often. I flirt a lot but somehow it seldom gets much further. Which I suppose is why he didn't exactly have to over-exert himself to get me into the equipment store.

We sat facing each other on the blue judo mats that smell of rubber and cheesy feet. The heating system clicked and purred intermittently.

I watched the sharp edges of his white teeth bite the base off one of the chocolates and crunch it; then he leant forward and slowly poured the liqueur on to my tongue. It trickled into my mouth, filling me with a decadent sweetness. Still leaning towards me, our knees touching, he put the empty chocolate shell on to the tip of my tongue and pushed it on with his lips. The chocolate began to melt as he sucked my tongue into his mouth, mingling intoxicatingly with the liqueur that dripped like desire from our lips.

His hands moved to my shoulders then slid down my breasts, sending hot waves to my pussy. Without taking his mouth from mine he pulled up my T-shirt, undid my bra and pushed his thumbs on to my nipples. I clenched my thighs. Then, in a single fluid movement, he removed my top and pushed me back on the mat. My nipples hardened at the cold shock of the rubber on my flesh but I was too distracted to care about the other sweaty bodies that had rolled and grappled on the mat's unsavoury surface.

He straddled my hips, his jeans rough on my bare skin. Lust seeped through the denim, igniting my groin. Pulling the box of chocolates closer he took two more out and bit the ends off them. Eyes glinting with amusement, he held them above my breasts and tipped out the liqueur. The thin, honey-coloured stream coated my nipples and trickled down the pale curves of my breasts. He slid off me and put the empty shells over my nipples then, biting gently into the chocolate, he began to suck. As the chocolate melted he swirled it with his tongue across my breasts, making little peaks like miniature walnut whips. His tongue teased and tantalised, tormenting me with tiny flicking movements almost too light to feel. I was desperate for his teeth to nip and nibble me; desperate for the pull of his lips that would draw shivers from deep in my belly.

I groaned and he raised his head. He was smeared with chocolate like a badly made-up clown. I started giggling. He wiped his palm down his face and grinned, then stood and pulled me to my feet.

'Get the rest of your kit off, gal, I'm going to give you a real good freshening up!'

He hoisted me up on to the vaulting box that they use for gymnastics and made me lie on my back. Using various bits of badminton net and strings, he tied weights to my wrists and ankles and let my limbs dangle off the box. I tried to move my arms but couldn't; the weights kept me firmly pinned down, pulling on my joints and stretching me taut.

He tugged me to the end of the box and pushed my legs to either side, leaving me wide and exposed. It felt vulgar, like a scene in a porn movie where too much is revealed and too much is accessible. I tried to pull my legs back together but there was no way I could shift the weights.

Suddenly I felt vulnerable and scared. I wanted to speak to him but realised I didn't even know his name. How had I let myself get in this position? What was I doing spread-eagled on a piece of gymnastic equipment, with a man I didn't even know, planning to do God knows what with me. My heart was banging against my ribs like a trapped bird and I started to feel sick.

Then I felt his fingers opening me up. Fuck! He was pushing something inside me. I tried to clench and squeeze him out but I was so wet he could have shoved his whole arm up there. Again his fingers probed and slid something into me.

I craned my neck. 'What the hell are you...'

But he couldn't answer. At that moment he buried his face between my thighs and ran his tongue thickly up my slit, sending a shudder through my whole body. My back arched instinctively. He pressed his hand softly on my belly and looked up, with chocolate streaked wetly over his nose and chin.

'You have the sweetest little pussy in the universe,' he said, sounding as if he genuinely meant it. Hardly surprising – he seemed to have shoved the rest of the box of chocolates up there.

'Just relax so I can get in there.'

I let the weights pull on my limbs and imagined they were bindings holding my torso in place, a torso that existed solely for sexual purposes. My arms and legs were superfluous. I had been pared down till my whole being was concentrated in my sex and every nerve ending was hotwired to my clitoris.

His mouth was bringing me to screaming point. I

could feel my hips straining to drive his face harder into me. I no longer cared what he did, so long as he didn't stop.

He pulled away, face damp and flushed, and began to undo his jeans. The moment of reckoning. He'd certainly charmed his way into getting a crafty shag out of me. I lifted my head again, but couldn't see beyond my own bush.

'Don't worry, I've got a rubber,' he whispered.

Panic wrapped my body in a cold shroud when I heard the tearing of foil and watched him fumble below my field of vision. Like I said earlier, despite my active solitary sex life and Angie's suspicions of promiscuity, I'd not actually gone 'all the way' more than a couple of times.

It was suddenly all too much. I knew I should tell him to stop, to tell him to untie me, to say I wasn't experienced and wanted to go home; to say it was all a mistake, but I couldn't. He glanced up and held my eyes briefly, then took me by the hips and slid me towards him. I shut my eyes tight when I felt the tip of his cock brush my thighs and I clenched my sex muscles but the weights took over and dragged me down on to him.

As he slid into my chocolate-coated muff my body suddenly relaxed as if I'd been immersed in a warm bath, and the cold band of fear that had been crushing my belly was replaced by the warmer, unfamiliar sensation of his cock.

I volunteered to do the late shift on the Sunday – surprise, surprise – then spent the whole evening panicking. He wouldn't come; he'd think I was a slapper, a slut, a tart.

Worse – he *would* come, knowing I'd be gagging for it, that I'd be ripping my knickers off, throwing myself at his feet, begging him to shag me. It was so degrading. I was suicidal with shame when I thought of how easily I'd succumbed and what I'd let him do to me.

Then I'd swing to the other extreme and replay the memories in slow motion. Sucking the chocolate off my nipples; sliding me sweetly on to his thrusting manhood (I liked that phrase even if it was corny) and I replayed the image till my crotch was sodden; the unexpected kiss when he slid out of me, so tender it was almost chaste. Please God, make him come, don't let me down.

And then the anxieties again. He'd think I was a slapper, a tart ... I should go home before he arrived. Better still, ring for a taxi now, don't wait!

Then he was there. The slightly too-long hair, the slightly too-thin body, the lopsided, cheeky smile.

'You look cute in that top,' he said, cheeky as ever.

I'd chosen it deliberately, of course – tight over the boobs and showing off my belly – then spent the entire shift regretting it. It was so predictable, so frigging 'girly'. A pulse throbbed in my groin and I didn't dare look at him. Go home, go home, my brain was saying.

'Er ... thanks.'

Leave now before it all comes apart, before the disappointment, before he tells you it was all a mistake, before he mentions the pregnant girlfriend, the wife and kids, his previous twelve marriages. Probably why he'd been so keen on using a rubber.

I snatched up my jacket. 'Actually I've got to go now. Got to, er, wash my hair ... meeting friends later.' No, I don't believe I said that! That is the most ...

He leant on the counter and stared at me with a half frown, half smile, like he didn't know whether I was for real or what.

'You know, that has to be about the most pathetic excuse ever,' he announced.

I felt myself blush.

'I've had a hard-on all bloody day thinking about last night. I've been really looking forward to seeing you. What's this all about? Boyfriend on the scene, is there?'

I felt such a shit I couldn't even deny it. I fumbled with the buttons on my jacket and avoided his eyes. After a few moments of deafening silence he stood up.

'Guess I'd better get on with the cleaning, then.'

I listened to the muffled slap of his footsteps echoing down the corridor. Why had I suddenly gone weird on him? He said all the right things, he was cute and he had a mouth to die for. I hadn't had too many second thoughts yesterday, so what was I so bothered about now? Was it fear of commitment or rejection?

My belly was buzzing like a hive of bees had taken up residence. Had I gone insane?

I found him shifting equipment around in the store. He stopped when he saw me and we stood staring at each other. Finally he spoke.

'I don't even know your name.'

'Hayley.'

'Hay-lee' he repeated slowly. The heating fan started buzzing and clicking. Neither of us moved.

'Take your top off, Hayley.' His voice was low and seductive, making my skin tingle. 'And the bra.'

I shivered as I let it drop.

'Touch them like you do in the toilet.'

I hesitated, self-conscious.

'Please, Hayley.' There was an erotic huskiness to his voice. I ran my palms over my nipples then rolled them between my fingers till they stood up.

'Come over here.' He patted the vaulting box beside him.

I felt unaccountably shy.

'Now turn around.' He slid his arms around my waist and moved his hands up to my breasts, squeezing my nipples gently. I could feel the warmth of his breath on my shoulder and smelt the spiciness of after-shave.

'Undo your jeans.' It was whispered in my ear hoarsely and made my chest tighten.

'Now move my hand like you do it to yourself.'

I took one of his hands and pushed it down the front of my jeans then placed my fingers over his and began to rub him against me. Gradually the movements became his own, and his fingers began to slip into my wetness. I relaxed and felt his erection against my buttocks. He kissed the side of my neck.

'What I really want is to tie you up and take you from behind,' he said. He was a right dirty little sod. A tremor ran through my body. He slid a finger inside me.

'I could tie your wrists to one of the bolts on the climbing wall. What do you say?' The finger was joined by a second.

'Then I can bend you over like this.' He tilted me forward. 'And pull your butt up and just slide in where you want me.' The fingers scissored inside me and I moaned.

He pushed my jeans down and I stepped out of them. He led me over to the climbing wall, pulled down the loose end of a rope that went up over a pulley in the ceiling, and bound my wrists. The knots were secured and he pulled on the other end of the rope till my arms were stretched up above my head. I was strung up like an offering, naked and helpless; he could do what he liked to me. The thought was scary, yet it filled me with such excitement. For a part-time cleaner, he had an inventive mind. There was something intensely erotic about being totally in his hands, at the whim of his sexual desires. I think it was because, however kinky he may be, I knew intuitively that he liked me a lot. He was friendly.

He took his time running his hands over my body, as if inspecting livestock he might be about to buy, before pushing them roughly between my thighs.

'Open your legs.'

Belly churning, I leant back against the climbing wall and felt the lumpy protuberances of the holds dig into my back. I spread my feet apart. Suddenly I wanted him to do something depraved to me. I wanted to *feel* my helplessness. I wanted him to exert his control; to exploit me and do something I'd normally resist.

'Do something to me,' I whispered. 'Something ... you know ...' I couldn't bring myself to say more. He looked at me for a moment then went purposefully to the equipment store, returning almost immediately with a badminton racket. He didn't speak or look at me again but knelt on the floor between my legs with the racket across his lap.

I shut my eyes and his warm breath tickled my pubes. I felt his thumbs in my slit, peeling my lips apart and opening me up. Then the cold hard end of the racket was pressing against me, pushing. My muscles contracted involuntarily and I clenched my buttocks. His tongue, wet and soft, delicately explored my folds, soothing my fears and weakening my resistance. As I relaxed he eased the racket slowly and smoothly inside me until I could feel its coldness along the whole length of my pussy.

'I bet that feels good,' he murmured into my pubic hair and began to nudge the head of the racket a centimetre or so, so that it moved inside me. With his tongue flicking my clit as he worked the handle my sex exploded into an orgasm more intense and dirty than anything I'd ever done to myself in the toilet.

I slumped, and could have just hung from my wrists recovering, but he now had an urgency about him. He eased the racket out of me, loosened the rope and tied my wrists to a bolt at waist height, then pulled my hips back towards him. The tearing of foil was followed by the sound of his zip and I was grateful that one of us had some sense. I knew guiltily that I had been beyond the point of caring.

He straightened my hips abruptly, pulled my buttocks apart and ran his penis down the crack of my arse, pressing it impatiently at my muff. My internal muscles felt stiff but I was well wet, and he shoved his cock all the way in till I could feel his pelvis rubbing against my backside. His fingers dug sharply into my hips, pushing and pulling me on to him, pumping away at me till I thought I'd split open. He fucked me with a raw, animal passion, then collapsed over my back as he came, covering me with kisses.

When he'd recovered his senses, he slipped out and stepped back. I slid to the floor, waiting for him to untie me, but he started wandering around picking up my clothes. Finally he dropped them in front of me and pulled on his jeans. They hung low on his hips, revealing a narrow stripe of hair reaching up to his navel. He might be skinny but he was definitely cute. I noted with interest that he didn't bother with underwear and I found it incredibly sexy. Nothing but a zip between me and his cock!

My hands were beginning to throb from the knots and I held them out to him.

He put his head on one side and smiled. 'You know, I kind of like you like that, naked and helpless.' He bent down and drew me to his mouth, pushing his tongue between my lips. I could smell the slight saltiness of sweat on him, mingled with my own juices.

'Maybe I should take you home with me and keep you tied to my bed.'

You bet!

He trailed his fingers over my breasts and followed

with his eyes. 'And while you're sleeping –' he dropped his voice to a whisper '– I'd creep over and put little silver rings through your nipples with Sam and Hay tags on!'

My pussy contracted hungrily at the thought. I pictured his name on a cold metal disc dangling from my nipple and wanted him to shag me again, right there and then.

'So it's Sam, is it?'

Pulling back, he stared at me in mock horror. 'You mean to say you go *this* far without even knowing a bloke's name?'

I laughed. 'Well, you've always had your mouth full when I've wanted to ask!'

The following day I was on middle shifts but told Karl I didn't mind stopping on till ten that night. He raised his eyebrows and I shrugged.

'I could do with the extra cash right now.' No way was he going to argue when it meant extra drinking time.

I heard the door go at just before ten – the state I was in I'd have heard it half a mile away in a thunderstorm. I wriggled my shoulders back surreptitiously so my T-shirt was tight across my boobs, then I turned round.

I was gutted to discover a grizzly old bloke in green overalls gawping at me. He raised his eyebrows leerily. 'The top looks a bit on the small side, but it's an improvement on Ange,' was his introduction.

'Caretaker' was written all over him. And dirty old man.

'Sent a relief, did they?'

I nodded, still stunned.

'Ay, they generally do. Usually that half-baked skivver from Chesterfield.'

His eyes were still fixed on my tits but my brain was busy processing this last bit of information.

'You mean he normally works at the Centre in Chesterfield, that cleaner guy?'

'Don't know that I'd call it working . . .'

OK, he'd seen enough. I'd got the info I needed. I pulled on my jacket and picked up my bag. 'Better not keep you then. Ta ra.'

Ange was back on Friday, though looking at her you'd never have known she'd been away; face still the colour of a lump of dough.

'What's this about you leaving, Hay?'

Doesn't take long for news to get round our grapevine; she'd only been in about two minutes.

'I've asked for a transfer to Chesterfield. On lates. I've a hunch the prospects are going to be better over there.'

Lovely Cricket Jan Bolton

It was Dad who started it off. I blame him. He was the one who badgered me into signing up for the Rothermere Eleven. I told him I wasn't interested in cricket – or bloody football or hockey – but he never listened to me. I'd been dragged – well, driven – protesting to the practice nets twice a week and, even though I never seemed to be putting that much effort into it, I cultivated a medium-pace spin technique that Dad said reminded him of Daniel Vittori's. I'm long in the leg and I soon perfected the timing of letting the ball free from my grasp, making sure it carried full momentum behind it. By the time the batsman had realised he'd underestimated me, the bails were already on the ground. I'm no slouch at the crease, either. I hit fours every game, much to everyone's surprise, not least my own and bounded down the wicket in fewer strides than it took most of my opponents. By mid-March I was in the elite squad. Me – Chris Cavendish. I could barely believe it.

The upper and lower sixth cricket tournament happens every June, when we play the equivalent teams from Sir William Levington. It's a school tradition – part of sports week. All the old crocks get wheeled up there for the day in their MCC and old school ties, straw trilbies and cravats and blazers. There's always a reception afterwards in the long room opposite the pavillion and, if it's a hot day, drinks are served by the lower years on the perimeter lawn. It's all very English and polite.

Dad was overjoyed when I made the upper eleven. He kept going on about having my name on that cup, like his had been thirty years back. The photo has been up in his study since I can remember – him and his hairy classmates back in the mid seventies, proud jaws and great prospects, prog rock on vinyl in the evening and Brian Johnston on long wave in the afternoon.

It's a bit late now to say it would never have happened if I hadn't been in the team. But how was I to know that the sight of me in my whites would be the final spark that would ignite the Roman candle of emotions in Melinda Parry – mother of my classmate Jason and the owner of the finest pair of tits in the borough, the South East, the country – to fizz and combust in a torrent of brief but beautiful flames.

As I sit here now, in my bedroom, waiting for the fallout, I try to tell myself I don't really give that much of a toss about it, 'cos I'm off to university in September, and they'll have forgotten about it by Christmas. I hope. But I don't think I can rely on that little nest-egg Dad promised me a couple of months back. The sight of his face when he caught us was something I'll never forget. And now I've been grounded pending a serious chat when he gets back here in about an hour.

I still can't believe it happened. It felt so right but, of course, I realise now that it was very, very wrong. I should have talked about it with someone, but it's not something you chat about with your parents, is it? How would it go? 'All right, ma, I've got the raging horn for my best mate's mum. Leave us alone for a bit, will you.' No, it just wouldn't be right.

I guess that's the thing about suburban life ... no one dares speak about sex but it occupies a large amount of the residents' daily thoughts – the not getting it, that is. It's the not getting it that landed me in hot water. Whatever happens I'm not going to blame her for seducing me, which she did, kind of, but it was hardly rape of a minor. I mean, it wasn't illegal – just immoral. I've never been one for false modesty and 'Oh, I shouldn'ts'. I always hated hearing my female relatives say that at birthdays and Christmas whenever Mum had wrapped up some cheapo toiletries to give out to them, supposedly from me. 'Oh, you shouldn't have!' they'd trill. Well I'm not going to say that, 'cos I did, and I have no regrets. And I'd do it all over again. If I could . . .

Jason's mum stopped me dead in my tracks the first time I met her – nearly three years back. I was besotted, but I kept it well hidden. I don't think Jase suspected anything. He was usually head down in one of his snow-boarding magazines or playing Grand Theft Auto. I'd never been that bothered about gaming before, but once I'd clocked Jason's mum I cultivated an interest that had me round their place all hours after school. I was happy to smack up some CGI pimps if it meant I could see Melinda. I'd be invited to tea, and to Sunday lunch sometimes.

Jason's parents were divorced. His dad was the competitive type, the opposite temperament to Jason and his mum. I guessed that Melinda liked that kind of powerful man who would lavish her with fine things – jewellery and fancy holidays and perfume and knickers. But I was wrong about that. I distinctly remember staring into a fruits of the forest Pavlova and drifting off to thinking what I could give her as a little present and thinking I didn't have a chance of impressing her. And then I realised I had turned into a romantic fool. Early on in my visits I bought her a bunch of flowers – for having me round to tea so often – and I went purple with embarrassment when she leant in to kiss me thanks. But the touch of her hand on my shoulder sent me into paroxysms of delight and I shivered under the warmth of it.

I recall being in the Parrys' garden, at dusk, late last year – just me and Melinda, sitting on the padded sun swing, gently rocking back and forth. Jason was having his Sunday bath and I was acutely aware of being alone with Melinda, who had her neat, tanned bare legs curled under her. I couldn't help my eyes from darting to where her dress had been pushed up. I was ten centimetres from luscious female thigh flesh and I was in pain from wanting to touch her. By this time I was besotted with her, and there was no stopping the tide. We were talking about the future; about my studies and what universities I was applying for, but all I wanted to talk about was how lovely I thought she looked. I must have been sounding less than confident because – and I remember it as if it were yesterday – she brushed her hand through my thick blonde hair and told me everything would be fine.

At that moment I wanted to fall upon her; to kiss her deeply and rip the light cotton dress from her shoulders and roll her down on to the grass. I wanted to be a beast with her and offer her my virginity and tell her she was beautiful. Her hair was shining in the early evening light and she looked so tempting – I sensed a wealth of erotic treasures could be mine, if only I could make the right connection. She was a woman in the prime of her life and she needed to be worshipped. I didn't have experience, and that was obviously what she would want from a lover, but I had plenty of enthusiasm. If only I had known then what she was like – that she too had strong desires, especially for younger men – I may well have acted upon my lusts a lot earlier. But I gritted my teeth and smiled thinly and pressed my hands between my knees in discomfort and shame at having my hair tousled by my mate's mum. There I was, thinking that she saw me as 'sweet' or something, and all the time she was planning on taking things a lot further.

Humans are cursed by shyness. Where does it come from? Why is it the most difficult thing in the world to tell someone you fancy them? I don't understand why it causes so much fuss. Unless a person is obviously displaying signs of arousal – and, personally, I find it very difficult to tell if a woman is aroused – potential couples can go through their lives never taking that essential chance that can make all the difference to one's sexual history. And that kills me.

A year makes a lot of difference when you're my age and, to be honest, I was gagging for some action. I'd been on a few dates and read enough to know what not to do in bed, but I craved an experience with someone older. My girlfriends in the neighbourhood were great company but, try as I might, I just couldn't get worked up about them the way I did about Melinda. I'd taken to pulling myself off about twice a day thinking of her. And after a couple of weeks of this she started looking at me differently – taking her time to listen to me, her eyes slowly looking me over when I'd stand in the kitchen waiting for Jason in the mornings, or whenever I called round. I convinced myself I must have been sending out powerful signals of sexual energy, drawing her to me with all that concentrated thought.

Melinda didn't work, and she always looked stunning, with long, dark, lustrous hair and a great line in low-cut tops made of materials you wanted to stroke. She never looked brash or too old for her outfits; she had a grace about her that was ageless and her smile would melt my insides at twenty paces. The family was minted; they even had an electronic gate and a driveway. It was so different from the way my family lived. We had a nice house and stuff but it was always chaotic and noisy. Two younger sisters squealing on their karaoke machine and Dad endlessly drilling and doing DIY and my mum trying to keep a semblance of order. The Parrys' place was tranquil – Jason was their only kid – and Melinda spent most of her time refining the interior design. Even the floral displays were colour coordinated and bursting with life. Everything she came into contact with seemed to bloom into ripe sensuality.

I like to flatter myself with the notion that I orchestrated the seduction with my irresistible looks, but the most likely truth was that she was bored. When I think back to her body language, her carefully chosen expressions and her flirtatious laughter, it all seemed too obvious for anything to happen between us. But she was clever; it was a double bluff. I always know which of my friends are seeing which girl because, after months of giggling and whispering and teasing each other, there's suddenly silence between them – overcompensating to put their mates off the scent. It's the first sign someone's having sex. So I never read Melinda's hands-on behaviour as anything other than affection. The unthinkable happened out of the blue – and it kind of scuppered my theory. I now know that when your best mate's mum shows up to watch the cricket match her son is not even playing in, wearing a skirt that's short enough to be a low-slung belt, and settles herself in with a pair of binoculars, realisation should kick in that something unusual is afoot.

The Parrys' house is right near the school sports ground and, by early April, Melinda had started to watch me at practice, which I initially found odd and then occasionally distracting, and then a major turn-on. She told me she was interested in the game, which I found hard to believe, especially when she said I'd take at least five runs and score a half century of wickets. I laughed at her mix-up and tried to teach her the difference, but I could see it wasn't sinking in. But she was beginning to have an effect on my performance.

There was no getting Jason down there as a chaperone – he just wasn't interested in traditional sports, and I could hardly tell him what was beginning to blossom. In fact, there was no one I could talk to. I thought I was imagining things and I wasn't about to tell her to back off as I was enjoying the attention too much. I mean, what young man in his right mind would have had asked for protection from a sexy housewife he had fallen in love with?

She'd taken to giving me a lift home after practice, dropping me off and chatting innocently as you like with my mum and dad. I got a couple of sly comments from Scott, the team captain and the most worldly-wise of the lads, and I spotted the others giving her the occasional lustful glance, but they had no reason to be leery. Everything was innocent, in deed if not in thought. Summer was almost underway and she'd taken to wearing skimpier clothes. In the car I couldn't take my eyes off her legs and she wouldn't stop grazing my knee every time she changed gear.

The atmosphere had definitely become sexually charged. She wasn't just my mate's mum any more; she was a potential conquest. My first proper woman. She'd started to ask me about my girlfriends; what sort of women did I like; what pop stars and celebrities. I mentioned Angelina Jolie, only 'cos I couldn't really think of anyone else, but subconsciously I might have been thinking of Melinda when I said it. Melinda's about a foot shorter than AJ but the hair and the complexion are the same, and I prefer unusual, strong dark women to cutesy blondes. She smiled at that, and then came out with it: 'So, how many lovers have you had?' I fumbled. I faffed and mumbled. I shrugged and stuttered words that weren't in any vocabulary. Eventually I came out with the outrageous 'a few', although she knew I was being economical with the truth.

'I don't want you to be scared,' she said. 'You know I'm genuinely fond of you and care about you doing well...'

Yes, I was thinking. *And ... but ...*

'But the fact is I've become attracted to you. In the way that a woman is attracted to a man. I cannot bear not touching you any longer, Chris. You have become more than my son's friend.'

I knew the right thing would be to say thanks and get out of the car and leg it. Or text Jason and tell him his mum was losing it. Or give her my dad's number and say she'd be better off with a real man. But of course I did none of these. Instead I took a quick look in the rear view mirror, thought of all the wanking I'd done over her in the past year and, seeing no one I recognised, pulled her towards me by the shoulders and snogged her. My mate's mum.

And my world burst into a supernova of delight as the reality of the situation filtered through to my consciousness. How cool was this! With my mouth still pressed to her lips I let my fingers stray to her breast. I nearly passed out with the joy and relief of finally laying hands on this goddess. I kept saying, 'Oh my God' and slapping a hand to my forehead. I was grinning like a loon and trying to remember whether I had packed any rubbers in my cricket bag. I was as nervous and excited as a shivering pup yet my ample rangy body felt as if it was expanding to giant size. I was becoming too big for the car. Not to mention the crotch of my cricket pants.

'Chris, listen to me,' she continued, 'I want to do it as much as you do. But we can't go to either of our houses and I'm not going to clamber into the back of the car with you.'

I was experiencing joy and desperation in equal measure. She wanted to 'do it' – but it wasn't going to happen this evening. When, then, when?

'No, of course not. I understand,' I managed to blurt out. 'It's just that I want to touch you so badly.'

My dick was flexing against the constraining cloth and Melinda had seized upon it. She must have known what agonising thrills were coursing through me. I practically had my head between her cleavage and I was not going to last long in that position, especially not with her touch firmly pressed on to my flesh. I had to get out of the car.

'I have to go, Melinda,' I said. 'I'm sure you know why. I'm not going to say anything to anyone.'

She smiled and caressed my cheek. 'I know you won't. And I've got an idea. Something to improve your cricket,' she teased. 'If Rothermere wins the match, meet me behind the scoreboard just after the game, and I'll be there with a surprise for you.'

I didn't know whether to believe her or not – or indeed what to think after this extraordinary turn of events – but I walked briskly home with my cricket jumper in front of my crotch and a spring in my step. I couldn't wait to lock myself in the bathroom as soon as I got home and I lazily pulled on my cock in the bath thinking about Melinda's beautiful breasts as I shot a stream of vigorous sperm up on to the surrounding tiles.

Come the day of the tournament a couple of weeks later the sun was blazing and everyone's parents and friends were seated in deck chairs around the pitch. The lower years were serving refreshments to local dignitaries and the image was one of suburban serenity. Melinda was there with Jason and the sight of them together as mother and son turned my stomach into knots. Had she been shitting me about the special treat? Surely she wouldn't risk anything with Jason there. And my mum and dad were sat next to them. I had to put my love-struck thoughts out of my head and concentrate on the game – a limited 40-over innings each.

Levingtons won the toss and opted to bat first. Scott

chose me to open the bowling and I gave the new ball a long slow rub along my thigh, hoping that Melinda was watching through her binoculars. The opposing side's team captain was first man at the crease and he was a big bastard for his age. I'd heard from Scott that he was South African, so I was already faced with a challenge. It wasn't like sending a ball down to Bradshaw or Neville from our own side: normal British lads who'd cut their teeth on the indoor nets at the local prep school. Guys like Levington's captain had the whole of veldt to practice in under a searing sun. Bugger.

I gave it my all and so did he – sending a couple of fours in the third over up to the boundary as our chaps slid their level best along the grass to stop the ball before it trundled into the refreshments tent, but failing. I'd managed to bowl one maiden over but Blankenfeld shamed me by hitting those two fours. After I'd bowled five overs Scott shifted position and I was moved into the slips. Crouching in the midday heat my thoughts kept jumping to what Melinda was planning, making polite conversation with my mum and dad and scoffing cheese and pickle sandwiches. I spent a few fretful minutes wondering what Jason would think if he knew what wheels had been put in motion. But he wouldn't know, would he? Because neither Melinda nor I were about to tell anyone what was occurring. If, indeed, anything was.

There was a sudden roar as the side of Blankenfeld's bat clipped a nice spin delivery from Neville. It rebounded at an awkward angle and my practice came into its own as I took one great leap for Rothermere College to stretch my right hand out at the perfect place. The leather orb smacked down nicely into my palm and their captain was dismissed for 28. It was a turning point. With the captain gone the rest of their lot fell like nine pins and we dispatched them for 92 all out.

It was back to the pav for refreshments and a consultation with the team for our innings tactics but my mind was on Melinda, and whether she'd seen my lucky catch. We must have looked the epitome of youthful vigour as we strode across the pitch, slapping each other on the back and showing congrats all round, exaggeratedly replaying the near misses and flukey triumphs. I caught sight of her with my dad, waving to me, and I flexed inside my cricket box, safe at least in the knowledge that if I got a hard-on it would be shielded by that essential cup of plastic that's protected a man's tackle and modesty since the game was invented.

Our innings in bat got off to a modest start, with Scott hitting safety strokes and notching up ones and twos nice and steady. Levington's bowling was a bit shoddy and, apart from their prize seam bowler, Haynes, setting up a couple of catches off our boys, we inched towards victory as the sun cast long shadows over the green. I went in as fourth man and determined to liven things up. After a frustrating start I got my chance on the final ball of the over when their bloke bowled short and I had time to really get behind my stroke. In a resounding crack, I was rewarded with the perfect sound and sensation of hitting the ball in the optimum part of the bat and I sent the ball flying over the boundary for the first six of the game.

The spectators got to their feet and their encouragement spurred me on to greater heights. As my partners changed through being caught out, and we suffered one LBW, I went on to realise that the game would be ours within the half hour, if I managed to keep my head and play it steady. Just as I predicted, their strategy fell apart under the onslaught of our tactical game and I began to feel as if I was in the right place at the right time. I wondered fleetingly if I'd ever feel like that when I went to university but I didn't have the luxury of idle reveries;

we had a game to finish off. With two men on our side still to pad up and 80 runs on the scoreboard, I put my all into it. I was paid back in full, and as the minutes clocked by and the chances of Levington's taking any more wickets looking decidedly slim, victory was in sight.

The large white numbers came round on the scoreboard and we'd done it. Levington's were all bluff and bluster with their fancy South African batsman, but they couldn't play the long game. The cup was ours and my name would have a place in the school records. The spectators got to their feet and cheered and the headmaster made his cheery announcements over the loudspeaker system. As we walked back to the pavilion I waved my bat high in the air and felt like a young god. Then I heard my name being called and Melinda was at my side. She was nodding her head vigorously and mouthing me to join her. I mouthed back 'scoreboard' and she nodded. It wasn't easy to slip away so, to avoid suspicion, I went into the pavilion and shot out the back door so I wouldn't be noticed by the others. She was waiting for me for me in the appointed place.

I hadn't had time to shower, and yet she told me how good I smelt. It takes a real woman to appreciate the scent of schoolboy sweat. I bounded off in my grass-stained clothes with much haste. At least she allowed me time take off my box.

Before I knew what was happening she had dragged me into the allotments that back on to the sports ground. The college grounds cover a huge area and there are riding stables and a tennis club as well as an ancient stretch of woodland within easy reach. As we jogged across the allotment – over the patches of string beans and cabbages – one or two eager gardeners glanced our way and we nodded to them. They probably thought we were mother and son. I didn't dwell on the fact Melinda was more than twice my age. There was only now and this moment that I'd waited a good couple of years for. I wasn't about to put obstacles in front of my imminent pleasure.

Once we were out of sight of anybody she took my hand and we slipped lightly into the woods. Every crackle of every twig set my heart pounding. I was excited beyond a level I had ever experienced and nervous as hell. When Melinda ducked down into the undergrowth she gave me a flash of her brown legs and I couldn't wait to get my hands around them. She came to a stop by a small sheltered clearing surrounded by overgrown brambles, fell against a tree and spun round to face me as I advanced on her.

I must have looked incongruous in my sports gear – adrift from my teammates and intoxicated with lust and joy – the happy cricketer in the woods. I eased my hands around her tiny waist and she wriggled against me, feeling for me between my legs. She hooked a leg up around my thigh and then, for the first time, I made contact with her private parts. Even the feel of it – like a plump hot fruit – drove me near to the edge of letting go too soon. I needed the real thing and I hoped to all the gods that she wouldn't back out on me now.

I kissed her deeply, feeling electrified by my desire. I'd looked at a lot of porn on the net and had a good stash of magazines but that fabricated stuff can never convey the feeling of a woman's heat and the beguiling softness of her touch. Her tiny hand was rubbing me along the length of my extremely hard penis. She was cooing and smiling; telling me how big I was. After a minute of this I could stand it no longer.

'Can I?' I breathed raggedly into her ear, picking up on her lemony perfume.

'I think so,' she said. 'I mean, you are old enough,

aren't you? Seventeen? I should have done this a year ago.'

'I think a year ago it would have been all over in the car the other day and I'd had to have done my own laundry again.'

She laughed and told me to kneel at her feet and pull her knickers down. With absolute determination not to press against the seam of my trousers too ardently I slowly prolonged the delicious agony – and the earthy scent of her womanliness drifted into the air and seduced me. I pressed my face to her sex and breathed gently on it, before taking my chances and allowing myself the thrill of poking my naughty little tongue between her lips. She began grinding her hips against me, clawing her fingers through my hair and telling me to work it faster.

At the same time I eased two fingers along her slit and was shocked by how damp she was. Which was nothing compared to the moisture that coated my hand as I slid into the silky interior, pressing my knuckles up against her pubic bone. I was in her at last – a dress rehearsal for the real thing that surely would be mine in a matter of minutes. I became more creative with my tongue, using its muscular dexterity to bring her to a climax as quickly as I could. I was worshipping her to be allowed my own release. But she was to have hers first – and oh my God did she go for it! If I hadn't have been so aroused by feeling her give under my ministrations, I might have been concerned that someone would hear us. But at that moment I didn't care; I had waited too long.

I was so hard by the time I managed to extricate myself from my white trousers that I was shaking with need. Melinda had sunk down the tree to squat on her haunches, and in that position she parted her knees to allow me to see her in all her glory. I stretched out an arm and aimed my thumb towards her clit. She seemed to like it so I rubbed her softly, feeling the warmth and moisture she had just oozed from her orgasm. I tilted her gently over on to her back, into the leaf mulch and ready for me. I nudged my cock against her, and I knew I would have to exercise supreme control not to spurt my hot liquid over her. The sight of her lying there with her wispy satin panties stretched between her knees and her ripe, plump lips glistening in the shadow between her thighs was a living porn tableau. I held myself tight in my hand, rubbing the slippy moisture that had seeped from the eye over my shaft. I was ready to blow.

I reached in my pocket for the condom but she told me not to worry about it; she was on the pill. And she then announced rather than asked, 'This is your first time, isn't it?'

At least she hadn't used the 'V' word. I nodded my head, unable to look her in the eyes. But she insisted I relax; that there was no shame.

'The first time should be a tribute. I want to feel you let go inside me. I want to feel the seed of a virgin. It's my first time, too. I've never taken a boy's cherry before.'

I felt a brief moment of panic but it didn't stop me; nothing would have. I wanted to come so badly. And then it was there; the first silky feel of her smooth moist slit on my dick was all it took to send me to heaven.

We looked into each other's eyes. She played the coquettish maiden, biting a finger and drawing her breath in sharply. She was driving me insane.

'Talk to me, Chris,' she said.

I didn't know what to say. I just kept telling her she was beautiful.

'I love it that you've still got your cricket whites on,' she continued. 'I've got a special thing about cricketers. I like to watch them slowly rub the ball along the inside of their thighs. I watched you do that earlier and it made me wet for you.'

It was her that was doing all the talking but I didn't mind.

'I was so ready for it when we were in the car. I knew I wouldn't take long to come. I loved it just now when you flicked your tongue into my cunt. This is your reward, Chris.'

That was it. I felt the molten fire build in my balls and began to push harder.

'Oh God,' I panted. 'Oh, that's it, I'm coming, I'm coming.'

And with my hands roaming over her breasts and the sound of the lewd words she had uttered in my ear still ringing in my consciousness as being such a very wrong thing for your mate's mum to say, there was an explosion of exquisite excitement as I let it all go inside her. To look up and stare directly into the face of my dad.

So now I'm sitting here biting my nails and feeling a mixture of elation at finally losing my V and terror at what he's going to do? Will he tell mum? Surely not! And Jason. Will he know about it? I did the only thing a boy would do, and legged it. I said thank you over and over to Melinda and sorry about twice that amount. They couldn't really blame me, could they? I was man of the match, after all.

Oh God, that's the front door. Oh Christ, Cavendish, you've really dropped yourself in it.

There's a knock at my door.

'Come in,' I croak, standing up ready to face the music and the wrath.

'Surprise!'

In fall Melinda and my dad. Dad's swigging from an

open wine bottle and the pair of them look beside themselves with glee.

'What?' I begin. 'What's going on?'

'Look, son. Don't you worry. Nothing's going to happen. Mum doesn't know a thing.'

'And neither does Jason,' said Melinda.

'And that's the way it's going to stay?' I suggest.

'In one,' says Dad. 'The thing is, I was so determined to see your name on that cup, I knew that a little incentive would work wonders.'

'It was no chore, Bill,' says Melinda. 'He's a beautiful boy.' She looked at me with genuine affection, and the worry eased out of my body. But I was still confused.

'We'd better be getting back to the grounds, before there's any hoo-ha,' said Melinda.

'Chris needs to come back too, don't you, son? Mingle with the local nobs and celebrate with your team mates.'

'But, how . . .?'

'Look, let's just say me and your mum are a bit friendlier with a select few neighbours than we might have let on. You're going off to university and you'll have your fun. We need ours too, you know. What fun would there be in suburbia without a bit of swinging?'

'You mean, you and Melinda . . .?' I ventured.

'No, *you* and Melinda,' he said. 'We met socially recently at an informal group. I'm not going into details but let's say we were talking about what a shame it was that most young men have to fumble around with girls their own age when they're, you know, that age when they get all emotional and silly on them. What better than to revert to the ancient ways of a lovely older woman deflowering the young heroes of the village! And then we got to talking about the match. We'd had a few drinks and one thing led to another and so Melinda and I concocted a fiendish plan.'

He said it with such gusto. I guess he's always been a

bit of an old pagan, with his fondness for real ale and Morris dancing. All that 'deflowering' stuff was pagan, after all, wasn't it? Not exactly sanctioned by the C of E.

'Let this be your summer solstice ceremony,' he said. 'So come back and take the cup for the college. You went into bat a boy, and you return to take the cup as a man!'

So now I'm standing by the pavilion, and the headmaster is holding the microphone to my dad as an old boy of the school to say a few words.

'I've waited years for this day,' he began.

And as the sun set over the pavilion and the sounds of glasses tinkled around the green, all was well with England and my future. I was beaming.

'And so have I, believe me,' I chipped in. 'So have I.'

WICKED WORDS ANTHOLOGIES –

THE BEST IN WOMEN'S EROTIC WRITING FROM THE UK AND USA

Really do live up to their title of 'wicked' – Forum

Deliciously sexy and explicitly erotic, *Wicked Words* collections are guaranteed to excite. This immensely popular series is perfect for those who enjoy lust-filled, wildly indulgent sexy stories. The series is a showcase of writing by women at the cutting edge of the genre, pushing the boundaries of unashamed, explicit writing.

The first ten *Wicked Words* collections are now available in eye-catching illustrative covers and, as of this year, we will be publishing themed collections beginning with *Sex in the Office*. If you never got the chance to buy all the books when they were first published, you can now complete your collection and be the envy of your friends! Look out for the colourful covers – guaranteed to stand out from everything else on the erotica shelves – or alternatively order from us direct on our website at www.blacklace-books.co.uk or through cash sales – details overleaf.

Full of action and attitude, humour and hedonism, they are a wonderful contribution to any erotic book collection. Each book contains 15–20 stories. Here's a sampler of what's on offer:

Wicked Words

ISBN 0 352 33363 4
£6.99

- In an elegant, exclusive ladies club, *fin de siècle* fantasies come to life.
- In a dark, primeval forest, a mysterious young woman shapeshifts into a creature of the night.
- In a sleazy midwest motel room, a fetishistic female patrol cop gets dressed for work.

More Wicked Words

ISBN 0 352 33487 8
£6.99

- Tasha's in lust with a celebrity chef – it's his temper that drives her wild.
- Reverend Billy Washburn needs salvation from Sister Julie – a teenage temptress who's set him on fire.
- Pearl doesn't want to get married; she just wants sex and blueberry smoothies on her LA poolside patio.

Wicked Words 3

ISBN 0 352 33522 X
£6.99

- The seductive dentist – Nick's encounter with sexy Dr May turns into a pretty unorthodox check-up.
- The gender-playing journalist – Kat lusts after male strangers whilst cruising as a gay man.
- The submissive PA – Mandy's new job fulfils her fantasies and reveals her boss's fetish for all things leather.

Wicked Words 4

ISBN 0 352 33603 X
£6.99

- Alexia has always fantasised about being Marilyn Monroe. One day a surprise package arrives with a sexy courier.
- Bridget is tired of being a chef. Maybe a little experimentation with a colleague is all she needs to get back her love of food.
- A mysterious woman prowls the back streets of New York, seeking pleasure from the sleaziest corners of the city.

Wicked Words 5

ISBN 0 352 33642 0
£6.99

- Connor the tax auditor gets a shocking surprise when he investigates a client's expenses claim for strap-on sex toys.
- Kate the sexy museum curator allows a buff young graduate to make a thorough excavation of her hidden treasures.
- Melanie the interior designer and porn fan swaps blokes with her best mate and gets up to nasty fun with the builders.

Wicked Words 6

ISBN 0 352 33690 0
£6.99

- Maxine gets turned on selling exquisite lingerie to gentlemen customers.
- Jules is stripped naked and covered in cream when she becomes the birthday cake for her brother's best mate's 30th.
- Elle wears handcuffs for an indecent liaison with a stranger in a motel room.

Wicked Words 7

ISBN 0 352 33743 5
£6.99

- An artist's model wants to be more than just painted, and things get pretty steamy in the studio.
- A bride-to-be pays a clandestine visit to the bathroom with her future father-in-law, and gets much more than she bargained for.
- An uptight MP has his mind (and something else!) blown by a charming young woman of devious intentions.

Wicked Words 8

ISBN 0 352 33787 7
£6.99

- Adam the young supermarket assistant cannot believe his luck when a saucy female customer needs his help.
- Lauren's first night at a fetish club brings out the sexy show-off in her when she is required to wear an outrageously daring rubber outfit.
- Cat's fantasies about hunky construction workers come true when they start work opposite her Santa Monica beach house.

Wicked Words 9

ISBN 0 352 33860 1

- Sarah gets a surprise when she and her husband go dogging in the local car park.
- The Wytchfinder interrogates a pagan wild woman and finds himself aroused to bursting point.
- Miss Charmond's charm school relies on old-fashioned discipline to keep wayward girls in line.

Wicked Words 10 – The Best of Wicked Words

- An editor's choice of the best, most original stories of the past five years.

Sex in the Office

ISBN O 352 33944 6

- A lady boss with a foot fetish
- A security guard who's a CCTV voyeur
- An office cleaner with a crush on the MD

Explores the forbidden – and sometimes blatant – lusts that abound in the workplace where characters get up to something they shouldn't, with someone they shouldn't – someone who works in the office.

Sex on Holiday

ISBN O 352 33961 6

- Spanking in Prague
- Domination in Switzerland
- Sexy salsa in Cuba

Holidays always bring a certain frisson. There's a naughty holiday fling to suit every taste in this X-rated collection. With a rich sensuality and an eye on the exotic, this makes the perfect beach read!